Ferdinand Praeger

# Wagner as I Knew Him

Ferdinand Praeger

**Wagner as I Knew Him**

ISBN/EAN: 9783337386801

Printed in Europe, USA, Canada, Australia, Japan

Cover: Foto ©Andreas Hilbeck / pixelio.de

More available books at **www.hansebooks.com**

# WAGNER

# AS I KNEW HIM

BY

FERDINAND PRAEGER

NEW YORK
LONGMANS, GREEN, AND CO.
15 EAST SIXTEENTH STREET
1892

TO

## THE RIGHT HONOURABLE

# THE EARL OF DYSART,



My Lord : —

If an intimacy, an uninterrupted friendship, of close upon half a century during which early associations, ambitions, failures, successes, and their results were frankly discussed, entitles one to speak with authority on Richard Wagner, the man, the artist, his mental workings, and the doctrine he strove to preach, then am I fully entitled so to speak of my late friend.

To vindicate Wagner in all things is not my intention. He was but mortal, and no ordinary mortal, and had his failings, which will be fearlessly dealt with. My sole purpose is to set Richard Wagner before the world as I knew him ; to help to an honest understanding of the man and his motives as he so often laid them bare to me ; and I unhesitatingly affirm that, when seen in his true character, many a hostile, plausible, and unsparing criticism, begotten of inadequate knowledge or malice, will shrivel and crumble away when exposed to the sunlight of truth.

The daring originality of Wagner's work could not help provoking violent opposition. Revolution in art as in aught else has ever been wedded to storm and tumult.

Of all things, Wagner was a thinker.   The plot, construction, and logical development of his dramas, the employment of those wondrous character-descriptive tone-themes, their marvellous combination, his ten volumes of serious matter, especially "The Work and Mission of my Life," emphatically testify to his deliberate studied thinking, and friend and foe alike readily acknowledge the *originality* of his thought.

Here then entered the art world, in the person of Richard Wagner, a quite natural subject for discussion.   Here was a thinker, an original thinker, and Carlyle says that "the great event, parent of all others, in every epoch of the world, is the arrival of a thinker, an *original* thinker."   No matter for marvel, then, that the air thickened with criticism as soon as the Thinker proclaimed himself.

The persistency and vigour with which Wagner pursued the end, — an end to which, primarily, he was unconsciously impelled by instinctive genius, — the emphatic enforcement of the Gospel it was the sole purpose of his thinking manhood to inculcate, led him to reject worldly advancement, to endure painful privation, to utter fierce denunciation against pseudo-prophets, and to be the victim of malignant insult and scornful vituperation.   And why?   Because his mission was to preach *Truth*.

Wagner was "terribly in earnest."   His earnestness forces itself home to us through all his works ; and in his strenuous striving to accomplish his task, he involuntarily said and did things seemingly opposed to the very principles he had so dogmatically enunciated.   But on investigating the why of such apparent contradictions, it will be found that they are but paradoxical after all, and that never has Wagner swerved from the direct pursuit of his ideal.   Thus he says, "I had a dislike, nay, a positive contempt, for the stage, its rouge and tawdry tinsel," and yet within its precincts he was spell-bound.   He was chained to it by indissoluble links.   It was the pulpit from which he was to expound his gospel. Again, he accepted from friends the most reckless sacrifices without the simplest acknowledgment or gratitude, yet it was not ingratitude as is commonly understood; he accepted the service not as done to himself, but for the glorification of true art, and in that consummation he felt they were richly recompensed. He, when he felt it his duty to speak plainly, spared the feelings of none by an incisive criticism which cut to the core, and yet an oversensitiveness made him writhe under the slightest censure.

Towards Jews and Judaism he had a most pronounced antipathy, and yet this did not prevent him from numbering many Hebrews among his most devoted friends. Pursued with the wildest ambition, he steadfastly refused all proffered titles and decorations. He formulated most positive rules for the music-drama, and then referring to "Tristan and Isolde," states: "There I entirely forgot all theory, and became conscious how far I had gone beyond my own system."[1] With Meyerbeer in view, he emphatically insisted that after sixty no composer should write, as being incapacitated by age and consequent failure of brain power, and then when long past this period he not only writes one of his greatest works, but when seventy and within the shadow of death, was engaged upon another of engrossing interest, viz. on the Hindoo religion. Lastly, whilst vehemently protesting the inseparability of his music from its related stage representation and scenic accessories, compelled by fate, he traversed Europe from London to St. Petersburg to produce in the concert room orchestral excerpts from the very works upon whose inviolability he had in such unequivocal terms insisted, — selections too, though arranged by himself, which give but the most incomplete conception of the dramas themselves.

This seeming jarring between theory and practice in so

---

[1] Letter to F. Villot.

powerful a thinker requires explanation, and in due course I shall exhaustively treat the same.

Wagner and I were born in the same town, Leipzic, and within two years of each other. This was a bond of friendship between us never severed, Wagner ever fondly delighting to talk about his early surroundings and associations. His references to Leipzic and prominent local characters were coloured with strong affection, and to discuss with one who could reciprocate his deep love for the charmed city of his birth, was for him a certain source of happiness.

Wagner's first music-master, properly so called, was Cantor Weinlig of Leipzic. From him he received his first serious theoretical instruction. Weinlig, too, was well known to me. He was an intimate friend of my father, Henry Aloysius Praeger, director of the Stadttheater and conductor of the famous Gewandhaus concerts, the latter post being subsequently filled by Mendelssohn among other celebrities. Between Weinlig and my father, whom the history of music has celebrated as a violinist of exceptional skill and as a sound contrapuntist, constant communications passed, and I was very often the bearer of such.

Common points of interest like this — striking Leipzic individualities, the house at Gohlis, a suburb of Leipzic where poor Schiller spent part of his time, the masters of St. Nicolas' School, where we both attended, though at different periods — I could multiply without end, each topic of absorbing interest to us both, and productive of much mutual expansion of the heart, but I will here refer to one only — that connected with Carl Maria von Weber.

" Der Freischütz " was first performed at Dresden, the composer conducting, on the 22d January, 1822. Wagner, then in his ninth year, was living at Dresden with his family. In his letter to Frederick Villot, he says of Weber: " His melodies filled me with an earnestness, which came to me as a bright vision from above. His personality attracted me with enthusiastic fascination; from him I received my first musical baptism. His death in a distant land filled my childish heart with sorrowful awe." "Der Freischütz" was almost immediately produced at Leipzic, and Weber came to Leipzic personally to supervise the rehearsals and to acquaint my father, then the conductor of the theatre, as to the special reading of certain parts. The work excited the utmost enthusiasm in Leipzic, and was performed there innumerable times. I, the son of the conductor, having free entry to the theatre, went nightly, and acquired thus early a thoroughly intimate acquaintance with the work, such as Wagner also had gained by his frequent visits to the Dresden theatre through his family's connection with the stage. In after-life we found that Weber and his works had exercised over both of us the same fascination. In 1844, the remains of the loved idol, Weber, were removed from Moorfields Chapel, London, to Dresden. At that time I was residing in London, and, in conjunction with Max von Weber, the composer's eldest son, and others, obtained the necessary authority and carried out the removal. Wagner was in Germany. There he received the body, and on its final interment pronounced the funeral oration over the adored artist.

In this country, where I have now lived for an unbroken period of fifty-one years, I was Wagner's first and sole champion, and, notwithstanding all the calumny with which he was persistently assailed (which even now has not entirely ceased), stood firmly by him.

It was through my sole exertions that the Philharmonic Society in 1855 offered Wagner the post of conductor. His acceptance and retention of the post for one season are now matters of history.

Wagner returned to London in 1877 to conduct the " Wagner Festival " concerts at the Albert Hall. As his sixty-fourth birthday fell during these concerts, some ardent friends promoted a banquet in his honour at the Cannon Street Hotel on the 23d May. To that banquet I was invited, and great was my amazement when Wagner, the applauded of all, spontaneously and without the least hint to me, warmly and affectionately said : —

" It is now twenty-two years ago since I came to this country, unacknowledged as a composer and attacked on all sides by a hostile press. Then I had but one friend, one support, one who acknowledged and boldly defended me, one who has clung to me ever since with unchanging affection ; this is my friend Ferdinand Praeger."

My Lord, I have felt it desirable to address these preliminary remarks to you as indicative of the manner in which I propose to treat my friend's life and work. Wagner was extremely voluble, and, with his intimate friends, most unreserved. He was a man of strong affections and strong memory, and to those he loved he freely spoke of those whom he loved, and thus I believe I am the sole recipient of many of his early impressions and reminiscences, of his thoughts and ambitions in after-life. Therefore shall I tell the story of his life and work, as he made me see it and as I knew him, keeping back nothing, believing as I do that the world has a right to know how its great men live : their lives are its lawful inheritance.

It is with deep affection that I undertake a work prompted by your Lordship's love for the true in art, and it is to you that I dedicate the result of my labour.

FERDINAND PRAEGER.

LONDON, 15th June, 1885.

# CONTENTS.

## CHAPTER IV.

### LEIPZIC, 1827–1831.



## CHAPTER V.

### 1832–1836.

## CHAPTER VI.

### 1836–1839.



## CHAPTER VII.

### EIGHT DAYS IN LONDON, 1839.



## CHAPTER VIII.

### BOULOGNE, 1839.

## CHAPTER IX.

### PARIS, 1839-1842.



## CHAPTER X.

### PARIS, 1839-1842. *Continued.*

The Paris sojourn the crucial epoch of Wagner's career — The grand opera the hothouse of spurious art — Concessions to anti-artistic influences — Realism of the historic opera irreconcilable with his own poetic idealism: why? — Is infected with the revolutionary spirit of the age — From now we date the wondrous change in his art work — Protests through the "Gazette Musicale" against Italian

## CHAPTER XI.

### DRESDEN, 1842-1843.

## CHAPTER XII.

### 1843–1844.



## CHAPTER XIII.

### 1845.

## CHAPTER XIV.

### 1848.

## CHAPTER XV.

### 1849–1851.



## CHAPTER XVI.

### 1850–1854.

## CHAPTER XVII.

### " JUDAISM IN MUSIC."

## CHAPTER XVIII.

### 1855.

## CHAPTER XIX.

### 1855. *Continued.*

## CHAPTER XXIV.

### 1865-1883.

PAGE

# WAGNER AS I KNEW HIM.

## CHAPTER I.

1813–1821.

SELDOM has the proverb "The child is father to the man" been more completely verified in the life of any prominent brain-worker than in that of Richard Wagner. The serious thinker of threescore, with his soul deep in his work, is the developed school-boy of thirteen lauded by his masters for unusual application and earnestness. All his defects and virtues, his affections and antipathies, can be traced to their original sources in his childhood. No great individuality was ever less influenced by misfortune or success in after-life than Wagner. The mission he felt within him and which he resolutely set himself to accomplish, he unswervingly pursued throughout the varied phases of his eventful career. Beyond contention, Richard Wagner is, I think, the greatest art personality of this century,—unequalled as a musician, great as a poet as regards the matter, moral, and mode of expression, whilst in dramatic construction a very Shakespeare. With an ardent desire to reform the stage, he has succeeded beyond his hopes; and well was he fitted to undertake such a gigantic task. His family — father, step-father, eldest brother, and three sisters — and early surroundings were all connected with the stage. Cradled in a theatrical atmosphere, nurtured on theatrical traditions, with free access to the best theatres from the first days his intellect permitted him to enjoy stage representations, himself a born actor, and with earnestness as the rule of his life, it is no matter for surprise that he stands foremost among the great stage reformers of modern times.

By birth he belonged to the middle class. A son of the people he always felt himself; and throughout his career he strove to soften the hard toil of their lot by inspiring in them a love for art, the power to enjoy which he considered the goal of all education and civilization. To him the people represented the true and natural, untainted by the artificiality that characterized the wealthy classes.

Painstaking, energy, and ability seem to have been the attributes of Wagner's ancestors. His paternal grandfather held an appointment under the customs at Leipzic as "thorschreiber," *i.e.* an officer who levied toll upon all supplies that entered the town. Family tradition describes him as a man of attainments in advance of his station, a characteristic which also distinguished his son Frederick (Richard's father). Frederick Wagner, born in 1770, also held an appointment under the Saxon government. A sort of superintendent of the Leipzic police, he spent his leisure time in studying French. Although unaided, he must have attained some degree of proficiency; as subsequently he was called upon to make use of it, and it proved of great service to him. He was a man of literary tastes, and was famed in Leipzic for his great reading and knowledge. Goethe and Schiller were then the beacon-lights of young German poetry. Their pregnant philosophical reasoning, clothed in so attractive, new, and beautiful a garb, fascinated Frederick Wagner, and he made them his serious study — a love which was inherited by his son Richard, who oft in his literary works refers to Goethe and Schiller as the two greatest German poets.

Like all natives of Leipzic he was passionately fond of the stage. The enthusiasm of all classes of society in Leipzic for matters theatrical is historic. Frederick Wagner attached himself to a company of amateur actors, and threw himself with such zest into the study of the histrionic art as to achieve considerable distinction and court patronage. The performances of this company were not unfrequently open to the public; indeed, at one time, when the town theatre was temporarily closed, the amateurs replaced the regular professionals, the Elector of Saxony evincing enough interest in the troupe to pay the hire of the building specially engaged for their performances.

When the peace of Europe was disturbed by the wild, ambitious plottings of Napoleon, a body of French troops were quartered at Leipzic under Marshal Davoust. It was now that Frederick Wagner's self-taught French was turned to account, as he was appointed to carry on communications between the German and the French soldiers. The Saxon Elector submitting to the French conqueror, the government of the town passed into French hands. Davoust, with the shrewd perspicacity of an officer of Napoleon's army, saw the solid qualities of Frederick, and directed him to reorganize the town police, at the same time nominating him superintendent-in-chief. He did not retain this appointment many months, as he died of typhoid fever, caught from the French soldiers, on the 22d of November, 1813.

Of his "dear little mother" Wagner often spoke to me, and always in terms of the fondest affection. He described her as a woman of small stature, active frame, self-possessed, with a large amount of common sense, thrifty and of a very affectionate nature.

The Wagner family consisted of nine children, four boys and five girls. Richard, the youngest of all, was born on the 22d May, 1813, at Leipzic. At the time of his father's death he was therefore but six months old. The eldest of the children, Albert, was born in 1799. He went on the stage as a singer at an early age, having a somewhat high tenor voice. In 1833 we find him stage manager and singer at Wurtzburg, engaging his brother Richard as chorus director. He afterwards became stage manager at Dresden and Berlin, dying in 1874.

Three of Wagner's sisters, Rosalie, born 1803, Louisa, born 1805, and Clara, born 1807, were also induced to choose the stage as a profession, each being endowed with unmistakable histrionic talent. Although not great they were actresses of decided merit. Laube, an eminent German art critic and writer, has given it as his opinion that Rosalie was to be preferred to Wilhelmina Schroeder, afterwards the celebrated Schroeder-Devrient, but this praise Wagner considered excessive, attributing it to the critic's friendly relations with the family.

The unexpected death of Frederick Wagner threw the family into great tribulation. A small pension was allowed the widow by government, but with eight young children (one, Karl, born some time before, had died), the eldest but fourteen years of age, the struggle was severe and likely to have terminated disastrously, notwithstanding the watchful thrift of Frau Wagner, had not Ludwig Geyer, a friend of the dead Frederick, generously helped the widow. Geyer was a favourite actor at Leipzic. A man of versatile gifts, he was poet, portrait-painter, and successful playwright. For two years he continuously identified himself with the Wagner household, after which, in 1815, he assumed the whole responsibility by marrying his friend's widow. Shortly after his marriage Geyer was offered an engagement at the Royal Theatre, Dresden, which would confer on him the highly coveted title of " Hofschauspieler," or court actor. He accepted the appointment, and the whole family removed with him to the Saxon capital. At this time Richard was two years old. Frederick Wagner, as a thorough Leipzic citizen, had already interested his family in theatrical matters ; now by Geyer becoming the head of the household, the stage and its doings became the every-day topic, and therefore the next consequence was its adoption by the eldest children, Albert, Rosalie, Louisa, and Clara. What wonder then that Richard was influenced by the theatrical atmosphere in which he was trained.

From the first Geyer displayed the tenderest affection towards the small and delicately fragile baby. Throughout his life Wagner was a spoilt child, and the spoiling dates from his infancy. Both step-father and mother took every means of petting him. His mother particularly idolized him, and seems, so Wagner told me, to have often built castles in the air as to his future. They were drawn towards the boy, first, because of his sickly, frail constitution; and secondly, owing to his bright powers of observation, which made his childish remarks peculiarly winning. As the boy grew up he remained delicate. He was affected with an irritating form of erysipelas, which constantly troubled him up to the time of his death.

Ludwig Geyer's income from all sources, — acting, portrait-painting, and play-writing — did not amount to a sum sufficient to admit of luxuries. Poor Madame Geyer, with her large, growing family, had still to keep a watchful eye over household expenditure. Portrait-painting was not a lucrative occupation, and play-writing less so, yet she contrived that the girls should receive pianoforte lessons. It was customary for needy students of the public schools to eke out their existence by giving lessons in music, languages, or sciences; indeed, it was not uncommon to find some students wholly dependent on such gains for the payment of their own school fees. The fees usually paid in such instances were sadly small, and not unfrequently did the remuneration take the form of a "free table." At that time there was scarcely a family in Germany that had not its piano. A piano was then obtainable at a cost incredibly small compared with the sums paid to-day. True, the cases were but coloured deal or some common stained wood, whilst the mechanism was of the least expensive kind.

In shape they were square, with the plainest unturned legs. Upright instruments had not then been introduced.

The Wagner family went to Dresden in 1815, and from that time, up to the date of his entering the town school at the end of 1822, Richard received either at school or at home no regular tuition. The boy was sickly and his mother was content to let him live and develop without forcing him to any systematic school work. It would seem that he received irregular lessons in drawing from his step-father, as Wagner told me that Geyer had hoped to discover some talent in him for the pencil, and on finding he had not the slightest gift, he was very much disappointed. As a boy, he continued to be a pet with Geyer, accompanying hisstep-father in his rambles during the day or attending with him the rehearsals at the theatre. Such home education as he did receive was of the most fragmentary kind, a little help here and there from his sisters or attention from Geyer or his mother. Music lessons he had none. All he remembered in after-life was having listened to his sisters' playing, and only by degrees taking interest in their work. His own reminiscences of his boyhood were plain in one point — he certainly was not a musical prodigy. He fingered and thumbed the keyboard like a boy, but such scraps as he played were always by ear.

Anxieties for a second time now began to thicken round the Wagner family. The court actor Geyer was laid on a sick-bed. He was not of a robust constitution, and conscious of failing health and apprehensive of death, sought anxiously to find some indication in young Richard of any decided talent which might help him to suggest as to the boy's future career. He had tried, as I have said, to find whether his step-son possessed any skill with the pencil, and sorrowfully perceived he had none. In other directions, of course, it was difficult for Geyer to determine as to any particular gift, if we remember the tender years of the boy. As to music, it would have been nothing short of divination to have predicted that there lay his future, since up to that time Richard had not even been taught his notes. But the court actor was an artist, and with unerring instinct detected in a simple melody played by Richard from memory that in music "he might become something."

Richard had been fascinated by a snatch of melody which was constantly played by his sisters. He caught it by ear, and was one day strumming it softly on the piano when alone. His mother overheard him. Surprised and pleased at the boy's unsuspected accomplishment, Geyer was told, and the melody was repeated in a louder tone for the benefit of the invalid in the next room. It was the bridal chorus from "Der Freischütz." Although a very simple melody and of easy execution, it must have been played with unusual feeling for a child to prompt Geyer almost to the prophetic utterance, "Has he perhaps talent for music?" Wagner heard this, and told me how deeply he was impressed by it. On the next day Geyer died, 13th September, 1821. Richard was then eight years and four months old, and preserved the most vivid remembrance of his mother coming from the death chamber weeping, but calm, and walking straight to him, saying, "He wished to make something of you, Richard." These words, Wagner said, remained with him ever after, and he boyishly resolved "to be something." But he had not then the faintest notion in what direction that something was going to be. Certainly music was not forecast as the arena of his future triumphs, since in his letter to F. Villot, dated September, 1860, he tells us that it was not until after his efforts in the poetical art, and subsequent to the death of Beethoven, 1827, *i.e.* six years after Geyer's death, that he seriously began to study music.

For a second time was the family thrown into comparative adversity. But the embarrassment was less serious than in 1813, since the three eldest children were now at an age to contribute materially to the general support. A trifling annuity was again awarded to the widow, and with careful thrift she resumed her sway of the household. The family at this time consisted of the widow; Albert, twenty-two years; Rosalie, eighteen; Julius, seventeen, apprenticed to a goldsmith; Louisa, sixteen; Clara, fourteen; Ottilie, ten; Richard, eight and four months; and Cecilia Geyer, six, the only child of Frau Wagner's second marriage. The two eldest girls and Albert had already embraced the theatrical profession. Family circumstances were therefore not so pinched as at the death of Frederick Wagner.

No plan having yet been devised as to the future of Richard, he was sent on a visit to an uncle Geyer at Eisleben, between which place and his mother's home at Dresden, he spent the next fifteen months, when it was decided to enter him at the Kreuzschule (the Cross School), Dresden.

# CHAPTER II.



His first visit to Eisleben — the going among strange people, new scenery, and for the first time sleeping away from his mother's home — was the first great event of his life, and left an indelible impression on him. The details he remembered in connection with this early visit, at a time when he was not nine years old, point to the vividness of the picture of the whole journey in his mind and his strong retentive memory.

The story I had from Wagner in one of our rambles at Zurich in 1856.

"My first journey to Eisleben," said Wagner to me, "was in the beginning of 1822. Can one ever forget a first impression? And my first long journey was such an event! Why, I seem even to remember the physiognomy of the poor lean horses that drew the jolting 'postkarre.' They were being changed at some intermediate station, the name of which I have now forgotten, when all the passengers had to alight. I stood outside the inn eating the 'butterbrod,' with which my dear little mother ('mein liebes Mütterchen' was the term of endearment invariably used by Wagner, when referring to his mother) had provided me, and as the horses were about to be led away, I caressed them affectionately for having brought me so far. How every cloud seemed to me different from those of the Dresden sky! How I scrutinized every tree to find some new characteristic! How I looked around in all directions to discover something I had not yet seen in my short life! How grand I felt when the heavy car rolled into the town of Eisleben! Even then Eisleben had a halo of something great for my boyish imagination, since I knew it to be the birthplace of Luther, one of the heroes of my youth, and one that has not grown less with my increasing years. Nor was it without a reason that, at so early a period, religion should occupy the attention of a boy of my age. It was forced upon my family when we came to Dresden. The court was Roman Catholic, and in consequence, no inconsiderable pressure was brought to bear upon all families who were connected in any manner with the government to compel them to embrace the court-religion. My family had been among the staunchest of Lutherans for generations. What attracted me most in the great reformer's character, was his dauntless energy and fearlessness. Since then I have often ruminated on the true instinct of children, for I, had I not also to preach a new Gospel of Art? Have I not also had to bear every insult in its defence, and have I not too said, 'Here I stand, God help me, I cannot be otherwise!'

"My good uncle tried his best to put me through some regular educational training. It was intended that he should prepare me as far as he could for school, as the famous Kreuzschule was talked of for me. Yet, I must confess I did not profit much by his instruction. I preferred rambling about the little country town and its environs to learning the rules of grammar. That I profited little was, I fear, my own fault. Legends and fables then had an immense fascination over me, and I often beguiled my uncle into reading me a story that I might avoid working. But what always drew me towards him was his strong affection for my own loved step-father. Whenever he spoke of him, and he did so very often, he always referred to his loving good-nature, his amiability, and his gifts as an artist, and then would murmur with a tearful sigh 'that he had to die so young!'

"It was arranged that I should enter the Dresden school in December, 1822, just at a time when my sisters were busy with the exciting preparations for the family Christmas-tree. How good it was of my mother then to let us have a tree, poor as we were! I was not pleased to go to school just three days before Christmas Day, and probably would have revolted had not my mother talked me over and made me see the advantages of entering so celebrated an academy as the Kreuzschule, pacifying my disappointment by allowing me to rise at early dawn to do my part to the tree. Now I cannot see a lighted Christmas-tree without thinking of the kind woman, nor prevent the tears starting to my eyes, when I think of the unceasing activity of that little creature for the comfort and welfare of her children."

Wagner was deeply moved when, on Christmas Day, he found amongst the usual gifts, such as "Pfefferkuchen" (ginger-bread) and "Stolle" (butter cake), a new suit of clothes for himself, a present from his thoughtful mother for him to go to school with. Throughout his life Wagner was always remarkably prim and neatly dressed, caring much for his personal appearance. The low state of the widow's exchequer was well known to Richard, and he could appreciate the effort made for him. He was no sooner at school than he attracted to himself a few of the cleverest boys by his early developed gift of ready speech and sarcasm. "Die Dummer haben mich immer gehasst" (the stupid have ever hated me) was a favourite saying of his in after-life. The study of the dead languages, his principal subject, was a delight to him. He had a facility for languages. It was one of his gifts. History and geography also attracted him. He was an omnivorous reader, and his precise knowledge on any subject was always a matter of surprise to the most intimate. It could never be said what he had read or what he had not read, and here perhaps is the place to note a remarkable feature in Wagner's disposition, viz. his modesty. Did he require information on any subject, his manner of asking was childlike in its simplicity. He was patient in learning and in mastering the point. But it should be observed that nothing short of the most complete and satisfactory explanation would satisfy him. And then would the thinking-power of the man declare itself. The information he had newly acquired would be thoroughly assimilated and then given forth under a new light with a force truly remarkable.

In stature Wagner was below the middle size, and like most undersized men always held himself strictly erect. He had an unusually wiry, muscular frame, small feet, an aristocratic feature which did not extend to his hands. It was his head, however, that could not fail to strike even the least inquiring that there he had to do with no ordinary mortal. The development of the frontal part, which a phrenologist would class at a glance amongst those belonging only to the master-minds, impressed every one. His eyes had a piercing power, but were kindly withal, and were ready to smile at a witty remark. Richard Wagner lacked eyebrows, but nature, as if to make up for this deficiency, bestowed on him a most abundant crop of bushy hair, which he carefully kept brushed back, thereby exposing the whole of his really Jupiter-like brow. His mouth was very small. He had thin lips and small teeth, signs of a determined character. The nose was large and in after-life somewhat disfigured by the early-acquired habit of snuff-taking. The back of his head was fully developed. These were according to phrenological principles power and energy. Its shape was very similar to that of Luther, with whom, indeed, he had more than one point of character in common.

In answer to my inquiries about his school period at Dresden, he told me that he was remarkably small, a circumstance not unattended with good fortune, since it served to increase the favour of his school professors, who looked upon his unusual mental energy in comparison with his pigmy frame as nothing short of wonderful.

As a boy he was passionate and strong-headed. His violent temper and obstinate determination were not to be thwarted in anything he had set his mind to. Among boys such wilfulness of character was the cause of frequent dissensions. He rarely, however, came to blows, for he had a shrewd wit and was winningly entreating in speech, and with much adroitness would bend them to his whims.

Erysipelas sorely tried the boy during his school life. Every change in the weather was a trouble to him. As regards the loss of his eyebrows, an affliction which ever caused him some regret, Wagner attributed it to a violent attack of St. Anthony's fire, as this painful malady is also called. An attack would be preceded by depression of spirits and irritability of temper. Conscious of his growing peevishness, he sought refuge in solitude. As soon as the attack was subdued, his bright animal spirits returned and none would recognize in the daring little fellow the previous taciturn misanthrope.

Practical joking was a favourite sport with him, but only indulged in when harm could befall no one, and incident offered some funny situation. To hurt one willingly was, I think, impossible in Wagner. He was ever kind and would never have attempted anything that might result in real pain.

His superabundance of animal spirits, well-seconded by his active frame, led him often into hairbrained escapades which threatened to terminate fatally. But his fearless intrepidity was tempered and dominated by a strong self-reliance, which always came to the rescue at the critical moment.

On one occasion when the boys of the Kreuzschule were assembled in class for daily work, an unexpected holiday was announced for that day. A chance like that was a rare thing at schools on the continent. The boys, wild with excitement, rushed pell mell from the building, and showed their delight in the usual tumultuous manner of school-boys freed from restraint. Caps were thrown in the air, when Wagner, seizing that of one of his companions, threw it with an unusual effort on to the roof of the school-house, a feat loudly applauded by the rest of the scholars.   But there was one dissentient, the unlucky boy whose cap had been thus ruthlessly snatched.   He burst into tears.   Wagner could never bear to see any one cry, and with that prompt decision so characteristic of him at all periods of his life, decided at once to mount the roof for the cap.   He re-entered the school-house, rushed up the stairs to the cock-loft, climbed out on the roof through a ventilator, and gazed down on the applauding boys.   He then set himself to crawl along the steep incline towards the cap.   The boys ceased cheering at the sight and drew back in fear and terror.   Some hurriedly ran to the "custodes."   A ladder was brought and carried up stairs to the loft, the boys eagerly crowding behind.   Meanwhile Wagner had secured the cap, safely returned to the opening, and slid back into the dark loft just in time to hear excited talking on the stairs.   He hid himself in a corner behind some boxes, waited for the placing of the ladder, and "custodes" ascending it, when he came from his hiding-place, and in an innocent tone inquired what they were looking for, a bird, perhaps?   "Ja, ein Galenvogel" (yes, a gallows bird), was the angry answer of the infuriated "custodes," who, after all, were glad to see the boy safe, their general favourite.   He did not go unrebuked by the masters this time, and was threatened with severe chastisement the next time he ventured on such a foolhardy expedition.

Wagner told me that whilst on the roof, which, like all roofs of old houses in Germany, was extremely steep, he felt giddy, and was seized with a dread of falling. Bathed in a fever of perspiration, he uttered aloud, "liebe mütterchen," upon which he felt transformed. It acted on his frame with the power of magic, and helped him to retrace his steps from a position which would appall a practised gymnast. Many years after this, Wagner's eldest brother, Albert, when referring to Richard having taken part in the rising of the people of Saxony in 1849, which he personally strongly deprecated, told me the above story in illustration of Richard's extreme foolhardiness. The episode was fully confirmed by Wagner, who then told me of his fears on the roof.

It was not in climbing only that Richard excelled. He was known as the best tumbler and somersault-turner of the large Dresden school. Indeed, he was an adept in every form of bodily exercise; and as his animal spirits never left him, he still performed boyish tricks even when nearing threescore and ten. The roof of the Kreuzschule was not infrequently referred to by me, and when Wagner proposed some venturesome undertaking, I would say, "You are on the roof again."

"Ah, but I shall get safely down again, too," was the answer, accompanied with his pleasant boyish laugh.

Richard early began to exhibit his love of acrobatic feats. When as young as seven, he would frighten his mother by sliding down the banisters with daring rapidity and jumping down stairs. As he always succeeded in his feats, his mother and the other children took it for granted that he would not come to grief, and sometimes he would be asked to exhibit his unwonted skill to visitors. This no doubt increased the boy's confidence in himself — a self-reliance which never left him to the time of his death.

Wagner's affection for his mother was of the tenderest. It was the love of a poet infused with all his noblest ideality. The dear name, whenever uttered by Richard Wagner, was spoken in tones so soft and tender as to bespeak at once the sympathy and affection existing between the two. A halo of glory ever encircled "mein leibe mütterchen." Nothing can give a better idea of this gentle love than the passages in "Seigfried," the child of the forest, where the hero demands of the ugly dwarf, Mime, who had brought him up, "Who was my mother?" an inquiry he repeated after he had killed the hideous dragon, Fafner, and thereby became able to understand the song of the birds. If ever music could give an idea of love, here in these passages we have it. In what touching accents comes, "How may my mother have looked? Surely her eyes must have shone with the radiant sparkle of the hind, but much more beautiful!" Every allusion to his mother in this scene is expressed in the orchestra with an ethereal refinement and originality of conception to which one finds no parallel in the whole range of music of the past. I verily believe that Richard Wagner never loved any one so deeply as his "liebe mütterchen." All his references to her of his childhood period were of affection, amounting almost to idolatry. With that instinctive power of unreasoned yet unerring perception possessed by women, she from his childhood felt the gigantic brain-power of the boy, and his love for her was not unmixed with gratitude for her tacit acknowledgment of his genius.

One of his early developed affections was a strong love for animals. On this point, and what I know of its strong sway with him in his dramas, I shall have something to say hereafter. Now I shall confine myself to the recital of an incident of his boyhood. To see a helpless beast ill-treated was to rouse all the strong passion within him. Anger would overcome all reason, and he would as a child fly at the offender.

One of his first impressions was a chance visit he paid with some of his school-fellows to a slaughter yard. An ox was about to be killed. The butcher, stripped, stood with uplifted axe. The horrible implement descended on the head of the stately animal, who gave a low, deep moan. The blows and moans were repeated. The boy grew wild, and would have rushed at the butcher had not his companions forcibly held him back and taken him away from the scene. For some time after he could not touch meat, and it was only when other impressions effaced this scene that he became reconciled by his mother reasoning that animals must be killed, and that it was perhaps preferable to dying slowly by sickness and old age. When a man, he could not refer to this incident without a shudder.

In after-life he rarely missed an opportunity of pleading for better treatment of animals, drawing the attention of the municipal authorities to the prevention of wanton cruelty, and arguing that animals, to be killed for human food, should be despatched with the minimum of pain.

# CHAPTER III.



FROM the record of the Kreuzschule it appears that Wagner entered that famous training college on the 22d December, 1822, as Richard Wilhelm Geyer, son of the late court actor of that name. He would then be nearly ten years old.

He told me that he well remembered the eager delight with which he looked forward to the prospect of enjoying systematic instruction. He hoped to be placed high in the school, yet dreaded the entrance examination, conscious how very patched was *then* his store of information. During his first seven years' residence in Dresden, from 1815–1822, the Kreuzschule, had been an every-day object to him, and yet on entering the building for the first time as an intending student, a feeling of awe took possession of him. The unsuspected majesty of the building, the echo of his footfall on the stone steps, made his young heart beat with expectant wonder. The result of the examination was to place him in the first form, his bright, quick, intelligent replies proving more valuable than his disconnected knowledge. For the masters of the Kreuzschule he ever retained an affection, their genial bearing and friendly tuition comparing favourably with the pedantic overbearing demeanour of the masters of the St. Nicholas school in Leipzic, where he went later on, men who represented a past and effete dogmatic German pedantry.

The direction of his school studies was almost entirely classic. For Greek he evinced a strong affection. Many a time has he told me that he was drawn towards the history of the Greeks by their refined sense of beauty, and the didactic nature of their drama, embodying as it did their religion, politics, and social existence.

Wagner never lost an opportunity of dilating upon, by speech and pen, what might accurately be described as the basis of all his art work. The drama of a nation, he persistently contended, was a faithful mirror of its people. Where the tone of the drama was base the people would be found degraded either through their own acts or the superior force of others. Where the mission of the national drama was the inculcation of high moral lessons, patriotism, and love, there the people were thrice blessed. This idea of a national drama for his fatherland possessed him. He longed to lift the German drama from its "miserable" condition, and his model was "the noble, perfect, grand, and heroic tragedy of the Hellenes." These words I have quoted from a pamphlet, "The Work and Mission of my Life," written less than ten years ago by Wagner. Their meaning is so clear and they summarize so accurately what Wagner in his younger days oft discussed with me that I am glad to add my testimony to what I know was the ambition of his life.

In his ardent struggles to found a national drama we clearly trace the young Dresden student. Here, indeed, is a plain incontestable instance of the boy as the father of the man. His school studies were pre-eminently

Greek language and literature, and it was this which dominated almost the whole of his future career. Hellenic history permeated his entire being, and he gave it forth in the form and model of his immortal music-dramas, in the mode of their development, and in their close union between the stage story and the life of the people.

At school, translations of Æschylus by Apel, a German writer of mediocrity, constituted his chief text-books. The tragedies suited so well the boy's nature that he soon became possessed with a longing to read them in the original. So real and fruitful was his earnestness, that by the time he was thirteen he had translated at home, and entirely for his own gratification, several books of the "Odyssey." This private home work was, he remembered, greatly encouraged by his mother, who, although untutored herself, revered, with a divination characteristic of women of the people, his efforts after a knowledge which she felt would surely be productive of future greatness. This piece of diligent extra school work is another of the many examples of the boy Wagner, "father to the man." Hard worker he always was. Persistency of application characterized him throughout his life, and when it is stated that during this very period of the "Odyssey" translation, he was also privately studying English to read Shakespeare, who is not amazed at the extraordinary energy of the boy? No wonder that the school professors spoke flatteringly of him, and looked for great things from him, and no wonder that the fond mother felt confirmed in her belief that Richard "would become something," and that Geyer's dying utterance would not be falsified.

Wagner's nature was that of a poet. The metrical skill of the Hellenes fascinated him and fostered his strongly marked sense of rhythm.

As regards mathematics, I never remember him in all our discussions to have uttered anything which might lead me to suppose he had ever any special liking for that branch of education, but at the same time I should add that his power of reasoning was at all times strong and lucid, as if based upon the precision acquired by close mathematical study. In all he did he was eminently logical.

His effort as a poet dates from a very early period. The incident, the death of a fellow-scholar, was just that which would touch a sensitive nature like Richard's. A school prize was offered for an elegy, and Wagner, eleven years old, competed. The presence of death to him was at all times terrible in its awful annihilation of all consciousness. Whether in man or beast, it was sure to set him pondering on the "whither?" a question to which at a later period of his life he devoted much labour to satisfactorily answer. Although not twelve years old, death had robbed him of his father and step-father, and their dark shadows flitted before him, reviving sad memories which time had paled. It was under this spell that the elegy was written, and it is not astonishing that the prize was adjudged to him. The poem was printed, but, unhappily, not preserved. In telling me of this early creative effort, and in reply to a naturally expressed desire to hear his own opinion about it, he said that beyond the incident he had not the faintest remembrance of the style or wording of the poem, jocularly adding that he would himself much like to see his " Opus I."

There was a halo of poetry about the Dresden school. Theodore Körner, the poet of freedom, was a pupil at the Kreuzschule up to 1808. His inspiriting songs were sung by old and young. Loved by all, his death, at the early age of twenty-two on the battle-field fighting for German freedom, made him the idol of his countrymen. The boys of his own school were intensely proud of him. To emulate Körner was the eager wish of every one of them, and into Wagner's poetic nature the poetry of the man and the cause he sung sank deeper than with the rest. The battle-songs of the fiery young patriot received an immortal setting by Wagner's idol, Weber.

The admiration of the future poet of " Tristan " for the genius of Shakespeare impelled him, as soon as he had sufficiently mastered English, to produce a metrical translation of Romeo's famous soliloquy. This was done when he had hardly completed his fourteenth year. Up to this period, poetry unquestionably dominated him. All his essays had been literary. Nothing had been done in music. It was now, however, that his latent music forced itself out of him. Up to the time that he entered the Dresden school, in his ninth year, he had received absolutely no instruction in music, and during his five years of school life a few desultory piano lessons from a young tutor, who used to help him at home with his school exercises, embraced the whole of his musical tuition up to the age of fourteen. For the technical part of his music lessons he had a decided dislike. The dry study of fingering he greatly objected to, and to the last never acquired any rational finger method. When joked about his ridiculous clumsy fingering, he would reply with characteristic waggishness, " I play a great deal better than Berlioz," who, it should be stated, could not play at all.

# CHAPTER IV.



FOR some time Rosalie and Louisa, Richard's two sisters, had been engaged at the Leipzic theatre, where they were very popular. Madame Geyer, desirous of being near her daughters and within easy reach of assistance, returned to Leipzic with the younger children and Richard with them. For ten years, from about 1818 to 1828, my father held the post of Kapelmeister at the Stadttheater, under the management of Küstner, a celebrated director. The period of Küstner's management is famous in the annals of the German stage for the high intellectual tone that pervaded the performances under his direction. The names of some of the artists who appeared there are now historic. So high was the standard of excellence reached in these truly model performances, that the whole character of German stage representations was influenced and elevated by it. This was the theatre at which Rosalie and Louisa were engaged. These were the high artistic performances which the youthful poet Richard witnessed, and which deeply affected the impressionable embryo dramatist.

Of this period, actors, plays, and incidents, I had the most vivid remembrance from the close connection of my father with the theatre and the friendly intercourse of my family with the actors. Wagner would take great delight in discussing the performances and actors. He was fond, too, of hearing what I, in my boyhood, thought of the acting of his sisters, and from our frequent and intimate conversations, bearing on his youthful impressions of the stage, he uttered many striking and original remarks which will appear later on. A popular piece then was Weber's "Sylvana," in which Louisa performed the part of the forest child. This part apparently won the youthful admiration of both of us. Wagner's remembrance of certain incidents connected with it was marvellous to me.

On his return to Leipzic, his first impulse drove him to visit the house in the Brühl in which he was born. Is it not possible that even at that early stage of his life his extraordinary ambition of "becoming something great" might have foreshadowed to him that the humble habitation of his childhood would later on bear the proud inscription, "Richard Wagner was born here"? What struck him at once as very strange was the foreign aspect of that part of the town where the Jews congregated. It was continually recruited by an increasing immigration of the nomadic Polish Jews, who seemed to have consecrated the Brühl their "Jerusalem," as Wagner christened it and ever referred to it when speaking to me. The Polish Jews of that quarter traded principally in furs, from the cheapest fur-lined "Schlafrock" to the finest and most costly furs used by royalty. Their strange appearance with their all-covering gabardine, high boots, and large fur caps, worn over long curls, their enormous beards, struck Wagner as it did every one, and does still, as something very unpleasant and disagreeable. Their peculiarly strange pronunciation of the German language, their extravagantly wild gesticulations when speaking, seemed to his æsthetic mind like the repulsive movements of a galvanized corpse.

I was sorry to find that Wagner, although generally averse to acts of violence and oppression, was but little shocked at the unreasoned hatred and contempt of the Leipzic populace (especially the lower classes) for the Jews. Their innate thrift, frugality, and skill in trading, were regarded as avarice and dishonesty. Tales of unmitigated cruelty and horror perpetrated by the Jews floated in the brains of the lower Christian (?) populace. The murder of Christian infants for the sake of their blood, to be used in sacrifice of Jewish rites, was a commonplace rejoinder in justification of the suspicion and hatred against this unfortunate race. Crying babes were speedily silenced by the threat, " The Polish Jew is coming." What wonder, then, to see what was almost a daily occurrence, — a number of Christian boys rush upon an unprotected, inoffensive Jew boy and mercilessly beat him to revenge the imaginary wrongs which the Jews were said to have done to Christian infants. Nor, I am sorry to add, did the fully grown Christian burgher interfere in such brutal scenes ; the poor wretched victim, beaten by overwhelming numbers and rolled howling in the mud, was but a Jew boy ! Strange to say, Wagner had imbibed some intuitive dislike to the Egyptian type of Hebrew, and never entirely overcame that feeling. No amount of reasoning could obliterate it at any period of his life, although he counted among his most devoted friends and admirers a great many of the oppressed race. Still considerably more odd is it that Wagner's first attachment was for one of the black-eyed daughters of Judah. When passing in review our earliest impressions of school life, we naturally came to that never-to-be-forgotten period of the earliest blossoms of first love, which then revealed to me this remarkably strange episode. Events of every-day occurrence, which in the lives of ordinary mortals scarcely deserve mentioning, are invested with a significance in the lives of men whose destiny points to immortality. When Wagner came to this curious incident of his school life, amazed, I ejaculated, "a Jewess ?" in a tone of "impossible !"

It was after a discussion of Jew-hating, and my pointing to the many friends and adherents he had among the Jews, he with his joyous outbreak of humor said, "After all, it was the dog's fault," referring to "Faust," where Mephisto, as a large dog, lies "unter dem Ofen." Then followed the story.

He had called at his sister Louisa's house (by the way, he had an affection for this sister which, in our intimate converse, he likened to that which Goethe in his case speaks of as having for its basis the frontier where love of kin ends and love of sex commences), went to her room, where he found an enormous dog which attracted his attention. Any one acquainted with Wagner knew of his devoted attachment to dogs, of which I shall have more to say hereafter. Not many could understand an affection which included every dog in creation. Wagner would engage in long conversations with dogs, and in supplying their answers would infuse into them much of that caustic wit which philosophers of all ages and countries have so often and pow-

erfully put into the mouth of animals.  Richard Wagner
delighted to make dumb pets speak scornfully of the
boasted superiority of man, thinking that after all the
animal's quiet obedience to the prescribed laws of
instinct was a surer guide than man's vaunted free
will and reasoning power.  He was fond, too, of quoting
Weber on such occasions, who, when *his* dog became
disobedient, used to remark, " If you go on like that, you
will at last become as silly and bad as a human being."

The dog so wholly engrossed Richard's attention
that he failed to notice a visitor, Fräulein Leah David,
who had come to fetch her dog, left at her friend's
house whilst paying visits in the neighbourhood.  The
young Jewess was of the same age as Richard, tall, and
possessed that superior type of Oriental beauty more
frequently found among the Portuguese Jews.  She was
on intimate terms with Louisa Wagner, who shortly
after married one of the celebrated book publishers of
Germany.  Leah David made an immediate conquest
of Richard.  "I had never before been so close to so
richly attired and beautiful a girl, nor addressed with
such an animated eastern profusion of polite verbiage.
It took me by surprise, and for the first time in my life
I felt that indescribable bursting forth of first love."

Wagner was invited to the house of her father, who,
like most wealthy Jews, surrounded himself with artists
of every kind.  Indeed, it was there that Richard made
many acquaintances which subsequently proved useful
to him.  There was an extravagant luxury in the osten-
tatious house of Herr David, which made the ambitious
young student poignantly feel the frugal economy practised in his own home.  Wagner's imaginative brain

always made him yearn for all the enjoyments that life could supply. Unlimited means was the roseate cloud that incessantly hovered before his longing fancy. In this respect he differs largely from most other creative great minds, who, by force of inventive genius, have conjured up worlds of power and riches, and yet have lived contentedly on the most modest fare and in the lowliest of habitations.

Richard's new-found friend was an only daughter, and having lost her mother, she was free to do as she willed ; the enthusiastic young musician was allowed to visit the house and proved a very genial companion, fond of her dog, and adoring art. Wagner did not declare his passion, feeling that in the sympathetic, friendly treatment he received it was divined and accepted. But he was regarded more in the light of a boy than as a lover, small and slight in stature, dreamy and absorbed as he was then. If the young lady chanced to be out when he called, he either went to the piano or occupied himself with the dog, Iago, if at home. The visits becoming frequent, the attachment ripened into an intimacy. At such a house, with a daughter fond of music, *soirées musicales* were constantly occurring. At one of them a young Dutchman, nephew of Herr David, was present. He was a pianist, and had just that gift which Wagner lacked, dexterity of fingering. Flatteringly applauded, the jealous Wagner intemperately and injudiciously launched out about absence of soul and similar expressions. Taunted into playing, his clumsy, defective manipulation provoked a sneer from the Dutchman and a titter from the assembly. Wagner lost his temper. Stung in his tenderest feelings before the

Hebrew maiden, with the headlong impetuosity of an unthinking youth he replied in such violent, rude language that a dead silence fell upon the guests. Then Wagner rushed out of the room, sought his cap, took leave of Iago, and vowed revenge. He waited two days, upon which, having received no communication, he returned to the scene of the quarrel. To his indignation he was refused admittance. The next morning he received a note in the handwriting of the young Jewess. He opened it feverishly. It was as a death-blow. Fräulein Leah was shortly going to be married to the hated young Dutchman, Herr Meyers, and henceforth she and Richard were to be as strangers.

"It was my first love-sorrow, and I thought I should never forget it, but after all," said Wagner, with his wonted audacity, "I think I cared more for the dog than for the Jewess. Whilst under the love-spell I had paid little heed to much that soon after, in pondering over the episode, revolted me. The strange characteristics of the Jews were unpleasant to me. Then it was that I first perceived that impassable barrier which must always rise up between Jews and Christians in their dealings with the world. One cannot help an instinctive feeling of repulsion against this strange element, which has been gradually creeping into our midst, growing like misletoe upon the oak tree, a parasite taking root wherever it can fasten but the smallest fibre, and clinging with a tenacity entirely its own, drawing in all nutriment within reach, and yet remaining, notwithstanding, a parasite. Such is the Jew in the midst of Christian civilization."

His entrance to the St. Nicolas school in 1827, where

he remained three years, was as the passing through a dark cloud. The whole training here differed vitally from that at the Kreuzschule. The masters and their mode of tuition was unsympathetic to him. I did not wonder at this when he told me. I had been at the school, too, and experienced similar feelings of resentment. The Martinet system of discipline was irksome to high-spirited boys. No attempt was made to develop individuality of character. This was unfortunate for Wagner. He was just then at an age when personal interest and sympathetic guidance would have been invaluable. Filled with wild dreams of a glorious future that was to follow his self-dedication to the drama, he threw himself with ardour into the completion of a play he had begun to work at. Ambition had prompted him to base it on the model of Shakespeare's tragedies. The plot was as wild and impossible as the unrestricted exuberance of so extravagant a fancy might suggest. It occupied him for upwards of two years, and greatly interfered with his legitimate school work. When in later life he surveyed this period he describes himself as "wild, negligent, and idle," absorbed with one thought, his great drama.

From the St. Nicolas school he passed to St. Thomas's school, where he stayed but a few months, leaving it for the University. At the University he attended occasional lectures only, showing none of that assiduity which distinguished him at the Kreuzschule. His University days were marked by a profligacy to which he afterwards referred with regret and even disgust. He was young and wild, and had determined with his insatiable nature to drain to the dregs the cup of dissoluted frivolity.  I should not be performing the duty of an honest biographer were I to omit an incident which occurred at this period, regrettable as it might seem.  His mother still received her modest pension. On one occasion Richard was commissioned to receive it for her.  Returning home with the money in his pocket he chanced to pass a public gambling house. *There* was one sensation he had not yet experienced. At that moment he felt that in the throw of the fascinating dice lay the fateful omen of his future.  The money was not his, yet he entered and risked the hazard of the dice.  He was unfortunate; lost all but a small sum he had kept back.  Yet he could not resist the alluring excitement.  He staked this too.  Fortune, happily for the wide world of art, befriended him, and he left the debasing den with more than he had entered, "But," inquired I, "what would you have done had you lost all?"  "Lord!" he replied, "before going into the house I had firmly resolved that should I lose I would accept the omen and seek my end in the river."  A man in years calmly telling me this so long after the incident had occurred urged me again to ask, "Would you really have done that?"  "I would," was the short determined answer.  He was unable to keep the story back from his mother, and at once on his return told her all.  "Instead of upbraiding me," Wagner said, "she fell with passionate love around my neck, exclaiming, 'You are saved.  Your free confession tells me that never again will you commit so wicked a wrong.'"  This Wagner related to me when I was staying with him at Zurich in 1856.  This hazardous throw of the dice was not the only occasion on which he had boldly defied fate. He was ever buoyed up with an implicit faith in his destiny, which sustained him through many trials, though at the same time it urged him to act in a manner where more thoughtful minds would have hesitated.

I now come to what was undoubtedly the crisis of Wagner's artistic career. It was the practice at German theatres, between the acts, for the orchestra to play movements of Haydn's symphonies or similar excerpts by other masters. The rule was to hurry through them in the most indifferent manner. Not the slightest attention was paid to expression, and if it happened that the manager's bell rang while the " playing " was going on, the performance would terminate with a jerk, each artist seemingly anxious not to play a note more, and heedless of finishing the " phrase " together.

At Leipzic, the entire music was particularly slovenly, played under the cynical Matthey. And yet the very men who played so reprehensibly in the stage orchestra, when performing at the famous Gewandhaus concerts seemed to be moved by feelings of reverence for their work, unknown to them in the theatre. It would be an interesting investigation to discover why this was. The symphonies of Beethoven in the concert-room compelled their whole worship; the symphonies of Haydn in the theatre were treated like " dinner " music. Perhaps the explanation is, that the symphonic movements played in the theatre bore no relation to the drama enacted, whereas music played for itself went with a verve and spirit, and attention to its meaning quite unknown to the stop-gap-music-scrambling of the theatre.

From the unsatisfying scrambling performances of the theatre, Wagner, fifteen years old, went to the Gewandhaus concerts. There he heard Beethoven's symphonies. What a revelation were they to him, played with the artistic perfection for which that orchestra was so justly celebrated, although there was room for improvement. They forced open in him the floodgates of a torrent of emotion. A new world dawned upon him. Music that had hitherto lain dormant, suddenly awakened into a vigorous existence truly electrifying. His future career was decided. Henceforth he, too, would be a musician. And what was there in Beethoven that should so startle him into new life? He had heard Haydn, Mozart, and earlier masters without being so completely awed and fascinated. What was there in these symphonies that should exercise such a determining influence over him? It was the overpowering earnestness of the unhappy composer. Beethoven dealt with life problems according to the spirit of his age — the demand for freedom of thought and liberty of the person. Beethoven had been baptized in that mighty wave, the struggle for freedom, which rolled over Germany at the beginning of this century. He could not help being eloquently earnest. He was the creature of his time, and when called upon to declare himself, was not found wanting in rugged, bold earnestness. Yet although Haydn and Mozart, too, were earnest, their utterances were of a subjective character. The world to them presented none of the doubts and philosophic speculations which convulsed Beethoven's period. Their view of life was pure optimism. A vein of bright joyousness runs through all their works, aye, even their most serious. But Beethoven was a pessimist, and his works betray him. When he has a sunshiny moment it serves only to show how deep is his prevailing gloom. Wagner at fifteen was a poet, and the energetic, suggestive music of Beethoven was mentally transformed into living personalities. He has said that he felt as if Beethoven addressed him "personally." Every movement formed itself into a story, glowed with life, and assumed a clear, distinct shape. I do not forget the earlier influence of Weber over him, but then that was more due to emotion than to reason. The novelty of "Der Freischütz," the freshness of its melodic stream, and the wild imaginative treatment of the romantic story captivated his first affection and enchained it to the last. The whole of his impressions of Beethoven (whom, by the way, Wagner never saw) were embodied by him in a sketch written for a periodical and entitled, " A Pilgrimage to Beethoven." Although the incidents painted there are not to be taken as having happened to the pilgrim, Wagner, yet the story is clear on one point — the unbounded spell Beethoven exercised over him.

As he was now determined to become a musician, and seeing the necessity of acquiring some theoretical knowledge of his new art, with his usual perseverance he began studying alone. His progress was so disappointing that he made arrangements with a local organist, with whom, too, he advanced but little. However, he was resolved. Music he wanted for his own play; without music he felt it was incomplete, and although he worked assiduously, theory seemed a long, dreary road which, instead of helping him to the goal he yearned to reach, presented innumerable obstacles in the path.  He wanted to compose, yet all the grammarian's rules were so many caution-boards, warning him against doing this or that, impediments that prevented him accomplishing what he strove to perform.  It was always what should *not* be done instead of what should be done.  With youthful impetuosity he then revolted against all grammarianism, and to the end of his life maintained an attitude of derisive defiance towards all who fought behind the shield inscribed fugue, canon and counterpoint.

Although conscious of how unsatisfactory his theoretical progress had been, ambition prompted him to write an overture for the orchestra.  The young composer was seventeen.  The overture is characterized by Wagner's besetting sin — extravagance of means.  Through his sister's connection with the stage he became acquainted with the music director of the Leipzic theatre, a young man, Heinrich Dorn, a few years older than Wagner.  I knew Dorn as a friendly, easy-going, good-tempered fellow.  Impressed with the unusual enthusiasm of the youth, Dorn kindly offered to perform his overture at the theatre.  It was performed.  The audience laughed at it, and Wagner was not slow to admit the justice of its reception.

Of the caligraphy displayed in this work I must say a few words.  The score was written in different-coloured inks, the groups of strings, wood, and brass, being distinguished by special colours.  His extreme neatness and care at all times of his life, when using the pen, was wonderful.  Before putting word or note to paper every thought had been so fully digested that there was never any need of erasure or correction. In strange contrast with Richard Wagner's clean, neat, distinct writing, stand Beethoven's hieroglyphics, whole lines of which were sometimes smudged out with the finger.

Wagner accepted the judgment upon his overture, though not without a painful feeling of disappointment. But as he was determined to be a musician, his family now encouraged him, and for that purpose placed him under Cantor Weinlig of Leipzic. The Cantor was on intimate terms with my father, and therefore was well known to me. He had a great name as a skilled contrapuntist. Gentle and persuasive in demeanour, he soon won the affection of his pupil, and although his tuition lasted for about six months only, it was sufficient to cause Wagner to refer with affection to this, his only real master.

The immediate result of Weinlig's tuition was the production of a sonata for the pianoforte. It is in strict form, but Wagner's conscientious adherence to the dogmatic principles he had learned seem to have dried up all sources of inspiration. He was evidently in a straight jacket, for the sonata does not contain one original idea, not one phrase of more than common interest. It is just the kind of music that any average pupil without gift might have written. Time was wanting before the careful, orthodox training of Weinlig could thoroughly assimilate itself to the peculiarity of Wagner's genius.

It is curious that he should have produced such a very inferior work as regards ideas and development while he was at the same time a most ardent student of Beethoven. It can only be explained by regarding the period as one of transition and receptivity. He was not full grown nor strong enough to wing himself to independent flight.

Beethoven was his daily study. He was carefully storing up all the grand thoughts of the great master, but his fiery enthusiasm had not yet come to that burning-point when it should ignite his own latent powers. His acquaintance with the scores of Beethoven has never been equalled. It was extraordinary. He had them so much by heart that he could play on the piano, with his own awkward fingering, whole movements. Indeed, beyond Weber, the idol of his boyhood, and Beethoven, there was no master whose works interested him at that period. His family considered him Beethoven-mad. His eldest brother, Albert, then engaged actively in the profession, and more of a practical business man, particularly condemned the exclusive hero-worship of a master not then understood or acknowledged by the general public. But Richard persevered with his study, and as a testimony of his affection for Beethoven it may be mentioned that, at eighteen, he produced a pianoforte arrangement of the whole of the " Ninth Symphony."

In the school of Weber and Beethoven did Wagner form himself. The musical utterances of both his models were in harmony with their time. Weber was romantic, Beethoven pessimistic. The cry for liberty which ran throughout Europe at the end of the eighteenth century affected the republic of letters sooner than the world of music. It was Wagner's "idol," his "adored" master, who first musically portrayed the revolutionary spirit of the dawn of this century. It was he who founded the romantic school of musicians. His ideality, his "romantic" genius, taking that word in its highest and noblest sense, place him in an entirely separate niche of the temple of art. His inventive faculty, the irresistible charm of his melody, his entirely new delineation and orchestral colouring of character, are immeasurably superior to anything of the kind which preceded him. He was the basis, the starting-point of a new phase in the art of music. And yet, with it all, the great Weber fell short in one important feature of his art — the consequential development of his themes. All his chamber music testifies to this. Even in his three great overtures, " Der Freischütz," " Euryanthe," and " Oberon," the " working-out " of the subjects is feeble and unskilful, and only compensated for by the ever gushing forth of new and potent ideas. Weber had not passed through the crucible of a serious study of the classical school. In his early·period he had treated music more as an amateur than as an earnest-thinking musician. Nor was he gifted with the brain power of Beethoven. It was the latter master's causal strength of brain, combined with his deep, serious studies and his incessant striving to express exactly what he felt, which have secured for him that exceptional position in modern tonal art.

Coming now to Wagner, we find him possessing, to a truly remarkable degree, the special powers of both. His wondrous inventive genius was controlled by a brain power as solid as rare. It enabled him to fuse in his own work the gifts of the idealist, Weber, and of the thinker, Beethoven. The latter's mastery of workmanship, his reasoned sequence of ideas, are vastly surpassed in Wagner's dialectic treatment. As an instrumental colourist Weber was superior to Beethoven. The deafness of the latter sometimes led him to mark the wrong instrument in his scores.   He could not hear, and therefore was not fully able to comprehend the qualities of every instrument, like Weber.   The greatness of his power as an orchestral writer is undeniable, yet many instances could be quoted where he has misapplied a particular instrument of whose character, through his deafness, he had lost the exact knowledge.   Wagner based his instrumentation on that of Weber.   In spite of an almost unlimited admiration of Beethoven, Wagner has not refrained from pointing to certain defects of scoring in him.   He shows that whilst Beethoven modelled his orchestra after Hadyn and Mozart, his conceptions went immeasurably beyond them and clashed with the somewhat inadequate means of their orchestra. Beethoven had neither the modern keyed brass instruments to support the wood-wind against the doubled and trebled strings, nor did he dare to venture beyond the then supposed range of the wood, brass, and string instruments.   Often when reaching what was thought to be the topmost note on either, he suddenly jumps in an almost childishly anxious manner to an octave below, interrupting the melody and producing an irritating effect.   Wagner has asserted that had Beethoven heard the tonal effect of portions of his marking, he would unquestionably have rewritten them or altered the instruments.   But whilst deploring his great predecessor's deafness as the cause of certain defective instrumentation he renders unstinted homage to the general orchestration of the symphonies.   The enormous amplification of deeply reasoned detail in those nine grand works demands from each individual of the orchestra an attention and refinement of expression to be expected only from an orchestra composed of virtuosi.

It was shortly after his return to Leipzic that Wagner began to study instrumentation. The Gewandhaus concerts and Beethoven's symphonies had stirred him. He thumped the piano, was conscious of his lack of skill, but nevertheless bought the scores of the symphonies and studied them with heart and soul. The magnificent colouring charmed him. To work the score at the piano, and see where the secret lay, was his careful study, and then, when he found it, he saw how necessary was individual excellence of performance. Even the Gewandhaus performances failed to completely satisfy him. The members of the orchestra were familiar with the works, yet was the performance far from conveying that lasting impression which the delineation of the intensely grand ideas were capable of, and which from his piano-reading he expected. The dissatisfaction he experienced induced him to seek further for the explanation, and after careful thought he fixed the blame on the shortcomings of the conductor. The head of an orchestra, he asserted, should study the work to be played under him until every phrase, its meaning, and bearing to the whole composition were thoroughly assimilated by him. He should, further, have a perfect acquaintance with the capabilities of every instrument, and an excellent memory. Works performed under conductors not possessing these qualifications never produce their legitimate effect. "It was only when I had conducted Mozart's works myself," says Wagner, "and had made the orchestra execute every detail as I felt it, that I took real pleasure in their performance."

# CHAPTER V.



HAD Wagner's youthful enthusiasm been fired at the Dresden Kreuzschule with love for Germany and hatred of the French oppressor, a feeling which flew through the land like lightning, had the songs of Körner's "Lyre and Sword," set to vigorous music by Weber, inspired him, his patriotism was intensified tenfold when, returning to his native city, he came into the midst of a population that had suffered all the horrors and privations of actual war. His study of modern literature, assimilated with surprising facility in a brain where all was order and consecutiveness, gave him an insight into the deplorable state of his beloved country, whilst indicating the direction in which future efforts should be directed. He found that the revolutionary spasm of the end of the eighteenth century had shattered time-honoured traditions, roughly shaken the creeds of the past, and indeed had left nothing untouched, infiltrating itself into every great and small item of human existence. The impetus of the time was "revolution!" To throw down the trammels of moral and physical slavery, to free man and raise him to the throne of humanity, was the desire of all European peoples. All worked towards one common goal; there was not one movement of importance then that was not influenced by the revolution. In literature the tendency was to make letters a concrete part of the national mind, just as the great French revolution called into existence the first notion of national life by investing the people with the controlling power of their country's interests. All the master-minds of the time of Louis the Fourteenth were in some measure connected with the king; but with the nineteenth century revolution a third state was developed, which enriched national life, and, acting upon literature, drove the hitherto secluded savants and their works into the vortex of popular life. Before this upheaval, literature had been the exclusive property of the professional savant and his high-born protector. The tendency of modern social life was to enthrone mind and genius. The third state was actually breaking down social barriers, the line of demarcation between them and so-called "good society," the monarch and aristocracy. That such a violent change at the beginning of the century should have unsettled and bewildered some otherwise remarkably gifted men is not surprising. The turbulent state of society, and the confused investigation and awkward handling of important moral questions, led to doubt and despair. Men like the brothers Schlegel became Roman Catholics, hoping by so doing to cast the responsibility of their life on a religion which closes every aperture to the reasoning powers. Ludwig Tieck, another German savant, followed their example, whilst men like Zacharias Werner, after having given proofs of the highest capability, destroyed their mental being by pursuing a most dissolute and reprehensible course; or, like Hoffman, by an over-indulgence in wine, helped

to create an unæsthetic phase in German literature
which, alas, serves only to show how sadly distorted
gifted brains can become. Kleist was driven to commit suicide. I could cite more unhappy victims of that
troublous epoch, existences blighted by the powerful
wave of romanticism and freedom that swept over the
land. The only man who remained unaffected by the
movement was Goethe. In his striving for plastic
beauty and classicism, he never became enthusiastic
for the romantic school. He even stood somewhat
aloof from Shakespeare ; nor would he, in his cold simplicity and placid grandeur, see in all the romantic movement aught but a remnant of revolution against his
"legitimate" supremacy.

Those early years of Wagner were passed in a scene
of unusual activity and excitement. His native city a
great battle-field the year of his birth, people hardly
recovered from the shock of the 1793 revolution, when
again they are startled by its reverberation in July,
1830. Then Wagner was seventeen, of an age and
thoughtful enough to be impressed by the struggle carried on around him, or, to quote his own words, "all
that acted more and more on my mind, on my imagination and reason." This was the spirit which he brought
to bear on his study of orchestration, — ideality controlled by strong reasoning power. He had studied
under the first professor of Leipzic, had had an overture performed in public, and now, in 1832, he essayed a
grand symphony for orchestra, which ever remained a
pleasing work to him, and to which he would refer
with evident satisfaction. Its history is a curious one.

Though not twenty, he, with his usual self-reliance,

boldly took the score and parts to Vienna. He wanted his work to be heard. His daring ambition was not satisfied with a lesser centre than the Austrian capital. Vienna was then, as it is now, the city of pleasure and light Italian music. As Beethoven himself could command but a small section of adherents among the pleasure-seeking Viennese, it is not surprising that the untried and unknown young composer was ignored. But undaunted, he took his treasure to Prague, where Dionys Weber, conductor of the Conservatorium, performed it to Wagner's unbounded delight. Returning home, he had the proud satisfaction of hearing it played at the classical Gewandhaus concerts and also at its rival but lesser institution, the " Euterpe." This was a promising augury, and to Wagner amply sufficient for assuming that later his work would be repeated. Therefore, when in 1834 Mendelssohn was appointed conductor at the Gewandhaus, Wagner unhesitatingly took the symphony to him. For a long time nothing was heard of it. Wagner became anxious, and applied to Mendelssohn, when to his indignation he was informed that the score had unfortunately been lost. Wagner never alluded to this incident without indulging in one of those bitter ironical attacks upon Mendelssohn in which he was such an adept. The incident rankled in the memory of the over-sensitive composer, and no amount of external amiability at a later period from Mendelssohn was ever able to efface it. This symphony was Wagner's first acknowledged work and acknowledged, too, by men of weight, whose commendation had, not unnaturally, elated him. "My first symphony!" How often have I heard that phrase? and spoken with such satisfaction that on several occasions I tried to induce Wagner to play some reminiscences of it to me.  He could not; he had lost all remembrance of it.  Accident or fate willed it that shortly before his death the orchestral parts were discovered at Dresden.  A score was arranged and the fifty-year-old work performed *en famille* in 1882, under the revered old man's bâton at Venice.

Though proud of his success as a musician, the poetic side of his nature was not repressed.  He was a poet as well as musician.  Suddenly the poesy within him leaped forth and impelled him to write words already wedded in his own heart to sounds.  Its appearance was as a revelation disclosing an allied power which was to exalt him to a pinnacle to which no other composer in the whole history of art could possibly lay claim.  He wrote a libretto to "The Wedding."  This was to be his first opera, and the same year, 1833, in which he wrote the words he also began the music.  However, he composed but three numbers, still in existence, the introduction, a chorus, a sextet, and then was dissuaded by his sister from proceeding further with it.  The story and its treatment were both pronounced ill-adapted for stage representation.  The book was the veriest hyper-romantic scum, a mixture of the gloomy fatalist Werner and the wildly extravagant Hoffman.  The opera was abandoned with regret, and a living was sought in any form of musical drudgery.  He was willing to "arrange," to "correct proofs," or do anything but teaching, to which he always had the strongest antipathy.  To my knowledge, he never gave a lesson in his life.  When, therefore, the post of chorus master at the Würzburg theatre was offered to him, he readily accepted it.  His eldest brother, Albert, was then engaged at Würzburg as singer, actor, and stage manager. It was the practice of Albert all through life to assume the rôle of mentor to his younger brother, but against this Richard strongly rebelled, though at the same time readily admitting his brother's abilities as a manager and singer. Possessed of a remarkably high tenor voice, Albert was unfortunately subject to intermittent attacks of total loss of vocal power. But the singer's loss was the actor's gain, for to compensate for this defect he exerted himself and succeeded in shining as an actor.

This Würzburg engagement was Richard Wagner's first real active participation in stage life. He had entered upon his new duties but a short time when an opportunity presented itself wherein he could exhibit his practical skill as a musician. Albert was cast for the tenor part in Marschner's "Vampyre." According to his notion, his chief solo finished unsatisfactorily. Richard's aid was invoked, and the result was additional words, some forty lines and music, too, which enabled Albert to display his unusually fine high tones.

The life to Wagner was novel, attractive, and full of bright promise. The friendly relations that existed between the chorus and their director, the habitual banter of the players, their studied posing, their concealing home miseries beneath a simulated gaiety, attracted and charmed the inexperienced neophyte. He was yet blind to all the wiles, trickeries, and petty infamies that seem inseparable from stage life. In the theatre the meannesses and jealousies that clog human existence under all forms are focused and exposed to the glare of publicity, whereas in the wide world they are lost among the crowd. It was not long before Wagner began to hate the shams and petty meannesses of the stage with ten-fold the intensity he had at first been bewitched by it.

During his stay at Würzburg, urged by his brother he again thought of composing an opera. Casting about for a fitting subject, he alighted upon a volume of legends by Gozzi. One, "La Donna Serpente," attracted him, and seemed to invite operatic treatment. He resolved to write his own text, and within the year produced what was his first complete opera, which he called "The Fairies." The musical treatment was entirely in the romantic style of Weber and Marschner, but Wagner frankly confesses it did not realize his expectations. He had thought himself capable of greater things than his powers were yet equal to. Nevertheless, he strove to obtain a hearing for it, but without success. French and Italian opera ruled the German stage, and native productions were not encouraged. However, an ardent aspirant for fame like Wagner was not to be discouraged by the cold slights offered to his first stage work. He returned to Leipzic, 1834, again energetically endeavouring to get it accepted, but only to be disappointed once more.

It was during this visit to Leipzic that an event occurred which was destined to strongly influence his future career. He heard that great dramatic artist, Schroeder-Devrient. The effect of her performance upon him was startling, although the operas in which she appeared, "Romeo" and "Norma" of Bellini, were of the weakest. He saw what a striking impression could be produced by careful attention to dramatic detail. The poorest work was elevated into the realms of high art by the grand style of the inspired artist. For the first time he realized the immense value of perfection of "style." The lesson was not lost, and the high point to which Wagner artists have subsequently carried it by the master's imperative insistence upon the most thorough and exhaustive attention to every detail of art, has formed the undying Wagner school.

Fired by enthusiasm, he began the composition of a new opera, in which he ambitiously hoped the great actress would perform the principal rôle. This was his second music-dramatic work, "Das Liebesverbot" ("The Novice of Palermo"), founded upon Shakespeare's "Measure for Measure." It took him about two years to write it. To Wagner this period was one of transition, alternately dominated by the serious Beethoven, the "romantic" Weber, Auber, and even the popular Italian school. He was as a tree through whose branches the winds rushed from all quarters, only the more firmly to consolidate the roots. He, too, was young, and a not unnatural desire to acquire some of the world's riches induced him to write his new work in a "popular" vein. The "Novice of Palermo" has but very faint indications of the Wagner of after-life, and in the composer's own judgment was but an indifferent work, although comparing favourably with the operas of its day.

After the termination of his Würzburg engagement Wagner went to Magdeburg, 1834, where he was appointed music director, a post he held for nearly two years, steadily working, meanwhile, at the "Novice of Palermo." The Magdeburg company was above the usual level of provincial troupes. The conductor was young and energetic, and soon secured the good will of his subordinates. But the Magdeburghers were apathetic in musical matters, and in the spring of 1836 the theatre announced its final performances. The "Novice of Palermo" was not then completed. After some discussion it was decided to perform it. Wagner hurried on his work, battling with innumerable difficulties which presented themselves thick and fast. First the theatre was threatened with bankruptcy. To escape this it was arranged to close the building a month earlier than the time originally announced. It left Wagner ten days for rehearsals. His book had not been submitted to the censor, and as it was now the Lenten season, there was a dread that the title might subject the libretto to vexatious pruning. The opera was given out as founded on one of the serious plays of Shakespeare, and by this means escaped all maltreatment. But what could be done in ten days? Little even where friendly will was engaged. However, after rehearsal upon rehearsal, the work was performed. Its reception was moderate. The tenor singer had been unable to learn his part in the short time and resorted to unlimited "gag." Perhaps hardly one was perfect in his rôle, and the whole work went badly enough. In after-life Wagner could afford to laugh at this makeshift performance, but at that time it was terribly real. He once gave me a representation of the tenor singer and other impersonators in a manner so ludicrous and mirth-provoking that he said, " You laugh now, but listen ! A second performance was promised for my benefit. We were assembled and about to begin, when suddenly a hand-to-hand fight sprung up between two of the characters, and the performance had to be given up." This put him in sad straits. He had hoped to receive such a sum of money from this "benefit" as would free him from all monetary difficulties, but no performance taking place he was worried in a most uncomfortable manner.

I suppose that if there be any feature in Wagner's character about which there is no difference of opinion it is his love for his native land. At critical junctures, he has not hesitated, by speech or action, to declare his pronounced feelings. At present, however, my purpose is not to illustrate this point, but to emphasize a phase of thought in Wagner's early manhood, which, boldly proclaimed at the time, gathered strength with increasing years, and forms one of the most important factors in his art-workings. He contended that the national life of a people was intimately entwined with their art productions. "The stage," said Wagner, "is the noblest arena of a nation's mind." This was a very favourite theme of his. . He would descant on it unceasingly. The stage was the mirror of a people. Shakespeare he worshipped, and gloried that such an intellect was counted in the republic of letters. England should be proud of her great man. He thought Carlyle right when he said Shakespeare was worth more to a nation than ten Indias. But poor Germany! What could she show? Where was her race of literary giants? The war of liberation had fired every German heart with the intensest patriotism. Young Germany had fought with unexampled ardour, and the hateful Napoleonic yoke was victoriously cast off. Liberty, patriotism, and fraternity were the watchwords of every German, and they found their art expression in the inspiriting strains of the soldier-poet, Körner, and the vigorous melodies of the patriotic Weber.   And German potentates looked on bewildered. Where would this torrent of enthusiasm end?   Were they themselves secure on their thrones?   Would it not sap the foundations of their own rule?   And, as history too sadly shows, fear developed into despotism. The princes turned, and with the iron heel trampled upon the very men who had valiantly defended them against the ruthless invader.   They were fearful of the German mind awakening to a sense of its political and social shortcomings.   They argued that this uncontrolled enthusiasm for liberty of speech and person was a menace to their thrones; therefore they strove to crush it out.   Their conduct Wagner later stigmatized as "replete with the blackest ingratitude," and their treatment of national art as dictated by "cold, calculating cruelty."   For the stage, alien productions were imported.   French frivolity reigned supreme.   Rossini's operas, licentious ballets, were patronized to the exclusion of Beethoven's works, and now, though half a century has elapsed, the baneful influence is still discernible. Such feelings greatly agitated Wagner's early manhood. By 1840 they had assumed definite shape, and we find him through the public journals deploring the want of a German national drama.   It was his effort to supply this want.   He went to work with a fixed purpose. How far he has succeeded posterity will judge.

# CHAPTER VI.



For nine months, from the Easter of 1836 to the opening of the new year, 1837, Wagner was without engagement. It was a period of hardship and suffering. In a most miserable plight he went to Leipzic and Berlin, energetically exerting himself to get his opera, "The Novice of Palermo," accepted. He met with plenty of promises but no performances. His needs became more pressing. Debts had been incurred and the prospect of paying them was of the gloomiest. An ordinary mortal would have sunk under such overwhelming trouble, but Wagner was made of sterner stuff. His indomitable self-reliance and pluck, based upon an abnormal self-esteem, ever kept alight the lamp of hope within him, and sustained him through sadder times than this. True, he had not proved to the world that he was a genius, but he, himself, was fully convinced of it. He had written two operas, a symphony, and other works, and though they did not surpass or even equal what had been accomplished by other artists, yet for all that he was strongly imbued with a consciousness of the greatness of his own power in the tonal and poetic arts. He was convinced that he had a mission to fulfil, a new art gospel to preach, and, too, that he would succeed. The death-bed prediction of his step-father that he would be " something " would be fulfilled.

As far as his art creations show, this was a period of non-productivity. But it is impossible to suppose that Wagner was idle. Genius is never inactive. If not visibly at work the reflective faculties are certain to be actively employed. Though beset with every conceivable worldly trouble, depending for daily wants on what he could borrow, he, with alarming temerity, married.

It was on the 24th November, 1836; the bride, Fräulein Wilhelmina Planer, leading actress of the Magdeburg company. She was the daughter of a working spindle-maker. It was not the known possession of any histrionic gift that caused her to become a professional actress, but a very natural desire, as the eldest of the family, to increase the resources of the household. Spindle-making was not a profitable calling, and with a family, other help was gladly welcomed. But, as necessity has oft discovered and forced to the front many a talent that would have lain hidden from the world, so now was Magdeburg astonished by the presence of an unquestionably gifted artist. Minna Planer played the leading characters in tragedy and comedy. When off the stage her bearing was quiet and unobtrusive. No theatrical trick or display indicated the actress. And, after she had finally quitted stage life, it had been impossible to suppose that the soft-spoken, retiring, shy little woman had ever successfully impersonated important tragic rôles.

Minna was handsome, but not strikingly so. Of medium height, slim figure, she had a pair of soft gazelle-like eyes which were a faithful index of a tender heart. Her look seemed to bespeak your clemency, and her gentle speech secured at once your good-will. Her movements in the house were devoid of everything approaching bustle. Quick to anticipate your thoughts, your wish was complied with before it had been expressed. Her bearing was that of the gentle nurse in the sick-chamber. It was joy to be tended by her. She was full of heart's affection, and Wagner let himself be loved. Her nature was the opposite of his. He was passionate, strong-willed, and ambitious : she was gentle, docile, and contented. He yearned for conquest, to have the world at his feet : she was happy in her German home, and desired no more than permission to minister to him. From the first she followed him with bowed head. To his exuberant speech, his constant discourses on art, and his position in the future, she lent a willing, attentive ear. She could not follow him, she was not able to reason his incipient revolutionary art notions, to combat his seemingly extravagant theories ; but to all she was sympathetic, sanguine, and consoling, — "a perfect woman, nobly planned," as Wordsworth sweetly sings. As years rolled by and the genius of Wagner assumed more definite shape and grew in strength, she was less able to comprehend the might of his intellect. To have written "The Novice of Palermo" at twenty-three, and to have been received so cordially was to her unambitious heart the zenith of success. More than that she could not understand, nor did she ever realize the extent of the wondrous gifts of her husband. After twenty years of wedded life it was much the same. We were sitting at lunch in the trimly kept Swiss chalet at Zurich in the summer of 1856, waiting for the composer of the then completed "Rienzi," "Dutchman," "Tannhäuser," and "Lohengrin" to come down from his scoring of the "Nibelungen," when in full innocence she asked me, "Now, honestly, is Richard such a great genius?" On another occasion, when he was bitterly animadverting on his treatment by the public, she said, "Well, Richard, why don't you write something for the gallery?" And yet, notwithstanding her inaptitude, Wagner was ever considerate, tender, and affectionate towards her. He was not long in discovering her inability to understand him, but her many good qualities and domestic virtues endeared her greatly to him. She had one quality of surpassing value in any household presided over by a man of Wagner's thoughtless extravagance. She was thrifty and economical. At all periods of his life Wagner could not control his expenditure. He was heedless, relying always upon good fortune. But Minna was a skilled financier, and he knew this. For years their lot was uphill, sometimes a hard struggle for bare existence, and through all the devotion and homely love of the woman soothed and cheered the nervous, irritable Wagner. When their means enabled them to enjoy the comforts of life without first anxiously counting the cost, Minna was possessed of one thought, her husband and his happiness. And Wagner knew it and gratefully appreciated the heart's devotion of the worshipping woman. Home was her paradise, her husband the king. Love, simple, trusting love, was her religion, and no greater testimony to the noble work of a genuine woman could be offered than that of the poet Milton in his "Paradise Lost":—

> Nothing lovelier can be found
> In woman, than to study household good.

Throughout his career Wagner shook off the troubles of daily life with an elasticity truly remarkable. But now he must do something. He had incurred the most sacred of all obligations, to provide for his wife, and employment of some description was a pressing necessity. Viewed from an artistic point, his lost appointment had been a success. He had acquired all the skill of an efficient conductor and had familiarized himself with a large number of opera scores. But what had he done with his own gifts? The miserable finale of the Magdeburg episode, and his increased responsibilities, made him seriously reflect on this past year and a half. True he had composed an entire opera. But of what material was it made? He had regretfully to acknowledge that it was not as he would wish it. He had thrown over his household gods to worship Baal. He had rejected Weber and Beethoven, "his adored idols," to dress his thoughts in attractive, showy, French attire. He had forsaken heartfelt truth for a graceful exterior. And what had he gained by imitating Auber and Rossini? Not even the satisfaction of public success. And why? His models spoke as they felt, whilst he clothed his thoughts in a borrowed garb. He was now conscious that he had but to express himself in his own language to convince others of the truth of his art gospel.

Some such similar post as at Magdeburg was what he now desired. There he would be Wagner himself. But in these early years smiling fortune was not always his happy companion. Nearly a year elapses before he again finds himself directing an operatic company. This time it is at Königsberg.

But before accompanying the weary artist to his new

home some mature reflections of Wagner on his Magdeburg period are worthy of notice. His elevation to the post of music director of the Magdeburg theatre was a joyful moment. For the first time he would be sole controller of operatic performances. When a youth he had been revolted by the slatternly manner in which theatre conductors had led the performances. Even the Gewandhaus concerts had not been altogether satisfactory. Something then was lacking in the ensemble. Now was his opportunity. The mechanical time-beating prevalent among conductors of opera houses would find no place with the ardent youthful composer. He first secured the affection of the singers by evincing a personal interest in their public success. His born actor's skill enabled him to illustrate how such a character should move, whilst with the orchestra he would sing passages and rehearse one phrase incessantly until he was satisfied. He was indefatigable. The secret of his success was his earnestness. He knew what he wanted, which was half-way to securing it. The company seems to have been fairly intelligent and to have responded freely to his wishes, but the audiences were phlegmatic. Magdeburg was a garrison city, and the audiences were domineered by the cold reserve observed by the military. Wagner thought of all publics the worst was a military one. Effusive exhibitions of joy they regard as indecorous and unseemly, and the absence of spontaneous enthusiasm exercises a depressing effect on artists. Among the operas he conducted were Auber's " Masaniello " and Rossini's " William Tell." Both of them were favourites of his. At that period, 1836, they stood out in bold relief from modern and ancient operas.

Their melodies were fresh and graceful, and a dramatic truthfulness pervaded them which to the embryo imitator of the Greek tragedy was a strong recommendation. Further, the revolutionary subjects were congenial to the outlaw of 1848. But Auber and Rossini were soon to be eclipsed by the clever Hebrew, Meyerbeer, and it is this last writer·who in a couple of years impels Wagner to leave his fatherland for Paris. It is Meyerbeer's works that he is now about to conduct at Königsberg, where we shall at once follow him.

The time he spent in Königsberg was a prolongation of the miserable existence which had followed the breaking up of the Magdeburg company, intensified now, alas, by anxiety for his young wife. It was unenlivened by any gleam of even passing sunlight. The time dragged heavily, and was never referred to without a shudder. In later years, in the presence of his first wife, he has compassionately remarked, "Yes, poor Minna had a hard time of it then, and after the first few months of drudgery no doubt repented of her bargain." To which the gentle Minna would reply by a look full of tender affection. Wagner's references to the devotion and untiring energy of his wife during the Königsberg year of distress always affected him.

He began his public life at Königsberg by conducting orchestral concerts in the town theatre. This led to his appointment as music director of the theatre. The operatic stage was then governed almost entirely by Meyerbeer, "Robert le Diable" and "Le Prophète," both recent novelties, being the great attraction. They met with an enormous success everywhere. Meyerbeer was in Paris, the idol of the populace. A man possessed of undeniable genuine merit, he bartered it away for gold. The real merit was over-laden with a thick coat of meretricious glitter. Attractive and dazzling show was what he set before the light-hearted public of the French capital, and they mistook the tinsel for pure gold. But, for all that, Meyerbeer was the hero of the hour, and what was fashionable in Paris was immediately reproduced in the fatherland towns and cities. In matters of art Paris was the acknowledged leader of Germany. From afar, the young ambitious music director of Königsberg heard of the fabulous sums which Meyerbeer received for his works. He was in the direst distress. The troubles of Magdeburg had followed him to his new home, and he looked with longing eyes towards Paris, the El Dorado of his dreams. He became haunted with visions of luxurious independence, startling in their contrast to his present penurious position. He looked about him and bestirred himself. With his accustomed boldness, not to say audacity, he promptly wrote to Scribe, hoping by one effort to emerge from all his trouble. What he sent to the famous French librettist was a plan he had sketched of a grand five-act opera based on a novel by König, "Die Hohe Braut" ("The Noble Bride"). He was anxious for the collaboration of Scribe, since in that he saw the *open sesame* of the Grand Opera House, Paris. The French writer did not reply. Wagner felt the slight. This was the second time the assistance of an acknowledged litterateur had been solicited, and it was the last. Laube did not satisfy him. Scribe did not notice him. Henceforth he would rely on himself.

His stay at Königsberg is marked by an event of

peculiar interest to Englishmen. Wagner had heard "Rule Britannia." He gave me his impressions of it. He thought the whole song wonderfully descriptive of the resolute, self-reliant character of the English people. The opening, ascending passage, which he vigorously shouted in illustration, was, he thought, unequalled for fearless assertiveness. The dauntless expressiveness of its themes seemed admirably adapted for orchestral treatment, and he therefore wrote an overture upon it. This he sent to Sir George Smart, one of the most prominent of English musicians, justly appreciated, among other things, for having introduced Mendelssohn's "Elijah" to England at the Liverpool festival of 1836. When Wagner related this incident to me in 1855, on his visit to London, he said that, having received no reply, he inquired and ascertained that the score seemed to have been insufficiently prepaid for transmission, and that Sir George Smart had refused to pay the balance, "and for all I know," continued Wagner, "it must still be lying in the dead-letter office."

A digest of Wagner's impressions of the world beyond the footlights, after his intimate connection with the provincial theatres of Würzburg, Magdeburg, and Königsberg, will explain how so serious a thinker could adapt himself to the slipshod existence of thoughtless, light-hearted play-actors. Among modern stage reformers Richard Wagner stands in the front rank. He was earnest. He was practical. He had experienced all evils arising from the shortcomings of the theatre, and he knew where to place his finger on the plague spot. His drawings and prescriptions were those of the practical worker; and he was enabled to make them so through the knowledge acquired during his early life behind the scenes.

What a curious medley stage life introduces one to! "My first contact with the theatre seems like the fantastic recollection of a masked ball," was Wagner's vivid description of his early stage experiences. The stage in Germany has too frequently, for the advance of dramatic art, been the last resort for gaining a livelihood. People of all ranks, highly educated, or with no more than the thinnest smattering of education, as soon as they find themselves without the means of existence, fly to the stage. To one individual endowed by nature for the histrionic vocation who thus adopts the profession, there are ten with absolutely no gifts and whose appearance is due to failure in other walks of life, or to want. All this motley group is, by the restricted stage precincts, brought *nolens volens* into daily contact and cannot avoid constantly elbowing each other. Their private affairs, their friendships, are an open secret. A special jargon is current coin among them. Cant phrases abound and their very occupation familiarizes them with sententious quotations on almost every subject. In no profession is there such an ardent catering for momentary praise. It is the food, the absolute nourishment of the actor; hence jealousy and envy exist stronger here than anywhere else, and Byron does not exaggerate when he speaks of "hate found only on the stage!"

To Wagner's impressionable and pageant-loving nature, the stage possessed fascinating attractions. The free and easy intercourse that existed between all the members of the company, actors, singers, and orchestral performers, the existence of a sort of masonic equality, and the general light-hearted exterior, was in accordance with the jocular temperament of the chorus master. He was familiarly joking and laughing with all his surroundings, a habit he retained to the day of his death. His self-esteem would at all times insist on a certain deference to his opinion, nor would he brook with equanimity any infraction of his ruling as music director. From the age of twenty, when he first ruled the chorus girls at Würzburg, down to the Bayreuth rehearsals for " Parsifal," at which he would illustrate his intention by gesture, speech, and song, he was eminently the commander of his company. His lively temperament, his love of fun, and remarkable mimetic gifts made him a general favourite. In the supervision of operas, musically distasteful to him, he was earnest and energetic, attending to detail and appropriate gesture in a manner that demanded the respectful admiration of all under his bâton. Respect and submission to his rule he exacted as due to his office, and he rarely had difficulty in securing it.

From Königsberg he paid a flying visit to Dresden, the city of his school-boy days. With his accustomed omnivorous reading, scanning every book within reach, he fell upon Bulwer Lytton's " Rienzi." Here was a subject inviting treatment on a large scale. Here was a hero of the style of William Tell and Masaniello. The spirit was revolution and moral regeneration of the people. It was a happy chance which led him to this story, the sentiment of which harmonized so perfectly with his own aspirations. Visions of Paris and its grand opera house had never left him. " Rienzi " offered the very situations calculated to impress an audience accustomed to the gorgeous splendour of the grand opera. Although his eyes were turned towards the French capital, and his immediate hope the conquest of the Parisians, it was not his sole nor ultimate desire. Paris was a means only. He saw that Paris governed German art, and he felt that only through Paris lay his hope of success in his fatherland. It was while under such influences that he began to formulate "Rienzi."

His stay in Königsberg was cut short owing to the company becoming bankrupt. This was the second experience of the kind he had met with in the provinces, and it helped to intensify his contempt for stage life. He was again in money troubles. Fortunately, his old friend Dorn was well placed at Riga and able to secure for him the post of conductor of the opera there. The company was a good one, and its director, Hotter, an intelligent and well-known playwright, who understood Wagner's artistic ambition. The young conductor was very exacting in his demands at rehearsals. To appeal to him was useless. He was earnest and inflexible. And yet, notwithstanding his earnestness and the trouble he took in producing uncongenial operas, he became weary of their flimsy material. Within him the sap of the future music-drama was beginning to rise. His own genius and artistic tendencies were in conflict with what was enacted before him. It was the difference between simulated and real feeling. What he was forced to conduct was stage sentiment, what he yearned for was life-blood. And this latter he strove to infuse into his "Rienzi," which was now assuming definite shape, words and part of the music being written.

When two acts were finished to his satisfaction, there was no longer any peace for him. Paris was the only fitting place where it could be adequately represented. But how to get to Paris? At Riga, as elsewhere, he lived beyond his means. I have before remarked on his incapability of controlling his expenses and living within a fixed income. Minna was thrifty and anxious, but her will was not strong enough to restrain her self-willed husband. She was in a constant state of nervous worry, but her devotion to Wagner prevented her making serious resistance. Now funds were wanting for the projected Paris trip, he had none. However, such a trivial item was not likely to thwart his ambition and to stand in his way. He borrowed again. He was without any letters of recommendation to Paris, spoke but very little French, and yet was full of buoyancy and hope of the success that awaited him when there. It was a bold, not to say reckless, venture. But it is characteristic of Wagner. At all great junctures of his life he risked the whole of his stakes on one card. His determination to leave Riga, and to turn his back on the irritating miseries of a provincial theatre, led him to embark with his wife and an enormous dog, in a small merchant vessel *Pillau* for London. Totally unprovided with any convenience for passengers, badly provisioned and undermanned, the frail trading-craft took the surprisingly long period of three weeks and a half to reach London. It encountered severe weather and on two occasions narrowly escaped foundering. The three passengers, Richard Wagner, his wife, and dog, were miserably ill. On one occasion the bark was driven into a Norwegian fiord; the crew and its passen-

gers — there were no others on board beside the Wagner trio — landed at a point where an old mill stood.
The poor wretches, snatched from the jaws of death,
were hospitably received by the owner, a poor man.
He produced his only bottle of rum and struck joy into
all their hearts by brewing a bowl of punch. It was
evidently appreciated by the hapless ship's company, as
Wagner was hilarious when he spoke of what he humorously called his "Adventures at the Champagne Mill."
When the weather had cleared sufficiently the ship set
sail for London and arrived without any further mishap.

# CHAPTER VII.



1839.

HIS first impression of London was not a pleasant one. The day was wretched, raining heavily, and the streets were thick with mud. At the Custom House Wagner was helped through the vexatious passport annoyance by a German Jew — one of those odd men always to be found about the stations and docks ready to perform any service for a trifling consideration. He recommended Wagner to a small, uninviting hotel in Old Compton Street, Soho, much resorted to by needy travellers from the continent. The hotel, considerably improved, still exists. It is situated a dozen doors or so from Wardour Street, and is opposite to a public house known then, as now, as the " King's Arms." Wagner would have gone straight away to a first-class hotel, but this time, feeling how very uncertain the immediate future was, he asked to be recommended to a cheap inn. He hired a cab, one of those curious old two-wheeled vehicles, where the driver was perilously perched at the side, and with his big dog, carefully sheltered from the weather under the large apron which protected the forepart of the vehicle, they started for Old Compton Street. Arrived there without incident, such of their luggage as they had been able to bring with them at once was carried upstairs, and Wagner and his wife sat down gloomily regarding each other. The room was dingy and poorly furnished, and not of a kind to brighten weary, seasick travellers. Wagner called his dog. No response. He opened the door, rushed down the narrow, dark staircase to the street. Alas! Neither dog nor cab were to be seen. He inquired of every one in broken English, but could learn nothing hopeful or certain about his dumb friend, the companion of his journey, and silent receiver of much of his exuberant talk. Returning to Minna, they came to the conclusion that the dog had leaped down from underneath the covering while the luggage was being transported upstairs. But where was he now? They had not the faintest clue, and knew not in which direction to seek for him. That evening, their first in London, was one of sorrow and discomfort. The next morning Wagner went back to the docks and gleaned tidings sufficient only to dishearten him the more. The dog had been seen the previous evening. Back to Old Compton Street, disconsolate; he had scarcely ascended the first flight of stairs when, his step recognised, loud barks of welcome greeted him from above. The dog was there. It had found its way into the room where his wife had remained during his absence. The poor beast was bespattered with mud, but this did not prevent Wagner affectionately fondling him. To Wagner the return of the dog was wonderful. How a dumb brute, that had seen absolutely nothing during the journey from the docks to Old Compton Street, could find its way back to the old starting-place, and then retrace its steps was a marvellous instance of canine instinct, and one which endeared the race to him deeper than ever, a love that endured to the last.

Wagner remained in London about eight days, time to look round and to arrange for passage to Boulogne, where Meyerbeer was staying, and from whom he hoped to receive introductions to Paris. Although Wagner could read English he was not sufficient master of it to understand it when spoken. This in some degree accounts for the slight interest he felt in his London visit. But he made the best use of his time. He was living within a quarter of an hour's walk of the house in Great Portland Street where his "adored idol," Weber, had died. To that shrine he made his first pilgrimage, to reverently gaze upon the hallowed house. He traversed all London, determining to see everything. The vastness of the metropolis with its boundless sea of houses oppressed him. He had strong, decided opinions as to what the dimensions of a town should be, attributing much of the poverty and misery of large towns to their overgrowth, and felt that when a township exceeded certain limits it was beyond the control of a governing body, and that neglect in some form or another would soon make itself felt. No city, he used to argue, should be larger than Dresden then was.

He was amazed and most disagreeably surprised with the bustle of the city. It bewildered him, and, as he expressed it, "fretted his artistic soul out of him." The great extremes of poverty and riches, dwelling in close proximity to each other, were a sad, unsolvable enigma. His lodgings were perhaps in one of the worst neighbourhoods of London. Old Compton Street

abutted on the Seven Dials.   There he saw misery
under some of its saddest aspects, and then, but a few
minutes' walk and he found himself amidst the luxury
of Oxford Street and Regent Street.   The feelings
engendered by this glaring inequality in his radical
spirit were never effaced.   He thought that the English
in their character, their institutions, and habits were
strangely contradictory, and the impressions of 1839
were confirmed on his subsequent visits to this country.
The grand, extensive parks, open to all, delighted him.
In Germany he had seen no parks, and where public
walks or gardens had been laid out, walking on the
grass was prohibited, whilst here no officious guardian
attempted to interfere with the free perambulation of
the visitor.   The bearing of the police, too, equally surprised him.   Here they were ready with information,
acting as protectors of the public, whereas in Germany
at that period they were aggressive and bureaucratic.
It is curious, but at no time do I remember Wagner
speaking of having visited any of the London theatres
in 1839, whilst in 1855, when he was here for the
second time, he went to almost every place of amusement then open, even those of third-rate order.   But if
in London he fell upon " sunny places," compared with
his German home, he also was sorely tried.   As I
have remarked, his rooms were in a very unaristocratic
quarter.   The bane of all studious Englishmen, especially musicians — the imported organ-grinder, unknown
in Germany — worried the excitable composer out of
all patience.   The Seven Dials was a favourite haunt
of the wandering minstrel, and the man who retired at
night, full of wild imaginings as to his " Rienzi," was

worked into a state of frenzy by two rival organ men grinding away, one at each end of the street.

The immensity of the shipping below London Bridge was a wonderful sight to him. He had come into dock in a tiny, frail sailing craft, the cradle of " The Flying Dutchman," after a hazardous passage across the North Sea. The size and number of the trading vessels appealed direct to his largely developed imaginative faculty. He pictured the mysterious Vanderdecken in this and that vessel, and was full of strange fancies of the spectral crew. The sea of sail so fascinated him that he took a special river trip to Greenwich, the closer to inspect the shipping, and with the further intent to visit the Naval Pensioners' hospital.

When it was known at the hotel in Old Compton Street that he was about starting for Greenwich, he was advised to go over the *Dreadnought* hospital-ship, then lying in the river just above Greenwich. He seized at the suggestion. The *Dreadnought* was one of the vessels of Nelson's conquering fleet in the famous battle of Trafalgar, in the year 1805. Wagner was a devoted worshipper of great men. An opportunity now presented itself to inspect one of the wooden walls of England. It is a widely known fact that hero-worship was a salient feature of Wagner's character. He always referred to Weber as his " adored idol " or " adored master," and for Beethoven he was equally enthusiastic. The " Dutchman," that weird story of the sea, had taken possession of him, and a visit to so celebrated a ship as the *Dreadnought* was an occasion of some importance. In his maturer age, when closer acquaintance with the English people had given him the right to express an opinion as to their nature, he said that in his judgment they were the most poetic of European nations. Poetry, with them, lay not on the surface as with the impetuous Gauls, nor was it sought after and cultivated as with the Germans; but with the English it was deep in their hearts and associated with their national institutions in a manner unknown among any other modern people. No nation has produced such a galaxy of poetic luminaries. The employment of the disabled battle-ship as a refuge for worn-out seamen, men who had fought their country's battles, was, he thought, an incontestable proof of a poetic sentiment founded in the heart of a nation and fostered by natural love. I am aware how much this is in opposition to the judgment of the English by a man who enjoyed a high social standing and intimate acquaintance with the best of Albion's intellect, viz. Lord Beaconsfield, whose famous dictum it was that the " English people care for nothing but religion, politics, and commerce," but the thoughtful opinion of a poet of acknowledged celebrity, Wagner himself, I have deemed it advisable to set forth.

The visit to the *Dreadnought* left an indelible impression upon Wagner. Arrived at the ship, he was in the act of ascending the pilot ladder put over the side of the vessel, by which passengers came on board, when his snuff-box fell out of his pocket into the water. The snuff-box was the gift of Shroeder-Devrient. He prized it highly and attempted to clutch it in its fall. In so doing, it seems he lost his hold of the ladder and was himself only saved from immersion by his presence of mind and gymnastic ability. The precious snuff-box was lost, but the composer of "Parsifal" was saved.

From the *Dreadnought* he went with the nervous Minna to the Greenwich hospital. Wagner had the habit of talking loudly in public, and while walking about the building, seeing a pensioner taking snuff, he said to Minna, "Could I speak English, I would ask him for a pinch." Wagner was an inveterate snuff-taker from early manhood. Imagine Wagner's surprise and delight when the Greenwich snuff-taker accosted him with, "Here you are, my friend," in good German. The pensioner proved to be a Saxon by birth, and, delighted to hear his native tongue, was soon at home with his interlocutor. He told him that he was perfectly contented with his lot, but that his companions, the English, were dissatisfied and were "a grumbling lot."

Wagner was filled with admiration at the generosity and beneficence displayed in the bounteous provision for the comfort of the pensioners. He told me his thoughts sped back to the German sailors on the East Prussian coast, their miserably poor and scanty food, their ill-clothed forms, and the general poverty of their position, when he saw the apparently unlimited supplies of good, wholesome provisions and substantial clothing; and yet, he said, the poor Germans are contented, while the Greenwich pensioners complain.

Wagner had been but two days in London in 1855, when he took me off to Westminster. This was not his first visit to the national mausoleum; he had been there in 1839, and recollections of that occasion induced him at once to revisit the Abbey. We went specially to pay homage to the great men in Poets' Corner, Shakespeare's monument being the main attraction. It will be remembered that his first effort in English had been a translation from Shakespeare, and I found that with increasing years such an enthusiasm for the great dramatist had been developed as was only possible in the ardent brain of an earnest poet. While contemplating the Shakespeare monument on his first visit, it seems he was led to a train of thought, the substance of which he related to me in our 1855 visit. At the time I considered it noteworthy as an important psychological feature and now relate it here. In reflecting over the work done by the British genius, and its far-reaching influence in creating a new form, he was carried back to the classic school of ancient Greece and its Roman imitator.

The ancient classic and the modern romantic schools were opposed to each other. The English founder of the modern school had cast aside all the rigid rules of the classical writers, which even the powerful efforts of the three Frenchmen, Corneille, Racine, and Voltaire, had been unable to revivify. In these reflections, referring to an antecedent period of sixteen years, I have often thought I could discern the germ of his daring revolution in musical form. Turning from the serious to the gay, as was his wont at all times, he added that his reverie had a commonplace ending. Minna plucked his sleeve, saying, "Komm, Lieber Richard, du standst hier zwanzig minuten wie eine Bildsaule, ohne ein Wort zusprechen" (Come, dear Richard, you have been standing here for twenty minutes like one of these statues, and not uttered a word), and when he repeated to her the substance of his meditations, he found as usual she understood but little the serious import of his speech.

Wagner's anxiety to reach the goal of his ambition left him no peace, and on the eighth day after his arrival in London he left by steamer for Boulogne.

The London visit charmed Minna. The quiet, unobtrusive manner of the English pleased her, but annoyed Wagner. He was irritated by their stolidity, and complained always of a want of expansiveness in them. Their stiff politeness he thought angular, and the impression did not wear off during his second visit. These first eight days were not wholly pleasant to him. He was anxious to get to Paris, and all his thoughts were turned towards the city of the grand opera. Minna carried away pleasant recollections, but Wagner thought his dog was the happiest of all, for in London he had been provided daily with special dog's fare, an institution unknown in Germany.

# CHAPTER VIII.



THE passage to Boulogne began pleasantly, but a bad sailor at all times, he did not escape the invariable discomforts of a channel journey. His large Newfoundland dog, for whom he had an affection almost parental, was on board, and excited general interest. Two Jewish ladies, named Manson, mother and daughter, hearing Wagner speak German to his wife and dog, soon entered into conversation with him through the medium of the dog. Speaking a vitiated German with a facility which seems to be the heirloom of the tribe of Judah, they discussed music, and with a familiarity also characteristic of the race they told Wagner they were going to spend a few days in Boulogne before proceeding to Paris. Interested in music, they at once blundered into the delusion, common to all the race, that every great composer was a Jew, supporting their assertion by naming Mendelssohn, Halévy, Rossini, and their personal intimate, Meyerbeer, including also Haydn, Mozart, and Weber. Wagner seized with such eagerness at the name of Meyerbeer that he did not stop to disprove the supposed Israelitic descent of Haydn, Mozart, and Weber. As the ladies were going to call on Meyerbeer, they promised to apprise him of Wagner's intended visit. In this opportune meeting, Wagner thought fate seemed to be stretching out a helping hand to the young German, he who had abandoned in disgust his post of conductor at Riga, to compel the admiration of Paris for his genius. With Meyerbeer at Boulogne and a friendly introduction to the ruler of the Paris Grand Opera, the future seemed promising. Notwithstanding his wife's misgivings he did not hesitate to accompany his travelling companions to their hotel. The expenses were so great, and out of all proportion to his scanty funds, that in a few days he sought a more humble abode.

He saw Meyerbeer, and though he was received amicably enough, yet were his first impressions not altogether agreeable. The ever-present smile of the composer of the "Huguenots" seemed studied and insincere, as though it was rather the outcome of simulated affability than of natural good feeling. Meyerbeer was a polished courtier, his manners bland and his speech unctuous. Diplomatic, committing himself to nothing, he seemingly promised everything. The impassioned language of the young idealist, his fervid outpourings on art, surprised and startled the worldly-wise Meyerbeer. The earnest expression of honest conviction rarely fails to excite interest even in the shrewd business man of the world. Meyerbeer listened attentively to Wagner's story of his early struggles, and of his hopes for the future, ending by fixing a meeting for the next day, when the "Rienzi" poem might be read. The subject and treatment pleased Meyerbeer greatly. From all that is known of him, it is clear that his great and only gift lay in the treatment of spectacle. The stage effects which "Rienzi" offered were many, and the situations powerful. Both features were then adjudged imperative for a successful grand opera in Paris, and in proportion as the " Rienzi " book promised spectacular display, so Meyerbeer grew eulogistic and generous in his promises of help.  Wagner was strongly of opinion that Meyerbeer's first friendly feeling was won entirely by the striking tableaux of the story.  Meyerbeer discussed with Wagner kindred scenes and situations in " Les Huguenots," and such comparison was made between the two books, that Wagner was forced to the conclusion that effect was the chief aim of Meyerbeer, and truth a subordinate consideration.

But to have won the unstinted praise of the enormously popular opera composer seemed to promise immediate and certain success.  It unduly elated him, so that when he experienced the difficulties of getting his work accepted at the Paris Grand Opera House, the shock was more severe and harder to bear.  But in Boulogne everything augured well.  Indeed, Meyerbeer expressed himself so strongly on the libretto as to request Scribe to write one for him in imitation of it.  When talking over this incident with me, Wagner said that he believed Meyerbeer's lavish praise of the book was uttered partly with a view to its purchase, but that Wagner's enthusiasm for his own work prevented Meyerbeer making a direct offer.  However this may have been, from Wagner's plain language to me there is no doubt at all in my mind that Meyerbeer did feel his way to purchase the " Rienzi " text for his own purpose.  Another meeting was arranged for trying the music.  On leaving Meyerbeer, he went direct to relate all to the expectant Minna.  As was his wont at all times after an event of unusual import, he made this a cause of festivity. With Minna he went to dine at a restaurant, and with juvenile exultation ordered his favourite beverage, a half bottle of champagne. To Wagner champagne represented the perfection of "terrestrial enjoyment," as he often phrased it. While sipping their wine they met their newly made acquaintances, the Mansons. Flushed with his recent success, he recounted the whole of the morning episode. The Mansons advised him to stay in Boulogne as long as he could whilst Meyerbeer was there, arguing that he was such an amiable man, and since his good-will had been won was sure to do all he could to promote Wagner's success; and they added significantly, "He has the power to do all."

The trying over of the "Rienzi" music with Meyerbeer was as successful as the reading of the book. Two acts only were then completed, but with these Meyerbeer expressed himself perfectly satisfied. It was just the music to be successful in Paris, and he prognosticated for Wagner a triumph with the Parisians. In discussing the incident with me, Wagner said he believed Meyerbeer's laudation of the music was perfectly sincere, "for," he cynically added, "the first two acts are just the very part of the opera which please me least, and which I should like to disown." It means that Meyerbeer committed the unpardonable fault in Wagner's eyes of praising the careful and neat writing of the composer when the score was opened. On all occasions Wagner would become irritated if his really remarkably neat writing were praised. He would say it was like praising the frame at the expense of the picture, and a slight on the intelligence of the composer.

Wagner took his place at the piano without being asked, and impetuously attacked the score in his own rough-and-ready manner. Meyerbeer was astonished at the rough handling of his piano. He was himself a highly finished performer on the instrument, having begun his public artistic career as a pianist. Wagner supplied as well as he could the vocal parts (with as little technical perfection as his piano-playing), whilst Meyerbeer carefully studied the score over the performer's shoulder. The opinion of Meyerbeer was most flattering, his admiration for Wagner intensifying greatly when at a subsequent meeting he went through the only complete work Wagner had brought with him to conquer Paris — "Das Liebesverbot." Before such lavish and warm praise Wagner's first distrust of Meyerbeer melted as snow before the sun's rays. Meyerbeer pointed to what he considered many admirable stage effects in the "Das Liebesverbot" libretto, and thought that a man so young who could write that and the "Rienzi" text was sure of future celebrity as a dramatist.

Meyerbeer was profuse in his promises of help, and proposed at once to recommend him to the director of a small Paris theatre and opera house, though he pointed out to Wagner that letters of recommendation were of little avail compared to personal introduction. But buoyed with such testimonials and a letter from the Mansons, he left Boulogne, where he was known as "le petit homme avec le grand chien," for Paris, again accompanied by his wife and dumb friend.

# CHAPTER IX.



THAT a young artist but six and twenty years of age, with a wife dependent on him for existence, unknown to fame, almost penniless, and even·without art works that he could show in evidence of his ability, should boldly assault the stronghold of European musical criticism, confident of success, often flitted before Wagner's mind in after-life as an act of temerity closely allied to insanity. "And ah!" he has added in tones of bitter pain, "I had to pay for it dearly: my privations and sufferings were as the tortures in Dante's ' Purgatorio.'" "But why did you undertake such a seemingly Quixotic expedition?" I asked. "Because at that time Paris was the resort of almost every artist of note, whether painter, sculptor, poet, or musician, and even statesmen, when all Europe clothed itself with the livery of Paris fashion." He felt within him a power which urged him forward without fear of failure, and so he came to Paris.

Germany offered no encouragement to native talent. Paris was the gate to the fatherland. First achieve success in Paris, and then his German countrymen would receive him with open arms. It is true, that even a short residence in Paris invested an artist with a certain superiority over his confrères.

As Wagner had but a very imperfect acquaintance

with the French language, he at once sought out the relative of the Mansons to whom he had been recommended. I have been unable to recall the surname of Wagner's new friend, but do remember well that he was spoken of as Louis. This Monsieur Louis was a Jew and a German. He proved an exceedingly faithful and constant companion of Wagner's during his stay in Paris, indeed played the part of factotum to the Wagner household. He must have been quite an exceptional friend, for on one occasion, when Wagner and I were discussing Judaism *per se*, he turned to me and with unusual warmth even for him, said, "How can I feel any prejudice against the Jews as men, when I sincerely believe that it was excess of friendship of poor Louis for me that killed him, — running about in all weathers, exerting himself everywhere, undertaking most unpleasant missions to find me work, and all whilst suffering from consumption. He did it too from pure love of me without any thought of self." Through the aid of Louis he found a modest lodging in a dingy house. The future was so much an uncertainty that with the remembrance of the first days of the Boulogne expensive hotel before him, he yielded to Minna's persuasiveness and reconciled himself to the new abode. He was told that Molière was born there; indeed, a bust of the great Frenchman did, I believe, adorn the front of the house, and this helped to make him accept his new quarters with a little more contentment than his own ambitious notions would have admitted.

Settled in his scantily furnished rooms, with ready business habits, so unusual in a genius, he made it his first duty to call wherever he had been recommended.

Difficult as it may be in any European city to gain access to the houses of prominent men, in Paris the troubles are greater, if only on account of that terrible Cerberus, the concierge, who instinctively divines an applicant for favours, and as skilfully throws obstacles in the way while angling for pourboires.

Disappointment upon disappointment met Wagner. Nowhere was he successful. In speech at all times he uttered himself *en prince*, and for a man seeking the favour and patronage of others this feature militated against him. Meyerbeer had told him in Boulogne that letters of introduction would avail him little or nothing, and that only by personal introduction could he hope to make headway. But though unsuccessful in every direction, he was not the man to give up without desperate efforts. In a few months his funds were entirely exhausted. Where to turn for the necessary money to provide the daily sustenance was the exciting trouble of the moment. His family in Germany had helped him at first, but material help soon gave place to sage advice. Barren criticism on his " mad" Parisian visit, and admonition on his present mode of existence, Wagner would not brook, and so communications soon ceased between him and Germany. But how to live was the harrowing question. It is with feelings of acute pain that I am forced to recall the deep distress that overwhelmed this mighty genius, and the humiliating acts to which cruel necessity drove him. After one more wretched day than the last he suggested to Minna the raising of temporary loans upon her trinkets. Let the reader try and realize the proud Wagner's misery and anguish, when Minna confessed that such as she had were already so disposed of, Louis having performed the wretched office.

This state of sad absolute poverty lasted for months. He could gain no access to theatres or opera house. He offered himself as chorus master, he would have taken the meanest appointment, but everything failed him. With no prospect of succeeding as a musician, he turned to the press. As he possessed a facile pen and a wide acquaintance with current literature, he sought for existence as a newspaper hack. Here he succeeded, and deemed himself fortunate to obtain even that thankless work. The one man to whom he owed the chief means of existence during this wretched Paris sojourn was a Jew, Maurice Schlesinger, the great music publisher and proprietor of the " Gazette Musicale," a weekly periodical. It is curious to note how again he finds a kind friend in a Jew. For Schlesinger he wrote critical notices and feuilletons upon art topics, one, now famous in Wagner's collected writings as " A Pilgrimage to Beethoven." The pilgrimage is wholly imaginary for as I have already stated Wagner never saw Beethoven. The paper itself contains some remarkable foreshadowings of the matured, thinking Wagner and his revolutionary art principles. He also wrote for other papers, Schumann's " Die Neue Zeitschrift," for a Dresden journal, and the " Europa," a fashionable art publication which occasionally printed original tonal compositions. For this last paper he wrote three romances, "Dors mon enfant," "Attente," and "Mignonne." He hoped by these to gain some entry into the Paris fashionable world, but, though he tried to assimilate his style to the popular drawing-room ballad of the day, his songs were pronounced "too serious," and met with no success.

But alas! his literary work was not financially productive enough, and dire necessity drove him to very uncongenial musical drudgery. For the same music-seller, Schlesinger, he made "arrangements" from popular Italian operas, for every kind of instrument. He told me that "La Favorita" had been arranged by him from the first note to the last. The whole of this occupation, to a man as intimate with the orchestra as he, was an easy task, yet very uninteresting and to him humiliating. But though suffering actual privation, he would not give lessons in music. Teaching was an occupation which, even in the darkest days, he would not entertain for a moment.

Such were the means by which Richard Wagner gained an existence during his Paris sojourn. But they were not productive enough. Often he was in absolute want. It was then in this hour of tribulation that the golden qualities of Minna were proved. Sorrow, the touch-stone of man's worth, tried her and she was not found wanting. The hitherto quiet and gentle housewife was transformed into a heroine. Her placid disposition was healing comfort to the disappointed, wearied musician. The whole of the Paris period is "a gem of purest ray serene" in the diadem of Minna Wagner. Thoughts of what the self-denying, devoted little woman did then has many a time brought tears to Wagner's eyes. The most menial house duties were performed by her with willing cheerfulness. She cleaned the house, stood at the wash-tub, did the mending and the cooking. She hid from the husband as much of the discomforts

attaching to their poor home as was possible.  She
never complained, and always strove to present a bright,
cheerful face, consoling and upholding him at all times.
In the evening she and his dog, the same that was temporarily lost in London, were his regular companions on
the boulevards.  The bustle of life and the Parisians
diverted him from more anxious thoughts, whilst supplying him with constant food for his ever-ready wit.

In dress Wagner was at all times scrupulously neat.
After nearly a year's residence in Paris, the clothes he
had brought with him from Germany were showing sad
signs of wear.  The year had been fruitless from a
money point, and his wardrobe had not been replenished.
His sensitiveness on this topic was of course well known
to Minna.  To give him pleasure she hunted Paris to
find, if possible, some German tailor in a small way of
business who, swayed by the blandishments of Minna,
provided her with a suit of clothes for her husband for
his birthday, 22d May, 1840, agreeing to wait for payment until more favourable times.  This delicate and
thoughtful attention on the part of Minna deeply touched
Wagner, and he related the incident to me in illustration
of the loving affection she bore him.  He said that during those three years of pinching poverty and bitter disappointments his temperament was variable and trying.
It was hard to bear with him.  Vexed and worn with
fruitless trials to secure a hearing for his " Rienzi,"
angered at witnessing the lavish expenditure at the
opera house upon works inferior to his own, he has
admitted that his already passionate nature was intensified, and yet all his outbursts were met by Minna in an
uncomplaining, soothing spirit, which, the first fury over,

he was not slow to acknowledge. Her sacrifices for him and all she did became only known years after, when their worldly position had changed vastly for the better. He never forgot her devotion, nor did he ever hide his indebtedness and gratitude to her from his friends.

During the three years that Wagner was in Paris, he was brought into communication with several prominent men in the world of art, men eminent in literature, in music, both as composers and as executants, in painting, and other phases of art. Of the dozen or so of men with whom he thus became more intimately acquainted, the greater portion were his own countrymen and about half were Jews. This constant close intimacy of Wagner with the descendants of Judah is a curious feature in his life, and shows that when he wrote as strongly as he did of Jews and their art work, his judgments were based upon close personal knowledge of the question. As may be supposed, the acquaintance of a young man between twenty-six and thirty years of age with these several thinkers and writers, could not fail to influence, more or less, an impressionable and receptive nature.

It was an odd freak of fortune that almost immediately after Wagner had settled in Paris, he should, by accident, meet in the streets an old friend from Leipzic, Heinrich Laube. It was in a paper edited by Laube that Richard Wagner's first printed article on the non-existence of German opera had appeared. That was when Wagner was about one and twenty. Laube was a political revolutionist who underwent several terms of imprisonment for daring to utter his thoughts about Germany and its government through his paper. But prison confinement never controlled the dauntless courage of the patriot.

He was a man of considerable and varied gifts. It is not only as a political demagogue that he will be known in future times, but as a philosopher, novelist, and playwright. In Leipzic he had shown himself very friendly to Wagner, whose sound, vigorous judgment attracted him, and now after hearing of Wagner's precarious situation, offered to introduce him to Heine. Such an opportunity could not be lost, and so the cultured Hebrew poet and Richard Wagner met.

A curious trio this: Laube, hard-featured and unpleasant to look upon, with a weirdness begotten possibly of frequent incarcerations, — a strange contrast to the handsome, regular-featured, soft-spoken Heine; and then the pale, slim, young Wagner, short in stature, but with piercing eyes and voluble speech which surprised and amazed the cynical Heine. When Heinrich Heine heard that Meyerbeer had given Wagner introductions, he doubted the abilities of the newcomer. Heine was strongly biassed against Meyerbeer and distrusted his sincerity. Although the meeting with Laube was a delight to Wagner, as it brought back to him all his youthful enthusiasm and hope, yet his appreciation of the accomplished writer, which in Leipzic amounted almost to reverence, had been by time and events considerably lessened. Wagner's greatest majesty, earnestness, was wanting in Laube. The litterateur in Wagner's estimation had no fixed purpose, no ideal. He frittered away considerable gifts in innumerable directions. Incongruities the most glaring not unfrequently appeared in his writings. A paragraph of sound philosophical reasoning would be followed by a page of the merest bombastic phraseology. In his dramatic efforts tragedy and farce were placed in amazing juxtaposition. He wrote a large number of novels, but not one proved entirely satisfactory. "Reisenovellen" was an imitation of Heine, but it fell immeasurably below the standard attained by his model. His best literary production was, without doubt, the history of his life in prison, which interests and touches us by its simplicity. However, Wagner could not resist the attraction which Laube's peculiarities possessed for him. The litterateur's unprepossessing pedantic exterior contrasted strangely with his voluptuous and imaginative mind. Possessed of a brain specially fitted for the conception of the noblest schemes for the freedom of human thought, he often childishly indulged in a roguish *plaisanterie.* From a thoughtful disquisition on the philosophy of Hegel he glides into the description of such unworthy topics as a ball-room, love behind the scenes, coffee-room conversation, etc. But, curiously, his revolutionary tendencies in all other matters were in strange contrast to his tenacious clinging to the then existing opera form, and Wagner's outspoken notions about the regeneration of the opera into that of the musical drama were vehemently opposed by him.

In Heinrich Heine Wagner found a more congenial listener to his advanced theories. Although Heine's appreciation of music was not based on any more solid ground than that of a general acquaintance with the operas then in vogue, he was far more affected, and was a greater critic on the tonal art than his contemporary, Laube. Heine had resided in Paris since 1830, and was thoroughly acclimatized to Parisian taste. He was accepted as the representative of modern German poetry, and his works, particularly " Les deux Grenadiers," " Les Polonais de la vraie Pologne," were popular amongst all classes. Heine was pre-eminently spiritual, a quality exceedingly appreciated by the French; hence his popularity. However serious or painful the topic, Heine could enliven it by his clever Jewish antithetic wit. Heine received Wagner with a certain amount of reserve. His respect for musicians was not great. He had found many who, with the exception of their musical knowledge, were uncultured. Wagner's thorough acquaintance with literature, especially that of the earlier writers, agreeably surprised him, and the composer's elevated idea of the sacred mission of music touched the nobler chords of the poet's nature. His opinion on Wagner, as quoted by Laube, presents an interesting example of Heine's perspicacity. As a specimen of unaffected appreciation from a critic like Heine, who rarely sat in judgment without giving vent to a vitiated vein of sarcasm, it is most interesting.

"I cannot help feeling a lively interest in Wagner. He is endowed with an inexhaustible, productive mind, kept almost uninterruptedly in activity by a vivacious temperament. From an individuality so replete with modern culture, it is possible to expect the development of a solid and powerful modern music." Heine could never refrain from employing a degenerated imitation of irony, called persiflage, as a weapon for the purpose of mockery, and for the production of effect. Heine's imagination is bold, and his language idiosyncratic, though not affected. His sentiment is deep, but his fault is the want of an ideal outside the circle of his own ideas. In his poems, effeminate tenderness is contrasted by a vigorous boldness, the purest sentiment by sensual frivolity, noble thought by the meanest vulgarity, and lofty aspirations by painful indifference. Whilst overturning all existing theories and institutions, he failed to establish any one salutary doctrine.

It was a happy chance for Wagner that a man in the prominent position of Schlesinger should have interested himself in a young musician, whose nature was the opposite of his own. A shrewd music-seller, with an eye always to the main chance, and an art enthusiast in close intimacy, was a strange spectacle, only to be accounted for by the fact that opposite natures attract, whereas similar characters repel each other. Schlesinger admired in Wagner the very qualities of earnestness and enthusiasm which were lacking in his own being. Meyerbeer was his deity. It was one day in a mail coach that I found myself the travelling-companion of Schlesinger. He talked the whole day, of Meyerbeer principally. He said that Meyerbeer showed a commercial sagacity in composing his works which was remarkable. Behind the stage he was as painstaking with artists and the *mise-en scène* as he was careful in the comfortable seating of critics. Not the smallest journalist, nor even their relations, failed to be seated well. Meyerbeer was the embodiment of the art of *savoir faire.* It seemed to me, then, a curious contradiction in my companion's character, that he could regard such phases in a man's character as wonderful, and at the same time have listened to the intemperate outpourings of the earnest Wagner. But it was so.

At the back of Schlesinger's music shop was a room where artists casually met for conversation. Wagner, owing to the "musical arrangements" for the firm and being writer for Schlesinger's "Gazette Musicale," was a frequent visitor. He met many known men and noted their speech. It all tended one way. The French were light-hearted, persiflage was a principal subject of their composition, and for such a public only light dainties were to be provided. They wanted the semblance and not the reality. Amusement first and truth after. His own romances, penned, as he hoped, in a fittingly light manner, were not light enough and as a consequence were not pleasing enough.

With Berlioz his relations were less happy. The two men met often, but were mutually antagonistic. They admired each other always. Both were serious and earnest, but their friendship was never intimate. In after-life the same strained bearing towards each other was maintained. From close observation of the two men under my roof, at the same table, and under circumstances when they were open heart with each other, I should say however that the constraint arose purely from their antagonistic individualities. Berlioz was reserved, self-possessed, and dignified. His clear, transparent delivery was as the rhythmic cadence of a fountain. Wagner was boisterous, effusive, and his words leaped forth as the rushing of a mountain torrent. Wagner undoubtedly in Paris learned much from Berlioz. The new and refined orchestration taught, or perhaps I should rather say indicated, to Wagner what could be done with the orchestra. Indeed, Wagner has said that the instrumentation of Berlioz influenced him, but disagrees with the use to which the orchestra was put. To Berlioz it was the end: to Wagner, a means.

Berlioz expended his ideas in special colouristic effects, whilst Wagner's pre-eminent desire was truthfulness of situation, the orchestra serving as the medium for the delineation of his ideas.  Wagner paid Berlioz a tribute in Paris by declaring that he was distinguished from his Parisian colleagues, that he did not compose for money, and then in the same breath sarcastically asserts that "he lacks all sense of beauty."  This I think unfair, nor do I consider it as representing what Wagner really wished to convey.  Berlioz was undoubtedly possessed of ideality, his intentions were noble and earnest, but in their execution he fell short of his conceptions.  However, he towers above all French composers for earnestness of purpose and strength of intellect.

Although Wagner often and strongly disagreed with Heine's judgment in matters of art, yet with one, the poet's racy notice dated April, 1840, published in "Lutèce," a miscellaneous collection of letters upon artistic and social life in Paris, he felt that the pungent criticism was not altogether wide of the truth.  Wagner kept the notice, and when he and Berlioz were in this country together in 1855, he gave it to me, remarking that though grotesque it was in the main faithful.  As it is very interesting I reproduce it : —

We will begin to-day by Berlioz, whose first concert has served as the début of the musical season, as the overture, so to speak.  His productions, more or less new, which have been performed, found a just tribute of applause, and even the most indolent present were aroused by the force of his genius, which revels in creations of the " grand master."  There is a flapping of wings, but it is not of an ordinary bird, it is a colossal nightingale, a skylark of the grandeur of the eagle, as it existed, it is said, in the primitive world. Yes, the music of Berlioz, in general, has for me something primitive, if not antediluvian, and it makes me think of extinct gigantic beasts, of mammoths, of fabulous worlds, and of fabulous sins; indeed, of impossibilities piled one upon another. His magic accents recall to us Babylon, the suspended gardens of Semiramis, the marvels of Nineveh, the bold edifices of Mizraim, such as are seen in the pictures of the Englishman, Martin. Indeed, if we seek for analogous productions in the realms of the painter's art, we find a perfect resemblance with the elective Berlioz and the eccentric Englishman. The same outrageous sentiment of the prodigious, of the excessive, of material immensity. With one brilliant effect of light and darkness, with the other thundery instrumentation: with one little melody, with the other little colour, in both a perfect absence of beauty and of naïveté. Their works are neither antique nor romantic, they recall to us neither the Greek pagan, nor the mediæval catholic, but seem to lift us to the highest point of Assyrico-Babylonio-Egyptian architecture, and bear us back to those poems in stone which trace in the pyramids the passion of humanity, the eternal mystery of the world.

Of the other notabilities in the art world with whom Richard Wagner came into contact in Paris, the chief were Halévy, Vieuxtemps, Scribe, and Kietz. For Halévy he had great admiration. His music was honest. It had a national flavour in it. It was of the French, French. There was a visible effort to reflect in tones the mind and sentiment of a people which was highly meritorious. He was the legitimate descendant of Auber, the founder of a really national French opera. If conventionality proved too strong for Auber, Halévy made less effort to throw off the thraldom. The latter was wholly in the hands of opera directors, singers, ballet masters, etc. Had he been a strong man, an artist of determination, governed more with the noble desire to elevate his glorious art than of pleasing popular favourites, he might have done great things. Opera comique represented truly the national taste of the Gauls. Auber and Halévy were the men who, assisted by Boildieu, could have laid a sure foundation, but conventionality proved too powerful for all three.

It is not difficult to understand why Wagner so constantly made a "national music-drama" the subject of discourse. In his judgment a drama reflecting the culture and life of a people was the noblest teacher of men. It appeals direct to the heart and understanding. It is the mirror of themselves, purified, idealized, and as such cannot fail to be the most powerful and effective moral instructor. "National drama" was an undying subject with Wagner. His constant effort was the founding of a national art for his own compatriots. It was the ambition of his life, so that after the first and so grandly successful festival performance of the "Niebulungen" in the Bayreuth theatre, 1876, his address to the spectators began, "My children, you have here a really German art." No wonder, then, that he spoke in Paris with such earnestness of the absence of a true national opera, and of the destruction of such as there promised to be through the attention lavished on Rossini and Donizetti. Halévy's "La Juive," a grand opera, Wagner considered a particularly praiseworthy work, and thought it promised great things. So much did he consider it worthy of notice, that when later on he became conductor of the Dresden Opera House, he devoted great attention to its production and adequate rendering.

Vieuxtemps, Wagner met occasionally, but was on less intimate terms with him. He admired him as a virtuoso on the violin; he had a grand style, but in his conversation and writings he was without any distinguishing or attractive ability, adhering so steadfastly to the rigid classical form that there was little sympathy between them. In Scribe he admired the skill and esprit of his stage works. He saw that the Frenchman most accurately gauged the taste of his public and was dexterous in the manipulation of his matter. Scribe was not then at anything like the zenith of his power, yet was possessed of a finish and delicacy in writing that Wagner admired. Lastly, Kietz, a painter from Germany, of a certain merit, was perhaps one of his most intimate friends. He painted a portrait of Richard Wagner which is now regarded as very excellent. Full of fun, his jocularity harmonized completely with Wagner's own humour, and, united with Louis, the three were ever at their most comfortable and happy ease.

# CHAPTER X.



VIEWED from an art standpoint, those dreary years of misery, spent in the centre of European gaity, were the crucial epoch of Richard Wagner's career. Then, for the first time, was he filled with the consciousness of the complete impossibility of the French operatic stage and its kindred institutions outside France, ever becoming the platform from which he could preach his doctrine of earnestness and truth. The Paris grand opera was the hothouse of spurious art. The master who would succeed there must abandon his inspiration and make concessions to artists and to managers. He found the so-called grand opera tainted, an unreal thing which dealt not with verities, but was the handmaid of fashion. It had no heart, no living, free-flowing blood, but was a patchwork of false sentiment rendered attractive by its gorgeous spectacular frame.

But it was not at one bound that Wagner arrived at this conclusion. The turning-point was not reached until after he had himself essayed a grand opera success, and found how inadequate and imperfect fettered utterances were to free thoughts. Indeed, by degrees he discovered that realism, the prime element of the grand historic opera, was completely antagonistic to the tenderness of his own poetic instinct, idealism. He looked too, to the grand opera for expression of the feelings of a people, and found works manacled by a rigid conventionality.

He had come to Paris with the " Das Liebesverbot " (the manuscript of which, by the by, I believe passed into the possession of King Ludwig of Bavaria : it would be interesting to see the score of this early work written in 1834) and a portion of " Rienzi." His aspirations were to complete this latter in a manner worthy of the Paris stage. He attended much the productions of the opera house. He heard Auber, Halévy, Meyerbeer, Rossini, and Donizetti, and, as the months rolled by he grew sick in heart at seeing the sumptuous settings devoted to works that were paltry, mean, and artificial compared with his own.

Wagner was now a young man rapidly nearing thirty winters of life. He was in a foreign land, earning a bare existence, but withal full of earnest enthusiasm and vigorous work. A thinker always, he set himself the problem in the midst of pinching poverty, why was it that an unmistakable and growing aversion for the grand opera had been awakened in him? He pondered over it. For months it exercised his mind and then, suddenly, the revolutionary spirit of the age took possession of him, and he threw over once for all preconceived operatic notions, and resolved to be no longer the slave of a form walled in by conventionality, nor the puppet of an institution like the grand opera house, controlled by innumerable anti-artistic influences. It is from this time that we date that glorious change in his art work which has made music an articulate language understood by all, whereas hitherto it had been but a lisping speech, with occasional beautiful moments undoubtedly, but for all that, an imperfect art.

Poor Wagner, what sorrows did he not pass through in 1840 and 1841! Now he has stolen into the opera house to listen to the sensuous melodies of Rossini and Meyerbeer, and afterwards wended his way home dejected and disconsolate, with his heart a prey to the bitterest pangs. He could vent a little of his imprisoned indignation in the "Gazette Musicale," and availed himself of this channel of publicity. He fell upon Rossini and Donizetti. Why should they, aliens, dominate the French stage to the exclusion of superior native worth and pure national sentiment? In his opinion Auber was badly treated by the Parisians, "La Muette de Porticci" (Masaniello), contained germs of a real national French opera. It was a work of excellence and merited a better reception at the hands of the composer's countrymen. "Poor Wagner!" I feel myself again and again unconsciously uttering, when I remember that his championship of Auber nearly cost him the little emolument his newspaper articles brought him, for Schlesinger administered a sharp rebuke, and told him that if he wished to enter the political arena he must write for a political and not a musical journal. That Wagner's attitude toward Auber was based on purely artistic grounds will be admitted, I think, when it is known that during these three years of Paris life the two men never met.

But if the grand opera procured him no pleasure he was compensated by the orchestral performances at the Conservatoire de Musique. Wagner has often related an incident connected with one of his visits to the miserable rooms of the Conservatoire in the Rue Ber-gère, that will never fail to make affection's chords vibrate with compassionate sympathy for the beloved master. I remember well Wagner telling the story to me. It was during his worst hours of poverty. Disappointments had fallen thick around him. For two whole days his food had been almost nothing. Hungered and wearied, he silently and unobtrusively entered the Conservatoire. The orchestra were playing the " Ninth Symphony." What thoughts did it not recall ! It was more than ten years since he had heard the symphonies of Beethoven. Then he was in his Leipzic home. How changed were all things now ! But the music was the same ! The old enchantment overcame him. The genius of Beethoven again dazzled his senses, and he left the concert-room broken down with grief, but more determined and with a fixity of purpose more resolute than he had had at any time during the Paris period. " It was," he says, " as a blessed reality in the midst of a maze of shifting, gloomy dreams." He went home invigorated with the healthy, refreshing draughts of the " Ninth Symphony," bent upon pouring out the feelings of his early manhood, but falling sick, his original intentions were abandoned.

The concerts at the Conservatoire afforded him genuine pleasure. The director, Habeneck, seems to have been a zealous, painstaking artist, all works conducted evidencing the very careful study they had received at his hands. It was at the Conservatoire that Wagner's soul of music was fed, his heart and mind satisfied, the eye was gratified by the magnificent mise-en-scene of the grand opera. These two institutions exercised a vast and wholesome influence over him, though he rebelled wholly against the dicta of the grand opera. Perhaps had it not been for the violent antagonism the Paris opera excited within him, and the deep feeling of revulsion that it engendered, Richard Wagner would not so soon have come to that invaluable knowledge of himself, nor the art-fire within have glowed with such clearness and intensity.

To Wagner the Gallic character was at once the source of attraction and repulsion. He admired the light-hearted gaiety, the racy wit, and agreeable tact which seems to be the birthright of even the lowest and least educated. Such qualities were akin to his own being. At all times he sparkled with witty remarks, and as for tact, the times are without number when I have seen him display a discretion and dexterity of tact which belong only to the born diplomat. It was not tact in the common understanding of the term, but a keen sense of perceiving when to conciliate, when to hit hard, and when to stop. I have been present on occasions when his language has been so intemperate and severely sarcastic that I have expected as the only possible consequence an unpleasant dénouement ; but his fine discernment, aided by undoubted skill and adroitness of speech, have produced a marvellous change, and I am convinced that the happy termination was only arrived at because of the tone of conviction in which he expressed himself. His words bore so plainly the stamp of unadulterated truth, that those who could not agree with him were captivated by his enthusiasm and earnestness. On the other hand, he was repelled by the frivolous tone with which the Parisians characteristically treated serious topics. There was a want of causality in them. His conception of the world with its duties and obligations was in complete contrast to theirs. Moreover, he felt they lacked true poetic sentiment. Their poesy was superficial. It was replete with grace and charm, nor was beauty occasionally wanting. But it did not well up from their hearts. They associated it closely with every action of life but it was more often the veneer than the thing itself that shone. And again, their proclivities were in favour of realism, whereas his own sentiments were entwined round a poetic ideal. It was during this Paris period that the aspiration for the ideal burst forth with an intensity that never afterwards dimmed. The longing for the ideal was no new sensation. Flashes had been observed earlier at Leipzic when under the fascination of Beethoven's symphonies, but, ambition, love of fame, and a not unnatural youthful desire to acquire wealth had diverted him from the ideal to the real, and it was not till saddened with disappointments and sorely tried in the crucible of misfortune that he emerged purified, with a vision of his ideal beautified and enthroned on high, resolved henceforth never to tire in his efforts to achieve his purpose.

I should not omit to refer to certain observations Wagner made upon the military and police element in these early Paris years. He was a keen scrutinizer of men and manners, and failed not to observe the power wielded by the army. The French were a pageant-loving people, but were heavily burdened to maintain their large military force. Poverty was a natural result, and bitter feelings were engendered towards a government which employed the army as an awe-inspiring power towards peaceful citizens. Though the soldier was drawn from the people, yet as the unit of an army he came to be regarded as an enemy of his class. Nor was Wagner more satisfied with the police. He said he never could be brought to regard them as custodians of the peace and protectors of the rights of citizens. Instead of being well-disposed, they assumed a hostile attitude towards civilians. Perhaps these may seem items of no great importance, but to me the shrewd, perceptive Wagner of 1840–41, with his revolt against an overbearing military and police is the father of the revolutionist of 1848. It is but a short space of seven years.

With all its attendant suffering and weariness Wagner was accustomed to regard his first sojourn in Paris as the most eventful period of his life in the cause of art. There he burnt the ships of the youthful aspirant for public renown. Worldly tribulation tried and proved him, and the art genius emerged from the conflict purified and strengthened. As he says in his short autobiographical sketch, " The spirit of revolution took possession of me once forever." As it is not an uncommon fact in history that great events have often been brought about by most trifling incidents, so now did the first step in this wondrous development arise out of an apparently unimportant conversation to which I shall shortly refer. He had come to Paris sustained by an over-sanguine conviction of compelling French admiration by a rich display of its own art proclivities. Omitting for the moment his " Faust " overture, he first completed " Rienzi," in the all-spectacular spirit suited to the grand opera house. Then, as far as actual production went, ensued nearly a year of sterility, only to be followed by the advent of the poetic ideal which, when once cherished, was never afterwards cast aside. It was the poet who was now asserting his power. Poesy was claiming its birthright with the tonal art, and as the holy union of the twin arts manifested itself before his seer-like vision, so the artist, Wagner, the creator of a music whose every phase glows with the blood of life, so the poet-musician clearly perceiving his ideal, strove towards its attainment and never abated his efforts to realize his object, nor turned aside from its pursuit.

It is a matter of vast interest to learn how he was led in this direction. Some months after he had been in Paris, with little prospect of obtaining a hearing at the grand opera house, and suffering the keenest pangs of poverty, he heard the "Ninth Symphony," at the Conservatoire. He had heard it years ago, but now its story, its "programme," was clear before him. He too would write a symphony. He would speak the feelings within him, and music should be a "reality" and not the language of mysticism.

Overburdened with such feelings as these, a few days later he entered the music shop of Schlesinger. There was news for him. The publisher had a proposition which he thought promised well for Wagner. Deeply interested in his penniless, enthusiastic compatriot, he had almost brought to a successful conclusion an arrangement by which Wagner was to write a piece for a boulevard theatre. The conditions were that the trifle should be light and showy, nothing serious, but attractive. Such an offer at any other period prior to this,

Wagner said he would have gladly welcomed. The time, however, was inopportune. Unfortunately for him, but to the incalculable gain of the art, just now he was under the magnetic influence of the " Ninth Symphony." He seems to have burst into an uncontrollable onslaught upon the trivialities that ruled the French stage. He would have none of them. Music now for him was a "blessed reality," and the hollow fictions of the boulevard theatres were unworthy of a true artist. Schlesinger reasoned with him, urged the wisdom of accepting the offer, though at the same time uncompromising in his demand that the proposed piece must not be serious, and must be written to suit the tastes of the uneducated public. But Wagner was not to be won over, quoting the dictum of Schiller, a great favourite with him, that "the artist should not be the bantling of his period, but its teacher." No arrangement come to, Wagner went home. It was raining heavily. Excited and wet through, he talked wildly to Minna, the result being that he was put to bed with a severe attack of erysipelas. Brooding over his position, angered with the world and himself, caring not for life, his thoughts reverted to the " Ninth Symphony," and he, with the energy of a sick, strong-willed man, resolved to write forthwith that which should be the expression of his pent-up rage with the world, and, as by magic, he fell upon the story of Faust. To Wagner, then, as to the aged student, "Life was a burden, and death a desired consummation." And so he plunged with his woes thick upon him into the composition, superscribing his work with the words of Faust :—

Thou God, who reigns within my heart,
Alone can touch my soul.

While writing this, Wagner told me, that then for the first time did music speak to him in plain language. The subjects poured hot out of his heart as molten metal from a furnace. It was not music he wrote, but the sorrows of his soul that transformed themselves into sounds. His illness lasted for about a week, the erysipelas attacking his face and head. The forced reflection upon the past that his confinement induced was bitter, but his floating ideas about the poetic drama were cemented. That sick-chamber was the hothouse of the "romantic" Wagner. There the revolutionary views first gathered strength and the germs of the "art of the future" consolidated themselves. All his thoughts and feelings upon the future he communicated to his gentle nurse, Minna, who was always a ready listener to his seemingly random talk. This quality of "a good listener," of always lending a sympathetic ear, was perhaps more soothing and valuable than a criticising, discerning companion might have been to him, especially during his days of sickness. He had also another ever-ready and attentive auditor, his dog, the companion of his voyage from Riga to London and thence to Paris. How fond he was of that dumb brute! The innumerable times he addressed it as if it were a human being! And Wagner was not forgetful of its memory. During the worst hours of want he wrote for a newspaper a short story entitled, "The end of a German Musician in Paris"; in that one sees with what affection he regarded his devoted friend. The principal character in this realistic romance is himself, whom he causes to die through starvation. In that the sorrow and suffering endured by Wagner are set forth in a mànner that touches one to the quick.    As soon as he was sufficiently recovered, he did not, as the majority of natures would have done, rest from all active mental work, but at once vigorously attacked his unfinished " Rienzi," the remaining acts of which were completed by the end of the year 1840.    A curious fate Wagner's.    He had embarked upon a hazardous voyage to the French capital with the view of producing "Rienzi" there, and yet no sooner was the work quite finished than he despatched it to Germany, hoping to get it performed at Dresden.    A glance at the music reveals the gulf that separates the Wagner of the first two acts — composed before he came to Paris — from the writer of the remaining three. Yet another composition, a complete opera, was given to the world in Paris in the end of 1841.    It has the unique distinction of being the work of Wagner that occupied the shortest time in writing.    From the time of its inception — I am now speaking only of the music — to its completion, about seven weeks sufficed for the work.    The poem had been completed some months earlier.    He had submitted "Rienzi" to the director of the grand opera, who gave him no tangible hope of its being accepted, but promised to do his best in producing a shorter opera by him.    This engagement on the part of the director, though not couched in unequivocal terms, was not to be allowed to drop.    Wagner went to Heine and discussed the situation.    Among the subjects proposed for an opera was Heine's own treatment of the romantic legend of " The Flying Dutchman " and his spectral crew.    The story was not new to Wagner.    He had heard it for the first time from the lips of the sailors on his voyage to London. Then it had impressed him. Now it took hold of him.

How this legend of the ill-fated mariner came to form the basis of an opera text is curious and interesting. There are few, perhaps, who have any notions from what crude material the significant "Dutchman," as we know it, was fashioned.

There existed in England, and a copy can still be obtained from French, the Strand theatrical publisher, a melodramatic burlesque by Fitzball, a prolific writer for the English stage, entitled "Vanderdecken, or The Phantom Ship." To mention the names of three of the original dramatis personæ, Captain Peppersal, the father of the Senta, Von Swiggs, a drunken Dutchman in love with Senta, and Smutta, a black servant, the character and mode of treatment of the story will be at once perceived. Vanderdecken retains much of the legendary lore with which we are accustomed to surround him, except that Fitzball causes him occasionally to appear and disappear in blue and red fire. Vanderdecken too is under a spell ; the utterance of a single word though it be joy at his acceptance by Senta, will consign him again to his terrible fate for another thousand years.

It was a perusal of this medley, of the spectral and burlesque, which led Heine to treat the story after his own heart, and it was the discussion with the poet that determined Wagner in his choice of subject. The libretto was finished and delivered to the director, who, whilst expressing entire satisfaction at the work, only asked its price so that he might deliver it to a composer to whom a text had been promised, and whose opera had the next right of being accepted. The poem was not sold, and Wagner turned again to his "arranging" drudgery. Later, however, he retook his text. The subject-legend was in the highest manner adapted for musical treatment. Whilst writing the poem he had felt in a very different mood than when writing the "Rienzi" text. In the latter, his object was a story so arranged as would admit of the then orthodox operatic treatment with its set forms of solos, choruses, ensembles, etc., etc. Wagner was a man of thought. He did not perform things in a haphazard manner. He saw his mark and flew to it. The historic opera, he reasoned, demanded a precise and careful treatment of detail incidents. This was not the province of music. The tonal art was a medium for the expression of feelings, to illustrate the workings of the heart. Now with legend the conditions are entirely opposite to those demanded by the historic opera. It is of no consequence among what people a particular legend originated. Place and period are equally unimportant. Romantic legends possess this superlative advantage over historical subjects ; no matter when the period, or where the place, or who the people, the legends are invested with none of the trammelling conditions of nationality or epoch, but treat exclusively of that which is human. This is an immense gain to both poet and musician. By this process of reasoning, Wagner gradually came to exclude word-repetition. In the "Dutchman" much verbal reiteration is still indulged in ; but the story and treatment show us the real Wagner of the future.

As to the composition of the music, I have heard so much from Wagner on this particular opera, to convince me that, though it occupied but a few weeks, it was not done without much careful thought. The scaffolding upon which it was constructed is very clear. Indeed, the "make" of the whole work is most transparent. There are three chief subjects. (1) Senta's song, (2) Sailor's and (3) Spinning chorus, and those have been woven into an organic whole by thoughtful work.

In the summer of 1866, I was sitting with Wagner at dinner in his house at Munich. It chanced that the conversation turned upon the weary mariner, his yearning for land and love, and Wagner's own longing for his fatherland at the time he composed the "Dutchman," when going to a piano that stood near him, he said, "The pent-up anguish, the homesickness that then held complete possession of me, were poured out in this phrase," — playing the short cadence of two bars thrice repeated that preludes Vanderdecken's recital to Daland of his woeful wanderings. "At the end of the phrase, on the diminished seventh, in my mind I paused and brooded over the past, the repetitions, each higher, interpreting the increased intensity of my sufferings," and, Wagner went on, that with each note he originally intended that Vanderdecken should move but one step, and move only in time with the music. Now this careful premeditated tonal working in the young man of twenty-eight is indicative, as much as any portion of Wagner is, of his *style*, a word of pregnant meaning when used in relation to Wagner's works.

The "Dutchman" was written at Meñdon, a village about five miles from Paris. It was composed at the piano. This incident is of importance, since for several months he had not written a note, and knew not whether he still possessed the power of composing. He had left

Paris because of the noise and bustle, and to his horror discovered that his new landlord was a collector of musical instruments, so there was little likelihood of securing the quietude he so much desired. When the work was finished, conscious that realistic France was not the place where he could produce his poetic ideal, he despatched it to Meyerbeer, then in Germany, whose aid he solicited in getting it performed. Replies were not encouraging. Meanwhile, sorely harassed how to provide life's necessities, he sold, under pressure, his manuscript of the poem for £20.

The sole ray of hope, the one chance of rescue from this sad plight, lay in "Rienzi." It had been accepted at Dresden and in the spring of 1842 he was informed that it was about to be put into preparation and his presence would be desirable. He therefore left Paris for Germany after nearly three years of absence.

# CHAPTER XI.

## DRESDEN, 1842–1843.

From now begins a new epoch in Wagner's life. The call he had received from Dresden filled him with delirious joy. The world was not large enough to hold him. He trod on air. That Dresden, the hallowed scene of Weber's labours, possessing the then first theatre in Germany, famed alike for its productions, style, and artists, should accept his work, and request his presence to supervise the rehearsals, was an acknowledgment which transformed, as by magic, a sombre, cruel outlook into a gloriously bright and warm future.

He was very sanguine of succeeding with " Rienzi." It was completely in the style of the foreign operas then in vogue among his countrymen. Germany had no opera of her own. Mozart and Gluck both composed in the French and Italian style, and Meyerbeer, the then ruler of the German operatic stage, fashioned his popular works on the spectacular style of the grand French opera. " Rienzi " was spectacular, with plenty of the same description of material as " Les Huguenots." So Wagner's hopes ran high, and a vista of happiness spread itself before him as an enchanted fairy-land.

With joy he took leave of Schlesinger and his few Parisian intimates, and set out for Germany, his fatherland. His fatherland! what a sea of tumultuous feelings did that thought of returning home produce in him. He was going back a conqueror. The creative artist was at last recognized; he was rescued from desperate distress at the very moment it seemed as if he were going to succumb to the conflict. It is difficult to at all thoroughly understand what Wagner went through after he had been summoned to Germany. The transformation scene in his life's drama was taking place. Again and again has he expatiated upon it with an honesty characteristic of him, and with a volubility that laid bare all his heart's hopes and emotions at the time.

Paris had not accepted him. He came, he saw, but had not conquered. His soul had swelled with artistic ambition; he was enthusiastic, desiring a platform from which to expound his cherished tenets; and Paris ignored him, treated his projects and himself as nought, and for all it cared, he might have perished unheeded, with none but his dog to mourn his loss. And now, from an unacknowledged artist, he was the chosen of celebrated Dresden, still warm with the inspired accents of his "beloved" Weber. Well might he become delirious with joy.

His homeward journey was full of happy incident and profit. He heard his native language again as the common tongue. Of German as a language Wagner was always enamoured. He possessed a large vocabulary himself, was a poet of no mean rank, and had always a wealth of illustration ready at command. Now to hear German spoken about him was delight. He was in a happy frame, ready to be touched with whatever he saw. The Rhine unusually excited him. In later years, when writing of the period, he tells us that at sight of the Rhine he vowed eternal fidelity to his country.

He remarked to me, in his poetic language, that its eddying wavelets seemed to be telling him its legends, and dolefully inquiring, Why did you leave us? He was happy to come home. His escape from feverish, sensuous Paris, to his healthy, honest fatherland, was, to use his own graphic analogy, as Tannhauser emerging from the Venus grotto to breathe the invigorating, bracing atmosphere of the German mountains. It was the awakening from an oppressive nightmare. The unvarnished straightforwardness of the German character welcomed him with the affection of fond parents. With all its rude plainness and stolidity, he loved the German mind. It was sincere, true, and made the French courteous polish, which he had just quitted, seem as a thing unreal, a lacquer, an affection that became offensive.

The return of Wagner and his wife to Dresden was particularly agreeable to the latter. In Dresden, she had a reputation as an actress, though not in the first rank, yet she was somebody, and would be so recognized. Besides, there she could have the respect paid to her due to the wife of the composer of " Rienzi." Poor Minna! what a patient and gentle woman she was. To hear her unaffected talk of the change in her own position, on their coming to live in Dresden, was touching, indeed. In Paris she had been a drudge, and no one knew but Wagner the half of her heroism, self-denial, and suffering. Now for her, too, the horizon was clearing, and it was with difficulty that she endeavoured to restrain the overflowing hopefulness of Richard. But he would not be repressed, and on nearing Dresden the two who had suffered together consoled and encouraged each other with visions of prospective prosperity.

A change of scene was always conducive to happiness in Wagner. For the first few days he visited well-remembered spots. He had a veritable passion for at once setting off to see familiar places. The joy of Dresden homely life contrasted with the Paris mode of living, acted like a charm on him. His spirits were at their best, his health good, and the kindly greetings he met everywhere worked together to make him thoroughly enjoy life. His sister Rosalie, the actress, was dead, so that all that was really known of him when he came to Dresden was that he was born at Leipzic, had been educated at the Dresden Schule, and had wholly written and composed two operas, and was the brother of the late Rosalie Wagner.

One of his first visits was to Reissiger, chief conductor at the Royal Opera (where Wagner's "Rienzi" was to be performed), and of the Royal Chapel. Reissiger was some fifteen years older than Richard Wagner. He had been trained in the school of strict fugue and counterpoint at Leipzic, and as a musician was prolific and clever, but lacked poetical inspiration and intellectual power. He was eminently a professor. He received Wagner politely, praised the "Rienzi," the score of which he knew, but with it all maintained an attitude of reserve. Wagner, who was on the best terms with himself and the world, ready to embrace everybody, was cooled by his reception, and felt that he could never be intimate with Reissiger, who occupied the greater part of their first interview with complaints about his own non-success on the operatic stage, all of which he peevishly attributed to the shortcomings of the *libretti*.

If, however, Wagner was disappointed with his probable standing with Reissiger, he was amply compensated by the warmth and spontaneity of Fischer's greeting. Fischer was stage manager and chorus director. He was a musician of superior attainments, a man of sound reflection, and felt that theirs was to be a friendship for life. He was enthusiastic about "Rienzi," foretold a certain success, and showed his earnestness by untiring activity in training the chorus, so important in the new work. He proved of invaluable service to Wagner by describing the character and temperament of the many individuals connected with the theatre with whom he would come into contact.

There was yet another friend who affectionately greeted Wagner. Tichatschek, the "Rienzi" of the forthcoming performance. Tichatschek was of heroic stature, finely proportioned, and dignified in bearing. He was enraptured with his part. He saw in it one which fitted him to perfection, both as to physical appearance and vocal powers, which, in his case, were strong and enduring.

A passing cloud was the absence of the "Adriano," his womanly ideal, Schroeder-Devrient. But she soon came to Dresden and was present at the "Rienzi" rehearsals. Wagner related to her the episode of the *Dreadnought*, and the fate of her precious gift, the snuff-box, when she pleasantly rejoined that "Rienzi" would produce him a shower of golden snuff-boxes from all the potentates of Germany, so convinced was she of its success.

"Rienzi" was performed at the end of 1842. An unquestioned success, everybody enthusiastic, the orchestra played with an energy that went quite beyond the phlegmatic Reissiger who conducted. Apart from the effective situations, the well-treated story and verve with which the chief characters worked, there is no doubt that a great portion of the success was due to the splendid appearance of Tichatschek. Commanding in stature and clad in glittering armour, possessing a powerful voice which he used to advantage, the audience were enraptured with the hero and cheered him lustily. The processions, the conflagrations, and all those stage effects so skilfully calculated by Wagner and intended for the grand opera house, Paris, appealed to the spectacle-loving portion of the playgoers. The plot, the revolt of an oppressed people, was unquestionably in harmony with the spirit of the period, for revolution was in the air; all over Germany there were disquieting signs. It has often been suggested that " Rienzi " was a confession of faith of Wagner's political, so-called revolutionary, principles, and was a forecast of the democratic storm of 1848, but it need scarcely be said that it was mere coincidence.

I have now arrived at the time when my own acquaintance with Richard Wagner began. It was in the beginning of the spring of 1843. Wagner had been appointed in January of that year co-chief conductor at the opera with Reissiger, but the superiority of his intellectual and artistic abilities over the homespun plebeian Reissiger soon gave him the first position in Dresden. Their second in command was August Roeckel. Roeckel was my most intimate friend. We were of the same age, and had but one judgment upon music. He was the nephew of Nepomuck Hummel and possessed much of the talent of that celebrated pianist. He was also a composer of merit; indeed, it was by reason of the sound musicianly skill displayed in his opera " Farinelli " that he was appointed second music director at Dresden, similarly as Wagner had been appointed chief director through the success of " Rienzi." The director of the opera had accepted " Farinelli " and announced a performance, but so dazzled was Roeckel by the brilliancy of Wagner's genius that he withdrew " Farinelli " and would under no circumstances permit its production. This act of self-effacement accurately paints the character of the over-modest man. Between Wagner and Roeckel the closest intimacy sprang up. Through all that stormy period of the revolution, Wagner thought and spoke of none other as he did of Roeckel. They were twin souls. For range of knowledge, active intelligence, and similarity of thought, Wagner had met with no one more congenial to him, and, I must add, none worshipped Wagner as August Roeckel did. He had resided in London and Paris, and the literature of both countries was as familiar to him as that of his native land. The first description I had of Richard Wagner was from August Roeckel. I had such complete confidence in his perception and judgment that I was at once won over to Wagner's side by the tone of hero-worship that pervaded the letter. Happily it has been preserved and I now reproduce it : —

At last fortune smiles on me. Think, I have been appointed Sachsischer music director, at the head of the most celebrated orchestra of Germany, no longer doomed to give lessons, my horror and abomination. " Farinelli," after all, was the right thing, but what chiefly reminds me of your perspicacity was the encouragement in regard to my pianoforte playing. Now that is of the greatest importance in helping me to establishing a name here. It was but natural that I doubted my gift as a pianist, when Edward (his brother) was the favourite of uncle "Hummel," but when at Vienna, I remembered your prophecy, and worked at the piano harder than ever, and now it stands me in good stead. Henceforth, I drop myself into a well, because I am going to speak of the man whose greatness overshadows that of all other men I have met, either in France or England, — our new friend, Richard Wagner. I say advisedly, our friend, for he knows you from my description as well as I do. You cannot imagine how the daily intercourse with him develops my admiration for his genius. His earnestness in art is religious; he looks upon the drama as the pulpit from which the people should be taught, and his views on a combination of the different arts for that purpose opens up an exciting theory, as new as it is ideal. You would love him, aye, worship him as I do, for to gigantic powers of intellect he unites the sportive playfulness of a child. I have a great advantage over him in piano-playing. It seems strange, but his playing is ludicrously defective; so much so, that when anything is to be tried I take the piano and my sight-reading seems to please him vastly.

DRESDEN, March, 1843.

My correspondence with August Roeckel was at this period a large one. He had a religious reverence for the gift, intellectual attainments, and eloquence of his new friend, topics which constitute the main theme of his letters. That Roeckel had an equal sway over Wagner in another direction, viz. politics, arose, too, from that same earnest enthusiasm, the parent of Wagner's own successful art efforts. It is necessary that I should explain that Roeckel was Wagner's shadow. They were inseparable, visiting each other during the day and at the theatre together at night. They had, so Wagner told me afterwards, a life in common. He was as much fired by Roeckel's wealth of literary lore, his heroic notions of life and duty, and the claim of a people to be well governed, as Roeckel was sympathetic and appreciative of those art theories which, according to Wagner, formed the upper stratum of man's existence. Roeckel's view is therefore the judgment of Wagner's other self, and as such has a right of existence here. It is full of warm interest about Wagner, who, in later years, greatly enjoyed the perusal of the correspondence. The absolute worship of Roeckel for his chief shows itself in the following letter written under the influence of early relations :—

I have the most affectionate letter from Bamberg. They want me back there, offer me greater advantages, urging that I was the first and only conductor there, whilst at Dresden I am but second. But can they understand to whom I am second? Such a man as Richard Wagner I never yet met, and you know I am not inclined to Cæsar's maxim, that it were better to be the first in a village than the second in Rome. I have begun to rescore my opera under Wagner's supervision; his frank criticism has opened my eyes to some very important instrumental defects. His notions of scoring are most novel, most daring, and altogether marvellous; but not more so than his elevated notions about the high purpose of the dramatic art; indeed, they foreshadow a new era in the history of art.

Dresden.

An incident of interest in the first part of 1843 was a visit of Hector Berlioz to Wagner. The great Frenchman came to hear " Rienzi." Satisfied he was not; about the only number that he thought meritorious was the prayer. With the "Dutchman," which he also heard, he was even still less contented. He complained of the excess of instrumentation. This is curious, to put it gently, that a composer who employs four orchestras with twelve kettledrums in one work, whose own scoring is noted for excessive employment of means, should make such a charge. It is inexplicable. The truth is, Berlioz was jealous of Wagner. Roeckel had been intimate with Berlioz in Paris. The father of Roeckel was the impressario who introduced the first complete German opera troupe to Paris and London. He had been an intimate friend of Beethoven, had impersonated "Florestan" in "Fidelio," and, indeed, had been tutored by the composer for the tenor part. The elder Roeckel's company included Schroeder-Devrient when he went to Paris. August Roeckel was therefore well known to Berlioz, and Schroeder-Devrient, having travelled with Roeckel's father, and being known intimately by August, was also a link between Wagner and himself. When, therefore, Berlioz came to Dresden, August was delighted, and was always present at the friendly meetings of the two composers. He wrote to me that their meetings were embarrassed. Wagner was first attracted, but the cold, austere, though always polished demeanour of Berlioz checked Wagner's enthusiasm. He had the air of patronizing Wagner; his speech was bitter, freezing the boisterous expansiveness of Wagner. At times the conversation was so strained that Roeckel was of opinion that Berlioz intentionally slighted Wagner. The more they were together, the less they appeared to understand each other; and yet, notwithstanding the fastidious criticism, the constant fault-finding of Berlioz, he took pains to arrange meetings with Wagner, naturally fascinated by the vigour with which Wagner discussed art.

# CHAPTER XII.

1843–1844.

However inclined the Dresden musical press may have been to be captious and antagonistic towards Wagner, there were certain decided evidences of gifts whose existence they could not deny, and which they were reluctantly compelled to acknowledge, in spite of their openly pronounced hostility. The rehearsing and conducting of "Rienzi" and the "Dutchman" had established Wagner's reputation as a conductor of unusual ability. "But," said his censorious critics, "that proves nothing, for he worked with heart and soul to secure success, just because the operas were his own. Wait until he is called upon to produce a classic; then we shall see." They had not to wait long. Within a month, Gluck's "Armide" and Mozart's "Don Giovanni" were performed under his bâton. His reading of both was original. He had, first, his individual conception of the opera as an organic art work, and then very pronounced views as to the manner in which each should be studied and performed. He spared not the orchestra. This not unnaturally created among the less intelligent some amount of irritation. Custom had sanctioned a certain slovenly rendering, and they revolted at the revolutionary spirit of the new conductor. But the openly expressed appreciation of the unquestioned abili-

ties of the conductor by the leading members of the
orchestra, was not without effect upon the malcontents.
The friction did not last long; a marked improvement
was felt by all, and Wagner's irrepressible animal spirits
and jocularity won over even the drudges.  I have it from
August Roeckel, his colleague at the desk, that the intelligent members of the orchestra idolized Wagner,
and never wearied under his bâton.

Wagner was possessed of a keen sense of euphonic
balance.  The predominance of one section of the
orchestra over another, except where specially required
to produce certain effects, he would not tolerate, be the
defaulting instrument ever so difficult to control.  On
one occasion the trombones were excessively noisy at a
"Rienzi" rehersal in the overture, where they should
accompany the violins *piano*.  Their braying aroused
Wagner's anger; however, with ready wit, instead of a
reproof, a joke, and turning good-humouredly to the cul-
prits, he laughingly said, "Gentlemen, if I mistake not,
we are in Dresden, and not marching round Jericho,
where your ancestors, strong of lung, blew down the
city walls."  The humour of the admonition was not
lost, and after a moment's general hilarity Wagner obtained the desired effect.

Wagner was a born disciplinarian.  He held the
orchestra completely in the palm of his hand.  The
members were so many pawns which he moved at will,
responding to his slightest expressed wish.  The rigid
enforcement of his will upon the players became talked
of outside the doors of the theatre.  The critics could
not understand why he should wish to change the order
of things, have a greater number and longer rehearsals

than any one else, and have the works performed in his
heterodox way; and so, they first ridiculed him, and
then uncompromisingly attacked him, attacks which, it
is regrettable to add, lasted all the years he remained in
Dresden.   But for all this, he was not to be deterred
from his purpose.   He knew what he wanted, and
meant to have it, and in this Wagner has again and
again acknowledged to me his indebtedness to August
Roeckel, who so ably seconded his chief.   According to
Wagner's notions the masterpieces of German musicians
could never be properly understood by the music-loving
public, owing to their imperfect and faulty rendering
under conductors who were so many automaton time-
beaters.   Great works of all descriptions were produced
in a styleless manner, no regard, indeed, but very little
effort, being made to discover the intention of the composer.   All were rendered in the same pointless manner.
This was revolting to his sense of artistic probity, therefore when he held the office of conductor he altered this
almost dishonest state of things, for it was dishonest not
to seek to reproduce a composer's intention.   Thus the
works of all masters suffered.   Therefore Wagner made
it a rule that whatever he conducted should be, when
possible, entirely committed to memory.   His earnestness became infectious, until players and singers became
animated by one feeling.   They felt that he, at the desk,
was as much a worker as any of them, and the result
was a performance hitherto unknown for perfection.   It
happened, therefore, that when "Don Giovanni" was
given, according to his feelings and as he willed it, the
critics fell upon him fiercely, going so far even as to
declare he did not understand Mozart, so unexpectedly

new did they find his conception. The contest waged hotly. A large and important body of directors of art opinion selected the phlegmatic Reissiger as their idol, and lauded him indiscriminately. It is, to say the least, strange that there should have been found any one to prefer a man of the diminutive talents of Reissiger to Richard Wagner. The former was a pure mechanic, respectable in his way, but completely overshadowed by the mighty genius of Wagner. This study of conductors and conducting was a phase of his art to which Wagner devoted much careful thought, embodying at a later period his views in a pamphlet on the subject, which will be found invaluable by orchestral conductors of every degree.

An incident of this year, 1843, his first at Dresden, to which Wagner referred with pleasure, was the performance of the "Dutchman" at Cassel by Spohr. It was done entirely on its merits, without any solicitation from Wagner, the pleasure being intensified by reason of the ripe age of the conductor and his well-known reverence for the orthodox. Spohr was sixty-nine, and Richard Wagner thirty. Wagner felt and expressed himself as deeply touched at the interest a musician of such opposite tendencies should take in his work, particularly, too, on receiving later a letter from Spohr expressing the delight he experienced on making the acquaintance of a young artist who showed in all he did such earnestness and striving after truth. When Wagner related this to me, wondering at the curious contradiction in Spohr's character, I remarked that the solution seemed to lie in the gentle, almost effeminate nature of Spohr, which found its completion in the robust, manly vigour of Wagner's own conceptions.

How Spohr could have been attracted by Wagner, and repulsed by the "last period" of Beethoven, is a contradiction difficult to account for; but that it existed is beyond doubt, for the last time he was in London, about 1850–51, I put the question direct to him whether it was true, as asserted, that he had stigmatized the third period of Beethoven as "barbarous music," to which he promptly and emphatically replied, "Yes, I do think it barbarous music." After the performance at Cassel, Wagner endeavoured to get the "Dutchman" accepted elsewhere, but signally failed; from Munich, where a quarter of a century later he was to be the ruling spirit, came the discouraging response that "it was not German enough," though the composer thought this its distinguishing merit.

The acrimoniously bitter attacks that were made upon Wagner, during his first year at Dresden, increased in poignancy, as he showed himself uncontrolled by custom's laws. He affected a careless, defiant attitude towards all criticism, whereas he was abnormally sensitive to journalistic opinion. He could scoff, play the cynic, treat his opponent with derisive scorn, but it was all simulated; the iron entered into his soul, and he chafed and grew irritable under it. It was as though he suffered a bodily castigation. He brooded over the attacks, and there can be no doubt that they caused him moments of acute pain. It is true that in combat he could parry and thrust with as much vigour as his opponents; that the sting of his reproof was as torturing as any he suffered; perhaps even that his assaults were more annihilating than the occasion demanded; yet with it all, though he emerged from the contest victorious, he suffered deeply, acutely. There can be no doubt that the genesis of this hostile criticism was directed more against the man than his art work, and that wounded personality played an important part in it. Richard Wagner was seen to be a man of artistic taste, with proclivities which were exhibited in his domestic surroundings, novel, perhaps, to the somewhat heavy Dresdenites. First, Wagner's attire was different from that of the ordinary individual. He persisted in wearing in the house a velvet dressing-gown and a biretta, truly an uncommon head-gear. His apartments were asserted to be upholstered luxuriously. And in these things the art critics (?) saw a target for ridicule and sarcasm. Now that his apartments were furnished in a costly manner is absolutely untrue. Wagner had a keen appreciation of the beautiful, and loved tasty decoration, but it was secured at the minimum of cost. The thrifty Minna contrived and invented, to gratify Wagner's fancies, at an outlay which does credit to German thrift. And yet there were found Dresden journals that went so far as to discuss his mode of living, attributing all the apparent extravagance to gratification of an over-rated self-esteem, the appeasing of an inordinate vanity.

A year of vexation! a year of consolidation was 1844! From Wagner I have often heard it: "My failures were the stepping-stones to success"; and this year, when the hot blood of ambition coursed violently through his youthful veins, when he aimed as high as the heavens, and met with failures everywhere, when directors of German opera houses returned his scores "unopened" or pronounced them unripe and lacking in melody, truly, it was an epoch of bitter disappointment. Attacked relentlessly by journalistic hacks, imbued with the bitter feeling that he was the rejected of his countrymen; that for him there was not a glimmer of hope of success on the German stage, and yet convinced of his own exceptional gifts, and the living truth of the mission he was destined to accomplish, he, broken down in spirit, angered with the world, and fractious with himself, retired from all intercourse with his fellow-men, shunned society as the plague, appeared at the Dresden theatre only when absolutely necessary, and went into seclusion, accessible to none except August Roeckel. Of this gloomy period, and the devotion of his friend, Wagner has left it on record. "I left the world, retired from public life, and lived in the closest communion with one intimate companion only, one friend, who was so full of sympathy for me, so wholly engrossed in my artistic development, that he ignored his own unquestioned talents, artistic instinct, and inventive powers, and cast to the winds his own chances of worldly success. This companion of my gloom was Roeckel." In referring to his friend's self-abnegation, Wagner evidently alludes to Roeckel's opera, "Farinelli," which the composer had withdrawn from the Dresden repertoire through excess of modesty, over-awed, as he was, by his conception of Richard Wagner's genius.

This tribute to the constancy and humble workship of August Roeckel is not a whit too much. Roeckel idolized Wagner. The two men were the complement of each other; whilst the vivacious imagination of Wagner inspired admiration in Roeckel, the latter's placid, closely-reasoned logic soothed the excitable poet-musician. All Roeckel's letters to me of this period — and he was an excellent correspondent — might be summed up in the word "Wagner." The minutest incidents of work and details of their conversations are related. This poor Roeckel suffered thirteen years imprisonment, from May, 1849, when his friend Wagner escaped. At the termination of his confinement, the two friends met with a warmth of affection difficult to describe. Seeing, then, the intimacy of the men during this year of retirement, it is the letters of August Roeckel which will supply the faithfullest record of Wagner's life and work.

He tells me that Wagner spoke of himself as "one crying in the desert." But few sympathized with him, his breaking away from the "Rienzi" period being frowned upon, but that through all disappointment Wagner's inexhaustible animal spirits never left him. The following letter is dated March, 1844 : —

Wagner has returned from Berlin, very morose in temper; the "Flying Dutchman" did not touch the scoffing Berliners, who certainly have less poetical feeling than most Germans; they only saw in Schroeder-Devrient a star, and in the touching drama an opera like other operas; yet they pose as profound art critics. Bah! they are simply stupid!

Since then we have had "Hans Heiling" and "Vampyr." Wagner thinks much of Marschner's natural gifts, but finds that his general intelligence is not on a level with his musical gifts, and that this is often painfully evident in his recourse to commonplace padding. . . . I wish you could have witnessed the work of the old Gluck "Armide," most tenderly cared for by Wagner. I doubt that it ever was rendered with such reverence, — nay, not even in Paris. We have also had what Wagner considers the masterwork of Mendelssohn, "Midsummer Night's Dream," with which he also took considerable pains, although fully aware of the composer's unfriendly feeling towards himself.

## Later I find the following : —

You cannot conceive what a system of espionage has grown up about Wagner, how keenly all his actions are criticised. He deemed it advisable to rearrange the seating of the band (I send you a plan) ; but oh ! the hubbub it has produced is dreadful. "What ! change that which satisfied Morlacchi and Reissiger?" They charge Wagner with want of reverence for tradition and with taking delight in upsetting the established order of things.

In the middle of the year it seems the "Faust" overture was performed ; the reception was disheartening. It was another disappointment, and showed Wagner how little the public was in sympathy with his art ideal. Although performed twice, it produced no effect.

This is not to be wondered at [writes Roeckel]; for in the judgment of some here it compares favourably with the grandest efforts of Beethoven. Such a work ought to be heard several times before its beauties can be fully perceived.

Wagner day by day becomes to me the beacon-light of the future ; his depth of thought, his daring philosophical investigations, his unrestrained criticism, startle one out of the every-day optimism of the Dresden surroundings. The only ready ear besides myself is Semper, who, however, agrees with Wagner's outbursts only so far as they are applicable to his own art, architecture, as in music he is but a dilettante. Much of Wagner's earnestness in his demands for improvement in art matters is attributed by the opposition to self-glorification. At the head of it stands Reissiger, who can not and will not accept the success of "Rienzi" as *bonâ fide*. He is forever hinting at some nefarious means, and cannot understand why his own operas should fail with the same public, unless, indeed, he stupidly adds, it is because he neglected to surround himself with a "life-guard of claqueurs"; but he was a true German, and against such malpractices. You can imagine how such things annoy Wagner; and although he eventually laughs, it is not until they have left a scar somewhere. For myself, I wonder how he can mind such stuff. I keep it always from him, but nevertheless it always seems to reach him; and Minna is not capable of withholding either praise or blame from him, although I have tried hard to prove to her that it affects her husband deeply, whose health is none of the strongest. Another annoyance is the Leipzic clique, with Mendelssohn at the head, or, to put the matter into the right light, as the ruling spirit. He gives the watchword to the clique, and then sneaks out of sight, as if he lived in regions too refined and sublime to bother himself about terrestrial affairs. But the worst sore is that coming from our intendant. He has not the shadow of an idea upon music; takes all his initiative from current phrases learnt by heart; he is the veriest type of a courtier, and hates nothing so much as "revolutionary" suggestions from a subordinate, for as such he rates the conductors, nor has he a glimpse of discernment as to their relative merits, and finding Reissiger always ready to bow to his aristocratic acumen, he evidently thinks him the more gifted. The matter is not made better by the bitter tone of the press, which, arrogating to itself the office of defenders of true art, smites heavily the "iconoclast Wagner." Schladebach leads them, and unfortunately, his prominent position inspires courage in scribblers.

*       *       *       *       *       *       *

We have had a very interesting event here. Spontini came to conduct his "Vestal." It was done twice. He is a composer who has said what he had to say in his own manner. He commands respect, is full of dignity and amiability. Wagner had trained the orchestra well; his respectful bearing to the veteran composer incited them to exert themselves heart and soul. The result was a very satisfactory rendering. But after the second performance, a peremptory order came from Luttichon, that the "Vestal" was not to be repeated, and Wagner was to convey the decision to Spontini. Wagner prayed me to accompany him; first, because he does not speak French so fluently as I do; and secondly, since Spontini had shown himself very friendly towards me, and it was hoped my presence might calm the composer's expected anger, for Spontini is known for his irritability on such occasions. We went. The time was most opportune, for as a new dignity had just been conferred upon him by the Pope, his vanity was so flattered that he listened with unruffled temper to what was, for him, unpleasant news.

DECEMBER, 1844.

Perhaps the event of the year was the removal of the remains of Weber from London to Dresden. An earnest committee had been working some time towards this end; concerts and operatic performances had been given in Germany and subscription lists opened to provide the necessary funds. Wagner was truly enthusiastic in the matter, but August Roeckel merits equal tribute. It was arranged that the deceased musician's eldest son, Max von Weber, should come to London to carry out the necessary arrangements. He came in June, 1844, and was the guest of Edward Roeckel. We met daily. Max von Weber was a bright, intelligent man. Enthusiastic for the cause, I accompanied him everywhere, soliciting subscriptions from compatriots in this country and interviewing the authorities to facilitate the removal. August Roeckel writes : —

All Dresden was in excitement; the event produced a profound sensation. The body was received by us all. We had been rehearsing for some time a funeral march arranged by Wagner from themes in " Euryanthe." The loving care bestowed by Wagner on the rehearsals touched every one. It was clear that his whole heart was in the work. His own opinion is that he never succeeded in anything as in this. The soft, appealing tones of the wood-wind were wonderfully pathetic, and when the march was performed in the open air, accompanying the body, not a member of the cortège or bystander but was moved. And then the scene at the grave! Schulz delivered an oration, and Richard Wagner too. Wagner had composed and written his out. Think of the care! He wished to avoid being led away at the sight of the mourners' grief, and the great concourse which was sure to be present, and so he learned his speech by heart. The impression produced upon me was such a one as I never before experienced. Deep sympathy reigned everywhere; all the musicians adored Weber; and the towns-people, members of whom had known that lovable man personally, did honour to Germany's great son, for national sentiment played an important part in the matter. You know that in ordinary conversation, the strong accent of the Liepzic dialect is the common speech of Richard Wagner, but when delivering his oration, his utterance was pure German, his measured periods were declaimed in slow, clear, ringing tones, showing unmistakable evidence of histrionic power. As an effort of will it was remarkable, and surprised all his intimate friends.

This curious and interesting feature of dropping the somewhat harsh Leipzic accent and delivering himself in the purest German remained with Wagner to the last. On all what might be termed state occasions, when addressing an assembly his speech was clear, measured, and dignified; not a trace of his Leipzic accent was observable. It should be explained that the Leipzic accent is a sort of sing-song, almost whining utterance, with as strongly marked a pronunciation compared to pure German as that of a broad Somerset dialect to pure English.

# CHAPTER XIII.

1845.

THE story of the composition of "Tannhäuser," poem and music, is a forcible illustration of the proverb, that the life of a man is reflected in his works. Of the music and the performance of "Tannhäuser" in October, 1845, at Dresden, I wrote a notice for a London periodical, called the "English Gentleman." This was the first time, I believe, that Wagner's name was mentioned in England. They were exciting times, and it is of exceptional interest at this epoch to reflect upon the judgment of the composer at the birth of "Tannhäuser."

When the legend first engaged Wagner's attention, with a view to its composition, he was not thirty years old. It will be remembered that the transformation from Paris poverty to a comparative Dresden luxury infused new life into him. He tells me, " I resolved to throw myself into a world of excitement, to enjoy life, and taste fully its pleasures." And he did. It was in this mood of feverish excitation that the Venus love invaded him. His state was one of intense nervous tension. The poem was worked out, but not in the shape we now have it. The end was subsequently changed. The poetry and music simmered in his brain for three years. He began elated, filled with sensations of ecstasy. He ended dejected, fearing that death would intervene before the last notes were written.

Now wherein lies the explanation of this? Let me recount briefly his life during these three years, and the reason will at once be perceived. He had opened his Dresden career with brilliancy. "Rienzi" had proved a great success; he had been appointed conductor to the court, a competence of 1500 thalers or £225 yearly was guaranteed him, and his horizon seemed brighter; — but the reverse soon began to show itself. The "Dutchman," by which he had hoped to increase his reputation, proved a failure; even "Rienzi" was refused outside Dresden, and the press was violently inimical. His excited sanguine temperament had received a grievous shock. At Berlin, the "Dutchman" proved so abortive, that he took counsel with himself, and resolved that this "Tannhäuser" should not be written for the world, but for those who had shown themselves in sympathy with him. As "Tannhäuser" neared its completion, his state grew more morbid and desponding. His only solace, outside Roeckel, was his dog. It was a common saying with Wagner that his dog helped him to compose "Tannhäuser." It seems that when at the piano, at which he always composed, singing with his accustomed boisterousness, the dog, whose constant place was at his master's feet, would occasionally leap to the table, peer into his face, and howl piteously. Then Wagner would address his "eloquent critic" with, "What? it does not suit you?" and shaking the animal's paw, would say, quoting Puck, "Well, I will do thy bidding gently."

During the composition Tichatschek, who was to impersonate the hero, practised such portions as were already written. His enthusiasm was unbounded, and with Roeckel, he urged the Dresden management to provide special scenery.   The appeal was responded to, and painters were even brought from Paris.   On the 19th October, 1845, the opera was performed, Johanna Wagner, aged nineteen, the daughter of his brother Albert, singing the part of Elizabeth.   As an illustration of Richard Wagner's thoroughness and attention to detail, I would mention that for this performance he wrote a prefatory notice to the book of words, in which he explained the purport of the story, with the object of ensuring a better understanding of the drama by the public.   The performance, alas, was only a partial success, nor was a second representation, given within a fortnight, any more successful.   The music was unlike anything heard before.   It was noised abroad that passages had been written for the first violins which were unplayable, and the audience listened expectantly for the "scramble."   No doubt there were violin passages as difficult as original, but the heart of the leader, Lipenski, was in his work, and he set himself so earnestly to teach individually each violinist difficult phrases, even carefully noting the fingering, that the performance was anything but a " scramble."   Then the critics ridiculed the hundred and forty-two bars of repetition in the overture for the violins.   This confession of superficial intellect was not confined to Dresden critics ; a dozen years later, that sound musician, Lindpaintner, expressed the opinion to me that the first eight bars of the overture were "sublime," but that the remainder was all " erratic fiddling."   Such were the criticisms (?) passed upon the work.   Wagner saw there was no hope of its acceptation elsewhere, and thinking to bring it prominently before Germany, wrote in the following year for permission to dedicate the work to the king of Prussia. The reply was to the effect that if he would arrange portions of it for military performance, it might in that manner be brought to the notice of the king, and perhaps his request complied with. It is needless to say Wagner did nothing of the kind, and "Tannhäuser" sank temporarily into oblivion.

As the part which Richard Wagner played in the Revolution of 1848–49 is of absorbing interest, the incidents which led up to it are of importance to be carefully noted. The first sign of the coming opposition to the government appeared in 1845. In itself it was slight, when we think of the terrible struggle that was shortly to be carried on with such desperation, but it shows the embers of revolt in Wagner, which were later fanned into a glowing flame by the patriot, August Roeckel. Wagner's heart, as that of all men, revolted at the cause, but had it not been for the "companion of my solitude," as Wagner calls Roeckel, he would never have taken so active a part in the struggle for liberty. Upon this part, I cannot lay too much stress.

Throughout Saxony, a feeling had been growing against the restraint of the Roman Catholic ritual. One Wronger, a Roman Catholic priest, proposed certain revisions and modifications. To this the Dresden court, steadfastly ultramontane, offered violent opposition, and Duke Johann, brother of the king, showed himself a prominent defender of the faith.

The struggle was precipitated by the following incident. In his capacity as general commandant of the Communal guard, the Duke entered Leipzic one day in August, to review the troops. He and his staff were received, on the parade ground, by a large concourse of spectators with such chilling silence that, losing command of himself, the Duke at once broke off the projected review. Later in the day, while at an hotel on the city boulevard, some street urchins marched up and down singing, "Long live Wronger." In a moment a tumult arose, upon which the royal guard stationed outside the hotel, by whose order is not known, fired upon the citizens promenading in the town. "The street," writes Roeckel, "was bathed in blood." This caused a tremendous stir throughout Saxony. This wanton act of butchery was openly denounced by Roeckel and Wagner, in terms so emphatic that they were called upon to offer some sort of apology to the court. The two friends arranged a meeting with Reissiger, Fisher, and Semper, when the subject was discussed, with the result that it was deemed advisable, while holding service under the court, to express regret at the exuberance of the language, and the matter was allowed to drop. But it rankled in Wagner. His position of a servitor was irksome; he became restive in his royal harness, and vented his annoyance in anonymous letters to the papers. From this time his interest in the political situation increased; continually stimulated by Roeckel, his sympathies were always with the people, his pen ready to support his feelings. And so the time wore on till the outbreak of 1848.

In the spring of 1846 an event occurred which had a great deal to do with my subsequent introduction of Wagner to the London public. It was his conducting of the "Ninth Symphony." A custom existed in Dresden, of giving annual performances on Palm Sunday for the benefit of the pension fund of the musicians of the royal opera. Two works were usually produced, one a symphony, the two conductors dividing the office of conductor. This year the symphony fell to Wagner, and he elected to perform the "Choral." When a youth he had copied it entirely at Leipzic, knew it almost by heart, and regarded it as the greatest of Beethoven's works, the one in which the great master had felt the inadequacy of instrumental music to express what he wished to convey, and that the accents of the human voice were imperatively necessary for its full and complete realization. When it became known what symphony had been selected the orchestra revolted. They implored Wagner to produce another. The ninth had been done under Reissiger and proved a failure, in which verdict Reissiger had agreed, himself going so far as to describe that sublime work as "pure nonsense." But Wagner was inexorable. The band, fearing poor receipts, sought the aid of Intendant Luttichorn : to no purpose, however. Wagner's mind was made up, and he set to work with his usual thoroughness and earnestness. To avoid expense he borrowed the orchestral parts from Leipzic, learned the symphony by heart, and went through all the band parts himself, marking the nuances and tempi. As to rehearsals, he was unrelenting. For the double basses he had special meetings, would sing and scream the parts at them. He increased the chorus by choir-boys from neighbouring churches, and worked for the success of the performance with an energy hitherto unknown. To Roeckel he detailed the practice of the best portion of the band, whilst he persisted with the less skilful. The result was a performance as successful financially as artistically. More money was taken than at any previous concert, and the fame of Richard Wagner increased mightily. This performance brings out prominently certain features in Wagner's character which enable us to see how, through subsequent reverses, he was able to achieve success. First, witness his courage and indomitable will in overcoming the obstacles of Luttichorn's opposition and the ill-will of the orchestra, the want of funds ; then his earnestness and care in committing the score to memory, his energy at rehearsals, his forethought and wondrous grasp of detail evident in the programme he wrote explaining the symphony, and his untiring efforts to succeed. Such points of character show of what material the man was made, how in all he did he was thorough, and how firmly impressed with the conviction that he must succeed.

The analytical remarks he appended to the symphony were not those that the musical world now know as Richard Wagner's programme, but a shorter and more discursive exposition. The year was 1846, but two from the revolution. The spirit of the brotherhood of nations was in the air, and the references of Schiller to this world's bond of union were seized by Wagner as presenting the means of contemplating Beethoven's work from a more exalted elevation than that of an ordinary symphony. It was currently known that the poet had originally addressed his " Ode to Liberty ! the beautiful spark of heaven," but that the censor of the press had struck out " Freiheit " (liberty), and Schiller had substituted " Freude " (joy). The sentiment, then, was one shared by all, and there can be no question that the success of the final chorus was as much owing to the inspiriting language as to the tonal interpretation.

Of recent years much has been said of Wagner's attitude towards the opinions upon Italian opera. The years he served at the conductor's desk at Dresden, at the period when the sap of his art ambition was rising rapidly, truly brought him into intimate acquaintance enough with the fashionable works of French and Italian masters, but his resentment, I can vouch, was not directed against the composer. He often and often pointed out to me what, in his opinion, were passages which seemed to betoken the presence of real gift. What he did regret was that their faithful adherence to an illogical structure should have crippled their natural spontaneity. That the talent of the orchestra, too, should be thrown away on puerile productions annoyed him. But Wagner was nothing if not practical, and after a season of light opera, the conducting of which was shared by Reissiger and Roeckel, he writes, "After all, the management are wise in providing just that commodity for which there is demand." When his own "Tannhäuser" was produced with its new ending, he was charged in the press with being governed too much by reflection, that his work lacked natural flow, that he was domineered by reasoning at the expense of feeling. To this Wagner replied in very weighty words, significant of the thought which always governed the earnest artist, "The period of an unconscious productivity has long passed : an art work to endure the process of time, and to satisfy the high culture which is around us, must be solidly rooted in reason and reflection." Such utterances are clearly traceable to his elevated appreciation of poetry and keen reasoning faculties.

"Lohengrin," beyond contradiction the most popular of all Wagner's operas, or music-dramas, for it should be well remembered that Wagner in all his literary works, up to the last persistently applies the term "opera" to "Lohengrin," and its two immediate predecessors, whilst music-drama was not employed until 1851, and then only for compositions subsequent to that period. The popularity of "Lohengrin" is not confined to its native soil, Germany, but all Europe, England, Russia, Italy, Spain, Portugal, and Denmark (shameful to add, France alone excepted), and America and Australia, have received it with acclamations. And why? The secret of it? For learned musicians too, anti-Wagnerians though they be, accepted it. From notes in my possession, I think the explanation becomes clear. Wagner writes at that time, "Music is love, and in my projected opera melody shall stream from one end to the other." The form, too, does not break from traditions. It is the border between the old and new. When "Lohengrin" was composed, not one of his theoretical works had been penned. He was untrammelled then. The principles upon which his subsequent works were based can only be applied, he says, to the first three operas "with very extensive limitations." Hence he satisfies the orthodox in their two fundamental principles, "form and melody." "Lohengrin" is a love-poem; to Wagner, then, music was love, and he was intent on writing melody as then understood throughout the new work.

The network of connection that exists between Wagner's opera texts, is but one of the many examples which might be adduced of the sequential thought characteristic of the composer. Each was suggested by its predecessor. The contest of the Minnesingers' "Tannhäuser" was naturally followed by the story of the Mastersingers, first sketched in 1845, the year of the "Tannhäuser" performance, and then Elsa the love-pendant of innocence and purity to the material, voluptuous Venus.

In this story of "Lohengrin," Wagner wavered for a time whether the hero should not remain on earth with Elsa. This ending he was going to adopt, Roeckel informs me, out of deference to friends and critics, but Wagner told me that Roeckel argued so eloquently for the return of Lohengrin to his state of semi-divinity, that to permit the hero to lead the life of a citizen would clash harshly with the poetic aspect, and so Wagner, strengthened in his original intention, reverted to his first conception. Allusion is made to this by Wagner in "A Commutation to my Friends," written in Switzerland, 1851 ; the friend there referred to is August Roeckel.

During the composition of "Lohengrin " Wagner was at deadly strife with the world. He flattered where he despised. He borrowed money where he could. Just then the world was all black to Wagner. Of no period of his life can it be said that Wagner managed his finances with even ordinary care. He always lived beyond his means. Though he was in receipt of £225 a year from the Dresden theatre, a respectable income for that period be it remembered, he did not restrict his expenses. And so his naturally irritable temperament was intensified and he resolutely threw himself into the " Lohengrin " work, determined not to write for a public whose taste was vitiated by " theatres having no other purpose but amusement," but to pour his soul out in the love-strains with which his heart was bursting. The original score shows that the order of composition was Act III, I, II, and the prelude last, the whole covering a period of eleven months, from September, 1846, to August, 1847. It was unusual for Wagner to compose in this manner; indeed, as far as I am aware, it was the only work so written.

At the time Wagner was meditating upon the " Lohengrin " music, when it was beginning to assume a definite shape in his mind, weighed down with the feeling of being " rejected " by his countrymen and depressed in general circumstances, the following letter, written to his mother, throws a charming sidelight upon Wagner, the man. The deep filial tenderness and poetic sentiment that breathe throughout it, touch and enchant us.

My Darling Mother: It is so long since I have congratulated you on your birthday, that I feel quite happy to remember it once at the right time, which I have, alas, in the pressure of circumstances, so often overlooked. To tell you how intensely it delights me to know you body and soul among us; to press your hand from time to time; and to recall the memory of my own youth so lovingly tended by you. It is the consciousness that you are with us that makes your children feel one family. Thrown hither and thither by fate, forming new ties, they think of you, dearest mother, who have no other ties in this world than those which bind you to your children. And so we are all united in you: we are all your children. May God grant thee this happiness for years yet to come, and keep you in health and strength to see your children prosper until the end of your time.

When I feel myself oppressed and hindered by the world, always striving, rarely enjoying complete success, oft a prey to annoyances through failure, and wounded by the rough contact with the outer world, which, alas, so rarely responds to my inner wish, nothing remains to me but the enjoyment of nature. I throw myself weeping into her arms. She consoles me, and elevates me, whilst showing how imaginary are all those sufferings that trouble us. If we strive too high, Nature shows us that we belong to her, are her outgrowth, like the trees and plants, which, developing themselves from her, grow and warm themselves in the sun of heaven, enjoy the strengthening freshness, and do not fade or die till they have thrown out the seed which again produces germs and plants, so that the once created lives an eternity of youth.

When I feel how wholly I belong also to nature, then vanishes every selfish thought, and I long to shake every brother-man by the hand. How can I then help yearning for that mother from whose womb I came forth, and who grows weaker while I increase in strength? How do I smile at those societies which seek to discover why the loving ties of nature are so often bruised and torn asunder.

My darling mother, whatever dissonances may have sounded between us, how quickly and completely have they disappeared. It is like leaving the mist of the city to enter into the calm retreat of the wooded valley, where, throwing myself upon mossy earth, with eyes turned towards heaven, listening to the songsters of the air, with heart full, the tear unchecked starts forth, and I involuntarily stretch my hand towards you, exclaiming, "God protect thee, my darling mother; and when He takes thee to Himself, may it be done mildly and gently." But death is not here : you live on through us; and a richer and more eventful life perhaps awaits you through us than yours ever could have been. Therefore, thank God who has so plentifully blessed you.

Farewell, my darling mother,

Your son,

RICHARD.

DRESDEN, 19th September, 1846.

It was well for Wagner that his mind was occupied with the composition of "Lohengrin" during 1846--47, for by the summer of the latter year the pressure of circumstances had become so acute that notwithstanding his exceptional elasticity of spirits the mental worry must have resulted in a more distressing depression than that which we know did take hold of him.   This exuberance of youthful frolic is an important characteristic of Wagner.   It was his sheet anchor, a refuge from annoyances that would have incisively irritated or crushed another.   True, he would burst into a passion at first, — there is no denying his passionate nature, — but it was of short duration and once over the boisterous merriment of a high-spirited school-boy succeeded.   Though deeply wounded, as only finely strung sensitive natures can be, he was quick to recover, and whilst animadverting upon the denseness of those who slighted his art, he distorted the incident and treated it as worthy of affording fun only.   Wagner identified himself with his art body and soul, his breath of life was art, his pulse throbbed for art, and to wound him was insulting art.   His success was the triumph of art, and the sacrifices his friends made of mental energy, wealth, and time were regarded by him but as votive offerings to the altar of the divine art, honouring the donor.   Then when his scores of " Rienzi," the " Dutchman," and " Tannhäuser " were returned unopened by managers, he turned with undiminished ardour upon " Lohengrin," doubting his capacity to realize in tones his feelings, but with dauntless fortitude to write his " love-music " for the glory of art, conscious that its scenic interpretation was, for the present at least, a very improbable circumstance.

What, in Wagner's character at all times, inspires our admiration is his courage.   " He never knew when he was beaten."   Weighed down with monetary difficulties,

— though his poor means were made rich by the wealth of love and ready invention of Minna, whose patience and self-denial he was always ready to extol, — with a cloudy art horizon, he sought to approach the great public in a more direct manner than by stage representations, by publishing the three operas already composed. It was not a difficult matter; he was a local celebrity, and on the strength of his reputation he entered into an engagement with a Dresden firm, Messrs. Meser and Co. The large initial cost was borne by the firm, but the liability was Wagner's. Messrs. Meser and Co. predicted a success, and risking nothing, or comparatively nothing, urged the issue of "Rienzi," "Dutchman," and "Tannhäuser." The contract was signed, the works were produced, but alas, the forecast was pleasant to the ear but breaking in the hope. There was absolutely no sale, and claims were soon preferred on the luckless composer for the cost of production. Of course they could not be met. Wagner had no available funds, his income was insufficient for his daily needs, and so he borrowed, borrowed where he could, sufficient to temporarily appease the publishers. This debt, paid by instalments, hung over him as a black cloud for years, always breaking when he was least equal to meet it. How he has stormed at his folly, and regretted his heedlessness of the future, but the demand met, his tribulation was immediately forgotten. A brother of mine, passing through Dresden in 1847, wrote to me of his surprise at the state of Wagner's finances, and of the sum that was necessary to keep him afloat, which under my direction was immediately supplied.

It was then that Wagner wrote to me: "Try and negotiate for the sale of my opera 'Tannhäuser' in London. If there be no possibility of concluding a bargain, and gaining a tangible remuneration for me, arrange that some firm shall take it so as to secure the English copyright." I went off at once to my friend Frederick Beale, the head of the house Cramer, Beale and Co., now Cramer and Co. Though Frederick Beale was an enthusiast in art, with a sense beyond that of the ordinary speculator in other men's talent, yet "he could not see his way to publishing 'Tannhäuser.'" I knew Beale would have done much for me, our relations being of so intimate a character, but the times "were out of joint," his geniality had just then led him to accept much that proved a financial loss to the firm, and so the work which, as time now shows, would have produced a future, was rejected, yes, rejected, though on behalf of Wagner I offered it *for nothing*. It is the old, old story; Carlyle offering his "Sartor Resartus" for nothing, Schubert his songs, etc., etc., and rejected as valueless by the purblind publisher. The publisher invariably is the man of his period; he is incapable of seeing beyond his age, and thrusts aside the genius who writes for futurity. "Wouldst thou plant for eternity?" asks Carlyle, "then plant into the deep, infinite faculties of man, his fantasy and heart; wouldst thou plant for a year and a day? then plant into his shallow, superficial faculties, his self-love and arithmetical understanding."

# CHAPTER XIV.

1848.

I NOW come to perhaps the most important period in
Richard Wagner's life, full of deep interest in itself, and
pregnant with future good to our art.   Additional interest is further attached to it because of the incomplete
or inaccurate accounts given by the many Wagner biographers.   For this shortcoming, this unsatisfactory treatment, Wagner is himself to blame.   He has left behind
him rich materials for an almost exhaustive biography ;
he was a man of great literary power, a clear and full
writer, and yet, with reference to the part he played in
the revolution in Saxony, of 1848–49, he is singularly, I
could almost say significantly, silent, or, when he does
allude to it, his references are either incomplete or mis-
leading.

Wagner was an active participator in the so-called
Revolution of 1849, notwithstanding his late-day statements to the contrary.   During the first few of his eleven
years of exile his talk was incessantly about the outbreak,
and the active aid he rendered at the time, and of his services to the cause by speech, and by pen, prior to the
1849 May days ; and yet in after-life, in his talk with me,
I, who held documentary evidence, under his own hand,
of his participation, he in petulant tones sought either
to minimize the part he played, or to explain it away

altogether.   This change of front I first noticed about 1864, at Munich.   But before stating what I know, on the incontestable evidence of his own handwriting, his explicit utterances to me, the evidence of eyewitnesses, and the present criminal official records in the procès-verbal Richard Wagner, of his relations with the reform movement (misnamed the Revolution); I will at once cite one instance of his — to me — apparent desire to forget the part he enacted during a trying and excited period.

Wagner was a member of a reform union; before this body he read, in June, 1848, a paper of revolutionary tendencies, the gist of which was abolition of the monarchy, and the constitution of a republic.   This document, of somewhat lengthy proportions, harmless in itself, which was printed by the union, constituted part of the Saxon government indictment against Richard Wagner.   From 1871–1883 Wagner edited his " Collected Writings," published by Fritsch, of Leipzic, in eleven volumes;   these include short sketches on less important topics, written in Paris, in 1841, but this important and interesting statement of his political opinions is significantly omitted.   Comment is needless.

To help in forming an accurate judgment of Richard Wagner's " revolutionary tendencies " (?) a slight sketch of the outbreak, its objects, and the means employed, will be of assistance.   Secondly, as the head and front of Wagner's offending, according to the government, rested on a letter he had written from Dresden to August Roeckel at Prague, on the first day of the rise, which letter was unfortunately found on Roeckel when taken prisoner, references to Roeckel's participation will be necessary.   Indeed, from an intimate knowledge of the two men, I place my strong conviction on record, that had it not been for August Roeckel, the patriot, Wagner, revolutionary demagogue, would never have existed nor have been expatriated. True and undoubted it is, that Richard Wagner's nature was of the radical reformer's type, but in these matters he was cautious, and would not have played the prominent part he did, had it not been for the stirring appeals of "the friend who sacrificed his art future for my sake." The feeling already existed in him; it was fanned into a glowing flame by his colleague, Roeckel. When aroused, Wagner was not the spirit to falter.

Wagner has often been charged with base ingratitude towards his king. The accusation is absurd, and proceeds solely from ignorance, forsooth, indeed, it is disproved emphatically in the very revolutionary paper which forms part of the official government indictment against him. Although he therein argues in favour of a republic, his personal references to the king of Saxony are inspired by feelings of reverential affection. Wagner was no common trickster, or prevaricator, and when he speaks of the "pure virtues" of the king, "his honourable, just, and gentle character," of the "noblest of sovereigns," we may unhesitatingly acquit him of any personal animosity. He even seems to have had a prophetic instinct of this charge, and meets it by, "He who speaks this to-day, and . . . is most firmly convinced that he never proved his fidelity to the oath of allegiance he took to the king, on accepting office, more than on the day he penned this address."

In the year 1848 the kingdom of Saxony, and other German principalities, were in a state of much unrest.

The outbreak of the French Revolution caused an onward movement, and the German people clamoured for constitutional government, and demanded (1) freedom of the press, (2) trial by jury, (3) national armies, and (4) political representatives. A deputation set out from Leipzic, in February, 1848, and pleaded personally before the king of Saxony. He replied by a more rigorous press censorship. The people congregated in thousands before the Leipzic town hall, to hear the royal reply read. Enraged at the refusal of their requests, and at the tone of that refusal, they determined on sending a second deputation. Wagner was present when this arrived. They no longer prayed, but plainly told the king that the press was free, demanded another minister, and intimated that if the freedom was not officially recognized, Leipzic would march *en masse* on Dresden. Six other towns then sent deputations; the king was advised not to receive them, but they forced their way to the presence chamber, which the king left by another door, exclaiming, " I will not listen — go ! " As a reply to such unwise treatment, Wagner's townsmen prepared to make good their words, and marched on Dresden. Prussian aid was sought, and promptly given, troops mobilizing on the northern frontier, the Saxon soldiery being despatched to surround Leipzic. Other towns arranged mass deputations to the king, who despatched a minister to report on the attitude of Leipzic. The report came, " The people are determined and orderly." The whole report was favourable to the town; upon which, the king changed his ministers, abolished the press censorship, instituted trial by jury, and promised a reform of the electoral laws. The people became delirious with joy, and received the king everywhere with acclamations.

It was during these stirring times that Wagner and Roeckel became members of the "Fatherland Union," a reform institution with a modest propaganda. The Union was really a federation of existing reform and political institutions, adopting for its motto, "The will of the people is law," leaving the question of a republic or a monarchy an open one.

There was plenty of enthusiasm and strong determination among members of the Union, but they lacked organization. The drift of the government's attitude was clear, seemingly conciliatory, but really more oppressive. The Union felt that until the electoral laws were altered and national armies instituted, the people would never be in a position to cope with the government. It was not that they desired the abolition of the monarchy so much as the acknowledgment that capable, law-abiding citizens had a right to a voice in the selection of their rulers. The Union had its own printing-press, and distributed largely political leaflets, a proceeding carried on openly, though the members knew themselves exposed to every hazard.

It is a fact that one of the best papers read before the members of the Union was written by Richard Wagner. It was not possible that a man of Wagner's excitable temperament, with his love of freedom, his deep-rooted sympathy with the masses, would have joined such a society without actively exerting himself to further its objects. In his heart he was not a revolutionist, he had no wish to overturn governments, but his principles were decidedly utilitarian, and to secure these he did not scruple to urge the abolition of the monarchy, although represented by a prince he dearly loved. His argument was delivered against the office and not against the man. Among the many reforms he advocates in this paper are two to which democratic England has not yet attained: (1) manhood suffrage without limitation or restriction of any kind, and (2) the abolition of the second chamber. Though he urges the substitution of a republic for a monarchy, he strives at the impossible task of proving that the king can still be the first, the head of a republic, and that the name only would be changed, and that he would enjoy the heart's love of a whole people in place of a varnished demeanour of courtiers. His paper was read on the 16th June, 1848, before the Fatherland Union. It was ordered to be printed and circulated among the various federated societies. A copy of this paper was sent to me, of which I give a translation here. It will be noted that it is not signed Richard Wagner but only " A Member of the Fatherland Union." This mattered not, as the author was well known, and when Wagner was numbered among those accused by the government, this paper was filed as part of the indictment against him. It is entitled: —

"What is the Relation that our Efforts bear to the Monarchy?" and is as follows: —

As it is desirable that we become perfectly clear on this point, let us first closely examine the essence of republican requirements. Do you honestly believe that by marching resolutely onward from our present basis we should very soon reach a true republic, one without a king? Is this your deliberate opinion, or do you say so only to delude the timorous? Are you so ignorant, or do you intentionally purpose to mislead?

Let me tell you to what goal our republican efforts are tending.

Our efforts are for the good of all and are directed towards a future in which our present achievements will be but as the first streak of moonlight. With this object kept steadily in view, we should insist on the overthrow of the last remaining glitter of aristocracy. As the aristocracy no longer consists of feudal lords and masters who can enslave and bodily chastise us at their will, they would do wisely to obliterate old grievances by relinquishing the last remnants of class distinction which, at any moment, might become a Nessus shirt, consuming them if not cast off in time.

Should they answer us that the memory of their ancestors would render it impious to resign any privileges inherited by them, then let them remember also that we too have forefathers, whose noble deeds of heroism, though not inscribed on genealogical trees, are yet inscribed — their sufferings, bondage, oppression, and slavery of every kind — in letters of blood in the unfalsified archives of the history of the last thousand years.

To the aristocracy I would say, forget your ancestors, throw away your titles and every outward sign of courtly favour, and we will promise you to be generous and efface every remembrance of our ancestors. Let us be children of one father, brothers of one family! Listen to the warning — follow it freely and with a good will, for it is not to be slighted. Christ says, " If thy right eye offend thee. pluck it out and cast it from thee, for it is better that one of thy members should perish than that thy whole body should be cast into hell."

And now another point. Once for all, resign the exclusive honour of ever being in the presence of our monarch. Pray him to cease investing you with a medley of useless court offices, distinctions, and privileges; in our time they make the court a subject for unpleasant reflection. Discontinue to be lords of the chamber and lords of the robes, whose only utterance is " our king," — strip him of his tinsel, lackeys, and flunkeys, frivolous excrescences of a bad time — the time of Louis the Fourteenth, when all princes sought to imitate the French monarch. Withdraw from a court which is an almshouse for idle nobility, and exert yourselves, that it may become the court of a whole and happy people, which every individual will enjoy and will be ready to defend, and smile on a sovereign who is the father of a whole contented people.

Therefore, do away with the first chamber. There is but one people, not a first and a second, and they need but one house for their representation. This house, let it be a simple, noble building, with an elevated roof, resting on tall and strong pillars. Why would you disfigure the building by dividing it with a mean partition, thus causing two confined spaces?

We further insist upon the unconditional right of every natural-born subject, when of age, to a vote. The more needy he be, the more his right, and the more earnestly will he aid in keeping the laws which he himself assisted in framing and which, henceforth, are to protect him from any similar future state of need and misery. Our republican programme further includes a new system of national defence, in which every citizen capable of bearing arms shall be enrolled. No standing army. It shall be neither a standing army nor a militia, nor yet a reduction of the one nor an increase of the other. It must be a new creation, which in its process of development, will do away with the necessity of a standing army as well as a militia.

And when all who draw breath in our dear German land are united into one great free people, when class prejudices shall have ceased to exist, then do you suppose we have reached our goal? Oh, no ; we are just equipped for the beginning. Then will it be our duty to investigate boldly, with all our reasoning power, the cause of misery of our present social status, and determine whether man, the crown of creation, with his high mental abilities and his wonderful physical development, can have been destined by God to be the servile slave of inert base metal. We must decide whether money shall exert such degrading power over the image of God — man — as to render him the despicable slave of the passions of usury and avarice. The war against this existing evil will cause neither tears nor blood. The result of the foregone victory will be a universal conviction that the highest attainable happiness is commonwealth, a state in which as many active men as Mother Earth can supply with food will join in the well-ordered republic, supporting it by a fair exchange of labor, mutually supplying each other's wants, and contributing to the universal happiness. Society must be in a diseased state when the activity of individuals is restrained and the existing laws imperfectly administered. In the coming contest we shall find that society will be maintained by the physical activity of individuals, and we shall destroy the nebulous notion that money possesses any inherent power. And heaven will help us to discover the true law by which this shall be proved, and dispel the false halo with which the unthinking mind invests this demon money. Then shall we root out the miseries engendered and nourished by public and secret usury, deceptive paper money and fraudulent speculations. This will tend to promote the emancipation of the human race (whilst fulfilling the teachings of Christ, a simple and clear truism which it is ever sought to hide behind the glamour of dogma, once invented to appeal to the feeble understanding of simple-minded barbarians), and to prepare it for a state towards the highest development of which we are now tending with clear vision and reason.

Do you think that you scent in this the teachings of communism?

Are you then so stupid or wicked as to confound a theory so senseless as that of communism with that which is absolutely necessary to the salvation of the human race from its degraded servitude? Are you not capable of perceiving that the very attempt, even though it were allowed, of dividing mathematically the goods of this world, would be a senseless solution of a burning question, but which attempt, fortunately however, in its complete impossibility, carries its own death-warrant. But though communism fails to supply the remedy, will you on that account deny the disease? Have a care! Notwithstanding that we have enjoyed peace for thirty-three years now, what do you see around you? Dejection and pitiful poverty; everywhere the horrid pallor of hunger and want. Look to it while there is yet time and before it becomes too late to act!

Think not to solve the question by the giving of alms; acknowledge at once the inalienable rights of humanity, rights vouchsafed by the Omnipotent, or else you may live to see the day that cruel scorn will be met by vengeance and brute force. Then the wild cry of victory might be that of communism, and although the impossibility of any lengthened duration of its principles as a ruling power can be boldly predicted, yet even the briefest reign of such a thraldom might be sufficient to expunge for a long time to come all the advantages of a civilization of two thousand years old.

Do you believe I threaten? No; I warn! When by our republican efforts we shall have solved this most important problem for the weal of society, and have established the dignity of the freed man, and established his claim to what we consider his rights, shall we then rest satisfied? No; then only are we reinvigorated for our great effort. For when we have succeeded in solving the emancipation question, thereby assisting in the regeneration of society, then will arise a new, free, and active race, then shall we have gained a new mean to aid us towards the attainments of the highest benefits, and then shall we actively disseminate our republican principles.

Then shall we traverse the ocean in our ships, and found here and there a new young Germany, enriching it with the fruits of our achievements, and educating our children in our principles of human rights, so that they may be propagated everywhere. We shall do otherwise than the Spaniards, who made the new world into a papistic slaughter-house; we shall do otherwise than the English, who convert their colonies into huge shops for their own individual profit. Our colonies shall be truly German, and from sunrise to sunset we shall contemplate a beautiful, free Germany, inhabited, as in the mother country, by a free people. The sun of German freedom and German gentleness shall alike warm and elevate Cossack, Frenchmen, Bushmen, and Chinese. You see our republican zeal in this respect has no termination; it pushes on further and further from century to century, to confer happiness on the whole of the human race! Do you call this a Utopian dream? When we once set to work with a good will, and act courageously, then every year shall throw its light on a good deed of progress.

But you ask, will all this be achieved under a monarchy? My answer is that throughout I have persistently kept it in view, but if you have any doubts of such a possibility, then it is you who pronounce the monarchical death-warrant. But if you agree with me, and consider it possible as I realize it, then a republic is the exact and right thing, and we should but have to petition the king to become the first and most genuine republican.

And who is more called upon to be the most genuine republican than the king? *Res-publica* means the affairs of the people. What individual can be destined more than the king to belong with his whole soul and mind to the people's affairs? When he has been convinced of this undeniable truth, what is there possible that could induce him to lower himself from his exalted position to become the head of a special and small section only of his people.

However deeply any republican may feel for the general good, he never can emulate the feelings of the king, nor become so genuine a republican, for the king's anxiety is for his people as a whole, whilst every one of us is, in the nature of things, compelled to divide his attention between private and public affairs. And in what would consist a sacrifice, which it might be supposed the king would have to make in order to effect so grand and noble a change? Can it be considered a sacrifice for a king to see his free citizens no longer subjects? This right has been acknowledged and granted by the new constitution, and he who confirms its justice and adopts it with fidelity, cannot see a sacrifice in the abolition of subjects, and the substitution of " free men." Would it be possible that a monarch could view the loss of the idle, vapid court attendance, with its surfeit of extinct titles and obsolete offices, as a sacrifice? What a contemptuous notion we should have of one of the most gentle-minded, true-hearted princes of our period, were we to assume that the fulfilment of our wishes entailed a sacrifice on his part, when we feel convinced that even a real sacrifice might with safety be expected from him, and the more so, when it is proved to him that the love of his people depended on the removal of an obstacle. What gives us the right to suppose this? that by our interpretation of the feelings of so exceptional a prince, we are able to infer that he would grant our request when we could not dare act thus with one of our body? It is the spirit of our time, the new state of things, that has grown up, which seems to give to the simplest among us the power of prophecy. There is a decided pressure for a decision. There are two camps amongst the civilized nations of Europe; from one we hear the cry of monarchy; republic, is the cry of the other.

Will you deny that the time has come when a solution of this question must be arrived at, a question, the reply to which embodies all that which, at the present moment, excites human sympathies down to their lowest depths? Do you mean to say that you do not recognize the hour as inspired by God, that all this had been said and attempted before, and would again pass off like a fit of inebriation, and would fall back into its old place? Well, then, it would seem as though the heavens had stricken you with blindness. No; at the present moment we clearly perceive the necessity of distinguishing between truth and falsehood, and monarchy as the embodiment of autocracy is a falsehood — our constitution has proved it to be so.

All who despair of a reconciliation throw yourselves boldly into the arms of the republic; those still willing to hope, lift their eyes for the last time to the points of existing circumstances to find a solution. The latter see that if the contest be against monarchy, it is only in isolated cases against the person of the prince, whilst everywhere war is being waged against the party that lifts the monarch on a shield, under the cover of which they fight for their own selfish ends. This is the party that has to be thrown down and conquered, however bloody the fight. And if all reconciliation fail, party and prince will simultaneously be hit. But the means of peace are in the hands of the prince; if he be the genuine father of his people, and by one single noble resolution he can plant the standard of peace, there where war seems otherwise inevitable peace will reign. Let us then cast our glance around, and seek among the European monarchs those said to be the chosen instruments of heaven for the great work of paternal government, and what do we see? A degenerated race, unfit for any noble calling! What a sight we find in Spain, Portugal, or Naples. What heartache fills us when we look in Germany, on Hanover, Hesse, Bavaria. Let us look away from these! God has judged the weak and wicked; their evils extend from branch to branch. Let us turn our eyes towards home, There we meet a prince beloved by his people, not in the old traditional sense, but from a genuine acknowledgment of his real self, his pure virtues, his honourable, just, and gentle character; therefore, we cry aloud, "This is the man Providence has chosen!"

If Prussia insists on monarchy, it is to suit its notion of Prussian destiny, a vain idea that cannot fail to pale soon. If Austria is of the same mind, it is because she sees in her dynasty the only means of keeping together a conglomeration of people and lands thrown into an unnatural whole and which cannot by any possibility hold together much longer. But if a Saxon chooses monarchy, it is because he loves his king, is happy in calling such a prince his own, not from a cold, calculating spirit of advantage, but from genuine affection. This pure affection shall be our beacon-light, our guide not only during this troubled state of things, but for the future and forever. Filled with this unspeakably grand and important thought, we with inspired conviction courageously exclaim, "We are republicans!"

By what we have achieved we are rapidly nearing our goal, — the republic, — and although much anger and deception attach themselves still to the name, all doubts can be dispelled by one word from our sovereign. It is not we who shall proclaim the republic; it will be our king, the noblest of sovereigns; he shall say : —

"I declare Saxony to be a free state, and the first of this free state shall give to every one the fullest security of his station, and we further proclaim that the highest power in the land of Saxony is invested in the royal house of Wettin to descend from branch to branch by the right of the firstborn. And we swear to keep the oath that the law shall never be broken, not that our taking it will be the safeguard of its being kept, for how many oaths are continually broken to such covenants! No; its safeguard will be the conviction we had before we took the oath, that the law will be the beginning of a new era of unchangeable happiness, not only for Saxony, but the whole of Germany, aye, to all Europe will it carry the beneficent message."

He who speaks this to-day, emboldened by inspired hope, is most firmly convinced that he never proved his fidelity to the oath of allegiance he took to the king on accepting office more than on the day he penned this address. Does it appear to you that by this proposition, *monarchy would be altogether abolished? Yes, so it would!* But the kingdom would thereby be emancipated. Do not deceive yourselves, ye who clamour for "a constitutional monarchy on the broadest basis."

You are either not honest in reference to that basis, or if you are in real earnest, you will torture your artificial monarchy to death, for every step you take in advancing on that democratic basis will be an encroachment on the power of the monarch, viz. : his autocracy; and in this light only can a monarchy be understood, therefore every step you take in a democratic direction will be a humiliation to the monarch, since it will bespeak a distrust of his rule. How can love and confidence prosper in a continual conflict between totally opposed principles?  A monarch cannot fail to be thwarted and annoyed in a contest in which very often undignified measures are employed that cannot but produce an unhealthy state of things. Let us save the monarch from such an unhappy half-life.  *Therefore, let us abolish monarchy altogether*, as autocracy, *i.e.* sole-reigning, becomes impossible by the strong opposition of democracy, — the reign of the many, — but, on the other hand, let us set against this the complete emancipation of royalty.

At the head of the free state — the republic, the king by lineal descent, will be what he in the noblest sense should be, viz. the first of the people, the freest of the free!

Would this not be the grandest realization of Christ's teaching, " the highest among you shall be the servant of all," for in serving and upholding the liberty of all, he raises in himself the conception of liberty to the highest pinnacle, the divine.   The more earnestly we dive into the annals of German history, the more we become convinced that the signification of sovereignty, as we have given it, is but a resuscitated one.   The circle of historical development will be closed when we have adopted it, and its greatest aberration will be found in the present un-German conception of monarchy.

Should we wish to formulate our heartfelt wishes into a petition, then I am convinced we should have to count our petitions by the hundred thousands, for their contents would lead to a reconciliation of contesting parties, at least of all of them that mean well.  But only one signature is wanted here to be conclusive, that is, the signature of our beloved king, whom from the innermost depth of our hearts we wish a happier lot than he can at present enjoy!

A MEMBER OF THE FATHERLAND UNION.

16TH JUNE, 1848.

It may be supposed with such documents scattered broadcast by a great political institution, that the government would have shown discretion and endeavoured to conciliate the people by judicious concessions.   Their action, however, was in the contrary direction.   They were well aware they could crush the people at the first appearance of an outbreak, and cared not. As long as they had control of the army they felt secure. This question of natural armies was for the moment pressing. Wagner had endeavoured to solve it in his paper, but his were more suggestions than a detailed plan, so his talk with his friend, August Roeckel, led to the latter attempting a solution. Roeckel took for his basis the various military organizations in force in Switzerland. His paper was read before the Fatherland Union, and Wagner told me, he was loudly applauded. Like his own paper it was printed, and in thousands. He, too, signed his scheme, " A Member of the Fatherland Union," but it was an open secret who was the author. The result was that he was dismissed from his post of assistant court conductor, after five years of service. The Union then resolved to hold themselves in readiness for extreme measures, and with that view directed Roeckel to amplify his plan. As this was a question of technical skill and practical experience, the aid of officers in the army was sought. The movement was popular with the troops, and advice was readily forthcoming. The government, becoming aware of this, at once dismissed all military men who had aided in formulating the plan. From this time Wagner was what might be termed a marked man. It was known that " the companion of my solitude " was his offending assistant director, and means were taken to indicate the disapprobation of the court. August Roeckel was dismissed in the autumn of 1848, just at the time all Dresden was celebrating the three-hundred years' jubilee of its theatre. Among the favours bestowed by the king were decorations for Chapel Master Reissiger, (a man vastly the inferior of Wagner) and other subordinates, but Wagner was passed over. The slight was intentional.

But a few weeks later Liszt was going to produce "Tannhäuser" at Vienna. To secure as perfect a representation as possible, Jenasst, the Vienna stage manager, visited Richard Wagner, for consultation, and he relates how Wagner took him to a meeting of republicans where the men all wore large hats, and behaved themselves generally in a wild, excited fashion.

No longer a musician by profession, but engaged entirely in the cause of the people, August Roeckel founded a small weekly paper called the "Volksblatte" (People's Paper), naturally supported by the Union; it was narrowly watched by the government. Occasionally seizures were made, but no charge was brought against Roeckel. In this Wagner wrote, and I know that the tenour of his articles was, "Destroy an interested clique of flatterers who surround the King; and let the royal ear be open to the prayers of all the people." The government contemplated a prosecution of Roeckel, but refrained solely because of the difficulty of securing a conviction.

In November the *Prussian National Gathering* was dissolved. This procedure exasperated the people, upon which Berlin openly announced that any exhibition of revolt would be at once put down mercilessly by bayonet and cannon. August Roeckel was appealed to, and he wrote a letter to the Prussian military authorities on the subject, copies of which he sent to the public journals. For this the government arrested him and put him in prison, where he remained three days without trial; a generous unknown friend, putting ten thousand dollars as bail, secured his release. Shortly after, he was tried and acquitted, but to this day it is not known who was the benefactor on that occasion. So popular was August Roeckel with the people, that on his acquittal, he was met by a large concourse of friends, to which joined a detachment of Life Guards, some two dozen, from the barracks close at hand, and headed a procession through the town. As may be expected, the whole of the troop of soldiers were tried, punished, and dismissed from the army. I mention this incident as bearing upon the prominence of Roeckel in the eyes of the government; and because the charges against Wagner rested on his friendship with Roeckel, and on papers found at Roeckel's house, implicating Richard Wagner.

In the opening winter months of 1848, the air was thick with reform. A new chamber was to be elected; every one was straining his utmost for the cause. It was felt that on the result of the elections the fate of the people rested. The Fatherland Union determined to run as many candidates of their own as possible, and Roeckel was of the chosen number. He was elected deputy for Limbach, near Chemnitz, the electors purchasing and presenting him with the freehold property, which it was required all members should possess. The result of the elections gave an overwhelming majority for what were termed the people's candidates. Roeckel wrote me the result, which was as follows: —

> Government party, nil seats.
> Moderate liberals, one-tenth.
> Democratic party, nine-tenths.

The democratic party as a body had pledged itself to a revision of taxation. It was felt that the new chamber would not trifle with an iniquitously large court list, nor would it tolerate luxuries on the civil list. This was openly talked about. Wagner was in distress. The subsidy granted by the government to the theatre was one of the items of the civil list; was this to go? He saw Roeckel; there was the man most fitted to urge the wisdom of retaining the charge. His devotion to the cause of the masses was unhesitatingly admitted on all hands, and he knew the theatre and its necessary expenditure better than any one. It was decided that while Roeckel should work in the chamber, Wagner should, as conductor, draw out a scheme and submit it to ministers, independently of his coadjutor. The plan once begun assumed much larger proportions than was intended for the occasion. It was delivered, and he heard nothing of it for months, officially, but he knew that the discussion was being shirked. When it was returned to him, there was evidence in the shape of pencil-marks that he had been laughed at as a visionary, anticipating a great measure of reform when it was intended none should be granted. Communications had been opened up secretly with the Prussian government, who promised on the first show of discontent to enter Saxony with their troops and very effectively stamp it out; and so the king's advisers had no intention of considering any plan the newly elected chamber might submit. In itself the plan is a marvel of administrative and constructive ability. He entitled it, "Scheme for the Organization of a German National Theatre." There are many propositions advanced in it which are very moot points, in urging which Wagner, in my judgment, was in error ; *e.g.* private enterprise was to be discountenanced for the reason that an impressario might produce immoral pieces. To him the theatre was a great educator of a nation, and he would insist on all theatres being under the direct control of the government. But apart from this, which is a matter of opinion, the scheme is a logical and exhaustive treatment of the whole question of dramatic and vocal art, from the training-school for girls and boys to their retirement on a pension to be allowed by the government. I will briefly mention the main features of his plan : (1) Girls to enter training-schools at fourteen, boys at sixteen, for three years ; (2) curriculum to embrace dancing, fencing, and general culture ; (3) pupils to first appear in the provinces ; (4) pensions to be guaranteed, and innumerable details as to construction of chorus, orchestra, qualification of directors and instructors, practice, etc.

# CHAPTER XV.

1849–1851.

THE year of the Revolution, Wagner's flight and exile,
— to comprehend the full significance of these three
incidents of magnitude, the condition of society, the
determination of the masses, and the unwise prevari-
cation of the ministry must be understood. Before
stating what I know of Wagner's active participation
during the next few exciting months, I will describe the
events themselves, and then treat of Wagner.

The newly elected chamber met on the 10th January.  For weeks they struggled to make headway.
Whatever measure they passed was vetoed or postponed
by the king's advisers.  The excuse ever was, "Wait
until the constitution of the Frankfort diet has been
promulgated"; or, when the chamber insisted on reforms as regards the jury system and law procedure,
they were hung up on the miserable plea that the minister of justice was ill, and could not devote himself to
a careful study of the changes proposed.  The constitution as laid down by the federated German parliament
at Frankfort gave to every native German equal civil
rights and freedom of speech and press.  Special civil
privileges for the nobility were not recognized; all
Germans were to be governed by the same laws.  Out
of the thirty-four principalities, twenty-nine had ac-

cepted the enactment wholly, but Saxony held out. The Dresden chamber resolved on coming to close quarters; they insisted on its official recognition. Matters were assuming a cloudy aspect, but the king had no intention of granting what a representative parliament of the whole German people held to be the just rights of every man. The ministry, therefore, at the wish of the king, resigned on the 24th February. This purchased a short period of tranquillity. The new ministry would require time to examine the question. False hopes were held out, but nothing was done in the shape of advance or concession. The people refrained from breaking out, expecting the Frankfort diet to insist on the Saxon monarch acknowledging the constitution. But they leaned on a reed. The king of Prussia, aware of the disturbed state of Saxony, sent a note to the king, intimating that at a word from him he was ready to overrun Saxony with his soldiers. Thus supported, there was no hope of any reform passing into Saxon law. And so, on the 23d April, August Roeckel writes to me, "This day we have passed a vote of want of confidence in the king's advisers." Five days later, the 28th, I hear again that "the ministry had the temerity to demand the imposition of a new tax." This was fiercely resisted, and the king, to bring his unfaithful commons to their senses, issued a proclamation dissolving the chamber. This unconstitutional and high-handed act was protested against with vehemence, and was denounced in plain terms by Roeckel. The chambers would not dissolve then, but arranged a final meeting two days hence. Rough work was expected by the ministry; orders were given to confine all troops to barracks on the 29th April, the day before the final meeting arranged for ; armaments were to be held ready for use.

On the 30th April the angered and excited chambers met. The debate was stormy, for the members were aware that troops and police were held in readiness to seize certain of their members, immediately on the rising of the house. Richard Wagner still held his office under the government. In a sketch of these exciting days, written and published by Roeckel, at my instigation, he states that Wagner, by some means, became aware that his friend Roeckel was to be taken prisoner ; at once making his way to the house, he called Roeckel out, while the debate was in progress. Deputies had an immunity from arrest while the house was sitting, a privilege similarly enjoyed by English members of Parliament.

Roeckel desired to stay till the end of the sitting. He had long felt, he says, that the government wished to force a decision by an appeal to arms, and he was anxious to remain to the last, to hear what the intentions of the government were. To this Wagner would not listen, but finding his own entreaties not strong enough, he quickly brought a few friends together, Hainberger, Bakunin, and Semper, and to their unanimous decision he gave way. They urged that he should not even go home to take farewell of his wife and five young children, but escape at once. The question then was — where ? Roeckel proposed Berlin, as he thought there the revolt would first break out, but Bakunin advised Prague, where the cause had some staunch friends, as safer. It was decided then for

Prague.   Roeckel was to be recalled immediately there was need for his presence.

The men who advised this temporary flight were important leaders of the people during the outbreak. First, Hainberger, son of Herr von Hainberger, one of the eight imperial councillors of the emperor of Austria. A musician of gift, his father wished him to enter the law, his studies in which drove him into the ranks of democracy.   He came to Dresden, and took up his abode with August Roeckel, was a member of the Fatherland Union, addressed public gatherings, and though but twenty years of age, was of invaluable service in the organizing (such as it was) and controlling of the people.   He was on the staff, too, of Roeckel's paper.

Michael Bakunin, an historic revolutionary figure, was, by birth, a Russian.   Driven into exile by the severity of the laws in his own country, he had taken refuge in Dresden, where he was hidden by Roeckel. A man of imposing personality, high and noble-minded, of impassioned speech, he was one of the greatest figures during those terrible May days.   As gentle and inoffensive as a lamb, his intellect and energy were called into action by the unjust treatment of the people. He unfortunately gave Roeckel a letter addressed to the heads of the movement in Prague, urging no precipitation, but combination, unity of action.

Here, for a moment, I must turn aside to the most prominent of Wagner's biographers, Glasenapp.   In vol. 1, p. 267, it is stated that Roeckel had left Dresden to escape the consequences of a law-suit.   This is totally inaccurate.   My information is derived from manuscript now before me, under Roeckel's own hand, and I will produce textually what he says : —

I had scarcely been three days in Prague, when a premature outbreak recalled me. Richard Wagner, whose later long years of persecution can but find their explanation in that he dared to distinguish between his duties as a court conductor and his conscience as a citizen, he who as conductor insisted on being unfettered, had long since been wearied out in bitter disappointment, by the non-fulfilment of the promises of 1848. Wagner wrote to me during the feverish excitement of 3d May. "Return immediately. For the moment you are not threatened with any danger, but there is a fear that the excitement will precipitate a premature outbreak." These last words [Roeckel goes on to add], were held by his judges to imply a preconcerted plot to overthrow all German princes, whereas his letter had reference solely to Dresden. The inference was erroneous. As you know, no organization existed by which the principalities could be united.

Simultaneously with this incriminating note from Wagner, a messenger arrived from Bakunin urging Roeckel to return with all possible speed, as directing heads were sorely needed, and particularly popular men. This was on the 4th. He left Prague immediately, arriving outside Dresden on Sunday, the 6th May, whence he heard the booming of guns, ringing of church bells, fusillading of musketry, and saw two columns of fire rising to the sky. From his position, he discerned that one was from the site of the old opera house. His heart sank. Had the people grown wild? Were they reckless, and was the grand cause to be lost in fury and ill-directed efforts? The gates of the town were held open to him by citizens. He made his way at once to the town hall. In his patriotism he thought not of wife or children. The streets presented an appearance akin to

the sickening, horrible sight he had seen in Paris during the July Revolution of 1830, — shops closed, paving-
stones doing duty as barricades, strengthened by over-
turned carts, etc., etc., a miscellaneous collection of
domestic articles.

Hurrying along, he came suddenly upon Hainberger.
The incident is curious and characteristic. Rapid inquiries and answers passed. It appeared that Hainberger
was at the same barricades as Richard Wagner, who, he
said, had just returned to the town in charge of a convoy
of provisions, and a strong detachment of peasants, and
Hainberger was sent in search of an ice for the parched
Wagner. The significance of this incident should not
be lost sight of. The character of " Wagner as I knew
him " is herein painted accurately in a few lines. He
was fond of luxury; a sort of Oriental craving possessed
him ; and, whether weighed down with debt and the
horizon obscure, or in the midst of a nation's throes for
liberty, he would appease his luxurious senses. Hainberger was the messenger, first, because of his devotion,
and secondly, because of his long legs, which enabled
him to step over the barricades.

At the town hall he found the members of the provisional government — Heubner, Todt, Tzchirner — that
had been appointed on the flight of the king, 4th May.
With them were Bakunin and Heinze, a first lieutenant
in the army, who had thrown in his lot with the people,
and took the military lead during the outbreak. Heinze
had no means of communicating his orders to anybody.
Every man guarded the post he thought best, and left
it at his discretion. The commander had no notion how
many men he commanded ; it was a chaos, a seething

medley of uncontrolled enthusiasm.  Up to the 5th May
no one had realized the serious nature of the conflict;
masses streamed hither and thither, were in a rough
sort of manner marshalled and directed to defend certain
streets; but it was a terribly unorganized mass, each
man fighting as he thought best.

Roeckel placed himself at the disposal of the provisional government, and was appointed director of a
district, — that in which Wagner worked.  Roeckel
visited the barricades, encouraged the people, and to
open up communications with comrades in neighbouring
streets, he had walls broken down and passages made
through houses.  But his chief crime, according to the
government, was the making of pitch rings to be flung
burning into public buildings held by the soldiers.  The
actual facts of the case were these : The barricades were
too low; men could with little effort step over them.
He hurriedly consulted Wagner, and it was agreed that
a storming by the soldiers could only be prevented by
covering the top of the barricades with some substance
easy of ignition.  Then Roeckel suggested tar or pitch
rings; and while Wagner went off to his convoy supervision, Roeckel, with a body of men, set to work making
these rings in the yard opposite the town hall.  The
work had only proceeded an hour when he received a
message from the provisional government.  His presence
was urgently required elsewhere, so the ring-making was
discontinued at once.  This was on the Monday, or but
one day after he had entered Dresden.  That evening
information was received that a convoy of provisions
and a detachment of peasants were a few miles outside
the city waiting to enter.  It was raining hard, and very

dark ; only some person acquainted with the road and place would be of service. Roeckel knew both, and started with Hainberger. As their mission was of such importance, they deemed it advisable to wait until night had completely set in. The rain and darkness increasing, the utmost caution was imperative ; but alas! they were met by a patrol of the Saxon troops, and Roeckel was taken prisoner, his companion Hainberger escaping, owing to his nimbleness. Roeckel was immediately taken before an officer and searched. On him were found papers inculpating Wagner and others. A few lines, too, from Commander Heinze as to the conduct of the people in the event of a sortie taking place, caused him considerable discomfort. His hands were tied behind him with rope which cut the flesh, and for the night he was left in a barn. Next morning, still tied, he was sent down the Elbe to Dresden under a strong escort, for the importance of the capture was soon known. On his way down, he passed his own house ; his wife was at the window, and his children, attracted by the helmets of the troops, were on the banks, unconscious that their father was a prisoner on board. He was confined in a narrow, dark room, in his wet clothes, and saw no one for two days, by which time the firing in the town had ceased, and he knew then that the outbreak was at an end.

And now, to measure accurately the extent of Wagner's culpability or his claim to eulogy, the precise nature of the revolt should be understood, the class and character of the insurgents, and their avowed purpose, plainly stated. Further, the source of the government indictment against Wagner and the reason of their relentless persecution should both be fully comprehended.

First, the revolt. It began through pure accident. Naturally the townspeople were excited at the knowledge of the military being held in readiness to suppress, by force of arms, any public expression at the arbitrary dissolution of the chambers. They gathered in groups about the streets, the pressure being greatest near the town hall. As the crowd swayed, a wooden gate, opening upon a military magazine, gave way. The troops were turned out, and defenceless people fired upon, — men, women and children dying in the streets. This was May 3d. Then began that loose organization. And who took part in it? Let the official records supply the answer. I find that when the insurrection was suppressed the government indicted twelve thousand persons, this lamentably lengthy list including thirty mayors of different towns, about two-thirds of the members of the dissolved chambers, government officials, town councillors, lawyers, clergy, school-masters, officers and privates of the army, men of culture, position, and social influence.

Well might Herr von Beust, the king of Saxony's chosen prime minister during March and April, 1849, when speaking in the Dresden chamber on the 15th August, 1864, or fifteen years after the terrible May days of 1849 that condemned Richard Wagner to exile, describe this revolt as an "insurrection that embraced the whole of the people of Saxony." After such striking, conclusive testimony to the character of the revolt, from the highest minister of the crown, no stigma can attach to Wagner or any member who united in defence of the liberty of the subject, but rather is such action to be commended.

One more fact from the official report now before me : of Prussian and Saxon troops thirty-four are recorded dead and a hundred wounded ; whereas, of the people, or "insurgents," one hundred and ninety men, seven women killed, and a hundred and eleven men and four women wounded, besides "about fifty more" of the people admittedly killed by the soldiery, and then thrown into the Elbe, or a gross total of a hundred and thirty-four soldiers killed and wounded against three hundred and sixty-two people.

And now as to the source of the government charge and the reason of its intolerant bearing for thirteen years towards Richard Wagner. I have already referred to the note taken upon Roeckel, which Wagner wrote and addressed to him at Prague, urging his immediate return. Further, I have reproduced the revolutionary paper which Wagner read before the Fatherland Union, a copy of which figures in the official indictment *re* Wagner. There yet remain other incriminating documents, and occasional words uttered by prisoners under examination, besides the knowledge the government possessed of his close intimacy with that revolutionary directing spirit, Bakunin, and also with August Roeckel; and further, his membership in the Union. But the chief materials for the government accusation were furnished by poor Roeckel himself. There was, first, the letter taken upon him — "Return immediately . . . excitement may precipitate a premature outbreak." Then his house was sacked. He was the editor and proprietor of the "Volksblatte," the people's paper.

Naturally, therefore, documents and papers of every description were found in profusion, held to incriminate several persons.　Here copies were found of the June, 1848, paper, by Richard Wagner, on the "Abolition of the Monarchy," and articles written by him for the "Volksblatte," then minutes of meetings of the Fatherland Union and of the sub-committee.　In a letter from his wife to me, detailing the incidents of the sacking of his house in Dresden, she says, "Every paper, printed and in manuscript, was taken away by the police officer who accompanied the military guard"; and, further, she says, "When I was ordered to leave Dresden I went first to Leipzic and Halle, thence to Weimar, and at each town, when it became known who we were, I and my five children were received with every sign of affection; at Leipzic the townspeople coming out in a body to welcome us."

Roeckel's wife was ordered to quit Dresden so that she might not witness the execution of her husband. Both Bakunin and Roeckel were, by order of the Prussian commander, to be shot in the market place, an order only countermanded when it was thought that further information could be extracted from them.　Ten days after Roeckel's capture he was brought up for investigation, in company with Heubner, the head of the provincial government, Heinze, the military commander of the people, and Bakunin, directing spirit. These four men were all chained.　From this time each was examined and interrogated separately.　Roeckel's investigations were endless.　He could not at the time perceive why he was repeatedly cross-questioned on the same point.　Alas, it was too cruelly potent when, on the 14th January, 1850, or nineteen months after he was taken prisoner, for the first time he heard specifically with what he was charged, and his sentence, — death. He saw then clearly that the last part of Wagner's note to him had been interpreted as implying a general organized rising throughout Saxony at a moment to be decided upon by the leaders, Bakunin, Heubner, Todt, Wagner, and Roeckel — "return immediately . . . the excitement will precipitate a premature outbreak." The official interpretation was entirely wrong. No decision of the kind had been arrived at. There was a complete lack of organization. They wished to be prepared for emergencies, but a deliberate attack was not contemplated. However, it sufficed to include Wagner among the chiefs of the insurrection.

Then there were Bakunin's letters to the sympathizers at Prague, unaddressed. By all manner of cunning questions that legal ingenuity could suggest was it sought to drag out from Roeckel in his cell, the names of the leaders at Prague. The addresses of several personages were found in the sacking of Roeckel's house, and these were all arraigned. For a year these secret investigations were carried on, in June, July, and August at Dresden, and subsequently at the fortress of Königstein. On the last day of August, 1849, Heubner, Bakunin, and Roeckel seem to have been confronted separately by a witness who swore to the part actually played by Wagner during the rising. Refusing to utter a word that should incriminate their friend, they were transported that night in three separate wagons to the impregnable fortress of Königstein. Officers with loaded revolvers sat inside each conveyance, a troop of mounted soldiery forming the van and rear of the cavalcade. The night had been chosen, as these men were known to be beloved of the people ; they were martyrs in a nation's cause, and it was feared that, should it become known who were the prisoners being conveyed, a rescue might be attempted. Inside the prison house, Roeckel met with kind treatment and was permitted to receive letters from his friends. The nobility of his character, his integrity, fearlessness, and unselfishness had rendered him so popular that the directors of the Royal Library at Dresden placed their whole store of books at his disposal. Within the walls of his prison he was equally popular, warders and soldiers uniting to form a plan for his escape, and that of Heubner and Bakunin. Roeckel and Bakunin declared themselves ready, but Heubner refused, whereupon Roeckel and Bakunin declined to hazard the attempt without their friend. It is to these efforts of the soldiers that Wagner refers in a letter to Edward Roeckel, brother of August, which appears later on. The friendliness of the warders being perceived by the authorities, Roeckel was removed to that Bastille of Saxony, the fortress of Waldheim, and Bakunin to Prague.

And now for the first time was Roeckel brought before a properly constituted tribunal. It was on the morning of the 14th January, 1850, that he heard for the first time the charge formulated against him and the sentence. The official accusation of my friend is before me, and as Richard Wagner is concerned, I will summarize the charge. It consists of eight distinct counts to the effect that he, Roeckel, had placed himself at the disposal of the provisional government, constructed barricades, was present at military councils, received the convoys of men and provisions that were brought into Dresden by Wagner and others, prepared tar brands, was concerned in a plot for a general uprising in the principalities to overthrow the lawful rulers, as proved by the letter from Richard Wagner taken upon him, etc., etc. The sentence passed upon Roeckel was death, Heubner and Bakunin having been brought up for trial and sentenced at the same time. The friends shook hands for the last time.

Outside a party had arisen demanding a second trial. The clamour was strong, so that a rehearing was conceded, but the second court, on 16th April, 1850, only confirmed the judgment of the first, the extreme penalty, however, being commuted by the king, who had under all circumstances shown himself averse to capital punishment, to imprisonment for life. Roeckel was, however, reprieved after having been incarcerated nearly thirteen years.

And now for the actual part played by Wagner. Throughout he was most active. He was, as he says, "everywhere." His genius for organizing and directing, which we have seen carried to such perfection on the stage, proved of infinite value during those anxious days. An outbreak had long been expected, but not at the moment it actually took place, and when it came he was found ready to carry out the work appointed him. Though not on the executive of the provisional government, he was consulted regularly by the heads, and as he says, "it was pure accident" he was not taken prisoner with Heubner and Bakunin, as he had but "left them the night before their arrest to meet them in the morning for consultation."

His temperament, all who have come into contact with him well know, was very excitable, and under such a strain as he then endured it was at fever pitch. Hainberger related to me a dramatic episode which thrilled Wagner's frame and stirred the whole of the eye-witnesses. I recounted it subsequently to Wagner, and he agreed entirely as to the truth of Hainberger's recital. It was in the morning about eight o'clock, the barricade at which Wagner and Hainberger were stationed was about to receive such morning meal as had been prepared, the outposts being kept by a few men and women. Amongst the latter was a young girl of eighteen, the daughter of a baker belonging to this particular barricade. She stood in sight of all, when to their amazement a shot was suddenly heard, a piercing shriek, followed by the fall of the girlish patriot. The miscreant Prussian soldier, one of a detachment in the neighbourhood, was caught redhanded and hurried to the barricade. Wagner seized a musket and mounting a cart called out aloud to all, " Men, will you see your wives and daughters fall in the cause of our beloved country, and not avenge their cowardly murder ? All who have hearts, all who have the blood and spirit of their forefathers, and love their country follow me, and death to the tyrant." So saying he seized a musket, and heading the barricade they came quickly upon the few Prussians who had strayed too far into the town, and who, perceiving they were outnumbered, gave themselves up as prisoners. This is but one of those many examples of what a timid man will do under excitement, for I give it as my decided opinion, and I have no fear of lack of corroboration, that Richard Wagner was not personally brave. I have closely observed him upon many occasions, and though entering into a quarrel readily enough, — once in the London streets with a grocer who had cruelly beaten his horse, — he always moved away when it looked like coming to blows. This might be termed discretion ; well, he was discreet, there are no two opinions about that, but I distinctly affirm that what is commonly understood by personal bravery, Wagner possessed none of it.

He was ever ready to harangue the people ; his volubility, excitability, and unquenchable love of freedom instigating him at all times. This was well known to the government, as also the foregoing incident, I am convinced, for, be it remembered, Wagner and his companions only made the Prussian soldiers prisoners, and it is not supposing the impossible that on release they would have reported fully who it was that led, musket in hand, the people against them,

Another incident of the campaign, and this time the author is Wagner. When it was reported that the ammunition was running short, the not very original idea sprang from him in this instance to use the lead from the house-tops. That Wagner's very active participation was fully reported to the government, is proved by their attitude towards him. They expected to take him prisoner with Heubner and Bakunin, for he was constantly with them, and they were betrayed by the Prussians ; and, as Wagner says, it was "pure accident" only that he was not taken with them.

As soon as the leaders were taken, and Wagner saw there was no use in continuing the conflict, he fled. He knew not in what direction to turn, but the thought of his precious manuscripts which he had with him determined his course — Weimar, Liszt. And so it fell out. Liszt was good and sheltered him, and interested himself so far as to go to the police official at Weimar to try and discover whether any warrant had been issued for his apprehension. Wagner remained below while Liszt entered to inquire. He was not kept in suspense long. Liszt hurried out breathless and excited. " For the love of God, stay not a moment ; a warrant has been issued and is upstairs now waiting to be executed, but I have prevailed upon H ——, who out of friendship will not put it into execution for an hour." Under Liszt's advice he left for Paris, the Weimar virtuoso being intrusted with Wagner's precious manuscripts. He went to Paris, but remained a few weeks only, seeking an asylum in Zurich, of which city in the October following he became a naturalized subject.

In the summer of 1853 he thought of quitting Zurich, information which was soon conveyed to the Dresden government, who at once issued the following proclamation. I draw attention to the words "most prominent," and further to the date, June, 1853 ; or, it should be borne in mind, four years after the Revolution. It ran as follows : —

Wagner, Richard, late chapel master of Dresden, one of the most prominent supporters of the party of insurrection, who by reason of his participation in the Revolution of May, 1849, in Dresden, has been pursued by police warrant, this is to give notice that it having transpired he intends to leave Zurich, where he at present resides, in order to enter Germany, he should be arrested ; whereby, for the better purpose of apprehension, a portrait of the said Richard Wagner is hereby given, so that should he touch German land he may at once be delivered over to the police authorities at Dresden.

The question then arises, is it to be supposed that a man thus pursued by the Saxon government had taken little or no part in the insurrection? There cannot be any doubt as to the answer. As I have before stated, Richard Wagner was deeply implicated in revolutionary proceedings before the May days of 1849, facts within the cognizance of the government. They knew he was a member of the political society, Fatherland Union, the centre of Saxon discontent; it was notorious that the conductor, Wagner, had written and read a celebrated paper in June, 1848, before the society, advocating the abolition of the monarchy; his most intimate companion and confidant was the second conductor, Roeckel, dismissed from office by reason of his revolutionary (?) practices, and he, Wagner, had already expressed his regret for hasty language condemnatory of the powers, and what was even still more convincing evidence, did he not stand convicted by his own handwriting — the short note taken on the person of August Roeckel, besides the evidence of his having contributed articles to Roeckel's paper? It is then a matter of universal rejoicing, that the "pure accident" did prevent his meeting Bakunin and Heubner, for, judging from the sentence of death passed upon those two, and upon Roeckel, it is more than probable that the same sentence would have been pronounced against him.

That the government regarded Roeckel and Wagner in much the same light, is to my mind further shown by the similarity in time of their respective imprisonment and exile — August Roeckel serving nearly thirteen years, and Richard Wagner's amnesty dating March, 1862. Several persons of high rank interceded for him, among them Napoleon the Third, who, after the "Tannhäuser" fiasco in Paris of 1861, expressed himself amazed at the fatherland exiling so great a son. After the perusal of the following letter, dated by Wagner, Enge, near Zurich, 15th March, 1851, future biographers can no longer ignobly treat the patriotism of Wagner by striving to whitewash or gloss over the part he played during those sad days. It is addressed to my life-long friend, Edward Roeckel (the brother of August), now living at Bath, where he has resided since 1849.[1]

ENGE, NEAR ZURICH, 15th March, 1851.

MY DEAR FRIEND: Many a time have I longed to write to you, but have been compelled to desist, uncertain as to your address. But now I must take my chance in sending you a letter, as the occasion is pressing, and I have to claim your kindness in the interest of another. I will, therefore, at once explain matters, and so have done with the immediate cause of this letter.

A young man, Hainberger, still very young, half German, half Pole, at present my exile companion in Switzerland, originally found refuge in the Canton Berne. This canton has expelled all political refugees, refusing to harbour them any longer, and, indeed, no canton will now receive another exile, at most keeping those already domiciled there; thus Hainberger is obliged to seek sanctuary either in England or America. Being a good violinist, I had already secured for him several months' engagement in the Zurich orchestra. His present intention, if possible, is to go next winter to Brussels, in order to profit by lessons from de Beriot, but alas! for him, his most reactionary Austrian parents and relations are as yet too angry with him to permit him to hope of their furnishing the necessary money for that plan. Until he can expect a change in that quarter, he does not wish to go as far as America, but prefers London, there to await that happy reconciliation with his relations. Meanwhile, and in order to ensure the means of subsistence, he would much like to find an engagement in one of the London

---

[1] The original in the possession of Edward Roeckel, Bath.

orchestras. As he does not know a soul in London to whom he could apply for help in this case, I turn to you in friendship, to assist in procuring him such an engagement. And, further, besides knowing no one in London, my young friend does not speak English. If, therefore, you could indicate any house where he could live moderately, and make himself understood, you would confer a great favour on me. Could we not direct him at once to Praeger? I take a deep interest in this young man, as he is of an amiable disposition, and I have become closely acquainted with him at Dresden, where indeed he stayed for some long time, with August. He is really a talented violinist, and possesses letters of recommendation from his masters, Helmsberger and David (in the first instance, he was a pupil of Jansa), which he wishes to be known, as he believes the name of Helmsberger a guarantee. If you are willing to do me this service I beg, in my name, that he may be sustained in all power.

Now to another matter. During the last few years much has occurred of a most painful nature, and oft have I thought of your sorely tried brotherly devotion. We were all compelled to be prepared for extremes during those times, for it was no longer possible to endure the state of things in which we lived, unless we had become unfaithful to ourselves. I, for my part, long before the outbreak of the Revolution, was incapable of anything but contemplating that inevitable catastrophe. What in me was a mixture of contemplation, was with August all action. His whole being was impelled to energetic activity. It was not until the fourth day of the outbreak at Dresden that I saw him on a Monday morning for the first and last time. For some time after he was captured, I could get no news of him but what I gathered from the public journals. Although I had not accepted a special rôle, yet I was present everywhere, actively superintending the bringing in of convoys, and indeed, I only returned with one from the Erzgebirge[1] to the town hall, Dresden, on the eve of the last day. Then I was immediately asked on all sides after August, of whom since Monday evening no tidings had been received, and so, to our distress, we were forced to conclude that he had either been taken prisoner or shot.

I was actively engaged in the revolutionary movement up to its

---

[1] Neighbouring mountains.

final struggle, and it was a pure accident that I, too, was not taken prisoner in company with Heubner and Bakunin, as I had but taken leave of them for the night to meet in consultation again the next morning. When all was lost, I fled first to Weimar, where, after a few days, I was informed that a warrant of apprehension was to be put in motion after me. I consulted Liszt about my next movements. He took me to a house to make inquiries on my behalf. While awaiting his return in the street, I suddenly caught sight of Lullu,[1] who told me her mother had arrived at Weimar, was living close by, and gave me their address, I promising to call at once; but on Liszt returning he told me that not a moment was to be lost, the warrant of apprehension had been received, and I must quit Weimar at once. It became, therefore, impossible to call on August's wife; and only now, as I am writing, does it strike me that " Linchen "[2] might perhaps think my behaviour unfeeling. I beg of you, then, when you have an opportunity, if she may have considered me wanting in sympathy, to explain how the matter then stood, as I should feel deeply distressed at such a belief existing. I heard from Dresden that, thanks to your brotherly devotion, the family of the unhappy August have been well provided for. Where they at present reside I do not know. As regards August, from whom, alas, I have not yet received any detailed information, I can, thinking of the terrible trial he is now undergoing, have only one profound anxiety, that is, his health. Should he lose this, it would be the worst possible thing; for his imprisonment cannot last eternally, of that there is no doubt. I cannot speak of " plots," as of them I know nothing authoritatively, and most likely they even do not exist, but a glance at the affairs of Europe clearly shows that the present state of things can be but shortlived. Good health and patience are most to be desired for those who suffer the keenest under existing circumstances. Happily, August's constitution is of the kind that gives every hope for him. I know, from his manner of living, that neither an active nor a sedentary life affect him deeply. But one thing is to be feared, viz. that his patience will not last him; and alas, in this respect I have heard, to my sorrow, that he has been incautious, and suffers in consequence stricter discipline. Altogether, however, I believe that the political prisoners in Saxony are treated humanely,

---

[1] A daughter of August Roeckel.    [2] August's wife.

and we must hope that by prudent behaviour August will soon experience milder treatment, could we but influence him in respect to his easily understoood passionate outbreaks.

I live here very retired with my wife, receiving from certain friends in Germany just sufficient monetary assistance. My special grief is my art, which, though I had my freedom of action, I could not unfold. I was in Paris, intended even going to London, but the feeling of nausea, engendered by such art excursions, drove me back here; and so I have taken to write books, amongst others, "Das Kunstwerk der Zukunft," and, on a larger scale, "Oper und Drama," my last work. I could also turn again to composing "Siegfried's Tod," but after all, it would only be for myself, and that in the end is too mournful. Dear Edward, write to me. Perhaps I may hear much news from you, and I would greatly like to hear how you are getting on. Farewell. Be assured of my heartiest devotion.

RICHARD WAGNER.

And now for a few closing remarks upon this revolutionary epoch. I have alluded to the whitewashing, as it were, of Wagner by his biographers when treating of this period. If it were asked who is to blame, the answer might fairly be, "Imperfect or inadequate knowledge of the facts," fostered, I regret to add, by Wagner's own later utterances and writings upon the point. When Wagner visited London in 1855, the Revolution and the thousand and one episodes connected therewith were related and discussed fully and dwelt upon with affection, but as the years rolled on he exhibited a decided aversion towards any reference to his participation. Perhaps we should not judge harshly in the matter; he had suffered much and there were not wanting, and I fear it may be said there are still not wanting, those who speak in ungenerous, malignant tones about the court conductor being false to his oath of allegiance,

of the demagogue luxuriating in the wealth of a royal
patron.   Wagner's art popularity was increasing and his
music-dramas were gradually forcing themselves upon
the stage, and he did not wish his chance of success to
be marred by the everlastingly silly and spiteful references to the revolutionist.   But whether he was justified
in writing as he did, in permitting almost an untruth to
be inferred and history falsified, I should not care to
decide.   As, however, I am of opinion that the lives of
great men (their public actions at least) are the property
of posterity, I have stated what I know to have been
the true facts, and will bring my remarks to a close by
appending a few extracts from Wagner's early and later
writings upon this point which, read by the light of the
uncontrovertible facts, I leave for each to form his own
opinion : —

(1) Paper on the "Abolition of the Monarchy," read before the
     Fatherland Union, dated 16th June, 1848.

(2) Note to August Roeckel: "Return immediately; a premature
     outbreak is feared."—May, 1849.

(3) Letter to Edward Roeckel: March, 1851 :
     (*a*) "It was no longer possible to endure the state of things
          in which we lived."
     (*b*) "I was present everywhere, actively superintending the
          bringing in of convoys, etc."
     (*c*) "I was actively engaged in the revolutionary movement up
          to its final struggle."

(4) His active participation, related by himself to me, corroborated
     by Hainberger's testimony.   (I should add that Hainberger
     came to London in April, 1851, stayed with me, and that I
     secured for him lessons and a place in the orchestra of the
     New Philharmonic.)

(5) Max von Weber, son of Carl Maria von Weber, told me that he was present during the Revolution, and saw Wagner shoulder his musket.

As I have stated, the general drift of Wagner's references to the Revolution is to minimize his share; I content myself with two extracts only : —

1. From "Eine Mittheilung an meine Freunde" (a communication to my friends), vol. IV. of his collected writings, and dated 1851 : " I never had occupied myself really with politics."

2. "The Work and Mission of my Life," the latest of Wagner's published writings, written in 1876 for America: "In my innermost nature I really had nothing in common with its political side," *i.e.* of the Revolution.

The significant omission of "The Abolition of the Monarchy" paper from his eleven volumes of "Collected Writings," a collection which includes shorter papers written too at earlier periods than the above, may also be noted.

# CHAPTER XVI.



PURSUED by a police warrant, Wagner first sought refuge and a home in Paris. The French capital possessed alluring attractions for him, but his reception, in 1849, was no brighter or more promising than it had been ten years earlier. He therefore left Paris, after a few weeks, and went to Zurich. Here he found a true home and hearty friends, and felt, as far as was possible, so contented that in the autumn following he became a naturalized subject. And yet Wagner used to say his forced exile pressed sore upon him, and there is no doubt he did chafe under it, and strove hard to free himself from its galling chains. He could not settle to work. He endeavoured to open communications with August Roeckel, through influential friends in Dresden, but was unsuccessful. When in Paris, and whilst still under the influence of the multitudinous, unsettling thoughts that had pressed him into the ranks of liberty, making him one of its most energetic champions, he endeavoured to negotiate with the editor of a newspaper of standing, for a series of letters, on the interesting and timely topic of "The Revolution, and its Relation to Art." But the proposal came to nothing. He was told the time was inopportune. "Strange and silly people," was his comment, and he left the Parisians for the more homely, though heavier folk, of Zurich.

And still he could not tear himself away from Paris. The city and people fascinated him then and at all times, and he returned, in the early part of 1850, to make another effort in the cause of art. Though his invectives were frequent and bitter, yet I have seen enough, and know enough, of the inner Wagner, to state positively that he highly esteemed the French intellect and judgment in matters of art. This is one of those curious paradoxes in Richard Wagner's character. He could never refer to the French without some sarcastic allusion to their frivolity. At all times Wagner was "terribly in earnest," and he almost took it as a personal insult to see the French full of sensuous enjoyment, and regarding art as a pleasant, agreeable relaxation, at the end of the day's labour. And yet he strove to succeed there for all that; even in 1860, when he was again in Paris, his feelings were precisely the same. Writing on this point, some sixteen years later, he says : "I thought that it was there (*i.e.* Paris) only that I could find the atmosphere so necessary to the success of my art,[1] that element of which I so much stood in need."

His success in 1849–50, however, was no more than it had been hitherto. His vanity was piqued at his reception. He visited old acquaintances, and was received with a patronizing friendship, as one who had come to Paris, an aspirant for fame. They would not see in him the "Tannhäuser" composer, the prophet who had come to baptize them with the pure, holy water of the true in art. His pride was wounded.

---

[1] The Work and Mission of my Life, chap. ix.

He was envious, too, of that smooth, highly polished gracefulness which the French possess in the small matters of every-day life, and which he was conscious he lacked.  Though refined in intellect, courteous in bearing, carrying himself with majestic dignity when occasion demanded, yet Richard Wagner's natural characteristic was a plainness and directness of speech, which often took the form of abruptness.  " Amiability usually runs into insincerity," says Mr. Froude, when describing Carlyle's character in the " Reminiscences," and Wagner was at all times sincere.  Sensitive, too, as artists commonly are, he saw the Parisians resolving life and art into a pastime, and doing it with an elegant, natural gracefulness that was absent in his own serious utterances of the heart.  Impatient of incapacity, blunt in speech, and vehement in declamation, even with bursts of occasional rudeness, he was angered and jealous, that a people — his intellectual inferior — should take life so easily.

Sick in heart, he soon became sick in body ; seriously ill indeed:  On his recovery, feeling naught congenial to him in Paris, he left again for Zurich, via Bordeaux and Geneva.  At Bordeaux an episode occurred similar to one which happened later at Zurich, about which the press of the day made a good deal of unnecessary commotion and ungenerous comment.  I mention the incident to show the man as he was.  The Opposition have not spared his failings, and over the Zurich incident were hypercritically censorious.  The Bordeaux story I am alluding to, is, that the wife of a friend, Mrs. H——, having followed Wagner to the south, called on him at his hotel, and throwing herself at his feet, passionately told of her affection. Wagner's action in the matter was to telegraph to the husband to come and take his wife home. On telling me the story, Wagner jocosely remarked that poor Beethoven, so full of love, never had his affection returned, and lived and died, so it is said, a hermit.

Another adventure of this description took place at Berlin, which to my mind is a verification of the homeopathic doctrine, *similia similibus curantur*, for I often taunted him with possessing, though in homeopathic doses, just those very failings he denounced in others, viz. amorousness, Hebraic shrewdness, and the Gallic love of enjoyment. When he was in a jocular mood he would laugh heartily at my endeavour to prove the truth of my opinions by the citation of instances, and occasionally he would admit the impeachment, whereas, at other times, he would become irritated, and put an end to any such conversation by charging me with having lost all my German feeling under the pernicious influence of a London fog.

Back in Zurich, he could not force himself to compose. He could not, and never did, take kindly to his compulsory exile, even appealing himself to the authorities more than ten years later for permission to re-enter his fatherland. And yet I have no hesitation in asserting that the world should regard it as a boon for art that he was thus driven into exile. Away from the theatre and the busy activity connected with his office of conductor, he had time to reflect over the many schemes for the elevation of art that constantly held communion with his inner self. Freed from the contact of that vortex of petty agitation which constitutes the active life of the stage, and of which every individual, no matter how inferior his grade, thinks himself the chief attraction, he gained that repose which enabled him to see art matters in their just proportion. His state, he described to me, as that spoken of by both Aristotle and Plato : " One of the highest happinesses attained through the pleasures of the intellect by the contemplative life." Indeed, it can be maintained, that all the great works of his after-life were either completed or sketched during those years of exile.

To begin with his literary work. In this branch of thought he was remarkably active. For five whole years, the first five of his Zurich life, I remember he said he did not compose a bar ; all was literary outpouring, and so much was he given to reflection on the strange position in which he found himself in the art world, and the manner in which his operas had been received, that he even seriously considered the question whether music was his province, whether he should not reject tonal composition entirely in favour of the spoken drama. In a letter of that period he says, " I spend my time in walking, reading, and literary work." And when one considers what Wagner did during those years of banishment, it will be seen how hard a worker he was. His exile lasted for something like twelve years, and during that time he wrote those masterly expositions : " Art and Revolution," " The Art Work of the Future," " Art and Climate," " Judaism in Music," and " Opera and Drama," whilst, as regards the music-drama, he wrote the whole of the words and music of the " Nibelung's Ring," " Tristan and Isolde," the " Mastersingers" (1861–62), and a fragment of music subsequently embodied and amplified in "Parsifal."

Wagner met with many reverses in the early portion of his career, but he also, on occasions, enjoyed exceptionally good fortune. Though caged, as he said, like an angry, irritable lion in Zurich, longing to burst his prison door, yet he met everywhere with troops of friends. The personnel of the opera house united to do him honour, and individually he was treated with hearty good will. One of his ardent admirers and intimate friends was Madame Wesendonck, the wife of a wealthy retired merchant who had come, with her husband, to take up her abode in Zurich. Wesendonck was a musical amateur, but not so gifted as his wife, who was enthusiastic for Wagner. Wesendonck had purchased some land overlooking the beautiful lake, and was building himself a house there. For that purpose he had brought architects and upholsterers from Paris. While the building was in course of erection, a very pretty chalêt adjoining the property became untenanted, which it was stated was about to be used as an asylum. Such information was not pleasant to Wesendonck, and at the suggestion and wish of his wife he purchased it and rented it to Wagner for a nominal sum. This really charming villa was an immense delight to Wagner. Hitherto, living in the town, he had grown fractious under the infliction of noises and cries inseparable from the bustle of civic life, and the "Retreat," as he called the chalêt, afforded him a pleasure, and procured that quiet comfort invaluable to him at that period of thought.

At the house of his friends there were frequent gatherings of musicians from Zurich and neighbouring towns, at which, it seems, he often delivered himself of lengthy harangues on his view of art, to find that one only of those who applauded him comprehended the heart of the thing he spoke of.   He said it was with him, just as it had been with the unfortunate Hegel, the philosopher, who with facetious cynicism remarked, that "nobody understands me, except one disciple, and he misunderstands me."   Perhaps the fault was partly his own.   His fervid perorations were ambitious, and he spoke above the heads of his hearers.   They saw in him only the composer of "Tannhäuser" and "Lohengrin," whereas he felt within himself the embryo of the colossal tetralogy; and how could they comprehend, then, a man who addressed his inward clamourings rather than his auditors.   When I say the embryo of the tetralogy, I include the musical sketch of certain of the leading ideas, for the whole of the Nibelung poem was completed, and a few copies printed in 1853 for his intimate friends, of one copy of which I am the fortunate possessor.

On recalling the occasion, when in 1855 Wagner gave me a bound copy of his "Nibelung lied," one incident stands out prominently.   On studying the poem I had been struck with the keen dramatic insight displayed by Wagner throughout his treatment of the old Norse sagas : the laying out of the ground plan, the sequence of the story, the exclusion of extraneous and subsidiary matter, the many powerful and striking tableaux presented, the crisp dialogue and scholarly retention of the alliterative verse, the merit of these features being increased by the high literary standard attained throughout the work.   Now when I congratulated Wagner on the literary skill he had shown, he grew peevish ;

and indeed he resented at all times praise of his poetic ability, seeming to think that in some measure it was a denial of his musical power.

Some portion of the Nibelung poem Wagner read to his small circle of intimates in London. At that time Richard Wagner was forty-two years of age, and his histrionic powers, at all times great, were perhaps then at their best. With his head well thrown back, he declaimed his poem with a majestic earnestness that cast a spell over all. But of his histrionic and mimetic powers I shall have something to say later on.

At Zurich he interested himself largely in the opera house. He sought to control the local taste, but the directors were governed with one thought and that, that only such works as bore the hall-mark of Paris success could succeed in Zurich. Accepting the state of things, he conducted performances of " Robert le Diable," " Les Huguenots," " Guillaume Tell," Halévy's " La Juive," Donizetti's " La Fille du Regiment," and other works of similar type. He even conducted the rehearsals, attending and exerting himself at these for the benefit, however, of Hans von Bülow, who had become his pupil. I know he was deeply attached to Bülow; he spoke of him with enthusiasm, praised his wonderful reading at sight, and was much impressed by his general culture. There is no doubt that Bülow merited the high opinion Wagner held of him, as subsequent events have proved.

On Richard Wagner's fortieth birthday, 22 May, 1853, a grand Wagner festival was held at Zurich, musicians from neighbouring towns being invited. All the principal theatres responded with the exception of Munich, which through its conductor, Lachner, refused to permit orchestral members of the theatre to attend, giving as the flimsy pretext that journeymen, *i.e.* orchestral performers, could not be granted passports. Lachner as a composer has found his level, and there it is wise to leave him. I will only note the curious fate which later made Wagner supreme at Munich and, further, how odd it was that when Wagner was conducting the Philharmonic concerts in London, Mr. Anderson informed him that it was the wish of the directors he should produce a prize symphony of Lachner. The proposition startled Wagner and perhaps, somewhat contemptuously, he exclaimed, "What! have I come all this way to conduct a prize symphony by Lachner? No! no!" and he would not either, not because the composition was superscribed "Lachner," but because of the really wretched Kapellmeister music it was.

The Wagner festival at Zurich was very gratifying to him. For a whole week he was fêted, and at the close received an ovation that took all his self-control. He addressed the audience in faltering accents, and on bidding his friends farewell he broke down entirely — that they should return to the fatherland and he an exile. Such a wail of anguish went out from his heart as only those who have known the sensitive character of the man can understand.

From the time Wagner went into exile his health generally gave way. Constant brooding over his enforced isolation from his countrymen induced melancholia, and in its train a malignant attack of his old enemy, dyspepsia. His wife, fortunately, was of a homely nature with a buoyancy of spirits, the value of which cannot be over-estimated, nor, must I add, was Wagner insensible to her worth. But with these terrible fits of dyspepsia which prostrated him for days, there also came, as one ill upon another, attacks of erysipelas. When he had the strength, he fought against them, but more often he succumbed. He sought relief at hydropathic establishments, for which form of prevention and cure he retained a fancy for many years. The bracing air of the mountains, too, he sought as a means of removing the ills under which he suffered. He was fond, too, of taking "Peps" with him in these rambles. "Peps," it will be remembered, was the dog who, he used to assert, helped him to compose "Tannhäuser." He was passionately fond of his dog, referred to him in his letters with affection, and ascribed to him feelings and a perceptiveness only possible from a man loving the animal kingdom as he did. All who remember the last sad incidents connected with the interment at Wahnfried will think of the faithful canine creature (a successor of "Peps"), who came to lie on the grave, and could not be induced to quit the spot where his master was buried. As it was there, so it was at Zurich. He loved "Peps" with a human love. Taking his constitutional on the Zurich mountains, "Peps" his companion, reflecting upon his treatment by his fatherland, he would declaim against imaginary enemies, gesticulate, and vent his irascible excitement in loud speeches, when "Peps," "the human Peps," as he called him, with the sympathy of the intelligent dumb creation, would rush forward, bark and snap loudly as if aiding Wagner in destroying his enemies, and then return, plainly asking for friendly recognition for the demolition. Such an expression of sympathy delighted Wagner, and he was very pleased to rehearse it all to his

friends, calling in "Peps" to go through the performance, and I must say the dog seemed to understand
and appreciate it all. Numerous anecdotes of this
kind he could tell, and he generally capped them with
such a remark as, " 'Peps' has more sense than your
wooden contrapuntists," pointing his speech by naming
the authors of some concocted Kappelmeister music who
were specially objectionable to him.

# CHAPTER XVII.



"JUDAISM IN MUSIC."

As regards his literary productions, that which provoked most discussion and engendered a good deal of
acrimonious hostility towards him was "Judaism in
Music." No one knowing Wagner, and writing any
reminiscences of him, no matter how slight, could omit
reference to this subject. Any such treatment would
be incomplete, though it would be easy to understand
such omission, for no friend of Richard Wagner would
elect to put him in the wrong, nor care to admit that his
attitude towards the descendants of Abraham, in certain
phases, was as unreasoned, and perhaps as ungenerous,
as that of earlier anti-Semitic agitators of the fatherland. However, an impartial critic must confess that
in Wagner's attacks on the Jews and their treatment of
art, he has, in much that he says, force and truth on
his side. Unfortunately, much of the cogency of his
reasoning is weakened in the eyes of many by the
introduction of the names of two of his prominent
contemporaries, Mendelssohn and Meyerbeer, both of
Hebraic descent. His attack is put down to personal
spite, jealousy born of anger at the success of his rivals.
Never was charge more groundless. Richard Wagner
was high above such small-minded enmity. His was a
nature incapable of mean, paltry envy. Rancour was

not in him.   Yet how could an attack upon "Judaism in music" be maintained without indicating Semitic composers, in whose works supposed shortcomings and spurious art were to be found?   That he was not animated by any personal motive I am convinced, and that the things he wrote of lay deep, deep in his heart, I am equally persuaded.   Finding in me a partial antagonist, he debated the question freely.   Perhaps, too, it was a subject impossible of exclusion from our discussion, since, when he came here (London) in 1855, or three years after his Jew pamphlet had been published, the press spared not its sneers and satire for a man who only saw in the grand composer of "Elijah" "a Jew,"[1] the man Wagner, whom "it would be a scandal to compare with the men of reputation this country (England) possesses, and whom the most ordinary ballad writer would shame in the creation of melody, and of whose harmony no English harmonist of more than one year's growth could be found sufficiently without ears or education to pen such vile things."

To understand this "Jew" question thoroughly, one should remember the admiration, the just admiration, in which Mendelssohn was held in this country.   He was the idol of English musicians.   That he should have been "assailed" by Wagner because of his Hebraic descent was unpardonable.   This was the spirit of hostility with which the larger proportion of the press received him, seeing in him the personal enemy of the "Jew" Mendelssohn.   And thus it happened that references to this question were continually being made, and discussions, occasionally of an angry character, were

[1] Sunday Times, 6th May, 1855.

thrust upon us. What Richard Wagner wrote in 1852, the date the paper was first published, he adhered to in 1855, and what is more, in 1869, when he was master of the situation, he somewhat pertinaciously appended a letter to the original indictment, from which he did not recede one step.

When Wagner had almost attained the zenith of his fame, at a time when his weight and genius were admitted, he then deliberately placed on record that years of his earlier suppression and ostracism from great musical centres were due, and due alone, to the power wielded by the Jews, and their determination to keep his works out of sight where possible.

The article, " Judaism in Music," was originally published in " Die Neue Zeitschrift," under the nom de plume of " Freethought." At the time the journal was edited by Franz Brendel, and when the subject-matter of the article is known, it will be admitted that the editor was courageous, and perhaps no one will be surprised at the hostile acts which followed. Poor Wagner seems to have been much troubled at the difficult position in which he had placed his friend. No sooner had the article appeared, he told me, than about a dozen of Brendel's co-professors at the Leipzic conservatoire sent forward a petition to the directors of the Institute urging the dismissal of the editor, but, though the signatories of the document were such names as Moritz Hauptmann, David, Joachim, Rietz, Moschelles (all Jews), Brendel retained his post. Of course there was no attempt at withholding the name of the real author; it was at once admitted. It was a bold act to first publish the paper in Leipzic, for though Richard Wagner's birthplace, it had received, as it were, a Jewish baptism from the lengthened sojourn of Mendelssohn there.

Certainly the article contained enough to create enmity on the part of the Jews. It opened with an assertion that one has an involuntary and inexplicable revulsion of feeling towards the Jews ; that, as a people, there is something objectionable in them, their person repellant, and manner obnoxious. Now when it is remembered that Wagner's daily visitor during his first sojourn in Paris was Dessauer, a Jew, that the man who brought about his own death for love of Wagner was a Jew, and that the music-publisher Schlesinger, his friend, was also a Jew, it will be confessed that this was a startling charge to come from him. I must add that Wagner always insisted it was not a personal question, and pointed out that some of his staunchest friends were Jews.

Then he further asserted, in the " Judaism " pamphlet, that it mattered not among what European people the Jew lived, he was always a foreigner, and our wish was to have nothing to do with him. This, again, was surprising, for Wagner was not slow to admit the loyalty of the people of Shiloh to the government of the country in which they were domiciled, and there is no doubt they are eminently patriotic, calling themselves by the name of the country in which they live. Indeed, it cannot be contended that the Jews are one nation ; they are many.

Wagner's antipathy towards the Hebrew people was, he felt, partly inherited by him as a German. He knew them to be observant, discerning, energetic, and ambitious, yet he could not put away from him an instinctive feeling of repugnance, and could not understand why the "Musical World" and the London press should so severely flagellate him because of his attitude towards the Jews. He found the Semitic race regarded here in an entirely different manner from what it was in Germany. Here it was much the same as in France. Civil disabilities had been removed, and the Israelites had proved themselves as great patriots as English Christians, one, Mr. Solomons, filling the post of alderman of the city of London at the time Wagner was here. This Mr. Solomons had been, with others of his co-religionists, previously elected a member of Parliament, and Wagner used often to express his wonder how a man waiting for the advent of the Messiah could sit in a house of Gentiles. Wagner marvelled, too, how the citizens of London could permit the Jews to amass such a large proportion of the wealth of the country, but he soon came to admit the force of the argument, that special laws having been enacted against them, preventing the acquisition of land, denying them the professions, and restricting them to certain trades, it was unreasonable, after having driven them to mean occupations, to reproach them for not having embraced honourable professions. I pointed out to him that in bygone centuries, when the Germans were barbarians, this much-despised people had produced poets, men of letters, statesmen, historians, and philosophers, all, too, of such brilliant genius as would add lustre to any galaxy of modern luminaries. He was struck by this, and, as his bent was art, fully admitted the poetic fancy and genius of the harpist David, the imagination of Solomon, and other of the old Hebraic writers.

And yet he would insist on the truth of his own assertion in the pamphlet. "If in the plastic art a Jew has to be represented," he said, "the artist models after an ideal, or, if working from life, omits or softens those very details in the features which are the characteristic of the countrymen of Isaiah."

As regards the histrionic art, he laid it down that it is impossible to picture a Jew impersonating a hero or lover without forcing a sense of the ridiculous upon us. And this feeling he felt of an actor, irrespective of sex. It would not be difficult to destroy this argument now : the names of Rachel, Sarah Bernhardt, Patti at once cross the mind. He asserted that their strength in art lay in imitation and not in creation.

In speech, too, the Jew was offensive to him. The accent was always that of a foreigner, and not of a native. The language was spoken as if it had been acquired, as something alien, and had not the ring of naturalness in it; for language, he argued, was the historic growth of a nation, and the Jew's mother tongue, Hebrew, was a dead language. To the Jew, our entire civilization and art had remained a foreign language. He could only imitate it; the product, therefore, was artificial; and as in speech, so in song. "Notwithstanding two thousand years of contact with European peoples, as soon as a Jew spoke our ear was offended by a peculiar hissing and shrill manner of intonation." Moreover, he contended, in their speech and writing there was a wilful transposition of words and construction of phrases, characteristics of an alien people, also discernible in their music. These racial characteristics which Wagner asserted were repugnant, were intensified in their offensiveness in his eyes by an absence of genuine passion, *i.e.* strong emotion coming deep from the heart. In the family circle he allowed the probability of the Jews being earnest and impassioned, yet in their works it was absent. On the stage he would have it that the passion of a child of Israel was always ridiculous. He was incapable of artistic expression in speech, and therefore less capable of its expression in song; for true song is speech raised to the highest intensity of emotion.

It will not be difficult to call to the mind the names of celebrated Hebrews, great as histrionic artists, who at once appear to confute this statement; and for my part, one name is sufficient, viz. Pauline Viardot Garcia, though it will be admitted, on closely examining Wagner's feeling, there is a vein of truth in it, which grows upon one on reflection.

And then Wagner turns towards the plastic art, and examines the position of the Jew under that art aspect. He states as his opinion that the Hebrew people lack the sense of balance and proportion, and in this he sees the explanation of the non-existence of Jewish sculptors and architects. Now it is regrettable that Wagner should have committed himself to so faulty a statement. The sculptor's art was not practised by the Jews, because it was prohibited by the Mosaic law, and to this day strict Hebrews would not fashion "any graven image, nor the likeness of anything that is in heaven above, or in the earth beneath, or in the waters under the earth." But Wagner was of opinion that the Jew was too practical to employ himself with beauty, and yet he was unable to explain the Jew's acknowledged supremacy as a connoisseur in works of art.

In such a general indictment, it is hardly to be expected that Wagner would have omitted the vulgar charge of usury, nay, he even went so far as to assert that it was their chief craft. This, I told Wagner, was hardly generous or fair on his part. By persecution and restriction of the Jew to certain trades we had driven him to the tables of the money-changers, and then charged, as crime, the very vice persecution had engendered.

Nor was he less severe towards the cultivated Jew, charging him with a desire to disown his descent, and wipe out his nationality, by embracing Christianity, but whatever his efforts, he remained isolated in a society he did not understand, with whose strivings and likings he had no sympathy, and whose history and development had remained indifferent to him.

With such convictions, strong and deep, it follows that Wagner would not allow that Hebraic tonal art could be acceptable to European peoples. The Jew, he said, was unable to fathom the heart of our civilized life ; he could not feel for or with the masses. He was an alien, and at the utmost, the cultured Jew could only create that which was trivial and indifferent to us. Not having assimilated our civilization, he could not sing in our heart's tones. He could compose something pleasant, slight, and even harmonious, since the possibility of babbling agreeably, without singing anything in particular, is easier in music than in any other art. When the Jew musician tried to be serious, the creative faculty was entirely absent ; all he could do was to imitate the earnest, impressive speech of others, and then the imitation was of the parrot kind, tones, without the purport

being understood, and occasionally exhibiting an unconscious gibberishness of utterance. Now this seemed to
me the denial of pure feeling to the Jew, and so I
sought to get from Wagner precisely what he did mean
by his charges on this point in the "Judaism" pamphlet. Music, I urged, was the art of expressing feelings
by sounds ; did he deny feelings to the Semitic people?
"No." Then it is only the mode of utterance, I urged, to
which you so strongly object. But he would not wholly
subscribe to this view, though he confessed it was an important element in the question. His view was, that
the true tone poet, the genius, was he who transfixed in
immortal tones the joys and sorrows of the people.
"Now," said he, "where is the Jew's people to be
found, where would you go to see the Hebrew people,
in the practice, as it were, of unrestrained Judaism,
which Christianity and civilization have left untouched,
and where the traditions of the people are preserved in
their purity? Why, to the synagogue." Now if this be
admitted, Wagner has certainly made out a strong case.
Truly, the folk melody proper of the Hebrews is to
be found in the song service of the synagogue, and a
dreadful tortuous exhibition it is. As Wagner said, "it
is a sort of 'gargling or jodelling,' which no caricature
could make more nauseous than it is in its naïve seriousness." There was the proper sphere for the Hebrew
musician, wherein to exercise his art, and when he attempted to work outside his own people's world he was
engaged in an alien occupation. The melodies and
rythmical cadences of the synagogue are already discernible in the music of Jewish composers, as our folk
melodies and rhythm are in ours. If the Jew listened to

our music and sought so dissect its heart and nerves, he would find it so opposed to his own cult, that it were impossible for him to create its like from his own heart; he could only imitate it. Following up this reasoning, Wagner argued that the Hebrew composer only imitated the external of our great composers, and that his reproductions were cold and false, just as if a poem by Goethe were delivered in Jewish jargon. The Hebrew musician threw the most opposed styles and forms about, regardless of period, making what Wagner called, with his usual jocularity, a Mosaic of his composition. A real impulse will be sure to find its natural expression, but a Jew could not have that, since his impulse would not be rooted in the sympathies of the Christian people. Then he enters into a description of Mendelssohn and Meyerbeer, or of the men and their music. Of Mendelssohn he says : —

In this man we see that a Jew may be gifted with the most refined and great talent, that he may have received a most careful and extensive education, that he may possess the greatest and noblest ambition, and yet, with the aid of all these advantages, be unable, even once, to impress on our mind and heart that profound sensation we look for in music, and which we have so many times experienced as soon as a hero of our art intones one single chord for us. Those who specially occupy themselves with musical criticism, and who share our opinion, will, on analyzing the works of Mendelssohn, be able to prove the truthfulness of this statement, which, indeed, can hardly be contested.

In order to explain the general impression which the music of this composer makes upon us, it will be sufficient to state that it interests us only when our imagination, always more or less eager for distraction, is excited in following in its many shapes, a series of forms most refined, and most carefully and artistically worked. These several forms only interest us, in the same manner as the combinations of colour in a kaleidoscope. But when these forms ought to express the profoundest and most forcible emotions of the human heart, they entirely fail to satisfy us.

No one, judging dispassionately, will contend that Wagner has exceeded the legitimate limits of criticism. It is not dogmatism, since he appealed to the reasoning faculty and adduced proof in favour of his deduction. The context of the article naturally imparts additional force to his statements. Mendelssohn is credited with the highest gifts, natural and acquired, and yet falls short in the production of a masterpiece that appeals direct to the heart, because by ancestry and surroundings he has stood without the pale of our European civilization, and consequently has not assimilated the feelings of the masses.

In his observations upon Meyerbeer he says :—

A musical artist of this race, whose fame in our time has spread everywhere, writes his works to suit that portion of the public whose musical taste has been so vitiated by those only desiring to make capital out of the art. The opera-going public has for a long time omitted to demand from the dramatic art that which one has a right to look for from it.

This celebrated composer of operas to whom we are making allusion, has taken upon himself to supply the public with this deception, this sham art. It would be superfluous to enter upon a profound examination of the artistic means which this artist employs with profusion to achieve his aim; it will be sufficient to say that he understands perfectly how to deceive the public. His successes are the proof of it. He succeeds particularly in making the bored audience accept that jargon which we have characterized as a modern, piquant expression of all the trivialities already served up to them so many times in their primitive absurdity. One will not be astonished that this composer equally takes care to introduce into his works those grand catastrophes of the soul which so profoundly stir an audience, for one knows how much those people who are the victims of boredom seek such emotions. Whoever reflects upon the reasons which insure success under such circumstances, will not be surprised to see that this artist succeeds so completely.

The faculty of deceiving is so great with this artist, that he deceives himself. Perhaps, indeed, he wishes it as much for himself as for the public. We verily believe that he would like to create works of art, but that he knows he is not able of doing so. In order to escape from this painful conflict between his wish and his ability, he composes operas for Paris, and has them produced in other countries, which in these days is the surest means of acquiring the reputation of an artist without being one. When we see him thus overwhelmed by the trouble he gives himself in practising self-deception, he almost assumes, in our eyes, a tragical figure, were there not in him too much personal interest and self at work, the amalgamation of which reduces it to the comic. Besides the Judaism which reigns generally in art, and which this composer represents in music, he is distinguished by an impotence to touch us, and further by the ridiculous which is inherent in him.

This criticism upon Meyerbeer is caustic and unsparing. Yet even now public opinion has testified to its veracity. It is not making too bold a statement to say that no musician of taste, no musician — it matters not of what nationality or school — of to-day will accord Meyerbeer that exalted position he occupied when Wagner had the temerity to show the sham and unreal art in the man. At that time, now nearly forty years ago, Richard Wagner suffered severely for his fearless and outspoken criticism. Personal jealousy was freely hurled at him as the paltry incentive of his article. I frankly admit, with an intimate acquaintance of Wagner's feelings regarding Meyerbeer, that he despised the "mountebank," hating cordially the thousand commercial incidents Meyerbeer associated with the production of his works. Schlesinger told me indeed of well-authenticated instances where Meyerbeer had gone so far as to conciliate the mistresses of critics to secure a favourable verdict. It can easily be understood that Wagner could not help feeling contempt for such a man, for when he himself came to London in 1855, he absolutely refused to call on any single critic, notwithstanding I impressed upon him how necessary and habitual such custom was. The result we know. He offended them all.

# CHAPTER XVIII.

1855.

THE story of the invitation of Richard Wagner, the then dreaded iconoclast of music, to London, to conduct the concerts of the conservative Philharmonic Society, is both curious and interesting, in the history of the tonal art. Costa, the previous conductor, had resigned. The pressing question was, who could succeed so popular a man? The names of many German notabilities were proposed, and as soon dismissed. In England there was Sterndale Bennett, but he had quarrelled with the directors ; the field was therefore open. It was then that the appointment of Wagner was suggested and agreed to. The circumstances were as follows. Prosper Sainton, the eminent violinist, was both leader of the orchestra of the Philharmonic, and one of the seven directors of the society. He was and is [1] an intimate friend of mine, and to him I proposed Richard Wagner. At that time Sainton was living with Charles Lüders, a dear, lovable German musician, with whom he had travelled on concert tours throughout Europe. From the time the two men met in Russia, they lived together for twenty-five years, until the marriage of Sainton with Miss Dolby, since which time Lüders was a daily visitor at his friend's house,

[1] Written before his death in 1890.

Sainton administering always to his comfort, and tending him on his death-bed, in the summer of 1884. Lüders and I were heart and soul, and catching my enthusiasm he pressed Sainton so warmly, that the name of Wagner was at once proposed. Richard Wagner was then but a myth to the average English musician. However, as Sainton was a general favourite with his colleagues, and was, further, held in high esteem on account of his artistic perception, I was requested, through his influence, to appear before the directors. I had then been a resident in the metropolis for twenty-one years; I attended at a directors' meeting in Hanover Square, and stated my views.

Up to the present time, I have never been able to discover how it was that seven sedate gentlemen could have been so influenced by my red-hot enthusiasm as to have been led to offer the appointment to Richard Wagner. I found that they either knew very little of him or nothing at all, nor did I know him personally; I was but the reflection of August Roeckel; as a composer, however, I had become so wholly his partisan as to regard him the genius of the age. The crusade in favour of Richard Wagner, upon which I then entered with so much fervour, will be best understood by an article contributed by me at the time to the "New York Musical Gazette,"[1] parts of which I think it advisable to reproduce here, even at the expense of repeating an incident or two. The article was summarized in the London musical papers, and immediately a shower of virulent abuse fell upon me which, however, at no period affected in the slightest my ardour for Wagner's cause.

[1] 24th February, 1855.

The musical public of London is in a state of excitement which cannot be described. Costa, the autocrat of London conductors, is just now writing an oratorio, and no longer cares for what he would have sacrificed anything for before he got possession of it, namely, the conductorship of the Old Philharmonic; and whom to have in his place, has for some time sorely puzzled the directors of the said society. No Englishman would do, that is certain, for the orchestra adores Costa; and besides, it belongs to Covent Garden, where Costa reigns supreme (and where he really does wonders; being musical conductor and stage manager; looking after the *mise en scène* and everything else with remarkable intelligence). Whom to seek for, the government knew not. They made overtures to Berlioz, but he had already signed an engagement with the New Philharmonic, their presumptuous and hated rival. Things looked serious, appalling, to the Old Philharmonic; they were in danger of losing many subscribers, and a strong tide was setting in against them. At last, seeing themselves on the verge of dissolution, and the New Philharmonic ready to act as pall-bearers, they resolved upon a risk-all, life-or-death remedy, and Richard Wagner was engaged! Yes; this red republican of music is to preside over the Old Philharmonic of London, the most classical, orthodox, and exclusive society on this globe.

Mr. Anderson, the conductor of the queen's private band, and acting director of the Old Philharmonic, was despatched as minister plenipotentiary and envoy extraordinary to Zurich, where Wagner is staying, to open negotiations and conclude arrangements, and happily succeeded in his mission. Wagner agreed to give up certain previously made conditions (some correspondence had taken place on the subject), which required a second conductor for the vocal part of the concerts, and unlimited rehearsals. In regard to pecuniary considerations, Wagner rather astonished the entire John Bull; he coolly told Mr. Anderson that he was too much occupied to give that point much thought, and only desired to know at what time he (Wagner) would be wanted in London. The society has requested Wagner to have some of his works performed here. He, however, has written nothing for concerts on former occasions; he has arranged a suite of morceaux from each of his three operas, and these give a public, unacquainted with his works, some idea of his peculiarities.

To see Wagner and Berlioz, the two most ultra red republicans existing in music, occupying the two most prominent positions in the musical world of this classical, staid, sober, proper, exclusive, conservative London, is an unmitigatedly "stunning" fact. We are now ready for anything, and nothing more can astonish us. Some of our real old cast-iron conservatives will never recover from this shock — among others, the editor of the London " Musical World." This estimable gentleman is in a truly deplorable state, whereby his friends are caused much concern. The engagement of Wagner seems to have affected his brain, and from the most amiable of men and truthful of critics, he has changed to the — well, see his journal. He lavishes abuse, in language no less violent than vehement, upon Wagner and all who will not condemn " poor Richard " without hearing him. Wagner once wrote an article, " Das Judenthum in der Musik " ("Judaism in Music"), in which he conclusively proves that a Jew is not a Christian, and neither looks nor " feels," nor talks nor moves like one, and consequently does not compose like a Christian ; and in that same article, which is written with exceeding cleverness, Wagner makes a severe onslaught upon Mendelssohn and Meyerbeer, on Judaistic grounds. The editor of the London " Musical World," considering himself one of Mendelssohn's heirs, and Mendelssohn having (so it is said) hated Wagner, *ergo*, must the enraged editor also hate him? He certainly seems to do so, " con molto gusto."

*　　*　　*　　*　　*　　*　　*

Wagner is at Zurich, quietly industrious, and does not even know or care about the hue and cry concerning him, which is raised by a set of idlers, who wish to identify themselves with something new and great ; being nothing themselves, nor likely ever to be anything.

It having been decided that the directors were to make proposals to Richard Wagner, I wrote to him detailing the events that had occurred, and stating that he might expect at any moment to receive a communication from the society. He did hear almost immediately, and on the 8th January, 1855, he wrote to me from Zurich.

I enter into correspondence with you, my dear Praeger, as with an old friend.  My heartiest thanks are due to you, my ardent champion in a strange land and among a conservative people.  Your first espousal of my cause, ten years ago, when August[1] read to me a vigorous article, from some English journal,[2] by you on the " Tannhäuser " performance at Dresden, and the several evidences you have given subsequently of a devotion to my efforts, induce me to unhesitatingly throw the burden of somewhat wearisome arrangements upon your shoulders, as papa Roeckel[3] urges me in a letter which I inclose.

I must tell you that before concluding arrangements with the directors of the Philharmonic, I imposed two conditions : first, an under conductor ; secondly, the engagement of the orchestra for several rehearsals for each concert.  You may imagine how enchanted I am at the promised break of this irritating exile, and with what joy I look forward to an engagement wherein my views might find adequate expression ; but frankly, I should not care to undertake a journey all the way to London only to find my freedom of action restricted, my energies cramped by a directorate that might refuse what I deem the imperatively necessary number of rehearsals ; therefore, am I willing to agree with what papa Roeckel advises, if it meets, too, with your support, viz. to forego the engagement of a second conductor.  In such an event, I would beg of you to talk over, in my name, this affair with Mr. Hogarth,[4] and so far to arrange that only the question of honorarium be left open for settlement, for which I would then ask your friendly counsel.  Altogether, what specially decides me to come to London, is the certainty of your help in the matter, for, being totally incapable to do that which may be necessary there, I shall be compelled in many more respects to have recourse to your decision.  If you will venture to burden yourself with me, then tell me in friendship, and take your chance how you fare with me.  My position forces me to wish again to undertake something desirable, but in how far that is possible, without lending myself to anything unworthy, I have to find out.

Be not angry with me that I have thus bluntly cast myself upon you.  If you receive my entreaty, then act in my name as you con-

---

[1] Roeckel.        [2] English Gentleman.        [3] August's father.
[4] Secretary of the Philharmonic Society.

sider good. Heartily shall I be glad of such an opportunity of becoming more intimate with you.

With best greeting to you, yours heartily,

RICHARD WAGNER.

ZURICH, 8th January, 1855.

P.S. Hogarth's letter I received twelve days ago, and I answered immediately, but up till to-day I have had no reply, most likely for the reason which papa Roeckel surmises.

The inclosure to Wagner's letter was a long epistle from papa Roeckel, advising him to accept the Philharmonic engagement as a means of introducing some of Wagner's own works to a London public in a worthy manner, the orchestra of the Philharmonic having acquired a continental reputation. Wagner had respect for the opinion of old Mr. Roeckel, taking counsel with him immediately the Philharmonic conductorship was proposed to him.

The next letter is dated —

ZURICH, 18th January, 1855.

Hearty thanks, dear Praeger. You show yourself in your letter exactly as I expected, and that gives me great courage for London. You no doubt know that I have given my word to Mr. Anderson. He was anxious to telegraph it at once to London in order to have the advertisement printed. I received your letter after Mr. Anderson had left. I was glad to find from you that you had been informed officially of my having accepted the engagement. What I think of this engagement I cannot briefly explain to you. I feel positive, however, that I make a sacrifice. I felt that either I must renounce the public and all relations with it once and for all, and turn my back upon it, or else, if but the slightest hope were yet within me, I must accept the hand which is now held out to me. I have repeatedly experienced, however, that where I was most sanguine I have ever been most positively in error; and although I have again and again felt this, yet I have been induced by this offer to make a last attempt, and as such I look upon the whole transaction. That the directors of the Philharmonic have no idea whom they have engaged, I am perfectly sure; but they will soon discover. They might have been more generous, for if these gentlemen intentionally go abroad to find a celebrity, they ought to have been inclined to spend a little extra. As to the question of emolument, I answered Mr. Anderson with tolerable indifference. They seem to attach great importance to the performance of my works. You no doubt are aware that I have never written anything for concert performances, and only on special occasions have I arranged characteristic movements from my three last operas, and even those which might perhaps give a concerted impression would occupy a whole concert. By these means I have been enabled to give to a public unacquainted with the peculiarities of my music an intelligent first impression. I might have wished to have begun with such a concert in London, but as this would entail somewhat heavy expenses at first starting, the concert might be repeated. Do you think this is practicable, or do you think I, myself, could undertake it as an enterprise? In which case I would keep back my compositions from the Philharmonic. I surmise, however, that such a speculation would encounter insurmountable difficulties in London, and therefore I shall be obliged after all to give detached selections in the concerts of the Philharmonic, whereby my meaning will be considerably weakened. If you think it worth while to give me an answer on this point, I beg of you to tell me whether I should have the parts of my compositions copied out here (Zurich), or whether I should only bring the scores, or, perhaps, should I previously send them to you so that they might be copied in London. Of course you can only inform me as to this after an official interview with the directors of the Philharmonic. In any case the choral sections would have to be translated. As regards my lodgings and London diet, Mr. Anderson mumbled something that this could be arranged to be free for me. I was, however, so preoccupied that I did not pay much attention to it. Have I, after all, correctly understood? He spoke, I think, of a pleasant residence near Regent's Park which could be procured for me. Would you have the amiability, when opportunity presents itself, to question Mr. Anderson on this point? If they could provide me such a pretty, friendly, and quiet lodging, with a good piano, from the 1st March, it would suit me well, for I would then save you trouble, and it would free me from all anxiety on that score, especially about my supposed daintiness. Now I presume I shall soon have something more to say about this. Meanwhile, I pity you beforehand on account of my acquaintanceship, and for the trouble I shall be to you. May heaven help that I shall have something good and noble to offer you.

Yours,

RICHARD WAGNER.

On reading this letter, admiration for the fearless courage of Wagner grows upon one. A whole concert devoted to his own works! He little knew with whom he was dealing. Wagner's temper was quick, and I feared to irritate him by conveying the certain refusal of the directors, but it had to be done. It was a difficult and delicate matter to prevent friction between Richard Wagner, possessed with the exalted notion of his mission, on the one hand, and the steady-going time-serving directors on the other. I saw Mr. Anderson. Timorous of the leap in the dark he and his colleagues had made in engaging Wagner, they feared hazarding the reputation of their concerts by the devotion of a whole evening to Wagner's works, but a compromise — that some selections should be given — was readily effected. The conveyance of this news to Wagner brought from him the following letter : —

My best thanks to you for so amiably taking such trouble. That you sounded the directors of the Philharmonic as to the question whether they would fill up a whole evening with selections from those of my operas which I have arranged specially for concert performances, although fully authorized to do so, produced a somewhat disagreeable effect upon me. Heaven knows how strange it is to me that I should force myself upon any body, and originally, I only wished your opinion whether I had any chance to have one concert set apart for my works, for in such case I should have held back the various selections. I had a similar intimation from Hogarth, to whom I briefly answered that I would conduct the classical works only, and that if the directors later on wished to perform any of my compositions, they might tell me so, when I should select such as I deemed most appropriate, for which contingency I should bring the orchestral parts with me, some of which, no doubt, would require additional copies, the expense of which, in London, could not be of much account. I am quite satisfied with this arrangement, and the people will learn to know me there. On the whole, I have really no special plan for my London expedition, except to essay what can be done with a celebrated orchestra, and further, a little change for me is desirable, but under no circumstances can London even be a home for me. As you open your hospitable doors to me, I shall avail myself of your kindness, and if you will let me stay until I have found a suitable apartment, I shall be grateful to you, and shall heartily beg pardon of your amiable wife for my intrusion. I shall be in London in the first days of March. I sincerely repeat to you that I have no great expectations, for really I do not count any more upon anything in this world. But I shall be delighted to gain your closer friendship. The English language I do not know, and I am totally without gift for modern languages, and at present am averse to learn any on account of the strain on my memory. I must help myself through with French. Now for mutual personal acquaintance,

Yours very faithfully,

RICHARD WAGNER.

ZURICH, 1st February, 1855.

The following incident, as showing the enmity towards Wagner prior to his landing on these shores, should be noted. It was after receiving the previous letter that I met James Davison, the editor of the London "Musical World," and also musical critic of the "Times," at the house of Leopold de Meyer, the pianist. We had hitherto been on terms of friendship. The power of this gentleman was enormous. He told me, "I have read some of Richard Wagner's literary works ; in his books he is a god, but as long as I hold the sceptre of musical criticism, I'll not let him have any chance here." He did his utmost. With what result is matter of history.

The next letter from Wagner is dated Zurich, 12th February. In it he speaks of "wishing for some quiet room, free from annoying visitors, where no one but yourself, knowing of my existence, will come to pester me while scoring part of my tetralogy. Your house I will gladly make as my own, but as a number of strangers are likely to call, I hope to escape them in solitude of unknown regions. You must not think this strange, as I isolate myself at home the whole morning, and do not permit a soul to come near me when at work, unless it be 'Peps.' You will remember, too, when I did something similar to this at Dresden, and left the world to go into retirement with August Roeckel."

A few days after he left Zurich for London, his next letter being dated—

PARIS, 2d March, 1855.

I am on the road to you. I expect to leave here Sunday morning early, and shall accordingly arrive in London in the evening, probably somewhat late. If, therefore, without further notice, I must be so unceremonious with you, the friend, whom, alas, I am not yet personally acquainted with, as to tumble right into the house, then must I beg of you to expect me on Sunday night. Trusting that I shall not ill-use your friendly hospitality, if only for this night, for I suppose we shall succeed in trying to find on Monday morning an agreeable lodging, in which I might at once install myself, for from the many exertions, I fear I shall come very fatigued to you. I do not doubt that you will have the kindness to inform Hogarth that, dating from Monday morning early, I shall be at the disposition of the directors of the Philharmonic. In so doing I keep my promise to be in London a week before the first concert. With the entreaty to best excuse me to your wife, and in hearty joy of your personal acquaintanceship,

I am yours very faithful,

RICHARD WAGNER.

Wagner arrived at midnight precisely on Sunday, the fifth of March.

If I had not already acquired through the graphic letters of August Roeckel an insight into the peculiarities of Richard Wagner's habits of thought, power of grasping profound questions of mental speculation, whilst relieving the severity of serious discourse by the intermingling of jocular ebulitions of fancy, I was soon to have a fair specimen of these wondrous qualities. One of the many points in which we found ourselves at home, was the habit of citing phrases from Schiller or Goethe, as applicable to our subjects of discussion, as often ironically as seriously. To these we added an almost interminable dictionary of quotations from the plays and operas of the early part of the century. These mental links were, in the course of a long and intimate friendship, augmented by references to striking qualities, defects, or oddities, our circle of acquaintances forming a means of communication between us which might not inaptly be likened to mental shorthand. Nothing could have exceeded the hilarity, when, upon showing him, at an advanced hour, to his bedroom, he enthusiastically said, "August was right; we shall understand each other thoroughly!" I felt in an exalted position, and dreamed that, like Spontini, I had received a new decoration from some potentate which delighted me, but the pleasant dream soon turned to nightmare, when I could find no room on my coat to place the newly acquired bauble. The next morning I found the signification of the dream. Exalted positions have their duties as well as their pleasures, and it became my duty to acquaint Wagner that a so-called " Necker " hat (*i.e.* a slouched one) was not becoming for the conductor of so conservative a society as the Philharmonic, and that it was necessary that he should provide himself with a tall hat, indeed, such headgear as would efface all remembrance of the social class to which his soft felt hat was judicially assigned, for, be it known, in some parts of Germany the soft slouched felt hat had been interdicted by police order as being the emblem of revolutionary principles. I think it was on the strength of the accuracy of this last statement that Wagner gave way, and I at once followed up the success by taking the composer of "Tannhäuser" to the best West End hatter, where, after an onslaught on the sons of Britannia and their manias, we succeeded in fitting a hat on that wondrous head of the great thinker. I could not help sarcastically joking Wagner on his compulsory leave-taking with the " revolutionary " hat for four months, — the time he was to sojourn amongst us, — by citing from Schiller's " Fiesco " the passage about the fall of the hero's cloak into the water, upon which Verina pushes him after it with the sinister words, " When the purple falls, the duke must follow." As to Richard Wagner's democratic principles, I observed that the solitude of exile had considerably modified them. This I noticed to my surprise and no less pain, for, when I anxiously inquired after our poor friend, August Roeckel, he shrugged his shoulders and said, " Perhaps he tries to

revolutionize the prison warders, for the 'Wuhlers'"
(uprooters, a name of the period) "are never at rest in
their self-elected role of reformers!"  I, who knew the
unambitious, self-sacrificing nature of the poor prisoner,
felt a pang of disappointment at Wagner's remark, and
had often to suffer the same when the year 1849 was
mentioned.

We drove from the hatmaker straight to the city to
inquire after a box containing the compositions Wagner had been requested to bring over with him.  The
box had arrived, and then we continued our peregrin-
ation back to the West, alighting at Nottingham Place,
the residence of Mr. Anderson.  The old gentleman
possessed all the suave, gentle manner of the courtier,
and all went well during the preliminary conversation
about the projected programme, until Mr. Anderson
mentioned a prize symphony of Lachner as one of the
intended works to be performed.  Wagner sprang from
his seat, as if shot from a gun, exclaiming loudly and
angrily, "Have I therefore left my quiet seclusion in
Switzerland to cross the sea to conduct a prize symphony
by Lachner?  no; never!  If that be a condition of
the bargain I at once reject it, and will return.  What
brought me away was the eagerness to head a far-famed
orchestra and to perform worthily the works of the great
masters, but no Kapellmeister music;  and that of a
'Lachner,' bah!"  Mr. Anderson sat aghast in his chair,
looking with bewildered surprise on this unexpected
outbreak of passion, delivered with extraordinary volubility and heat by Wagner, partly in French and partly
in German.  I interposed a more tranquillizing report of
the harangue and succeeded in assuring Mr. Anderson

that the matter might be arranged by striking out the
"prize" composition, to which he directly most urbanely
acceded. Wagner, who did not fail to perceive the startling effect his derisive attack on the proposed work had
produced on poor Mr. Anderson, whose knowledge of
the French language was fairly efficient in an Andante
movement, but quite incapable of following such a
*presto agitato* as the Wagner speech had assumed,
begged me to explain the dubious position of prize compositions in all cases, and certainly no less in the case of
the Lachner composition, and Wagner himself laughingly turned the conversation into a more general and
quiet channel. After thus having tranquillized the
storm, the interview ended more agreeably than the
startling episode had promised. I, however, then clearly
foresaw the many difficulties likely to occur during the
conductorship of a man of Wagner's Vesuvius-like temper, and the sequel amply proved that I had not been
unduly prejudiced in this respect. Yet in all his bursts
of excitability, a sudden veering round was always to be
expected, should it chance that the angry poet-musician perceived any ludicrous feature in the controversy,
when he would turn to that as a means of subduing
his ebullition of temper, and falling into a jocular
vein, would plainly show he was conscious of having
exceeded the bounds of moderation. I was glad that
we had passed the Rubicon of our difficulties for the
present, for I was fully aware that whatever difficulties
might arise with regard to Wagner's relation to the
other directors, they would be easily overcome by Mr.
Anderson's support, for it was he who unquestionably
ruled the "Camarilla," or secret Spanish council, as

Wagner styled the "seven," when any work proposed by them for performance met with disapproval. I never could well understand how the Lachner episode became known, but it is certain that it did, for the German opposition journals, and there were many, made great capital out of the refusal of Wagner to conduct a prize symphony.

Our next visit was an unclouded one. We went to call on Sainton, who was as refined a soloist as he was an intelligent and energetic orchestral leader. His jovial temperament, Gasconic fun (born at Toulouse), his good and frank nature, pleased Wagner at once. Charles Lüders, a German musician, "le frère intime " of Sainton, formed the oddest contrast to his friend's character. Quiet, reflective, and somewhat old-fashioned, he nevertheless became an ardent admirer of Wagner's music, and proved that "extremes meet," for in his compositions, and they are many, known in Germany and in France, the good Lüders tenaciously clung to the traditions of a past period. We soon identified him in gentle fun with the "contrapuntista." Notwithstanding the marked contrast of the quartette, Wagner, Sainton, Lüders, and myself, we harmonized remarkably well, and many were our pleasant, convivial meetings during the time of Wagner's stay in London. As Sainton had always been very intimate with Costa, and was his recognized deputy in his absence, he accompanied us on the first visit to the Neapolitan conductor, Wagner expressing a wish to make Costa's acquaintance. This was the only visit of etiquette Wagner paid. He sternly refused to pay any more, no matter to whom, and I gladly desisted from advocating any, though he suffered severely in consequence from a press which stigmatized him as proud and unsociable.

We went home to dine. What a pleasant impression did the master give us of his childlike jollity. Full of fun, he exhibited his remarkable power of imitation. He was a born actor, and it was impossible not to recognize immediately who was the individual caricatured, for Wagner's power of observation led him at all times to notice the most minute characteristics of all whom he encountered. A repast in his society might well be described as a "feast of reason and flow of soul," for, mixed in odd ways, were the most solid remarks of deep, logical intuition, with the sprightliest, frolicsome humour. Wagner ate very quickly, and I soon had occasion to notice the fatal consequences of such unwise procedure, for although a moderate eater, he did not fail to suffer severely from such a pernicious practice. This first day afforded a side-light upon the master's peculiarities. Never having been used to the society of children, he was plainly awkward in his treatment of them, which we did not fail to perceive whenever my little boy was brought in to say "good-night."

As soon as we had discovered a fitting apartment at Portland Place, Regent's Park, within a few minutes' walk of my house, the first thing he wanted was an easel for his work, so that he might stand up to score. No sooner was that desire satisfied than he insisted on an eider-down quilt for his bed. Both these satisfied desires are illustrative of Wagner. He knew not self-denial. It was sufficient that he wished, that his wish should be gratified. When he arrived in London his means were limited, but nevertheless the satisfaction of the desires was what he ever adhered to.

He had not been here a day before his determined character was made strikingly apparent to me. In the matter of crossing a crowded thoroughfare his intrepidity bordered close upon the reckless. He would go straight across a road; safe on the other side, he was almost boyish in his laugh at the nervousness of others. But this was Wagner. It was this deliberate attacking everything that made him what he was; timorousness was not in his character; dauntless fearlessness, perhaps not under proper control, naturally gave birth to an iconoclast, who struck with vigour at all opposition, heedless of destroying the penates worshipped by others.

The rehearsal and the introduction of the band of the Philharmonic was a nervous moment for me. I knew the spirit of opposition had found its way among a few members of the orchestra; indeed, it numbered one at least, who felt himself displaced by Wagner's appointment. However, Wagner came. He addressed the band in a brotherly manner, as co-workers for the glory of art; made an apt reference to their idol, his predecessor, and secured the good-will at once of the majority. I say advisedly the majority only, because they had not long set to work when he was gently admonished by some that "they had not been in the habit of taking this movement so slowly, and that, perhaps, the next had been taken a trifle too fast." Wagner was diplomatic; his words were conciliatory, but, for all that, he went on his way, and would have the *tempi* according to his will. At the end he was applauded heartily, and henceforth the band apparently followed implicitly his directions.

The first concert took place on the 12th March; the programme was as follows:—

|                                             |              |
| ------------------------------------------- | ------------ |
| Symphony . 7 . . . . .                       | Hadyn.       |
| Operatic terzetto (vocal) . . .             | Mozart.      |
| Violin Concerto . . . . .                   | Spohr.       |
| Scena ("Ocean, Thou Mighty Monster"),       | Weber.       |
| Overture (" The Isle of Fingal ") .         | Mendelssohn. |
| The " Eroica " . . . . .                     | Beethoven.   |
| Duet (" O My Father ") . . .                | Marschner.   |
| Overture (" Zauberflöte ") . . .            | Mozart.      |

The effect of the concert will be best understood by the following notice, which I contributed at the time for the " New York Musical Gazette ":—

The eagerly looked for event has taken place. Costa's bâton, so lately swayed with such majestical and even tyrannical ardour, this self-same bâton was taken on Monday last (12th March) by Richard Wagner. The audience rose almost *en masse* to see the man first, and whispers ran from one to another: " He is a small man, but what a beautiful and intelligent forehead he has!" Haydn's symphony, No. 7 (grand) began the concert, and opened the eyes of the audience to a state of things hitherto unknown, as regards conducting. Wagner does not beat in the old-fashioned, automato-metronomic manner. He leaves off beating at times — then resumes again — to lead the orchestra up to a climax, or to let them soften down to a *pianissimo,* as if a thousand invisible threads tied them to his bâton. His is the beau ideal of conducting. He treats the orchestra like the instrument on which he pours forth his soul-inspired strains. Haydn's well-known symphony seemed a new work through his inexpressibly intelligent and poetical conception. Beethoven's " Eroica," the first movement of which used to be taken always with narcotic slowness by previous conductors, and in return the funeral march always much too fast, so as to rob it of all the magnificent *gran'dolore;* the scherzo, which always came out clumsily and heavily; and the finale, which never was understood. — Beethoven's "Eroica" may be said to have been heard for the first time here, and produced a wonderful effect. As if to beat the Mendelssohnian hypercritics on their own field, Wagner gave a reading of Mendelssohn's "Isle of Fingal" that would have delighted the composer himself, and even the overture of "Die Zauberflöte" ("Magic Flute") was invested with something not noticed before. Let it be well understood that Wagner takes no liberties with the works of the great masters; but his poetico-musical genius gives him, as it were, a second sight into their hidden treasures; his worship for them and his intense study are amply proved by his conducting them all without the score, and the musicians of the orchestra, so lately bound to Costa's reign at Covent Garden, and prejudiced to a degree against the new man, who had been so much abused before he came, and judged before he was heard (by those who are not capable of judging him when they do hear him!) — this very orchestra already adores Wagner, who, notwithstanding his republican politics, is decidedly a despot with the orchestra. In short, Wagner has conquered, and an important influence on musical progress may be predicted for him. The next concert will bring us the "Ninth Symphony" and a selection of "Lohengrin," which the directors would insist on, notwithstanding the refusal of the composer. The "Times" abuses Wagner and revenges the neglected English conductors; mixes up his music with the Revolution, 1848, and falsely states that he hates Mozart, Beethoven, etc., etc., and furthermore asserts, just as falsely, that he wrote his books in defence of his operas; but is so virulent against the man, and says so little about his conducting, that it strikes us the article must have been written some years ago, as an answer to "Judaism in Music." The "Morning Post" agrees perfectly with us as to Wagner being the conductor of whom musicians have dreamed, when they sought for perfection, hitherto unbelieved.

After the first concert, we went by arrangement to spend a few hours at his rooms. Dear me, what an evening of excitement that was! There were Wagner, Sainton, Lüders, Klindworth (whom I had introduced to Wagner as a pupil of Liszt), myself and wife. Animal spirits ran high. Wagner was in ecstasies. The concert had been a marked success artistically, and Richard Wagner's reception flattering. On arriving at his rooms, he found it necessary to change his dress from "top to toe." He had perspired so freely from excitement that his collar was as though it had that moment been dipped into a basin of water. So while he went to change his attire and don a somewhat handsome dressing-robe made by Minna, Sainton prepared a mayonnaise for the lobster, and Lüders rum punch made after a Danish method, and one particularly appreciated by Wagner, who, indeed, loved everything unusual of that description. Wagner had chosen the lobster salad, I should mention, because crab fish were either not to be got at all in Germany, or were very expensive. When he returned he put himself at the piano. His memory was excellent, and innumerable "bits" or references of the most varied description were rattled off in a sprightly manner; but more excellent was his running commentary of observations as to the intention of the composer. These observations showed the thinker and discerning critic, and in themselves were of value in helping others to comprehend the meaning of the music. What he said has mostly found its way into print; indeed, it may be affirmed that the greater part of his literary productions was only the transcription of what he uttered incessantly in ordinary conversation. Then, too, he sang; and what singing it was! It was, as I told him then, just like the barking of a big Newfoundland dog. He laughed heartily, but kept on nevertheless. He cared not. Yet though his "singing" was but howling, he sang with his whole heart, and held you, as it were, spellbound. There was the real musician. He felt what he was doing. He was earnest, and that was, and is, the cause of his greatness. Then when we sat at supper he was in his liveliest mood. Richard Wagner a German? Why, he behaved then with all that uncontrolled expansion of the Frenchman. But this is only another instance of those contradictions in Wagner's life. His volubility at the table knew no bounds. Anecdotes and reminiscences of his early life poured forth with a freshness, a vigour, and sparkling vivacity just like some mountain cataract leaping impetuously forward. He spoke with evident pleasure of his reception by the audience; praised the orchestra, remarking how faithfully they had borne in mind and reproduced the impressions he had sought to give them at the rehearsal. On this point he was only regretful that the inspiration, the divination, the artistic electricity, as it were, which is in the air among German or French executants, should be wanting here; or, as he phrased it, "Ils jouent parfaitement, mais le feu sacré leur manque."

Then followed his abuse of fashion. White kid gloves on the hands of a conductor he scoffed at. "Who can do anything fettered with these things?" he pettishly insisted; and it was only after considerable pressure, and pointing out the aristocratic antecedents of the Philharmonic and the class of its supporters, that he had consented to wear a pair just to walk up the steps of the orchestra on first appearing, to be taken off immediately he got to his desk. That evening, at Wagner's request, we drank with much acclamation eternal "brotherhood," henceforth to "tutoyer" each other, and broke up our high-spirited meeting at two in the morning.

But the second concert, 26th March, 1855, the programme was after Wagner's own heart. It was, perhaps, *the* one of the whole eight which delighted him the most, embracing as it did the overture to "Der Freischütz," the prelude and a selection from "Lohengrin," and Beethoven's "Ninth Symphony." It was the first time any of Wagner's music was to be performed in England, and Wagner was anxious. But the rehearsal was reassuring. At first the orchestra could not understand the *pianissimo* required in the opening of the "Lohengrin" prelude ; and then the crescendos and diminuendos which Wagner insisted upon having surprised the executants. They turned inquiringly to each other, seemingly annoyed at his fastidiousness. But the conductor knew what he wanted and would have it. Then came the overture to "Der Freischütz." Now this was exceedingly popular in England, and it was thought nothing could be altered in the mode of rendering it. Traditions, however, of the "adored idol," Weber, were strong in Wagner, and he took it in the composer's way ; the result was, that at the concert the applause was so boisterous, and the demands of the audience so emphatic, that a repetition was at once given. That the overture was repeated will show how insistent were the audience, for Wagner then, as afterwards, was decidedly opposed to encores ; however, upon this occasion there was no way of avoiding the repeat. Though, as I have said, the overture was extremely popular, yet the reading was so new and striking, the phrasing and *nuances* marked with such decision, that the people were startled, and expressed their appreciation heartily.

The reception of the " Lohengrin " selection, too, was unmistakably favourable.　The delicately fragile orchestration of the sweetly melodic prelude, followed by the bright and attractive rhythmical phrases of the bridal chorus, caused a bewildered, pleased surprise among the audience, who had expected something totally different. The "music of the future was noise and fury," so said the leading English musical journal, and this authority counted for something ; but the " Lohengrin " prelude was very inaccurately described, if that had been included, and Wagner felt pleased and contented at the impression which the first performance of any of his music had created in this country.

# CHAPTER XIX.



On the "Ninth Symphony," that colossal work, Richard Wagner expended commensurate pains.  I remember how surprised the vocalists were at the rehearsal, when he stopped them, inquiring did they understand the meaning of what they were singing, and then he briefly explained in emphatic language what he thought about it.  The bass solo was especially odd : the vocalist was taking it as though it were an ordinary ballad, when Wagner burst in fiery song, natural and falsetto, illustrating how it should go, singing the whole of the solo of Mr. Weiss (the bass vocalist) in such a decided, clean cut manner that it was impossible for the singer to help imitating him, and with marked effect too.  As for the band, that rehearsal was a revelation to them.  That symphony was a stupendous work, yet the conductor knew it by heart and was conducting without score.  They felt they were in the hands of a man whose artistic soul was fired with enthusiasm ; his earnestness infected them ; they caught it quickly and responded with a zealousness that only sympathetic artists can put forth, ably supported by Sainton, whom the Prince Consort complimented to Wagner as a splendid " Chef d'attaque."  The concert performance created, too, such a stir that even the most violent of all the anti-

Wagner critics spoke of it as an "intellectual and elevated conception." This concert placed Wagner permanently in the heart of his band; they loved to be under the command of such an earnest art worker and yielded willingly to his inspirations.

That evening after the concert, at our now established gathering, Wagner was positively jubilant. He had been able to produce the " Ninth Symphony " in London as he wished, and he hoped the "traditions" would remain. He emphasized "traditions" in a slyly sarcastic manner, and well had he reason to do so. Traditions of Mendelssohn and Spohr were omnipotent, and omnipotent with the orchestra, and Wagner hoped the conservative English mind would retain "his" traditions of the "Choral Symphony," among which would be found how he had sung the long recitative for the strings,— double-basses, — that ushers in the choral portion of the work. When Wagner first sang this part to the orchestra, they all engaged in a good-humoured titter, which speedily gave way to respect; for Wagner certainly was marvellously successful in explaining how he wanted a phrase played by first singing it, — a gift it undoubtedly was.

He said he would not do any work next day, and arranged that we should visit the city. We went first to the Guildhall. It was astonishing how he absorbed everything to himself, to his purposes, how his fancy freely exercised itself. Gog and Magog ! they were his Fafner and Fasolt ; then his humour leaped in advance of the period, and he laughingly asked me whether there was a "Götterdamerung" in store for the City Fathers, and whether Guildhall, their Walhalla, supported by the giants Gog and Magog, would also crumble away through the curse of gold. We next went to the Mint. There, too, the central figure was Wagner; the main theme of discussion, Wagner. When the attendant put into his hands, as was the custom, a roll of cancelled bank notes, amounting to thousands of pounds sterling, he turned to me and said, " The hundredth part of this would build my theatre, and posterity would bless me." His speech certainly savoured of the consciousness of genius. I do not think this is a euphemistic way of saying he had a good opinion of himself. I say it, because I feel it to be the truth. It was through this very consciousness that he triumphed over the many difficulties that beset him. Without it he could not have achieved what he did. The buoyancy of hope begotten of conscious strength is a powerful factor in the securing of success. The theatre he had in his mind then, I thought to be that which he had urged the Saxon authorities to establish, the scheme for which I was then well acquainted with, but his latter discourse showed how, during his exile, that original thought had amplified itself. Of our visit to St. Paul's Cathedral I can recall but one observation of Wagner, to the effect that it was as cold and uninspiring as the Protestant creed — a strange remark from one whose own religious tendencies were Lutheran, and who could express his religious convictions so powerfully and poetically in his last work, " Parsifal."

Richard Wagner's intense attachment to the canine species led him to make friends with our dog, a large, young, black Norwegian beast, given me by Hainberger, the companion of Wagner in the forward movement of

1848–9, and sharer of his exile. The dog showed in return a decided affection for his newly made acquaintance. After a few days, when Wagner found that the dog was kept in a small back yard, he expostulated against such "cruelty," and proposed to take the dog's necessary out-door exercise under his own special care — a task he never shirked during the whole of his London stay. Whenever he went for his daily promenade, a habit never relinquished at any period of his life, the dog was his companion, no matter who else might be of the party. Nor was the control of the dog an easy task. It was a curious sight to witness Wagner's patience in following the wild gyrations of the spirited animal, who, in his exultation of that semi-freedom, tugged at his chain, dragging the Nibelung composer hither and thither.

Part of Wagner's daily constitutional was to the Regent's Park, entering by the Hanover Gate. There, at the small bridge over the ornamental water, would he stand regularly and feed the ducks, having previously provided himself for the purpose with a number of French rolls — rolls ordered each day for the occasion. There was a swan, too, that came in for much of Wagner's affection. It was a regal bird, and fit, as the master said, to draw the chariot of Lohengrin. The childlike happiness, full to overflowing, with which this innocent occupation filled Wagner, was an impressive sight never to be forgotten. It was Wagner you saw before you, the natural man, affectionate, gentle, and mirthful. His genuine affection for the brute creation, united to a keen power of observation, gave birth to numberless anecdotes, and the account of the Regent's

Park peregrinations often formed a most pleasant subject of after-dinner conversation. I should explain that
though Wagner had rooms in Portland Place, St. John's
Chapel, Regent's Park, he only took his breakfast there,
and did such work in the matter of scoring in the morning, coming directly after to my house for his dog and
rolls, returning for dinner and to spend the rest of the
day under my roof, where also a room was provided for
him.

In our friendly talks upon the animal kingdom, we
soon came to a decided dissension. I casually remarked
on the ludicrous effects animals produce at times, and
under all circumstances on the stage; here I found myself in direct opposition to Wagner's notions on the subject. Had he not the dragon Fafner, the young bear
in "Siegfried," the Gräne, the steed of the Valkyrie,
even the fluttering bird in the tetralogy? Was not the
swan in "Lohengrin" another proof of his predilection
for realistic representation of animals on the stage? It
was in vain that I cited the lamentable failure of the
serpent in Mozart's "Magic Flute," which, even at the
best theatres in Germany, never produced other than a
burst of hilarity at its wriggling in the pangs of death,
when pierced by the three donnas; or again the two
lions in the same opera which are rolled on to the stage
like children's wooden horses; or Weber's mistake of
introducing a serpent in his "Euryanthe," which always
mars that scene! But I found myself obliged to cease
quoting examples, and seek a basis for establishing principles for my argument against the introduction of animals on the stage. Here more success awaited me on
the strength of Wagner's own exalted notion of the his-

trionic art ; viz. that an actor, to be worthy of the name, must possess the creative power of a poet, and become, as it were, inspired into the state impersonated, which might not inaptly be likened to that of mesmerism. The actor must believe himself another being, must be unconscious of aught else. One such artist, he asserted, was Garrick, in the delivery of monologues, when the great tragedian was said to have isolated himself to such a degree, that though with his eyes wide open, he became, as it were, visionless. It was on this ground that I attempted my argument against Wagner's illogical and intemperate introduction of the brute creation into his dramas. If, I argued, you will not accept an actor properly so-called, a reasoning man, unless his poetic creative fancy can enable him to transport his identity into a character entirely different from his own, how still less can you expect any animal to impersonate a set rôle in any performance? Whatever actions may be required from it, a dog will always represent a dog ; a horse, a horse. Wagner saw the argument, but reluctant as at all times to confess himself beaten, he advanced "training" as a defence. This, however, served only to destroy his case the more ; for he had previously reasoned, and with much force, that all training for the stage as a profession was useless, and but so much misdirected effort and waste of time, unless the student had given evidence of a genius, which nature, alas! is chary in bestowing. So much for the introduction of real animals upon the stage ; there the case is bad enough, and the results occasionally disastrous and ludicrous ; but when one has to make shift with imitation, the matter is still worse. Here, too, however, Wagner was reluctant to forego the semblance as much as he was the reality. Yet, let the case be tested by oneself. Recall the bear Siegfried brings with him into the smithy, think of the ridiculous effect produced by the actor's antics in his vain efforts to worthily perform his part and seem a real bear. There is no margin left for the imagination, and the sad attempt at a mistaken realism defeats its own purpose. It is an extraordinary feature in a poetic brain like that of Wagner, that he would cling persistently to such a realism. This subject remained always one on which we dissented, and I never failed to prognosticate a failure for his pets in the Nibelung tetralogy, which to my mind was fully proved even under his own supervision, and on the hallowed ground of Bayreuth at the performances there, which were, in all other respects, so marvellously perfect. Who is there that was terribly impressed by the sight of the dragon, or who could divest himself of the thought that a recital of the combat would have proved infinitely more impressive than the slaying of the snorting monster, however well Siegfried bears himself towards the pasteboard pitiful imitation of a fabulous beast? Who, again, would not sooner have heard a description of the wild, spirited steed, Gräne, than witness the nervous anxiety of Brünhilde in mounting and dismounting a funeral charger, which is the cynosure of all eyes while on the stage, to the loss of the music-dramatic setting? The attention of the dramatis personæ and audience is distracted from the action of the drama, and centred on the probable next movement of an animal unable to grasp the situation. This question of realism is a debatable point; but if it be not kept within strictly defined limits, I fear there will be danger of the ludicrous triumphing over the serious.

An inquiry into the probable causes of an exaggerated tendency to realism, in a man like Wagner, cannot but be interesting to those who, without bias, accept him as a master-mind. After many years of an ardent study of his character, compelled by his commanding genius, I am forced to a conclusion, the key to many of his actions, which is equally the explanation in the present instance, is the lack of self-denial. He yearned for unlimited means to achieve his purpose, and would have the most gorgeous and costly trappings, to set off his pictures of the imagination. It was the same in every-day matters of life. Nor, must I add, did he ever care from whence the means came. That this was the case in real life, all who know him will testify. How much more, then, would such a tendency be fed in realizing the vivid impressions with which his active poetical fancy so freely provided him. Unlimited means! that was the dream of his life, and up to a late period, when these means at last realized themselves by the astounding success of his works and the enormous sums they produced, his inability to curb his wants down to his actual means kept him in a state of constant trouble and yearning for freedom from those shackles.

He accepted his humble descent, fully convinced from earliest time of having the patent of nobility in his brain — in his genius! He ever bore himself with the consciousness of superiority, but as for titles and decorative distinctions, he disdained them all. Were they not bestowed on numskulls? therefore, he has loudly proclaimed genius should not dishonour its lofty intelligence in accepting empty baubles. But riches and the profuse luxurious splendour that can be purchased thereby would not have seemed too much for him, had they equalled the fabulous possessions of a Monte Cristo. The traditional humble state of the great composers, if not actual poverty, as compared with the fortunes amassed in other arts, was a continual source of complaint with him.

The programme of the third concert was as follows :—

THIRD CONCERT, 16TH APRIL.

| | |
|---|---|
| Symphony in A . *(Italian)* . | Mendelssohn. |
| Aria from " Faust " . . . . | Spohr. |
| Concerto, pianoforte . . . . | Beethoven. |
| Aria . . . . . . . | Mozart. |
| Overture (" Euryanthe ") . . . | Weber. |
| Symphony in C minor, No. 5 . . | Beethoven. |
| Recitative and Aria . . . . | Spohr. |
| Overture (" Les deux journées ") . . | Cherubini. |

That evening, the 16th April, there was a stir among the Mendelssohnian supporters. They mustered in force ; for it had been rumoured that at the rehearsal Wagner had not stopped the orchestra once. But however Wagner may have regarded the works of the composer of " Elijah," he was straightforward enough to do with all his might what he put his hand to, as the sequel proved, since the " Daily News " reported that it "never heard the ' Italian ' Symphony go so well." That there were some whose prejudice was not appeased, is to be accepted as a matter of course, and Wagner was taunted in the " Times," "with a coarse and rigorously frigid " performance.

As for the overture to "Euryanthe," it is not too much to say the audience was startled out of itself; there was a dead silence for a moment on the work being brought to a close, and the enthusiasm, vigorous and hearty, burst forth. It was a new reading. Such was the surprise with which we witnessed the rapturous applause, that at the convivial gathering after the concert Wagner set himself at the piano, and from memory poured forth numerous excerpts from "Euryanthe." Then we learned that that opera was intensely admired by Wagner. He thought it "logical" and "philosophical," and throughout showed that Weber was a reflective musician, and, as he himself forcibly argued, that only works of reflection could ever be immortal. The plot, its treatment, and the language employed were, he felt, the causes of the opera's non-popularity, and that these wretched drawbacks dreadfully changed the intrinsically beautiful music.

Reflections upon the habits and customs of a past generation sometimes introduce us to situations that produce in the mind wonder and perhaps a feeling of disgust. Who can picture the composer of that colossal work of intellect, the "Nibelung Ring," sitting at the piano, in an elegant, loose robe-de-chambre, singing, with full heart, snatches and scenes from his "adored" idol, Weber's "Euryanthe," and at intervals of every three or four minutes indulging in large quantities of scented snuff. The snuff-taking scene of the evening is the deeper graven on my memory, because Wagner abruptly stopped singing, on finding his snuff-box empty, and got into a childish, pettish fit of anger. He turned to us in deepest concern, with "Kein schnupf tabac mehr

also Kein gesang mehr" (no more snuff, no more song);
and though we had reached the small hours of early
morn, would have some one start in search of this "necessary adjunct." When singing, the more impassioned
he became, the more frequent the snuff-taking. Now,
this practice of Wagner's, one cultivated from early
manhood, in my opinion pointedly illustrates a phase in
the man's character. He did not care for snuff, and
even allowed the indelicacy of the habit, but it was that
insatiable nature of his that yearned for the enjoyment
of all the "supposed" luxuries of life. It was precisely
the same with smoking. He indulged in this, to me,
barbarous acquirement more moderately, but experienced not the slightest pleasure from it. I have seen
him puffing from the mild and inoffensive cheroot, to
the luxurious hookah — the latter, too, as he confessed,
only because it was an Oriental growth, and the luxury
of Eastern people harmonized with his own fondness
for unlimited profusion. "Other people find pleasure
in smoking; then why should not I?" This is, briefly,
the only explanation Wagner ever offered in defence of
the practice — a practice which he was fully aware increased the malignity of his terrible dyspepsia.

There was in Wagner a nervous excitability which
not infrequently led to outbreaks of passion, which it
would be difficult to understand or explain, were it not
that there existed a positive physical cause. First, he
suffered, as I have stated earlier, from occasional attacks of erysipelas; then his nervous system was delicate, sensitive, — nay, I should say, irritable. Spasmodic
displays of temper were often the result, I firmly feel,
of purely physical suffering. His skin was so sensitive

that he wore silk next to the body, and that at a time
when he was not the favoured of fortune.   In London
he bought the silk, and had shirts made for him; so,
too, it was with his other garments.   We went together
to a fashionable tailor in Regent Street, where he ordered that his pockets and the back of his vest should
be of silk, as also the lining of his frock-coat sleeves; for
Wagner could not endure the touch of cotton, as it produced a shuddering sensation throughout the body that
distressed him.   I remember well the tailor's surprise
and explanation that silk for the back of the vest and
lining of the sleeves was not at all necessary, and that
the richest people never had silk linings; besides, it
was not seen.   This last observation brought Wagner
up to one of his indignant bursts, "Never seen! yes;
that's the tendency of this century; sham, sham in
everything; that which is not seen may be paltry and
mean, provided only that the exterior be richly gilded."

On the matter of dress he had, as on most things,
decided opinions!   The waistcoat he condemned as
superfluous, and thought a garment akin to the mediæval doublet in every way more suitable and comely, and
was strongly inclined at one time to revert to that style
of costume himself.   He did go so far as to wear an
uncommon headgear, one sanctioned by antiquity, the
*biretta*, which few people of to-day would have courage
to don.   Thus it was that from physical causes Wagner
preferred silks and velvets, and so a constitutional defect
produced widespread and ungenerous charges of affected
originality and sumptuous luxuriousness.

Wagner was greatly amused at the references to him
in the London Charivari "Punch," wherein his "music

of the future " was described as " Promissory Notes," and on a second occasion when it was asserted that " Lord John Russell is in treaty with Dr. Wagner to compose some music of the future for his Reform Bill."

The fourth concert on the 30th April nearly led to a rupture between Wagner and the directors. The programme was as follows : —

| | |
|---|---|
| Symphony in B flat . . . . . | Lucas. |
| Romanza (" Huguenots ") . . . | Meyerbeer. |
| Nonetto for string and wind instruments . | Spohr. |
| Recitative and Aria . . . . . | Beethoven. |
| Overture (" Ruler of the Spirits ") . . | Weber. |
| Symphony No. 7 . . . . . | Beethoven. |
| Duetto ("cosi fan Tutti ") . . . | Mozart. |
| Overture (" l'Alcade de la Velga ") . . | Onslow. |

Wagner had a decided objection to long programmes. The London public, he said, "overfeed themselves with music ; they cannot healthily digest the lengthy menu provided for them." This programme was distasteful, and what a scene did it produce ! During the aria from " Les Huguenots," the tenor, Herr Reichardt, after a few bars' rest, did not retake his part at the proper moment, upon which Wagner turned to him, — of course without stopping the band, — whereupon the singer made gestures to the audience indicating that the error lay with Wagner. At the end of the vocal piece a slight consternation ensued. Wagner was well aware of the unfriendliness of a section of the critics, and in all probability capital would be made out of this. At the end of the first part of the concert I went to him in the artists' room. His high-pitched excitement and uncontrolled utterances, it was easy to foresee, boded no good. And so when we reached home after the concert there ensued a positive storm of passion. Wagner at his best was impulsive and vehement ; suffering from a miserable insinuation as to his incapacity, he grew furious. On one point he was emphatic,— he would return to Switzerland the next day. All entreaties and protestations were unavailing. Sainton, Lüders, and myself actually hung upon him, so ungovernable was his anger. He knew how I had suffered in the press for championing his cause. "Chef-de-claque," "madman," and "tutto quanti" were the elegant epithets bestowed upon me in print; and if Wagner left now, the enemy would have some show of truth in charging him with admitted incompetence : however, after two or three hours' talking he engaged to stay and see whether he could not win success with the "Tannhäuser" overture, which was to be performed at the next concert.

A distorted report of this event appearing in certain German musical papers, he wrote an explanatory letter to Dresden, in which he stated, "I need not tell you that it was only the entreaties of Ferdinand Praeger and those friends who accompanied me home, that dissuaded me from my somewhat impulsive determination."

At the fifth concert, 14th May, the "Tannhäuser" overture was performed. It came at the end of the first part of another of those long programmes which Wagner disliked so much. In a letter to me to Brighton, where I had gone for a few days, he writes : "These endless programmes, with these interminable masses of instrumental and vocal pieces, torture me." The programme of the fifth concert was : —

| | |
|---|---|
| Symphony . . . . . . | Mozart. |
| Aria . . . . . . . | Paer. |
| Concerto (pianoforte) . . . | Chopin. |
| Aria . . . . . . . | Mozart. |
| Overture (" Tannhäuser ") . . | Wagner. |
| Symphony (" Pastorale ") . . . | Beethoven. |
| Romance . . . . . . | Meyerbeer. |
| Barcarola (vocal) . . . . | Ricci. |
| Overture (" Preciosa ") . . . | Weber. |

How those violin passages on the fourth string in the "Tannhäuser" overture worried the instrumentalists! But as Lipinski had done at Dresden, so Sainton did now in London, and fingered the passages for each individual performer. The concert room was well filled. At the close of the overture tumultuous applause followed, the audience rising and waving handkerchiefs; indeed, Mr. Anderson informed me that he had never known such a display of excitement at a Philharmonic concert where everything was so staid and decorous. As this overture has become perhaps one of the most popular of Wagner excerpts, it will be interesting to read what the two acknowledged leading musical critics in London, *i.e.* of the "Musical World" (who was also the critic of the "Times") and the "Athenæum," said with reference to it. The former wrote : " The instrumentation is always heavy and thick"; and the " Athenæum " said : " Yawning chromatic progressions. . . . a scramble ; . . . a hackneyed eight-bar phrase, the commonplace of which is not disguised by an accidental sharp; . . . the instrumentation is ill-balanced, ineffective, thin, and noisy."

On the morning of the 22d May, Wagner came to Milton Street very early. It was his birthday ; he was forty-two, and the good, devoted Minna had so carefully timed the arrival of her congratulatory letter, that Wagner had received it that morning. He was informed that her gift was a dressing-gown of violet velvet, lined with satin of similar colour, headgear — the *biretta*, so well known — to match, — articles of apparel which furnished his enemies with so much opportunity for charges of ostentation, egregious vanity, etc. Minna knew her husband well; the gift was entirely after his heart. He read us the letter. The only portion of it which I can remember referred to the animal world, — the dog, Peps, who had been presented with a new collar; and of his parrot, who had repeated unceasingly, " Richard Wagner, du bist ein grosser mann " (Richard Wagner, you are a great man).  Wagner's imitation of the parrot was very amusing.  That day the banquet was spread for Richard Wagner.  How he did talk! It was the never-ending fountain leaping from the rock, sparkling and bright, clear and refreshing.  He told us episodes of his early career at Magdeburg and Riga. How he impressed me then with his energy! Truly, he was a man whose onward progress no obstacles could arrest.  The indomitable will, and the excision of " impossible " from his vocabulary, were prominent during the recital of the stirring events of his early manhood.  Certainly it was but a birthday feast, and the talk was genial and merry; yet there went out from me, unbidden and unchecked, " Truly, that is a great man."  Yes, though it was but after-dinner conversation, the reflections were those of a man born to occupy a high position in the world of thought and to compel the submission of others to his intellectual vigour.

At the sixth concert, 28th May, another of those lengthy programmes was gone through, and comprised—

| | |
|---|---|
| Symphony in G minor . . . . | C. Potter. |
| Aria ("Il Seraglio") . . . . | Mozart. |
| Concerto, violin, Mr. Sainton . . | Beethoven. |
| Sicilienne . . . . . . | Pergolesi. |
| Overture ("Leonora") . . . | Beethoven. |
| Symphony, A minor . . . . | Mendelssohn. |
| Aria ("Non mi du") . . . . | Mozart. |
| Song, "O ruddier than the cherry" . | Handel. |
| Overture ("Der Berg-geist") . . | Spohr. |

Think of the anger of Wagner! two symphonies and two overtures in the same evening, besides the vocal music and concerto! This was the fourth concert at which a double dose of symphony and overture was administered to an audience incapable of digesting such a surfeit; it was these "full" programmes, reminding him of the cry of the London omnibus conductors, "full inside," which led him humorously to speak of himself as "conductor of the Philharmonic Omnibus." In the subjoined letter addressed to my wife, anent their daily promenade for the "banquetting," as he called it, of the ducks in the Regent's Park, he subscribes himself as above.

CARISSIMA SORELLA: Croyez-vous le temps assez bon, pour entreprendre notre promenade? Si vous avez le moindre doute, et comme l'affaire ne presse pas du tout, je vous prie de vous en dispenser pour aujourd'hui. Faites-moi une toute petite reponse si je dois venir vous chercher dans un Hansom, ou non?

En tous cas je gouterai des 4 heures des delices de votre table!

Votre cordialement, dévoúé frère,

RICHARD WAGNER,
*Conductor d'omnibus de la Société*
*Philharmonique,* 1855.

The letter was sent by hand, as his rooms were but ten minutes from my house. Perhaps I may here reproduce another short note from Wagner to my wife, with no other intention than showing the degree of close friendship that existed between him and us : —

MA TRÈS CHÈRE SŒUR LÉONIE : Si vous voulez je viendrai demain (Samedi) diver avec vous à 6 heures le soir. Pour Dimanche il m'a fallu accepter une invitation pour Camberwell, que je ne pouvais absolument pas refuser. Serez-vous contente de me voir demain?

Votre très obligé frère,

RICHARD WAGNER.

VENDREDI SOIR, 1865.

Reverting to the concert, the universal criticism was that Wagner had achieved great things with Cipriani Potter's symphony. The music Wagner thought the exact reflection of the man, antiquated but respectable. Potter was a charming man in daily intercourse, of short stature, thin, ample features, huge shaggy eyebrows, stand-up collars behind whose points the old man could hide half his face, and a coat copied from a Viennese pattern of last century. Wagner was genuinely drawn to the man ; and as the inimical "Musical World" said, "took great pains with the symphony" (p. 347). Wagner used to declaim greatly against Mendelssohnian tradition, in the orchestra, — that no movement should be taken too slow, for fear of wearying the audience. However, being a man of strong independent character, he would have his way, and movements were taken as slow as the spirit appeared to require. The critics abused him heartily ; indeed, to such an extent that when the Mozart symphony in E flat was to be done, the directors implored Wagner to allow the orchestra to take the slow movement in the quick *tempo* taught by Mendelssohn. Similarly, when Potter's symphony was to be done, Mr. Potter particularly requested Wagner to take the *andante* somewhat fast, otherwise he feared a failure. But Wagner, who, with his accustomed earnestness had almost the whole by heart, told the composer that the *andante* was an extremely pretty, naïve movement, and that no matter the speed, if the expression were omitted or slurred, the whole would fall flat ; but, added Wagner, it should go thus : Then he sang part to Mr. Potter, who was so touched that he grasped Wagner's hand, saying, " I never dreamed a conductor could take a new work so much to heart as you have ; and as you sing it, just so I meant it." After the concert Mr. Potter was very delighted.

But the work of the evening was the " Leonora " over-ture. Here again Wagner had his reading, one which the orchestra fell in with immediately, for they perceived the truth, the earnestness of what Wagner taught.

At the seventh concert, 11th June, the "Tannhäu-ser" overture was repeated, by royal command. The programme, again " full," included three overtures and two symphonies.

| | |
|---|---|
| Overture (" Chevy Chase ") . . . | Macfarren. |
| Air (" Jessonda ") . . . . | Spohr. |
| Symphony (" Jupiter ") . . . | Mozart. |
| Scena (" Oberon ") . . . . | Weber. |
| Overture (" Tannhäuser ") . . . | Wagner. |
| Symphony (No. 8) . . . . | Beethoven. |
| Song (" Ave Maria ") . . . . | Cherubini. |
| Duet . . . . . . . | Paer. |
| Overture (" Anacreon ") . . . | Cherubini. |

The press did Wagner the justice to state that he showed himself earnest in the matter of Macfarren's "Chevy Chase." His own overture, "Tannhäuser," was again a brilliant success. The queen sent for him into the royal salon, and, congratulating him, said that the Prince Consort was "a most ardent admirer of his." Richard Wagner was pleased at the unaffected and "winning" manner of Her Majesty, who spoke German to him, but as his own account of the interview, written to a friend at Dresden two days after the concert, is now before me, I will reproduce it.

. . . It was therefore the more pleasing to me that the queen (which very seldom happens, and not every year) had signified her intention of being present at the seventh concert, and ordered a repetition of the overture. It was in itself a very pleasant thing that the queen overlooked my exceedingly compromised political position (which with great malignity was openly alluded to in the "Times"), and without fear attended a public performance which I directed. Her further conduct towards me, moreover, infinitely compensated for all the disagreeable circumstances and coarse enmities which hitherto I had encountered. She and Prince Albert, who sat in front before the orchestra, applauded after "Tannhäuser" overture, which closed the first part, with such hearty warmth that the public broke forth into lively and sustained applause. During the interval the queen sent for me into the drawing-room, receiving me in the presence of her suite with these words: "I am most happy to make your acquaintance. Your composition has charmed me." She thereupon made inquiries, during a long conversation, in which Prince Albert took part, as to my other compositions; and asked if it were not possible to translate my operas into Italian. I had, of course, to give the negative to this, and state that my stay here could only be temporary, as the only position open was that of director of a concert-institute which was not properly my sphere. At the end of the concert the queen and the prince again applauded me. . . .

That evening after the concert our usual meeting included Berlioz and his wife. Berlioz had arrived shortly before this concert. Between him and Wagner I knew an awkward constraint existed, which I hardly saw how to bridge over, but I was desirous to bring the two together, and discussing the matter with Wagner, he agreed that perhaps the convivial union after the concert afforded the very opportunity. And so Berlioz came. But his wife was sickly; she lay on the sofa and engrossed the whole of her husband's attention, causing Berlioz to leave somewhat early. He came alone to the next gathering.

After such a triumph as Wagner had had that evening with the overture, he was unusually excited. Hector Berlioz, too, was of an excitable temperament, but could repress it. Not so Wagner. He presented a striking contrast to the polished, refined Frenchman, whose speech was almost classic, through his careful selection of words. Wagner went to the piano, and sang the "Star of Eve," with harmonies which Chellard, a German composer of little note (he had composed "Macbeth" as an opera), said "must be intended." The effect was extremely mirth-provoking, for Wagner could ape the ridiculous with irresistible humour.

That evening Wagner, who was always fond of "tasty" dinners, spoke so glowingly of the French, and their culinary art powers, that we arranged a whitebait dinner at Greenwich at the Ship, one such as the ministers sat down to. Edward Roeckel, the brother of August, came up from Bath for the occasion, and was the giver of the feast. We went by boat. I remember well the journey, for poor Wagner had an attack of *mal-*

*de-mer*, as though he actually were at sea ; the wind was blowing hard, and the water rough.  He appreciated highly the whitebait, especially the dish of devilled ones, and the much-decried cooking of the British ascended several degrees in his opinion.

The attitude of the bulk of the London press towards Wagner I have spoken of as unfriendly ; they condemned him, indeed, before he was heard.  Not content with writing bitterly against him, some persons were in the habit of sending him every scurrilous article that appeared about him.  Who was the instigator I could not positively say.  On one occasion, a letter was addressed to Wagner by an English composer, whom I will not do the honour of naming, who had sought by every possible means to achieve notoriety, stating that it was said Wagner had spoken disparagingly of his name and music, and desiring an explanation with complete satisfaction.  Wagner was excessively angry.  He had never heard the name of the composer, wanted to write an indignant remonstrance, but was dissuaded by me, for I saw both in this and the regular receipt of the anonymously sent papers, an attempt to draw Wagner into a dispute.  Of course the writer was but the tool of others.  In these matters Wagner yielded himself entirely into my hands, though he was often desirous of wielding a fluent and effective pen against his ungenerous enemies.

At that time I had in London a friend on a visit from Paris, a musical amateur of gift, named Kraus.  He was in the confidence of the emperor of the French, holding the position of steward to a branch of the Bonaparte family.  I invited him to meet Wagner, of whom he was an admirer. Now listen to what took place. Wagner did all that was possible by persuasive language to induce Kraus to move the emperor to do something for Berlioz. It was to no purpose that we were told the emperor was not enthusiastic for music, and that so many impossible difficulties were in the way. Wagner kept to his point ; Berlioz was poor, had been compelled to resort to pledging trinkets, etc., whereby to live, and that it was a crime to the art which he, Kraus, professed to love, that Berlioz should be in want. I have thought this incident worthy of notice, as showing the good-will of Wagner for a brother artist was stronger than the icy restraint that existed between them when they met.

Much has been written and said of Wagner's extravagance, his prodigality of luxury. Well, 'tis true, Wagner knew not self-denial, and that his taste was ever for the beautiful and costly. With such characteristics, his indulgence in the choice and elegant can be understood. Should something pretty attract his attention in the street, say in a shop window, he would stop suddenly and exclaim aloud what he thought, heedless of the people standing by. Wagner was not wealthy when in London, yet he spent freely ; silk for shirts for ordinary wear, and costly Irish laces for Minna. In these shopping expeditions my wife was his companion, and Wagner showed he possessed that kindly tact born of natural goodness of heart, in discovering what might be considered pretty, when it was straightway purchased and presented to her.

I now come to the last concert, the eighth, which took place on the 25th June. Again the programme included two symphonies and two overtures : —

| | |
|---|---|
| Symphony (No. 3, C minor) . . . | Spohr. |
| Scena ("Der Freischütz") . . . | Weber. |
| Concerto (pianoforte) . . . . | Hummel. |
| Song . . . . . . . | Haydn. |
| Overture ("Midsummer Night's Dream") | Mendelssohn. |
| Symphony (No. 4, B flat) . . . | Beethoven. |
| Duet ("Prophète") . . . . | Meyerbeer. |
| Overture ("Oberon") . . . . | Weber. |

At the close of this concert he met with applause, hearty from a section, but I cannot say it was universal. He had won many friends and had made many enemies, but on the whole, Wagner was satisfied. That evening our last festive gathering was very jovial. Wagner expressed himself with all the enthusiasm his warm, impulsive nature was capable of; he was deeply sensible of the value of his stay here. He had almost retired from the world, but now Paris and Germany would again be brought to hear of him. He regretted much the spiteful criticism that had fallen upon me, and which I was likely to meet with still more. We remained with Wagner until about three in the morning, helping him to prepare for his departure from London that 26th June.

I have refrained from making any quotations about myself. Those who are interested enough to know how a pioneer is treated by his contemporaries will discover many silly, impotent reflections upon me in the musical journals of the period. I will content myself with reproducing a few extracts about Richard Wagner and his music. The principal papers in London, those that directed public opinion in musical matters, were the "Musical World," "Times," "Athenæum," and "Sunday Times." Four days after Wagner had left, the following sad specimens appeared. The "Musical World," 30th June, 1855 :—

We hold that Herr Richard Wagner *is not a musician at all* . . . this excommunication of pure melody, this utter contempt of time and rhythmic definition, so notorious in Herr Wagner's compositions (we were about to say Herr Wagner's *music*), is also one of the most important points of his system, as developed at great length in the book of "Oper und Drama." . . . It is clear to us that Herr Wagner wants to upset both opera and drama. Let him then avow it without all this mystification of words — this tortuous and sophisticated systematizing. . . . He is just now cleansing the Augean stables of the musical drama, and meanwhile, with a fierce iconoclasm, is knocking down imaginary images, and levelling temples that are but the creations of his own brain. When he has done this to his own satisfaction, he will have to grope disconsolate among the ruins of his contrivance, like Marius on the crumbled walls of Carthage, and in a brown study begin to reflect, "What next?" For he, Wagner, can build up nothing himself. He can destroy, but not reconstruct. He can kill, but not give life. . . . What do we find there in the shape of Wagnerian "Art Drama." So far as music is concerned, nothing better than chaos — "absolute" chaos. The symmetry of form — ignored or else abandoned; the consistency of keys and their relations — overthrown, contemned, demolished; the charm of rhythmic measure, the whole art of phrase and cadence, the true basis of harmony and the indispensable government of modulation, cast away for a reckless, wild, extravagant, and demagogic cacophony, the symbol of profligate libertinage! . . . Look at "Lohengrin" — that "*best* piece"; hearken to "Lohengrin" — that "*best* piece." Your answer is there written and sung. Cast that book upon the waters; it tastes bitter, as the little volume to the prophet. It is poison — *rank poison.* . . .

This man, this Wagner, this author of "Tannhäuser," of "Lohengrin," and so many other hideous things — and above all, the overture to "Der Fliegende Holländer," the most hideous and detestable of the whole — this preacher of the "future," was born to feed

spiders with flies, not to make happy the heart of man with beautiful melody and harmony.  What is music to him, or he to music?
. . .  Who are the men that go about as his apostles?  Men like
Liszt — the apostle of Weimar and Professor Praeger, madmen, enemies of music to the knife, who, not born for music, and conscious
of their impotence, revenge themselves by endeavouring to annihilate
it. . . .  Wagner's theories are impious.  No words can be strong
enough to condemn them; no arraignment before the judgment-seat
of truth too stern and summary; no verdict of condemnation too
sweeping and severe. . . .  Not to compare things earthly with
things heavenly, has Mendelssohn lived among us in vain? . . .  All
we can make out of "Lohengrin," by the flaming torch of truth, is
an incoherent mass of rubbish, with no more real pretension to be
called music than the jangling and clashing of gongs and other
uneuphonious instruments. . . .  Wagner, on the contrary, who,
though a mythical dramatist, is no musician and very little poet.
. . .  He cannot write music himself, and for that reason arraigns it.
His contempt for Mendelssohn is simply ludicrous; and we would
grant him forty years to produce one melodious phrase like any of
those so profusely scattered about in the operas of Rossini, Weber,
Auber, and Meyerbeer. . . .  Wagner is as unable to invent genuine
tune as pure harmony, and he knows it.  Hence "the books." . . .
Richard Wagner and his followers — sham prophets. . . .  Listen
to their wily eloquence, and you find yourself in the coils of rattle-
snakes. . . .  There is as much difference between "Guillaume
Tell" and "Lohengrin" as between the sun and ashes.

## From the "Sunday Times," May, 1855 :—

Music is not his special birthgift — is not for him an articulate
language or a beautiful form of expression. . . .  Richard Wagner
is a desperate charlatan, endowed with worldly skill and vigorous
purpose enough to persuade a gaping crowd that the nauseous
compound he manufactures has some precious inner virtue, that
they must live and ponder yet ere they perceive. . . .  Anything
more rambling, incoherent, unmasterly, cannot well be conceived.
In composition it would be a scandal to compare him with the men
of reputation this country possesses.  Scarcely the most ordinary

ballad writer but would shame him in the creation of melody, and no English harmonist of more than one year's growth could be found sufficiently without ears and education to pen such vile things.

The "Athenæum," upon the fifth concert says : —

The overture to "Tannhäuser" is one of the most curious pieces of patchwork ever passed off by self-delusion for a complete and significant creation.

The critic, after finding a plagiarism of Mendelssohn and Cherubini, continues : —

The instrumentation is ill-balanced, ineffective, thin and noisy.

The "Musical World" of 13th October, 1855, says : —

TANNHÄUSER —We never before heard an opera in which the orchestra made such a fuss; the cacophony, noise, and inartistic elaborations!  We can detect little in "Tannhäuser" not positively commonplace.  It is tedious beyond endurance.  We are made aware, by a few bars, that he has never learned how to handle the implements; and that, if it were given him as a task to compose the overture to "Tancredi," he would be at straits to accomplish anything so easy, clear, and natural.

# CHAPTER XX.

## 1855–1856.

RICHARD WAGNER left London for Paris, from whence he wrote immediately the following letter. The humorously descriptive reference to the Channel passage is characteristic.

DEAREST FRIENDS: Heartiest thanks for your love, which after all is the one thing which has made the dull London lastingly dear to me. I wish you joy and happiness, and, if possible, to be spared the dreariness of the London pavement. Were it not that I regret to have left you, I would speak of the delightful feeling which has taken possession of me since I have returned to the continent. Here the weather is beautiful, the air balmy and invigorating. The past night's rest has somewhat recruited my strength after the recent fatigue. At present I am enjoying peace and quiet, which I hope will soon enable me to resume work, the only enjoyment in life still left to me.

I have not much to tell of adventures, except that when I went on board I felt rather queer. I lay down in the cabin and had just succeeded in getting into a comfortable position for sleep, hoping thereby to keep off the sea-sickness, when the steward shook me, wanting to look at my ticket. To comply, I had to turn over so as to get to my pocket. This movement caused me to feel unwell; and then the unhappy man claiming his steward's fee, I was obliged to sit up in order to find my money. This new movement brought on the sea-sickness, so that just as he thankfully received his gratuity, he also received the whole of my supper. Yet he still seemed quite content, notwithstanding, whilst I had such a fit of laughter that drove away both sickness and drowsiness so that I entered Calais in tolerably good spirits.

The custom-house visiting only took place in Paris. It was well for me that the lace I had secreted for Minna was not discovered. Here I soon found my friend Kietz, to whom I poured out my heart about you, dear friends. To-morrow I leave with a Zurich friend, who has waited for me. From Zurich you shall have news. As I write to you all, I beg you to divide my greetings, and do this from the depth of your hearts. To my sister Léonie, give her as well a hearty kiss for me.

Adieu, good lovable humankind, think with love of thy

RICHARD WAGNER.

PARIS, 28th June, 1855.

From Paris he went direct to Zurich, where Minna was waiting for him. He had scarcely arrived when he sent me the following. It is noteworthy, as it illustrates how a great man could interest himself in the small concerns of home life. His affection for domestic pets is once more touched upon, and that humour, which but rarely forsook him even in his pessimistic Schopenhauerian utterances, again playfully laughs throughout the letter.

Best greetings from Switzerland.

I hope you have already received tidings of me from Lüders. From you, however, I have not yet heard anything. You might at least have written to say you were glad to have got rid of me, how sister Léonie fares, and how Henry is, whether " Gypsy " (the dog) has made his appearance in society, whether the cat has still its bad cough. Heaven! how many things there are of which I ought to be informed in order to be perfectly at ease. As for me, I am still idle. My wife has made me a new dressing-gown, and what is more, wonderfully fine silk trousers for home wear, so that all the work I do is to loll about in this costume, first on one sofa and then on another.

On Monday next I go with my wife, the dog, and bird, to Seelisberg; there I think I shall at last get straight! If you could but visit me there. My address for the present is Kurhaus, Sonnenberg, Seelisberg, Canton Uri. I do not know how I can sufficiently express the pleasure which my wife wishes me to convey to you. Whilst I unpacked I chatted, and kept on chatting and unpacking. Several times she was deeply moved, particularly when we came to the carefully marked and neatly folded socks. Again and again she called out, " What a good woman that Léonie must be ! " and then when the needle-case came out and that beautiful thimble, both she and I were mightily pleased. We wish your wife the happiest confinement that woman ever had, and at least six healthy children all at once with heavenly organized brains, every one to be born with a pocket containing ten thousand pounds each, and further, that your wife shall be able on the same evening of the confinement to dance a polka in the Praeger drawing-room. May it please heaven that this reverential wish shall be tenfold fulfilled, then your love for children will be fully satisfied.

In a few days you will receive a box with three medallions in plaster of Paris. These were modelled by the daughter of " the Princess Lichtenstein," and are to be divided thus : one for the Praeger family, one for the family Sainton and Lüders (who I sincerely trust will never separate, and who are regarded by me as one family), and the other for the poor fellow of Manchester Street, Klindworth, the invalid, from whom I am expecting news about his performance of last Wednesday. I trust he is already at Richmond enjoying the benefit of hydropathy. I purpose writing to him as soon as I know his address. For the present greet the poor fellow heartily for me, and in my name try to console him for me. I will soon write to Sainton, and for that occasion I will pull together all the French I learned in London, so that I might be able to express to him my opinion that he is a splendid fellow. And what is dear Lüders about? I hear that he has headed the riot in Hyde Park. Is that true?[1] I hope he has not used my letter to Prince Albert in making lobster salad. I have often been unlucky with letters of mine. Even yesterday I found reproduced in Brendel's " Neue Zeitschrift " a letter I had written to my old friend, Fischer, at Dresden. It has most disagreeably affected me, for if I had wished to express myself about the London annoyances I should have done it in a different manner, but I had not the

---

[1] This is Wagner's characteristic jocularity, Lüders being a man of short and slight stature and most mild in temper.

slightest wish to do anything of the kind. However, I am heartily glad my time of penance is past, and forgive with my whole heart Englishmen for being what they are; still I am resolved, even in thought, never to have anything more whatsoever to do with them. But you, my dear friends, I will ever cherish in remembrance, and if all that is agreeable be but a negative of pain, then by the memory of your love and friendship is the period of my London tribulation blotted out.

A thousand hearty thanks for your love! Now you will, I hope, give me the joy of good news, and say that you love me still. To dear Edward [1] give my best greetings. It was a great pity I did not see him again.

Farewell, my dear Ferdinand; all happiness to yours, and to the dear wife good wishes.

RICHARD WAGNER.

ZURICH, 7th July, 1855.

The next letter, dated eight days later than the preceding, will be admitted a jewel in Wagner's crown. Picture this great intellect, the creator of the colossal Nibelung tetralogy (with its Gräne, the steed of the Valkyrie), crying "incessantly" over the grave of a dead dog, postponing the removal of his household to nurse the dying creature until its last moments, and then himself burying it in the garden. The whole of this touching recital bespeaks a tenderness, a wealth of human love and large-heartedness, which show Wagner, the man!

DEAREST FRIEND FERDINANDUS: A thousand hearty congratulations to the newly born. Right gladly I agree to become god-father and, if you think it will bring fortune, add my surname as well.

I arrived here in this paradise a few days ago. I read your letter on the left corner of the balcony of the hotel, the picture of which heads this letter. Occasionally, while reading, I raised my eyes

---

[1] Edward Roeckel of Bath.

and looked beyond upon the magnificent Alps, which you cannot fail to notice at the side of the hotel. I say that I looked from the letter occasionally, since its contents afforded me matter for reflection, and I found solace and comfort in the contemplation of the sacred and noble surroundings. You have no conception how beautiful it is here, how pure the air that one breathes, and how beneficially this wonderful spectacle acts on me. I fancy you would become delirious with joy at the prospect, so that the return to London would be a sad event; yet you must undertake this trip next year with your dear wife.

But how strange that the same incident should have happened to us both at about the same moment! You remember that I expected to see my old and faithful dog, "Peps."[1]  Well, shortly before my arrival he had been taken ill, but nevertheless he received me with the greatest delight, and soon began to improve somewhat in health. The day of our departure for Seelisberg was already fixed, where, as I wrote to you, I was going with my wife, my dog, and bird.[2]  Suddenly dangerous symptoms showed themselves in " Peps," in consequence of which we put off our journey for two days so as to nurse the poor dying dog. Up to the last moment "Peps" showed me a love as touching as to be almost heartrending; kept his eyes fixed on me, and, though I chanced to move but a few steps from him, continued to follow me with his eyes. He died in my arms on the night of the 9th–10th of the month, passing away without a sound, quietly and peacefully. On the morrow, midday, we buried him in the garden beside the house. I cried incessantly, and since then have felt bitter pain and sorrow for the dear friend of the past thirteen years, who ever worked and walked with me. It has clearly taught me that the world exists only in our hearts and conception. That the same fate should befall your young dog at almost the same moment has deeply affected me. I have often thought of " Gypsy,"[3] and wished I had taken him with me, and now that fiery creature too is also suddenly dead!!  There is something terrible in all this!!!  And yet there are those who would scoff at our feeling in such a matter!

[1] " Peps " was the dog which helped to compose " Tannhäuser."
[2] The parrot.
[3] Wagner used to take " Gypsy " out for a walk daily.

Alas! I am often tired of life, yet life is ever returning in a new guise, alluring us anew to pain and sorrow. With me now it is sublime nature which ever impels me to cling to life as a new love, and thus it is I have begun once more to work. You have again been presented with a new-born life. I wish you happiness with all my heart. I feel as though I had some claim to the boy, for it was during the last four months prior to his entering the world that I came a new member into your household. The affection I sought was vouchsafed to me in the highest degree; the mother's mind was no doubt much occupied with that strange, whimsical individual, whom, to his great joy, she so heartily welcomed. May it not be, perhaps, that before he saw the light, this may have influenced the little stranger! if so, my heartiest wish is that it may bring him blessings. Now give my best greetings to sister Léonie, and thank her heartily for all the kindness she showed me. I can but wish her the happiest motherly joys; remember me to Henry; he is to care for his little brother as if it were a sister.

Farewell, and let me soon know how you all are, Keep up, and above all, see well that you come to visit me next year; kindly remember me also to my few London friends. Lüders and Sainton I thank for their friendly letter; you will soon hear from me. Farewell, dear brother,

Your

RICHARD WAGNER.

P.S. Liszt will not come until October. Ask Klindworth to write to me. Thousand kind things from my wife.

SEELISBERG, CANTON URI, 15th July, 1855.

In the next letter he speaks sorrowfully of the demon of ill-health which had settled in his house. Poor Minna suffered with heart-disease, an illness to which she eventually succumbed, whilst he, too, was somewhat broken down, and shortly to be laid upon a sick-bed. His only relief from worry and trouble was work. Indeed, the major portion of his work was done at times when the horizon was dark for him.

Best thanks, dear friend, for your letter, which was, alas, sad enough to make me sad too.   The worst of misfortune in a life like yours is that in surveying all circumstances, it is positively unrectifiable: to revolt against it, even at the best, has still something ridiculous in it.   To him, who like you suffers keenly (and amongst your surroundings must perforce suffer the most), all I can say is, think, dear friend, no man is happy except he who is foolish enough to think that he is.   You and I are not fit for this life except to be tired of it; he who becomes so the soonest finishes his task the quickest.   All so-called "fortunate events" are but deceptive palliations, making the evil worse.   I know this is capable of being understood in a double sense, so that it might be interpreted either as a trivial commonplace or the deepest possible reflection.   I must leave it to chance how you will understand it.   The only ray of light in the dark night of our life is that which sympathy affords us.   We only lose consciousness of our own misery when we feel that of others.   Entire freedom from one's own sorrow is only possible if one could live solely for the sorrows of others, but the evil of it is, that one cannot do this continually, as one's own troubles always return the stronger to attack the feelings.   I, for my part, must say that since in London I have never had my mind free from troubles.   The demon of sickness has come to lodge in my house.   My wife, particularly, causes me great anxieties.   Her ever-increasing ill-health helps to render me very sad.   Worried and troubled, I resumed work.   I struggle at it, as work is the only power that brings to me oblivion and makes me free.   Only look to it that next year you come to Switzerland; meanwhile amuse yourself as much as you can in your polemical war against London music-artists and critics, not on my account, however, but only as I believe it is a good channel to absorb your otherwise sad thoughts.

From New York I have just received an invitation to go over and conduct there for six months; it would be well paid.   It is fortunate, however, that the emolument is not after all so very large, or else, perhaps, I might myself be obliged to seriously consider the matter.   But of course I shall not accept the invitation.   I had enough in London.   I am somewhat fidgety that you have not yet acknowledged my three medallions, one for you, one for Sainton and Lüders, and one for Klindworth.   I paid freight for them some time ago, and

thought they would have been in your hands long before this. If
you have not yet received them, I beg of you to make inquiries at
the post-office, since I sent the little box from Basle by the mail,
and your address was correctly written. Do not forget to speedily
inform me of its arrival.

Please send at once to Berlin the box which I left at your house,
containing my manuscripts, and address it to the Royal Music Director, Julius Stern, Dessauer Strasse No. 2. Do not prepay it. You
may have some expense on my account which I will settle with you
when we meet. Do not forget to mention it.

Perhaps you have heard already that " Tannhäuser " has created
a perfect furore at Munich. I felt constrained to laugh at the
sudden veering round in my favour when I remembered that only
two years ago Lachner contrived that the performance of the overture to " Tannhäuser " should be a complete fiasco. On the whole,
I live almost entirely isolated. Working, walking, and a little reading constitute my present existence. At present, I am expecting
Liszt at Christmas. How fares my sister Léonie? Well, I hope.
You write so ambiguously about it that I cannot make out the exact
thing. How is the boy? Is he really called Richard Wagner? Are
you not right glad to have him? Greet your dear wife for me with
all my heart, and tell her I often think of her with pleasure, and of
the friendly interest she took in me. My love to the poor hypo-
chondriacal Lüders. How well I ought to have felt myself in London. When he became excited, he was irresistible. I will write to
Sainton soon. He is happy, and finds himself best where he is.

Farewell, dear Ferdinand. A thousand thanks for your friendship. When things go badly with you, laugh at them.

Adieu,

Your

RICHARD WAGNER.

ZURICH, 14th September, 1855.

The next letter shows Wagner in a new light. It is
addressed to my wife in her native language, French.
Wagner has freely admitted in his published writings that he had no gift for languages, still he spoke
French well, truly, not as a born Frenchman, yet, as a

thoughtful man, and moreover as an earnest student he was able to express himself with clearness and freedom, and to a degree was master of the idiom. Intellect, combined with earnestness, will forge a path through difficulties where education alone would halt. Berlioz was an educated Frenchman, and expressed himself in elegant and polished diction — it was like music to hear him speak — yet he soon succumbed to Wagner's torrent of enthusiasm. Of course this in part finds its natural explanation in Wagner ever having something new to say, and "Wagner eloquent" was irresistible. But as he ever depreciated his ability in French, I have inserted the following in the original (with translation) so as to enable the reader to form his own judgment.

This letter is a well-drawn portrait of Wagner by himself. It shows the boy in the man. Picture this man, after a serious illness of some weeks, which must have been terribly irksome to a man of his active temperament, setting himself the task the first day of his convalescence to write in French and at such length. Instead of grumbling at the mental miseries such an illness must have caused him, through the interruption of that work so dear to him, he roused himself, in order to amuse by his boyish, humorous chat, "his sister Léonie," whom he knew was all sympathy for him. The boy's affectionate heart is plainly discernible in the man, tried and battered as he was by the world. It makes one think of the boy's gentle love for his "little mother," as he endearingly spoke of his mother. In him there were always glimpses of sunshine which would burst forth, aye, in the midst of the storms which, caused by disappointment and ill-usage, raged within himself or round about him.  It was impossible for those who knew Wagner not to love him, notwithstanding those defects of character which he possessed; they disappeared entirely in the love one bore him, and the worship his mighty genius compelled.  The sun itself has spots, which, notwithstanding, do not prevent it from glittering with radiance.  Why should not Wagner be allowed the privilege of the sun?

ANSICHT VOM KURHAUSE SONNENBERG AUF<br>SEELISBERG, CT. URI.

MA TRÈS CHÈRE SŒUR! Allons donc! Je vais vous écrire en français.  Dieu donne que vous en entendiez quelques mots — cequi ne sera pas chose facile.  Mais je ne serai pas si absurde de me donner de la peine, pour faire de bonnes phrases; cela sera l'affaire du Dr. Wylde, qui s'y entend probablement aussi bien qu'à la musique!  Plutôt je porterai sur ce papier quelques bêtises de mon genre, qui ne toucheront au caractère d'aucune langue, ni vivante, ni morte.

Enfin, je vous félicité, ma soeur, d'être doublement mère!  L'événement que Ferdinand m'a annoncé il y a quelque temps, était prévu par moi moyennant d'un pressentiment prophétique, qui me naissait pendant mon séjour à Londres; car, pendant que je me souhaitais au diable — c'est à dire: hors du monde — je m'avisais, que le bon Dieu se preparait à remplir la lacune attendue, en mettant au monde un remplaçant pour moi.  Mais ce bon Dieu s'est trompé, comme il lui arrivé quelques fois (en toute confiance soit dit!); le diable ne m'a pas encore accepté; je suis resté au monde, par obstination seulement, comme vous allez voir — et mon remplaçant est arrivé pendant que je vis encore, de la sorte qu'il y a maintenant deux Richard Wagner.  Ainsi, je ne suis pas surpris de cet événement, que j'ai plutôt préparé en quelque sorte (et sans la moindre offense pour Ferdinand!) seulement par ma résolution de quitter la terre, résolution, dont le changement me procure maintenant le plaisir passablement rare, de vivre ensemble avec mon remplacant future, de faire sa connaissance personelle, de m'entende avec lui sur la direction des concerts de la Société Philharmonique, enfin sur mille choses d'une importance extrême, qui ne s'arrangent pas si bien par une distance si énorme que celle de la mort à la vie. — Cette affaire a donc bien réussie. Seulement je plains de vous avoir causé tout de désagrements et de souffrances, comme vous les avez dû subir pour cela (je le dis vous savez toujours sans la moindre offense pour Ferdinand !). Jugez donc de la grande et intime satisfaction, que je viens d'eprouver à la nouvelle de votre rétablissement complêt, et croyez à la sincérité bien cordiale des félicitations, que je vous addresse.

Maintenant je n'ai pas d'autre soin, que de m'entendre aussitôt que possible avec ma doublette sur nos démarches réunies pour conquérir le monde avant de le quitter de ma part c'est-à-dire : de la part de Richard Wagner l'aîné. Ainsi je vous prie de me donner toujours des nouvelles bien promptes et exactes sur l'état du développement de mon remplaçant. J'ai déjâ très besoin de ses fonctions auxiliares. On m'a invité de venir en Amérique, pour faire de la musique à New York et à Boston on m'a promis des recettes très fortes, et mille autres choses. Mais il m'est impossible d'y aller : cela serait alors l'affaire de Richard Wagner le jeune ; quand pourra-t-il accepter l'invitation ? Expliquez-vous, je vous en prie, très clairement sur ce point là. Aussi j'ai une multitude de projets de sujets d'opéras dans ma tête : Ferdinand les croît sous le toît de ma maison ; il se trompe, ma maison c'est moi, et le toît c'est mon crâne. Je n'ai ni le temps, ni la tranquillité nécessaire pour les ôter de leur cage, là, où ils sont encore enfermés : ainsi, ce sera l'affaire de mon remplaçant de delivrer ces plans d'opéras et d'en donner ce qui lui plaît à son petit père pour qu'il en fasse la musique. Quand sera-t-il assez développé pour ce travail bien pressant ? Répondez-moi avec promptitude sur cette demande ; demandez à Ferdinand si elle est importante ! Ah ! mon dieu ! il y a encore tant d'autres choses à arranger ensemble qu'une conférence prochaine me parait indispensable. Connaissez-vous le Dr. Wylde ? Eh bien ! j'attends son invitation pour lui donner des leçons de "musique du future." Richard Wagner le jeune ne serait-il pas encore mieux avancé que moi pour instruire ce genre de musique, puis qu'il est encore plus du future que moi ? Que voulez-vous ? Il n'y a pas de temps à perdu. Dépechez-vous du peu d'education qu'il faudra pour mûrir les facultés de mon remplaçant, et écrivez moi aussitôt télégraphe quand le moment sera venu, ce moment de développement accompli que j'attends avec impatience. N'est-ce pas, chère soeur Léonie? N'est-ce pas, ma mère (entendez-bien !!) n'est-ce pas, vous n'oublierez pas cela par hasard? Et surtout vous ne manquerez pas d'instruire mon " alter-ego " de gagner de l'argent? le seul talent (entre autres) que, par une faute incomprehensible dans mon education, je n'ai pas cultivé dutout ce qui me cause quelquefois, *i.e.* toujours — des peines horribles, puisque je suis luxurieux, prodigue et dépensier par nature, beaucoup plus que Sardanapale et tous les empereurs Romains pris ensemble. J'ai donc besoin d'un autre moi! (" passez-moi le mot ") qui gagne énormément d'argent pour moi. Vous n'oubliez pas cela, et m'enverrez sous peu de temps quelques millions, volés par mon remplaçant aux admirateurs innombrables que j'ai l'aissé en Angleterre. J'y pense bien, je trouve que c'est là le point décisif, de la sorte que je vous donne le conseil final, de faire apprendre à mon remplaçant seulement ce que je n'ai jamais appris-moi; cela veut dire faire de l'argent — " make money " — mais beaucoup! Beaucoup! Enor-mément beaucoup!

Voilà ma bénédiction : — que Dieu m'exance !!

Quant à Richard Wagner l'aîné, je ne puis vous donner que des nouvelles peu agréables : il se traîne à travers la vie comme un far-deau. Sa seule réjouissance est son travail; son plus grand déplaisir est quand il perd l'envie de travailler; mais la cause de sa mort sera un jour le sort terrible auquel il lui faut livrer ses travaux, à la mutilation et à la destruction parfaite par des exécutants bêtes ou mérchants; contre lesquels il lui est défendu de protéger son œuvre, puisqui'il est exilé de là, où il est exécuté. (Pensez donc à mon remplaçant!) Tout autre malheur ne me touche plus forte-ment : mais celui-là me touche au cœur et aux entrailles. Sous de telles influences je perds quelques fois, l'envie de travailler parfaite-ment et pour longtemps : ces époques sont terribles, car alors il ne me resto rien, rien pour me soulager. Aux derniers mois j'ai regagné heureusement un peu mon ancien zéle, et je travaillais assez bien au second de nos drames musicals; que je voulais finir à Lon-dres (sot que j'étais!) Malheureusement j'étais forcé de passer les dernières sermaines au lit, en proie d'une maladie, long temps cachée en moi, et enfin éclatée — j'espère à mon salut. Je viens de quitter le lit hier, et me voilà aujourdhui à la table pour vous écrire. Soyez indulgent, et pardonnez-moi le tas de bêtises que je vous envoie avec cette lettre ; mon écrit ne sera pas probablement mieux que ma conversation, qui était bien triste et bêto. Mais néanmoins vous m'avez voué votre amitié, car vous savez lire entre les lignes de ma conversation. Soyez bien cordialement remercié pour ce bienfait ! Maintenant soyez heureuse, ce qu'on est qu'au milieu de désagrements et de souffrances de toute sorte — par un cœur plein de compassion, de cette compassion qui s'égaie aussi à l'apperception d'un sourire de l'autrui, même si ce n'était que le sourire exalté de la mélancolie. Par example : —

Vive le punch et la salade de hommard ! Vive Lüders qui la préparait ! Vive Ferdinand qui devorait les os ! Vive Sainton qui venait tard, mais qui venalt ! Vive Klindworth, quine mangeait et ne buvait pas, mais qui assistait ! Vive, vive Léonie, qui riait de compassion de notre hilarité ! Cela n'était pas si mal ! Soyons reconnaissants, et restons amis ! Et vous ma chère mère? restez ma soeur !                    Adieu.

Votre

RICHARD WAGNER l'aîné.

P.S.   La prochaine lettre sera à Sainton.   Je ne puis pas dépenser autant de Français dans un jour ! —

3D NOVEMBRE, 1855.

ANSICHT VON KIRHAUSE SONNENBERG AUF<br>SEELISBERG, CT. URI.

MY DEAR SISTER: Now, then, I am going to write to you in French. May heaven help you to understand something of it, for I fear it will not be an easy matter. I shall not, however, be foolish enough to give myself the trouble of making fine phrases. That I leave to Dr. Wylde,[1] who, no doubt, understands that much better than he does composing. Rather do I prefer to put down on paper some stupidities of my own, which will have no relation either to a dead or living language.

Now, I congratulate you, my sister, in being doubly mother.[2]

---

[1] Then conductor of the New Philharmonic concerts, at present director of the London Academy of Music.     [2] Meaning of two Richard Wagners.

The event, Ferdinand had announced to me some time ago, I had foreseen, by means of prophetic vision generated during my stay in London; for whilst I was wishing myself to the devil — that is to say, out of the world — I perceived that Providence was preparing to fill the gap, by sending into the world a substitute. But the same Providence made a mistake, as He occasionally does (this, remember, is quite confidential!); the devil has not yet wanted me; I have remained in the world, as you shall see, through sheer obstinacy, and my other self has arrived whilst I am still living, so that now there are two Richard Wagners!!

I am not surprised, then, at the event, which, by my resolve to quit the world, I had in some measure prepared (this without the slightest offence to Ferdinand); but fate having ordained otherwise, I have the rare pleasure of living at the same time with my future substitute, of making his personal acquaintance, of coming to some understanding with him about conducting the concerts of the Philharmonic Society; in short, upon a thousand things of the greatest importance, which could not conveniently be arranged at such an enormous distance as that of the other world to this. So the event has been quite a success. But I must ever regret to have caused you so much pain and suffering on that account. I say it, you know, always without any offence to Ferdinand. Think, then, of the great personal relief I have just experienced at the news of your convalescence, and believe in the warm-hearted sincerity of my congratulations.

I have no other care now but to come to an understanding as quickly as possible with my other self, respecting our united efforts to conquer the world before I myself (*i.e.* Richard Wagner the elder) leave it. I therefore entreat you to keep me well informed of the exact state of the development of my substitute. Even at this very moment I very much need his help.

I have received an invitation from America to conduct at New York and Boston. In addition to a thousand other things I have been promised very large receipts. It is, however, quite impossible for me to accept; that must be the province of Richard Wagner the younger. When will he be able to accept the invitation? I beg of you to be very explicit on this point. Further, I have a multitude of projects and subjects for operas in my head. Ferdinand imagines them under the roof of my house; he is mistaken, my house is myself, the roof my skull. But, alas, I have neither the time nor the requisite tranquillity to release them from the prison-house in which they are confined: that also, then, must be the work of my other self; and when he has liberated them he may give what he likes of them to his father to set to music. When will he be developed enough for this pressing work? Be prompt in your reply on this point. Ask Ferdinand if it is not important! Ah! good heavens! there are such a number of other things which we must arrange together that an early conference is imperative.

Do you know Dr. Wylde? Well, I am expecting an invitation from him to give him lessons in the " music of the future." But will not Richard Wagner the younger be better fitted than I to teach that kind of music, since he is still more closely connected with the future? What think you? There is no time to lose. Make haste with the little education absolutely nesessary for ripening the faculties of my *alter ego*, and telegraph to me the moment the time has arrived — that time of complete development so anxiously waited for by me. Is it not so, dear sister Léonie? Eh! my mother (you understand!) Now you must not fail to remember this.

But above all, you must not omit to teach my *alter ego* to make money, the one talent of all others which, by some incomprehensible fault in my education, has never been cultivated. And this causes me sometimes (*i.e.* always) horrible anxieties, since by nature I am luxurious, prodigal, and extravagant, much more than Sardanapalus and all the old Roman emperors put together. In this I am sadly in want of another self (pardon me for saying so), who will gain money enormously. Now be sure and do not forget this and send me as soon as possible a few millions, stolen by my double from the innumerable admirers I have left behind in England! On pondering over the situation, I perceive that herein lies the crucial point, so that my last entreaty is that you instruct my other self in that which I have never learnt, viz. making money — make money — but much! Much! Enormously much!

This is my prayer; may heaven hearken to me!

Of Richard Wagner the elder I can only give you poor news. He drags himself through life as a burden. His only delight is his work. His greatest sorrow, the loss of desire to work. The cause of his death will one day be the terrible fate to which he cannot help exposing his works, *i.e.* to their mutilation and complete destruction by stupid or wicked executants, from whom he is powerless of protecting them, since he is an exile from that land where they are being performed. (Think, therefore, of my *alter ego!*) No other misfortune affects me so keenly. This touches me to the heart, to the very core. It is when under such feelings that I occasionally lose completely — yes, even for a long time — the desire to work. These periods are terrible, for then nothing remains, nothing to comfort me. During the last few months I had happily regained a little of my old enthusiasm, and I had been working pretty well at the second of my musical dramas, which I had hoped to finish in London (fool that I was!). But alas, I have been confined, during the last few weeks, to my bed, a prey to a long latent illness, which, having at last broken out, I hope has been the saving of my life. I only left my sick-bed yesterday, and here I am to-day at my table, writing to you. Be indulgent, and excuse the mass of nonsense I am sending you in this letter. My correspondence will probably be no better than my conversation, which was very dull and stupid. But nevertheless, you vowed to me your friendship, for you know how to read between the lines of my conversation. I thank you very heartily for that kindness!

Now be happy, although one lives in the midst of annoyances and sufferings of all kinds — for it is only by a heart full of compassion which brightens up even at the perception of a smile from another, though it be but the forced smile of melancholy.

Three cheers for the punch and lobster salad! Long live Lüders, who prepared it! Long live Ferdinand, who devoured the bones! Long live Sainton, who came late, but who came! Long live Klindworth, who neither ate nor drank, but who was present! Long live, long live Léonie, who laughed sympathetically at our boisterousness! That was not so bad. Let us be grateful, and let us remain friends. And you, my dear mother, remain my sister.

Adieu.<br>Yours,

November 3d, 1855.         RICHARD WAGNER THE ELDER.

P.S. The next letter will be to Sainton. I cannot dole out so much French in one day.

The next letter, written three months after the preceding, is of interest in showing that Wagner kept up the practice of his daily promenade.

DEAREST FRIEND: Thanks for your beautiful London notice, which I have just read in Brendel's "Zeitschrift." As I am thoroughly acquainted with all the circumstances, I pronounce it excellent; in short, so important, and so always hitting the mark, that were I not the leading subject I should have much less restraint in praising it.

Be assured that the remembrance I seem to have left with you will always remain one of my most cherished thoughts. That I was so fortunate to create a good opinion in you, is to me exhilarating and touching. After all, what a lot of trouble we both had to endure. Be content with these few words, written immediately after reading your notice, and just before taking my accustomed stroll, and be assured that they contain much joy.

Farewell, dearest Ferdinand, and continue to love me.

Yours,<br>RICHARD WAGNER.

Many, many hearty greetings for sister Léonie and the godchild!

Adieu.

ZURICH, 15th January, 1856.

Again was Wagner laid upon a sick-bed. One anxiety seems to have possessed his mind — the longing to complete the "Walküre." The following letter is of importance, since it shows the composer's frame of mind during the composition of the above work, a state of "pure despair" which, says Wagner, could alone have created it : —

Best thanks, dearest friend for your letters. You are right; I have again been laid on a sick-bed, and when at last I became convalescent I was in a perfect rage to get to the score of my "Walküre" (in the composition of which I have been hindered for the last year). So much do I long to finish it that I have entirely ceased letter-writing. Altogether, the older one grows, that is to say, in sense and reason, the more the worldly events of every-day life dwindle away into nothingness. That which one experiences in the inward heart becomes more and more difficult to explain. I do not mean to say that the events one has passed through, and which have touched you most intimately, cease to exist to live on; no, no; therefore I assure you that you and your family are ever vividly before me, yet as soon as one commences to write one finds after all there is nothing of real worth to put down. On the whole, we can only agree with each other, then there remains nothing but actual occurrences, views, and intentions to discuss. In these my life at present is as poor as my art creations are prolific, and which, indeed, are surging to the surface and becoming richer and richer. When you come to me, and I play my works to you, you will agree with me. In so far as the world has a claim upon me I can point solely to my work. I have nothing else to offer to it.

If you read the poetry of the "Walküre" again, you will find such a superlative of sorrow, pain, and despair expressed therein, that you will understand me when I say the music terribly excites me. I could not again accomplish a similar work. When it is once finished, much will then appear quite different (looking at the work as an art whole), and will afford enjoyment, whereas nothing but pure despair could have created it. But we shall see!

Altogether I live so secluded and retired that I feel at a loss when I am anxious to talk to you about it. I look forward to the time of Liszt's coming to me as a bracing up of my heart. Alas! on account of illness, I was compelled last winter to put off the visit. About the illness in your little family I take a hearty interest. In your new garden I picture you gambolling with your children. How I wish that I had a little house with a little garden attached; alas! an enjoyment hitherto unattainable.

At first I was tolerably indifferent about the sad conflagration,[1] but when I thought of Sainton it became painful to me. Now I hear that Gye has managed to continue his opera notwithstanding, and therefore Sainton's income, no doubt, will not be endangered,

---

[1] Burning of the opera house, Covent Garden.

and the misfortune overcome! That he now plays under Wylde amuses me much. It was ridiculous that he had to resign the Old Philharmonic. After all, Costa has succeeded in this! When I recall my London visit, I find I do not remember much except the friends I left there; they are all that remind me of it — happily!

But now try and come to visit me. For my operas wait until you hear them produced by me. Now you can get a very inadequate impression of them. If, therefore, you desire more of me, come to me yourself; in so doing you will give me great pleasure. I remain here during the summer. If I can arrange it, I intend going in the autumn with Semper to Rome; at least, such is my present hope. But continue to give me frequent news of you, and be assured that in so doing you give the greatest gratification to

Your

RICHARD WAGNER.

Greet your dear wife heartily for me; she is to continue to hold me in good remembrance. Happiness and prosperity to my god-child!

Kiss poor Lüders a thousand times; I shall soon inquire more precisely after Bumpus.

Adieu,

R. W.

ZURICH, 28th March, 1856.

## The next letter is again dated from Zurich :—

That's right, dearest Ferdinandus, to determine to leave Richard Wagner of the future to come to the R. W. of the present. My *alter ego* will not regret it. When you are here I will hammer out the " Walküre " to you, and I hope it will force its way from ear to heart. Then there is a bit of the " Siegfried," and that, too, must I sing to you. How my head is full of projects for work!

Minna is very delighted at the prospect of seeing you, and says she will treat you as a brother. I have told her how heartily you enter into the mysteries of household matters, and are of just that temperament to agree with her, and appreciate that domestic skill for which I am totally unfitted. To me also your presence will be a delight, for I can talk to you with open heart, and have much to say to you.  Now see that you do not let anything intervene that shall prevent your coming.  I am just now full of work, and when you are here I shall work all the same.  Some hours during the morning shall be devoted to work while you shall be sent upstairs to deeply study Schopenhauer, and then shall we not argue and discuss like orators in the old Athenian lyceum!  Two months, and you will be with me! ah! that is good!  Then bring all your brain-power, all your keen penetration, for you shall explain to me some obscure passages in that best of writers, Schopenhauer, which now torment me exceedingly.  He will, perhaps, cause you many researches of the heart, so you must come fully equipped with all your intellectual faculties in the full vigorous glow of health, and then I promise myself some happy hours.  And what shall be your reward? Well, the " Walküre " shall entreat you, and man, the original man, " Siegfried " shall show you what he is!  Now, good, dear friend, come!

Mind, now, no English restraint and propriety; bother that invisible old lady, Mrs. Grundy, that hovers over the English horizon, ruling with a rod of iron what is supposed to be proper and virtuous!

Heartiest greetings to dear sister Léonie, and tell her that her son, Richard Wagner the elder, sends his best affection to the younger, and inquires whether he has yet been taught how to make money.

Yours,<br>
RICHARD WAGNER.

P.S.  Ferdinand, bring me a packet of snuff from that shop in Oxford Street, you know, where you got it before for me.

R. W.

ZURICH, May, 1856.

# CHAPTER XXI.

ZURICH, 1856.

In the summer of 1856 I spent two months under Wagner's roof at Zurich. As it was holiday time for me, and Wagner had no engagements of any importance, we passed the whole period in each other's society debating, in a most earnest, philosophical, logical manner, art matters, most of our discussions taking place during our rambles upon the mountains.

One figure I found in that quiet, tastily arranged chalet, who filled a large portion of Wagner's life; to whom, first, Wagner owed an unpayable debt, and then that wide world of countless ones which has been enriched by the artist's creations. But that solitary, heroic Minna is, it seems — judging from the many writings which have appeared of the master — likely to be forgotten. Her glory is obscured by the more brilliant luminary that succeeded her. Still a domestic picture of the creator of the " Walkyrie," whilst that work was actually in hand, is of interest, as herein we see the man, the actual man, the human being, with his irritabilities and good humour, all under the gentle sway of a soft-hearted, brave woman.

Nor should the reader think that the worth of Wagner's first wife is here over-estimated through partiality. There is another witness to her good qualities, who certainly will not be suspected of friendly feeling, viz. Count von Beust, the Saxon minister, who vigorously and unrelentingly persecuted the so-called revolutionist in 1849. Beust knew Minna in Dresden, and what he then learnt of the chapel master's wife was not obliterated by forty years active participation in the diplomatic subtleties of European politics. In his autobiography,[1] published the latter end of 1886, he speaks of Minna's amiable character, and describes her as an excellent woman.

Minna may be spoken of as a comely woman. Gentle and active in her movements, unobtrusive in speech and bearing, possessing a forethought akin to divination, she administered to her husband's wants before he knew them himself. It was this lovable foresight of the woman which caused such a horrible vacancy in Wagner's life when, later, Minna left him, a break which he so bitterly bemoaned, and which all the adoration and wealth of Louis of Bavaria could not atone for. As a housewife she was most efficient. In their days of distress she cheerfully performed what are vulgarly termed menial services. In this she is as fitting a parallel of Mrs. Carlyle, as Wagner is of Carlyle. Both the men were thinkers, aye, and "original" thinkers (which in Carlyle's estimation was "the event of all others," a fact of superlative importance). They both elected hard fare, nay, actual deprivation, to submission to the unrealities, and both are educators of our teachers: and Minna's efforts in the house and sustaining Wagner in the dark days is the pendant of Mrs. Carlyle's scrubbing

---

[1] An English translation of these memoirs by Baron de Worms was published in 1887.

the floors of the little house at Scotsbrig in the wilds of Scottish moors. But though Minna was not the intellectual equal of this cultured Scottish lady, she is not to be confounded with the German housewife, so often erroneously spoken of as a sort of head cook. She was eminently practical, and full of remedies for sickness.

In art, however, Minna could not comprehend the gifts of her husband. He was an idealist; she, a woman alive to our mundane existence and its necessities. She worshipped afar off, receiving all he said without inquiry. In their early years their common youth glossed over difficulties. Moreover, Wagner was not in the full possession of his wings. He knew not his own power. For him exile was the turning-point of his greatness, the crucible wherein was destroyed the dross of his art, the fire from which he emerged, the teacher of a purified art. Exile was the period of his literary achievements. There was the test of his greatness. "A man thinks he has something to say. He indulges in an abundance of spoken language, but when in the quiet of his study he seeks to transfix on paper the fleeting theories of his brain, then is he face to face with himself, with actualities. And in exile Wagner first sought to set down in writing the theories which hitherto, in a limited manner only, had governed his work."[1] From this self-examination Wagner rose up nobler and stronger. And here it was that Minna failed to keep pace with him. She had been a singer and an actress, and could, in a manner, interpret his work, but the meaning of it lay deep, hidden from her. It was not her fault, yet she was to suffer for it. Still I must point out that all Wagner's works were

[1] Letter to Mr. Villot, page 35.

created during the period of his first marriage. His union with Cosima von Bülow is dated 25th August, 1870, since which time "Götterdammerung" (a poem written in 1848) and "Parsifal" only, have been given to the world.

While I was with Wagner it was his invariable habit to rise at the good hour of half-past six in the morning. If Minna was not about, he would go to the piano, and soon would be heard, at first softly, then with odd harmonies, full orchestral effects, as it were, "Get up, get up, thou merry Swiss-boy." That was his fun. Early breakfast would be served in the garden, after which Wagner would hand me "Schopenhauer," with my allotted task for the morning study. This plan, though Wagner's, was one which coincided happily with my own inclinations. I was, as it were, ordered up to my room, there to ponder over the arguments of the pessimistic philosopher, and so be well prepared for discussion at the dinner-table, or later, during our regular daily stroll.

Now to me Schopenhauer was not the original great thinker that Wagner considered him. Some of his most prominent points I had found enunciated already by Burke, that eloquent and vigorous writer, in his "Enquiring into the Origin of our Ideas on the Sublime and Beautiful." The personally well attested statement that "the ideas of pain are much more powerful than those which enter on the part of pleasure," was so well reasoned by Burke, that Wagner induced me to read the whole of that author's work to him.

Wagner a pessimist! So he would have had every one believe then, and for some time later too. But my impression then and now is that, as with a good many people, pessimism is only pre-eminent when fortune fails to favour. This feeling is confirmed by an extract recently published from certain manuscripts found after Wagner's death : "He who does not strive to find joy in life is unworthy to live." Certainly this was not the utterance of Wagner in the dark days of his work. While on this subject I may recall one incident which has remained prominently with me because of the locality where it occurred. We were on the top of one of the heights overlooking the Zurich Lake, discussing the much debated Schopenhauer, when I observed that pessimism, in a well-balanced mind, could only lead to optimism, on the ground that, "what cannot be cured must be endured," and jocularly cited from Brant's "Narrenschiff," written in the quaint language of the fifteenth century : —

> Wer sorget ob die genss gaut blos,
> Und fegen will all goss und stross,
> Und eben machen berg und tal
> Der hat keyn freyd, raw überal.

> He who shall fret that the geese have no dress,
> The sweeper will be of street, road and mess.
> He who would level both valley and hill
> Shall have of life's gifts no joy, but the ill.

Wagner stopped, shouted with exultation, and then commenced probing my knowledge of one of our earliest German poets. He assumed the part, as it were, of a schoolmaster, and so when we arrived home, in a boyish manner, he, delighted, called aloud to Minna before the garden gate was opened, " Ach, Ferdinand knows all about my pet poets."

Every morning after breakfast he would read to Minna her favourite newspaper, "Das Leipziger Tage-blatt," a paper renowned for its prosy character. Imagination and improvisation played her some woeful tricks. With a countenance blameless of any indication of the improvisor, he would recite a story, embellishing the incidents until their colouring became so overcharged with the ludicrous, that Minna would exclaim, "Ah, Richard, you have again been inventing."

He had spoken to me of Godfrey von Strassburg, saying, "To-morrow I will read you something good." He did next day read me "Tristan" in his study, and we spoke long and earnestly as to its adaptability for operatic treatment. Events have shown it to have been the ground-work of the music-drama of the same name. But at the time he spoke, it appeared to me he had no thought of utilizing it as a libretto. This intention only presented itself to his mind while we three were at breakfast on the following day. He was reading the notices in the Leipzic paper with customary variation, when, without any indication, he dropped the paper onto his knees, gazed into space, and seemed as though he were in a trance, nervously moving his lips. What did this portend? Minna had observed the movement, and was about to break the silence by addressing Wagner. Happily, she caught my warning glance and the spell remained unbroken. We waited until Wagner should move. When he did, I said, "I know what you have been doing." "No," he answered, somewhat abruptly, "how can you?" "Yes; you have been composing the love-song we were speaking of yesterday, and the story is going to shape itself into a drama!" "You are right as to the composition, but — the libretto — I will reflect." Such is the history of the first promptings of that wondrous creation, "Tristan and Isolde."

But how, how did this Titanic genius compose? Did he, like dear old papa Haydn, perform an elaborate toilet, donning his best coat, and pray to be inspired before setting himself to his writing-table *away* from the piano? or were his surroundings and method akin to those of Beethoven? — a room given over to muddle and confusion, the Bonn master writing, erasing, re-writing, and again scratching out, while *at* the piano! Well, distinctly, Wagner had nothing in common with Haydn. The style of Beethoven is far removed from him as regards the state of his working-room. I am desirous there should be no misunderstanding on Wagner's method of composing, because I find that my testimony is in conflict with some published statements on this subject, from those whose names carry some weight.

Wagner composed *at* the piano, in an elegantly well arranged study. With him composing was a work of excitement and much labour. He did not shake the notes from his pen as pepper from a caster. How could it be otherwise than labour with a man holding such views as his? Listen to what he says: "For a work to live, to go down to future generations, it must be reflective," and again in "Opera and Drama," written about this time, "A composer, in planning and working out a great idea, must pass through a kind of parturition." Mark the word "parturition." Such it was with him. He laboured excessively. Not to find or make up a phrase; no, he did not seek his ideas at the piano. He went to the piano with his idea already composed, and made the piano his sketch-book, wherein he worked and reworked his subject, steadily modelling his matter until it assumed the shape he had in his mind. The subject of representative themes was discussed much by us, and he explained to me that he felt chained to the piano until he had found precisely that which shaped itself before his mental vision. I had one morning retired to my room for the Schopenhauer study, when the piano was pounded — yes, pounded is the exact word — more vigorously than usual. The incessant repetition of one theme arrested my attention. Schopenhauer was discarded. I came down stairs. The theme was being played with another rhythm. I entered the room. "Ah!" he exclaimed, "you have been listening!" "Who could help it?" was my answer. "Your vigorous playing fascinated me more than skilful philosophical dialectics!" And then I inquired as to the reason of the change of rhythm. The explanation astonished me. Wagner was engaged on a portion of "Siegfried," the scene where Mime tells Siegfried of his murderous intentions whilst under the magic influence of the tarn helm. "But how did you come to change the rhythm?" "Oh," he said, "I tried and tried, thought and thought, until I got just what I wanted." And that it was perseverance with him, and not spontaneity, is borne out by another incident. The Wesendoncks were at the chalet. Wagner was at the piano, anxious to shine, doubtless, in the presence of a lady who caused such unpleasantness in his career later on. He was improvising, when, in the midst of a flowing movement, he suddenly stopped, unable to finish. I laughed. Wagner became angry, but I jocularly said,

"Ah, you got into a *cul-de-sac* and finished *en queue de poisson.*" He could not be angry long, and joined in the laugh too, confessing to me that he was only at his best when reflecting.

The morning's work over, Wagner's practice was to take a bath immediately. His old complaint, erysipelas, had induced him to try the water cure, for which purpose he had been to hydropathic establishments, and he continued the treatment with as much success as possible in the chalet.

The animal spirits and physical activity of Wagner have before been referred to by me. He really possessed an unusual amount of physical energy, which, at times, led him to perform reckless actions. One day he said to Minna, "We must do something to give Praeger some pleasure, to give him a joyful memento of his visit; let us take him to Schaffhausen," and though I remonstrated with him on account of his work, he insisted, and so we went. We stayed there the night. Breakfast was to be in the garden of the hotel. The hour arrived, but Wagner was not to be found. Search in all directions, without results. We hear a shout from a height. Behold! Wagner, the agile, mounted on the back of a plaster lion, placed on the top of a giddy eminence! And how he came down! The recklessness of a school-boy was in all his movements. We were in fear; he laughed heartily, saying he had gone up there to get an appetite for breakfast. The whole incident was a repetition of Wagner's climbing the roof of the Dresden school-house when he was a lad. Going to and returning from Schaffhausen, Wagner took first-class railway tickets. Now in Switzerland, first-class travelling is confined to a very few, and those only the wealthiest, so that Minna expostulated with him. This was typical. As he described himself, he was more luxurious than Sardanapalus, though he lived then on the generosity of his friends to enjoy such comfort. Minna was the housewife, and strove to curb the unlimited desires of a man who had not the wherewithal to purchase his excess. And Wagner was not to be controlled, for he not only travelled first-class, but also telegraphed to Zurich to have a carriage in waiting for us.

At Zurich Wagner had a sense of his growing power, and he cared not for references to his early youthful struggles. I remember an old Magdeburg singer, with her two daughters, calling to see her old comrade. The mother and her daughters sang the music of the Rhine maidens, Wagner accompanying, and they acquitted themselves admirably. But when the old actress familiarly insisted on taking a pinch of snuff from Wagner's box, and told stories of the Magdeburg days, then did Wagner resent the familiarity in a marked manner.

When they finished singing, Minna asked me : " Is it really so beautiful as you say ? It does not seem so to me, and I am afraid it would not sound so to others." Such observations as these show where Minna was unable to follow Wagner, and the estrangement arising from uncongeniality of artistic temperament.

When I was at Zurich, Wagner showed me two letters from august personages. First, the Duke of Coburg offered him a thousand dollars and two months' residence in the palace, if he would score an opera for him. The offer was refused, for he said, " Look, now, though I want the money sadly, yet I cannot and will not score the duke's opera."

The second letter was from a count, favourite of the emperor of Brazil. The emperor was an unknown admirer of Wagner's, it appears, and was desirous of commissioning Wagner to compose an opera, which he would undertake should be performed at the Italian opera house, Rio Janeiro, under his own special direction. Wagner did not care to expatriate himself to this extent, but the offer spurred him on to compose an opera, which he said, "shall be full of melody." He did write his opera, and it was "Tristan and Isolde."

How was Wagner as a revolutionist at this time? Well, one of his old Dresden friends came to see him, Gottfried Semper. We spoke of the sad May days, and poor August Roeckel. Again did Wagner evade the topic, or speak slightly of it. The truth is, he was ready to pose as the saviour of a people, but was not equally ready to suffer exile for patriotic actions, and so he sought to minimize the part he had played in 1849. It appears from "The Memoires of Count Beust," to which I have before alluded, that Wagner also sought to minimize his May doings, by speaking of them as unfortunate, when he called upon the minister after his exile had been removed, on which Beust retorted, "How unfortunate ! Are you not aware that the Saxon government possesses a letter wherein you propose burning the prince's palace?" I am forced to the conclusion that Wagner would have torn out that page from his life's history had it been possible.

During my stay I saw Minna's jealousy of another. She refused to see in the sympathy of Madame Wesendonck for Wagner as a composer, that for the artist only. It eventually broke out into a public scandal, and filled the opposition papers with indignant reproaches about Wagner's ingratitude toward his friend. On leaving Zurich I went to Paris. There I wrote to Wagner an expostulatory letter, alluding to a couple of plays with which we were both familiar, viz. "The Dangerous Neighbourhood" and "The Public Secret," with a view of warning him privately in such a manner that Minna should not understand should she chance to read my letter. The storm burst but too soon. Wagner wrote to me while I was still in Paris: "The devil is loose. I shall leave Zurich at once and come to you in Paris. Meet me at the Strassburg station." . . . But two days after, this was cancelled by another letter, an extract from which I give.

Matters have been smoothed over, so that I am not compelled to leave here. I hope we shall be quite free from annoyance in a short time; but ach, the virulence, the cruel maliciousness of some of my enemies. . . .

I can testify Wagner suffered severely from thoughtlessness.

# CHAPTER XXII.



FROM the time I left Zurich in the autumn of 1856, to the untoward fate of "Tannhäuser," at Paris, in March, 1861, of the several letters which passed between Richard Wagner and me I reproduce the few following, as possessing more than a personal interest.

On the 17th July he writes : —

Hard have I toiled at "Siegfried," for work, work, is my only comfort. Unable to return to the fatherland! Cruel! cruel! and why? The efforts of the grand duke,[1] are fruitless; one hopes for the best, but that best comes not. Eh! is not Schopenhauer right? Is not the degree of my torment more intense than that of any joy I have experienced? Here I am working alone, with no seeming probability of my compositions ever being performed as I yearn for. My efforts are in vain, and then when I look round and see what is being done at the theatres, — the list of their representations *fills me with rage,* — such unrealities !

You tell me that Goethe says, " The genius cannot help himself, and that the demon of fate seizes him by the nape of the neck, and forces him to work *nolens volens.*" And must I work on without a chance of being heard? *Nous verrons. . . .*

But listen, Ferdinandus ! I am pondering over the Tristan legend. It is marvellous how that work constantly leaps from out the darkness into full life, before my mental vision. Wait until next sum-

---

[1] Alluding to the action taken by Frederick of Baden (whose wife was a lover of Wagner's music) to secure the reinstalment of Wagner as a citizen of Germany.

mer, and then you shall "hear something"! But now my health is poor, and I am out of spirits. . . .

Keep me in thy love.

Thine,

RICHARD WAGNER.

Not long after the above reached me, Wagner's health did begin to give way, so that his next letter is dated :—

VENICE, October, 1858.

Yes; I have been long in writing, but you are a second me and understand the cause. Since I have been here I have been very ill. I have sought to avoid all correspondence, and have endeavoured to restore my somewhat shattered self. Thank sister Léonie for her account of my *alter ego*. Poor little fellow! he is in terribly wondrous sympathy with me. Perhaps, were he here, we might together come through our pains triumphantly. . . . What was good news for me was that "Lohengrin" was done at Vienna, though I cannot understand how it can be adequately given without me. Only "hearty love and good-will could conquer. . . .

Your

RICHARD WAGNER.

Wagner appears to have stayed at Venice through the winter of 1858–59, going in the spring of 1859 to Lucerne. It was from this latter place he wrote to me that he meant to go to Paris.

Strange the fascination Paris possessed for Wagner! He always spoke against it, yet when his fortunes were at the lowest, it was towards Paris that he turned for succour. He has told me that he felt the French were in a manner gifted in art as no other European people; that they inherited a perception of the beautiful and sense of the delicate refinement to a degree beyond that of other nations, though he saw it in an artificiality which gave it an unsound basis. And thinking of Meyerbeer, he felt the French to be generous in their treatment of aliens. So, in the autumn of 1859, again he attempts the conquest of Paris. He wrote to me, asking for an introduction to certain friends who would assist him in securing the legal copyright of his compositions. I took steps to put him into communication with the desired advisers, and he then did his best to make friends in all directions. He became popular; gave musical parties, inviting art celebrities, beside musicians. Minna was with him. They brought some of the furniture and hangings from their Swiss chalet, and transformed the house of Octave Feuillet, which Richard Wagner had taken, into the same agreeable and pleasant abode as at Zurich. Of course there was the usual opposition party, and they made the most out of the upholstery, charging Wagner in the press with keeping his house like that of a *lorette*, and behaving altogether with the vanity and ostentation of an Eastern potentate.

" Look here," said he to me, when I was with him in Paris, "now you know this furniture, and how carefully Minna has preserved it, and yet see how I am treated." He was desirous of replying to the press notices, but I endeavoured to dissuade him. He went to the Rue Newton, a street situated on the left hand of the Champs Elysée, beyond the Rondpoint, because it was quieter than the Rue Martignan, and he had trees near him. The Rue Martignan was the first he went to on returning to Paris, and where I visited him. It was in the Rue Newton, however, that his reunions took place.

And who were present at these gatherings? Well, occasionally men of note : Villot, famed as the recipient of that lengthy exposition of Wagner's views in the shape of a letter ; Gasparini, a medical gentleman from the south of France; Champfleury, an enthusiastic pamphleteer who wrote then, and published his views of Wagner; and Olivier, the husband of Cosima Bülow's eldest sister. There doubtless were others, but I do not know. What I do know is that I marvelled much at some of the visitors who found themselves in Wagner's salon. A very mixed assembly. At one of his receptions, while Wagner was singing (in his way) and accompanying himself at the piano, I remember an old lady (a Jewess) who snored painfully audibly while Wagner was at the piano. Aroused by the applause of the others, she suddenly burst into grunts of approval, clapping her hands at the same time. I expostulated with Wagner. How could he sing and play before such an audience ? "How could he help it," was his reply ; to that lady he was under obligations for £200. She resided in Manchester, and had been introduced to him by a German friend, a Bayreuth figure, known to all pilgrims to Wahnfried. His singing was like that of a composer who tries over at the piano all the parts of his score. What among musicians and composers would be regarded as a grand boon seemed to me, before the uninitiated, as a profanation. He hardly liked such references to his performance, but conscious of their sincerity, he fully explained his position to me. The trials which a genius is sometimes compelled to undergo are bitter, very.

I was one day discussing with Wagner, when he was called away by a visitor. On his return, he told me I should never guess who it was. M. Badjocki, chamberlain of the Emperor Napoleon III., had been directed to arrange for a performance of "Tannhäuser" at the grand opera. The story of the "Tannhäuser" disaster is now known to almost every one. I therefore shall touch upon certain points, only particularly those with which I am acquainted as an eyewitness, and which have not been spoken of elsewhere. Richard Wagner told me that one day, at a reception, the emperor had asked the Princess Metternich whether she had seen the last opera of Prince Poniatowski. She replied, contemptuously, "I do not care for such music." "But is it not good?" doubtingly observed the emperor. "No," she said, curtly. "But where is better music to be got, then?" "Why, Your Majesty, you have at the present moment the greatest German composer that ever lived in your capital." "Who is he?" "Richard Wagner." "Then why do they not give his operas?" "Because he is in earnest, and would require all kinds of concessions and much money." "Very well; he shall have *carte blanche.*" This is the whole story.

After many fluctuations, as to whether the performance would take place or no, the translation was begun. On this were engaged at first one Lindau and Roche, who shaped it in the rough, but so badly that it had to be redone. This time Nuitre, a well-known poet, did it. Connected with Roche is an incident which Wagner related to me, and perhaps has an interest for all.

On Wagner's return to Paris, in 1859, he had some difficulty with his luggage at the custom-house. He spoke to an officer who seemed in command. "What is your name?" the officer inquired. "Richard Wagner." The French officer threw himself on his knees, and embraced Wagner, exclaiming, "Are you the Richard

Wagner whose 'Tannhäuser' I know so well?" It appears Roche was an amateur, and, alighting upon Wagner's "Tannhäuser," had studied it closely. This was a good beginning in Paris for Wagner.

Well, Nuiter was the poet. The translation was in progress while I was in Paris, and I was a daily witness of the combined efforts of Nuiter and Wagner at the translation. How Wagner stormed while it was being done. "Tannhäuser" teems with references to "love," and every time such words or references were to be rendered into French, Nuiter was compelled to say, "No, master, it cannot be done like that," — so many were the possible double interpretations likely to be put upon such by the public. To all Wagner's anger Nuitre posed a soft answer. "It shall be all right, master; it shall be done well, if I sit up all night;" and this was the frequent response of the poor poet.

The rehearsal began in September, 1860, and ended the first week in March, 1861. Wagner applied to the authorities for permission to conduct himself. The answer came: "The general regulations connected with the performances at the grand opera house cannot be interfered with for the proposed representation of 'Tannhäuser.'" This was communicated officially to Wagner, and he sent the letter to me. What did happen was that Dietsch, the composer for whom Wagner's poem, the "Flying Dutchman," had been purchased, conducted instead. Dietsch received Wagner's suggestions and hints in a good-natured manner, and worked as well as he could for the success of the performance. Before the rehearsals came to an end Wagner had become quite indifferent as to the possible reception of "Tannhäuser."

The first public representation was to take place on the 13th March, 1861.   On the 12th February Wagner wrote me the following : —

Come, dear old friend, now is the time when I want all my friends about me.   The opposition is malicious ; fair play is no part of the critic's stock in trade. . . .   I have had pressure put upon me from high quarters, urging me to give way, and that unless I bend before the storm my proud self-will will be snapped in twain. . . .   But I will have none of it.   I hear David[1] has been subsidized by the members of the Jockey Club to purchase tickets of admission for himself and gang of hirelings, who are going to protest vigorously against their exclusion.   We may, therefore, expect much rough work, and so I want you and others to be about me.   I care not for all the mercenaries in Paris.   The work of my brain, the thought and labour I have in solitude anxiously bestowed upon it, shall not (by my will, at any rate) be left to the mercy of a semi-inebriated, sensual herd.   Here are artists working zealously for the success of my work, men and women really exerting themselves in an astonishing manner.   There are truly some annoyances both on the stage and in the orchestra ; but on the whole, the energy shown is wonderful. . . .   My indignation was at a boiling-point when Monsieur Royer insolently observed that if Monsieur Meyerbeer contrived a ballet for half-past eight he saw no reason why I could not follow so popular a composer.   I ! . . .   Meyerbeer !   Never ! Fail me not then, Ferdinand.   You will find me in the most jubilant spirits, and well supported, but in the moment of trial it is the old faces one longs to see about.   Bring " ma mère Léonie " to witness the downfall of her son, and to console him in his anger.   If good old Lüders could only come, his quaint humour would be irresistible. Now come.

Yours,<br>
RICHARD WAGNER.

I returned, therefore, to Paris, and went with Wagner to the final rehearsals.   At the last, the dress rehearsal, one of the chief characters . . . walked on

---

[1] Then " Chef de claque."

the stage in ordinary morning attire, creating a laugh and some confusion. Wagner might have avoided what was almost the inevitable reception of the performance, for he told me he had received a visit from some manager, whose name I now cannot recall, of a theatre at St. Petersburgh, who had agreed to produce "Tannhäuser" there, provided the Paris representations were foregone. To this he refused. Thus the Paris performances took place.

On the 13th March we were all assembled. In a private box sat the Princess Metternich, whose influence with the emperor had brought about the performance. Before the princess showed herself in the box, the noisy hissing, which greeted her from a section of the audience, indicated the hostility present. The overture was, on the whole, well received. Indeed, altogether, the opera created a favourable impression among those who had not come with the avowed intention of making the performance a failure. When the dog-whistles of the "protectors" of the *corps-de-ballet* were first heard, a goodly portion of the audience rose indignantly, endeavouring to suppress the organized opposition, but to no purpose, and the work dragged itself on to a torturing accompaniment of strife among the audience.

How indignant was Wagner! His excitement and anger were great. Annoyed with himself for coming to Paris, with having so little perception in seeking to succeed with an opera opposed to the formality where tradition was king. But the second performance took place, all the same, on the 18th March. Then the opposition was but little up to the end of the first act, but from there it gathered in force. At the third and last representation, which was on Sunday, the 24th March, the members of the Claque appeared in force, paid again, it was commonly asserted, by the Jockey Club. This performance decided the fate of "Tannhäuser." At this last representation I was not present. The scenic artist, Monsieur Cambon, however, came to London and gave me a description of it. The whistles and toy flageolets of the enemy destroyed all hope of hearing any portion comfortably, but as far as he could gather from independent testimony of those musicians and artists outside the opera house, "Tannhäuser" was regarded as a great work, and but for the persistent tactics of the Jockey Club would have proved a success. Such was the enthusiasm the work inspired in some of the artists, that Monsieur Cambon told me he himself went specially to the Wartburgh, there to prepare his canvas for the performances.

There is now one point characteristic of Wagner's earnestness. He went through the score with me before the performances, I should add, and he told me, "I have been through it before and found many bald places, which required filling in, and which my long experience has taught me how to improve."

# CHAPTER XXIII.



From Paris Wagner went to Carlsruhe, whence he wrote to me the following letter. The allusion in the opening phrases of his letter is to my inability to stay for the third performance of " Tannhäuser."

You never heard such a din. It was a pity indeed you were away. I would it had been possible to prevent it; however, it could not be otherwise. But we did very well, until one whistle more shrill than the rest screamed for fully a minute. It seemed an hour. Horrible! horrible! — and my work was submitted to such an audience! Had I but the strength — but no, my indignation is now nearly over; the joy of being on my native soil once again, a free man, has removed a load from me that really at moments felt insupportable. Aye, those who have kept me from my fatherland little know how dearly they punished me for my, perhaps, imprudence in those early Dresden days. The sight is again reproduced before my vision, but in my joy at being free to go — except in Saxony — where I choose, poor August's earnest face appears before me; and he is still the political prisoner of a power that could crush him in a moment. It is unkingly. Those days have made me suffer so keenly in what I love the dearest and tenderest on earth, my art, that in my happiness at being once more home I could shut out forever that sad past. Now I may go forward with my work. I shall not rest contented until Saxony once again is free to me as to the birds of the air; but how my hopes are built upon the future, and I feel all the confidence of success. I am sick again in body just now, but I will be conqueror. Was ever work like mine created for no purpose? Is it miserable egoism, the stupidest vanity? It matters not what it is, but of this I feel positive; yes, as positive as that I live, and that is my "Tristan and Isolde," with which I am now consumed, does not find its equal in the world's library of music. Oh, how I yearn to hear it! I am feverish; I feel worn; perhaps that causes me to be agitated and anxious, but my "Tristan" has been finished now these three years and has not been heard. When I think of this I wonder whether it will be with this as with "Lohengrin," which now is more than thirteen years old, and has been as dead to me. But the clouds seem breaking — are breaking. The grand duke is good. He shows himself desirous of befriending me; no doubt intends well, and has even proposed that I shall return to Paris to engage singers to perform "Tristan." I am going to Vienna soon. There they are going to give me a surprise. It is supposed to be kept a secret from me, but a friend has informed me they are going to bring out "Lohengrin." You will hear about it.

Ah! I have so run away with my thoughts that I have nearly failed to tell you what I began to say; and that is, strong pressure was brought upon me to consent to a fourth performance of "Tannhäuser." I was officially informed that all the seats had been taken; the public were strongly desirous of hearing an opera which had caused such a stir in high circles, that the sale of tickets had been so brisk that now not one was unsold. But nothing, nothing would induce me to submit again to such debasing treatment. I would sooner lose all hope of assistance from imperial and noble personages, and fight my battle alone, than again appear before such tribunal. The royalty, £60, I left for Nuiter; it was a poor recompense. . . . Now commend me to sister Léonie; tell her that Minna is grateful for her thoughtful kindness, and bids me send her a thousand hearty greetings.

Always thine,

RICHARD WAGNER.

CARLSRUHE, April, 1861.

The next letter, August, 1862, is from Biebrich, near Mayence, on the Rhine.

MY DEAR FRIEND: It is a long time since I wrote to you; yes, but I have had a worrying, anxious time. I do not seem to be able to forge ahead. Each time I feel now I am within reach of my goal, it flies from me like a " will o' the wisp."

No, " Tristan " has not yet been done ; but it will, it will soon be done. I have found such a Tristan as charms my soul, such a one as will worthily enact my hero. He has been here with me for a few days studying it. Schnorr! Ah, the alighting upon him was miraculous! At one time last winter, so saddened and broken down was I by successive disappointments, that I had a presentiment of approaching death. I actually had rehearsals of "Tristan" at Vienna, and then the proposed performance does not take place. But now it will. Yet I dare not be too positive. It it does, Schnorr will be grand ; then you must come. Why can't you come now to me? I am going to stay here till the end of the summer ; that my poor second self is so weakly as to compel you to go to the seaside, I am concerned deeply. May the sea-breezes invigorate him, and soon give his mother no cause for anxiety. But I intended telling you how I heard Schnorr first.

He was going to sing " Lohengrin " at Carlsruhe. I did not want him or anybody to know I should be present, so I went secretly, for I feared a disappointment ; he is fat, and picture a corpulent Knight of the Swan ! I had not heard him before. I went, and he sang marvellously. He was inspired, and I was enchanted ; he realized my ideal. So come now and see him ; you will be delighted too. . . . I am staying here because I want to superintend the printing of my " Meistersinger."

Yours,<br>RICHARD WAGNER.

AH ! DEAR FERDINAND : I am faring tolerably well ; have made some good friends, influential ones too, but that is not what I crave. " Tristan "! that's it ! I am ready to go back to Vienna at any moment, am expecting information from there, but again have feelings that the performance will not take place. Here, as you have doubtless seen through the press notices, my music has been received with an enthusiasm beyond what it ever before achieved in Germany. Tell Lüders that I called on his friends and they behaved in the kindest manner to me. Give the dear fellow my heartiest greetings. I would Minna were here with me ; we might, in the excitement that now moves fast around me, grow again the quiescent pair as of yore. The whole thing is annoying. I am not in good spirits. I move about freely, and see a number of people, but my misery is bitter. Can you not arrange to come and be with me in the summer, wherever I may be? Write to me a long letter of how all is with you.

Yours ever,<br>RICHARD WAGNER.

St. Petersburgh, February, 1863.

I did not see him that year; matters could not be arranged. But since that time the storm was gathering in intensity which was to soon break. Minna had been in correspondence with me. Of her letters I publish nothing. But the next from Wagner tells its own sad story in plain language. It is dated —

Mariafeld, April, 1864.

And so she has written to you? Whose fault was it? How could she have expected I was to be shackled and fettered as any ordinary cold common mortal. My inspirations carried me into a sphere she could not follow, and then the exuberance of my heated enthusiasm was met by a cold douche. But still there was no reason for the extreme step; everything might have been arranged between us, and it would have been better had it been so. Now there is a dark void, and my misery is deep. It has struck into my health, though I carefully attend to what you ever insist is the root of my ills — diet. Yet I do not sleep, and am altogether in a feverish state. It is now that I feel I have sounded my lowest note of dark despair. What is before me? I know not! Unless I can shortly and quickly rescue myself from this quicksand of gloom, it will engulf me and all will then be over. Change of scene I must have. If I do not I fear I shall sink from inanition. I like comfort, luxury — she fettered me there — How will it end?

Write to me soon.

RICHARD WAGNER.

But a startling change was nigh at hand. The curtain was about to rise upon the " Wahnfried " act of the hitherto stormy drama of Richard Wagner's life. As far as the wit of man could devise, Wagner was henceforth to be relieved from all care and anxiety as to the future. His wants — and be it remembered they were not few, for, on his own confession, he stands described as "more luxurious than Sardanapalus" — were all about to be provided for with regal liberality. But the following extracts from a letter which conveyed to me the news, will be noted with interest, since they give a vivid picture of the man and his feelings, in a word, paint the human being in characters so striking, and lay bare the workings of the heart in a manner which was impossible for his most intimate friend to hope to achieve. It was not wealth he wanted. Luxury when he possessed it in abundance did not comfort him : the worship and close intimacy of a king solaced him not : the void was sympathy, such as only a loving woman could give. The gloomy picture he draws of desolation amidst plenty invokes our heartiest compassion.

DEAREST FERDINAND : I owe it to you that you should be informed of what my joy — clouded though it is by certain thoughts — has been during the last few weeks. Such a state of intoxication have I been cast into, that it has been as though I were another being than myself, and I but a dazed reflection of the real mortal. It is a state of living in another atmosphere, like that induced by the drinking of hasheesh. A message from the sun-god has come to me ; the young king of Bavaria, a young man not yet twenty years of age, has sent for me, and resolves to give me all I require in this life, I in return to do nothing but compose and advise him. He urges me strongly to be near him ; sends for me sometimes two and even three times in one day ; talks with me for hours, and is, as far as I can see, devoted heart and soul to me. There is but one name for him — a god-like youth. But though I have now at my command a profusion of unlimited means, my feeling of isolation is torturing.  With no one to realize and enjoy with me this limitless comfort, a feeling of weariness and desolation is induced which keeps me in a constant state of dejection terrible to bear.  The commonest domestic details now must be done by me; the purchasing of kitchen utensils and such kindred matters am I driven to—Ah! poor Beethoven!  Now is it forcibly brought home to me what his discomforts were with his washing-book, and engaging of housekeepers, etc., etc.  I who have praised woman more than Frauenlob, have not one for my companion.  The truth is, I have spoilt Minna: too much did I indulge her, too much did I yield to her; but it were better not to talk upon a subject which never ceases to vex me.  The king strives his utmost to gratify me, and if I do not seem happy when with him and show my appreciation of his wondrous goodness, I should deserve to be branded as " ingrate."

There is one good being who brightens my household—the wife of Bülow; she has been with her children.  If you can come to see me I shall be happy.  My god-child, Richard Wagner, is now eight years old, you tell me; bring him; the talk of a dear innocent child will do me good; to have him near me will, perhaps, comfort me.                    Your unhappy

Richard Wagner.

Starnberg, June, 1864.

The preceding letter is to me a landmark in Wagner's life.  The facts have only to be recited for it to be clearly perceived what a striking climax had been reached.  Upon them I make no comment.  They speak for themselves — the sudden transformation from a state of hardship into one of security; the powerful patronage and friendship of the king of Bavaria; the absence of Minna; the presence of Madame von Bülow.

New influences were now beginning to work upon Wagner; and — they were not weak.  I did not see Wagner until the next year, when the change was pronounced.    During the winter the attachment of the king grew in warmth, until in a manner Wagner may be said to have dominated the youthful monarch completely.    In the early spring of 1865, Wagner wrote me the following short note.    It was in reply to one from me, urging him to find some occupation for August Roeckel, who had been released since the January of 1862.    When Roeckel was at Dresden, in 1849, with Richard Wagner, he had effaced himself entirely for his friend.    Then Wagner was appreciative of sacrifices upon the altar of friendship, and regarded them as done on his behalf entirely; but he later grew so absorbed with his mission that no sacrifice did he regard as done to himself, but for the glory of his art, and in this no sacrifice could be too great.    The short note after a private reference to Roeckel run as follows : —

. . . At present I cannot.    Time may be when the good August shall feel that his old friend lives — now, all I can say is that the king loves me with a love beyond description.    I feel as sure of his love for me till the end, as I am conscious of his unbounded goodness to me now.    It is a trial, though, of the heaviest; the formation of his mind I feel it a duty to undertake.    He is so strikingly handsome that he might pose as the King of the Jews (and — this in confidence — I am seriously reflecting on the Christian tragedy; possibly something may come of it).    But you must forgive me any more correspondence just now, I am busy.

Yours,

RICHARD WAGNER.

MUNICH (London post-mark), 8th April, 1865.

It appeared later that he was deeply engrossed in preparations for "Tristan's" performance, his next letter — but a short invitation — bearing on the subject.

Dear Praeger: 15, 18, 22 May: Wonderfully fine representations of " Tristan " at Munich.　Come, if you can, and write first. I should be heartily glad to know you present at them.

Yours,<br>RICHARD WAGNER.

Munich, 7th May, 1865.

I found it impossible to be present at the " Tristan " performances, and was compelled to postpone my visit to the summer of the same year.　On the 27th July, Madame von Bülow wrote to me for " her friend," explaining that he was so much touched by the death of poor Schnorr (the Tristan of the recent performances), that he was unable to write any letters, but that Wagner would be at Munich up to the 8th August — though she " had advised Richard very strongly to retire to the mountains there to strengthen his nerves."

# CHAPTER XXIV.


1865–1883.

I went to Munich and found Wagner considerably
depressed. "Tristan," the work he evidently loved with
no ordinary affection, had, after seven years of hoping
against hope, but just been performed to his intense
satisfaction, when the ideal impersonator dies. The
happiness he had recently felt at the three "Tristan"
performances, coupled with the publication of the piano
scores of the "Walküre" and "Tristan" had, to an
extent, kept his mind free. These events passed, and
his friends departed, he fell into a desponding mood.
Minna, his wife, was not there. This was a constant
irritation to him. He affected to care nothing about it,
but his references to her absence showed how it
annoyed and preyed upon him. Then was he placed in
delicate relations with the young king of Bavaria. Louis
constituted Wagner his adviser — his Mentor. Questions of state were submitted to him. The king's personal advisers were aware of this, and resented it.
Wagner knew of the intrigues against him. He sincerely yearned for quietude; all the more because he
instinctively felt the coming storm. He showed me all
the letters that his royal devotee had written to him,
and this I can testify, that breathing as they did the
fervid adoration of a cultured, highly gifted youth for a

genius, Wagner on his side felt no less intense admiration and affection for the "god-like" king. So great was the influence it was assumed Wagner possessed over the monarch, that his good-will was sought by all classes of petitioners for the royal favour.

The house inhabited by Richard Wagner was detached, an uncommon thing for houses in Germany. It had been built, he told me, by an Englishman, and now that he could command practically "unlimited means," he did not restrict his wants. I may say he positively revelled in his grandeur like a boy. His taste in arranging his house once again provoked the hostile comments of an ever-ready opposition press. As I have before remarked, this charge of Oriental luxury was a stock one with some people. Even now, his velvet coat and biretta are made the subject of puerile attacks; but I cannot refrain from stating that Richard Wagner's house and decorations are far surpassed by the luxuriously appointed palaces of certain English painters, musicians, and dramatic poetasters. Wagner was fond of velvets and satins, and he knew how best to display them. The arrangements in the house, too, showed the unmistakable guiding of a woman. Madame von Bülow acted as a sort of secretary to Wagner. Wagner was a prolific correspondent, but during the early portion of the summer, he had, it seems, been busy finishing the score of the second act of " Siegfried."

Wagner laid bare his hopes and wishes to me. He merits eulogy for his fearlessness. With that trait I was particularly struck. In relating the subject of a certain interview with the king, I was of opinion he had been too blunt of speech, too outspoken in his criticism, and I asked what would he do were he to lose the royal favour, remembering how dark and mournful had been his days at the moment the king sought him out. His reply startled me. "I have lived before without the king, and I can do so again." Honour to Wagner! He was fearless here as he was in his music — no concessions to false art.

A born actor Wagner? Certainly. Out together one day he related to me the story of his climbing the Uri-rothstock in company with a young friend. Some distance up the mountain, his companion, who was following, exclaimed he was giddy and falling, upon which Wagner turned round on the ledge of rock, caught his friend, and passed him between the rock and himself to the front. The scene was reproduced very graphically. His presence of mind never left him. Truly, Wagner was born to teach actors.

I found that the same boyish love of fun remained with Wagner. He dearly loved a joke, a good story, a witty anecdote. Many did he tell me. Even when I was leaving Munich, his stories came out, so that on saying good-bye, he added, "Well, we have had some discomforts, but a good many jokes."

Towards the end of the year the intrigues of his opponents proved too strong for him. He left Bavaria; but I will give some few extracts from his next letter, which will tell the history in his own way. It is dated —

CAMPAGNE AUX ARTICHAUX.

. . . The stories you read in the papers of my flying the country are wholly untrue. The king did nothing of the kind. He *implored* me to leave; said my life was in danger; that the director of the police had represented to him the positive necessity for my quitting Munich, or he could not guarantee my safety. Think, so greatly did he fear the populace! The populace opposed to me? No; not if they knew me. My return, I am told, is only a question of time; until the king is able to change his advisers. May he come out of his troubles well. . . .

Yours,<br>RICHARD WAGNER.

GENEVA, 1866.

The next letter of interest is dated nearly six months later. It shows that Wagner and the king did not then always get on well together.

MUNICH, June, 1867.

MY GOOD FERDINAND: I will keep my promise about August. He is here. I will see to it, but there are so many obstacles. The king is influenced by innumerable enemies, who are jealous of me, and angered at my influence with him. I have, indeed, almost broken off our relations, only the scandal would be too great!

"Lohengrin" and "Tannhäuser" were to be produced with the best artists and dresses. I was anxious to have Tichatschek as Lohengrin. He had, however, been singing elsewhere, in "Masaniello," so that he was hoarse. The *entourage* of the king seemed to have conceived a thorough dislike of Tichatschek. But what is more true, they were, I am convinced, desirous of preventing my appearing with the king at the performance, because they feared a demonstration.

After the last rehearsal, a few days ago, the king, who was present, sent for me. Tichatschek had displeased him, and he asserted he would never again attend a performance or rehearsal in which that singer took part. As this dislike referred only to the stiff acting of Tichatschek (for he had sung splendidly), I felt that the king's enthusiasm inclined to the spectacular, and where this was defective, he could not elsewhere find compensation. But now comes the outrage. Without consulting me, he ordered Tichatschek and the "Ortrud" to be sent away. I was, and am, furious, and forthwith mean to quit Munich. Now you know the situation, you will understand the impossibility of doing anything at present.

Yours,<br>RICHARD WAGNER.

Nothing came of the promise to help Roeckel, though Wagner and the king were soon reconciled. Roeckel became editor of a democratic newspaper, ceasing all active participation in the musical world. The friendship of Louis grew stronger, if that were possible, and Wagner shows by his letters that he was quite "the guide, philosopher, and friend" of the young monarch. Of his communications to me during the next year, I select the following short note, as possessing a wider interest than a merely personal communication.

DEAR OLD FRIEND: The 21st June first performance of the "Meistersinger" (model). On the 25th the second, and repetition of it up to about the 20th July. Now see whether you can catch something of it. It will be worth while, and will give me great joy when you come. Many hearty greetings.

From yours, RICHARD WAGNER.

MUNICH, at Bülows, 11 Arcos Strasse, 11th June, 1868.

As the above note shows, Wagner was living in Bülow's house. I purposely pass over the next two years. Events were coming to a climax. He and I did not agree; but still his friendship never waned or abated one jot. Meanwhile his wife, Minna, had died at Dresden. The two following notes tell their own tale. The first is but a very short communication of what the world had foreseen; the second was the printed card announcing his second marriage, which I presume was sent to all his friends.

(1)

MY DEAR FERDINAND: You will be no doubt angry with me when you hear that I am soon to marry Bülow's wife, who has become a convert in order to be divorced.

Yours, RICHARD WAGNER.

JULY, 1870.

(2)

We have the honour to announce our marriage, which took place on the 25th August of this year, at the Protestant Church of Lucerne.

RICHARD WAGNER,<br>
COSIMA WAGNER, *née* LISZT.

25TH AUGUST, 1870.

In the following November Wagner wrote to me again. It was the first of a series of letters relative to the purchase of a costly edition of Shakespeare, in English, as a birthday present to Madame Wagner. I publish six of these. They show Wagner by the fireside, at home with wife and children. Nearly sixty, with the close of his life almost in sight, he first bathes in that unspeakable happiness — the presence of children constantly about him, ready to receive the pent-up affection of half a century. It seems to me that his state of mind will be best understood by a few words, taken from the closing paragraph of his letter of the 25th November, 1870: "God make every one happy. Amen!"

(I)

DEAR OLD ONE: If you are still alive, and not angry with me for various reasons, you could do me a right good service. I should like to make a present to my wife (you know the deep, serious happiness that has been mine) on her birthday, which falls just on Christmas Eve, — a present of one of the most beautiful editions of Shakespeare in English. I do not so much want one of those editions with a voluminous appendix of critical notes as a really luxurious edition of the text. If such an edition de luxe is only published with notes, and so forth, well, then I will have that. I know that in this respect the English have achieved something extraordinary, and it is just one of their grand editions I should like to possess. Further, it must be encased in a truly magnificent binding, and of the greatest beauty.  All this, I feel sure, can only be obtained for certain in London.  Now be so good as to occupy yourself in the most friendly manner for me.  Deem me worthy of a response and a note of the price, that we may arrange everything, and I will forthwith send you the necessary funds.

How are you all at home?  I hear that the English are making colossal profits by the war.  I hope something of the good may fall to you.  Your last letter coming after such a long time was a delightful surprise, and has given me much joy, for I perceive in it that you still are actively employed.  Often do I now think of you because of your love for children.  My house, too, is full of children, the children of my wife, but beside there blooms for me a splendid son, strong and beautiful, whom I dare call *Siegfried Richard Wagner.*  Now think what I must feel, that this at last has fallen to my share.  I am fifty-seven years old.

> Be most fondly greeted.
> From your
> RICHARD WAGNER.

LUCERNE, 11 November, 1870.

## (In pencil on the last page of the letter.)

Perhaps the director of the theatre might make me a present of a copy of Shakespeare.

### (2)

> When Ferdinand in pious rage,
> The Moors afar did chase!

Therefore, thou most excellent good one, quick to business!

Your recommendation seems to point to the Cambridge edition of Dyce.  You say that the cost will be about three guineas (*i.e.* £3. 3*s.*) therefore — let us stop at Dyce's — this Cambridge edition.  But you do not tell me, however, whether it is one volume or in several.  Further, how am I to decide about the binding?  I know that in London bookbinding is treated as an art, and I would much like to have a good specimen of London art work for my wife (for I cannot present her with anything else).  Acting upon the hypothesis that it is in one volume only, I have forwarded to you six pounds for disposal upon the work, and therefore three pounds less three shillings will be available for the binding. Should there be two volumes, then you must consider whether for the money you can still obtain something remarkably good. If not — then order unhesitatingly what is good, and write to me at once and I will send you a few pounds more immediately. The chief point to be kept in view is that you arrange with the bookbinder so as to have the work finished in time to enable me to present it here on Christmas Eve.

But now, above all, be not angry with me for thus earnestly importuning you. If you but think of Milton Street and Portland Terrace, lobster salad, punch, and Lüders, then shall I be pardoned. And lastly will come your good wife to the rescue, who, notwithstanding that she, as I see, has still little children, may yet have some kind remembrance for me.

I am glad that you write to me about yourself in full; one cannot do anything better than write about one's self to one's friends, for the more one reflects the less one seems to know of others. According to this, I ought to write a great deal about myself, but that I must defer for an ocular inspection by you; therefore, come and see me. My son is Helferich Siegfried Richard. My son! Oh, what that says to me!

*You* have plenty of children's prattle, are used to it like the English to hanging, but with me the hanging is only just beginning. Now I must prepare to live to a good old age, for then will others profit by it. Outside my home life, one thing only do I propose to accomplish, and that, the performance of my " Nibelungen " drama as I have conceived it. It appears to me that the whole German Empire is only created to aid me in attaining my object. Carlyle's letter in the " Times " has caused me intense satisfaction. The Messieurs Englishmen I have already learned to know through you. I need but refer to divers data I have from you to be at once clear about the character of this strangely ragged nation.

God make every one happy. Amen! Now greet mamma and children, and tell them of Milton Street. Come next summer into Switzerland and keep me in your heart as I do you.

Yours,<br>RICHARD WAGNER.

LUCERNE, 25th November, 1870.

(3)

MY GOOD FERDINAND:   Is it not too bad that I am still to give you so much trouble?   I thought there must be, especially in London, a central depot where one could quickly be informed about the most complicated matters of all kinds.   Does there not exist, *i.e.* in Regent Street, or in some other main thoroughfare, a bookseller who keeps on hand a stock of editions de luxe of celebrated authors, in elegant and costly bindings, ready for sale for certain festive occasions?   Certainly it would have been better could you have alighted upon such an edition of " Shakespeare " already bound.   That a bookbinder would now undertake such a task, I myself feel it is somewhat venturesome to hope.   But as you are such a good fellow I leave the whole business entirely in your hands.   Do not let the price frighten you, for when it is a question of a birthday gift for such a noble, dear woman, then, in honour of Shakespeare, one may afford to be liberal.   Yet on this occasion, I insist that the external must be the pre-eminent consideration, the thing to be first thought of, viz. beautiful, correct print on beautiful paper, artistic binding, and — the internal Shakespeare supplies himself; but do not trouble at all about the critical notes of English editors.

As the time is now very close upon us, it would be best if you could still discover, all ready and complete, a luxurious book, in a luxurious shop, in a luxurious binding; for the rest — go on!   I am not sending you any further money to-day, as I want to leave the matter entirely in your hands.   How much more I am to send you we will arrange later on.

Adieu for to-day !

Good old fellow !

Make sure that we see you next summer here !

Don't be melancholy, and keep me in your love.

Yours,

RICHARD WAGNER.

LUCERNE, 9th December, 1870.

(Herewith the addresses of the London banker: nice fellows those ! !)

(4)

DEAR GOOD PRAEGER : Ah, now all is right, and the trouble at an end.   You will have seen by my last letter that it seemed to me our only hope lay in finding an edition de luxe ready bound.   That this should have been in nine volumes, though not precisely an edition de luxe, is satisfactory ; therefore, have you acted most blamelessly and correctly.   Instead of having to transmit to you further subsidies, you tell me there is even a balance at my disposition.   Now I have cudgelled my brains as to what can be purchased with the remaining twelve shillings.   In this matter it will depend on the patience and perseverance of your wife, should she see some pretty trifling *article-de-mode* to put on the Christmas table, where it might look well, perhaps.   My wife has spoken to me about, and would like, if possible, an East India, or even Chinese, foulard dress, rich, highly-coloured patterns on satin ground, brilliant and luxurious, *i.e.* Orientally fantastic, such as is sure to be found in London.   Now if your good wife would be kind enough to look to this, and should it not go into the abnormal in cost, of which, naturally, there is no intention, since the proposed costume is not to serve for ostentation, but for the gratification of a fantastic taste, I would beg of you to make bold and send me about twenty metres of such a material, and to send it off at once.   The settlement of the transaction on my side would follow immediately.   I do not restrict the price, as that might hamper you ; but on the other hand, I beg you to understand that, in case it is really something beautiful and original, Oriental, do not stop at the price.   Only in respect of the design, I remember there must be no figures, nothing but flowers — that much do I remember. God knows to what new trouble I am putting you again.   Don't take it too seriously, but remain good to me, for this is the most important of your business.

Heart greetings to all of you, from yours,

RICHARD WAGNER.

LUCERNE, 11th December, 1870.


### (5)

DEAR OLD FRIEND : Yes, yes ! so it is, and I have neglected to inform you that " Shakespeare " rightly and well came into my hands.   It arrived somewhat late, but for the efforts on your part to fully gratify me I give you my thanks.   Altogether I am sorry I did not pay more thought to the gigantic proportions of London business, as I feel by that I have unknowingly thrown upon you a lot of trouble in this affair. But now that everything has turned out well, I thank you once more, and promise not to trouble you again with such commissions. I write to you in haste, as I am preparing for a journey; to-morrow I go with my wife into Germany, where I propose to try and discover how matters stand. Several things are in preparation, but all tend to one good, that is, the performance of the " Nibelung " *after my own way*. Leipzic, Dresden, and above all, Berlin, will be visited by me. In Berlin, where they have made me a member of the Academy, I shall deliver a discourse on the mission of the opera, etc.

I will send to you the " Kaisermarsch," and all else that comes out.

Now look to it that you pay me a visit next summer in our beautiful retreat. By the middle of May we shall have returned.

And now, farewell!

Be not angry with me!

Greet wife and children, and keep loving
Your faithful friend,
RICHARD WAGNER.

LUCERNE, April, 1871.

(6)

LEIPZIC, 12th May, 1871.

This I have carried about with me on a long journey, for, when I wanted to send it from Lucerne, I found I had mislaid your address. It is fortunate that in your last letter, sent after me from Lucerne, and which has just reached me, I have once again your address.

I am fatigued, and I return to-morrow.

As regards the proposals and offer of the English music-sellers, I would beg you to request them to address in the matter, Tausig, Dessauer Strasse 35, Berlin. He has urged me to let him manage many things in which I am always worsted. He will arrange with the publishers, O. F. Peters, music bureau, in a manner that I shall derive all possible advantage. Else, dearest, I am well, and my undertaking bodes well for a success.

Best greetings to wife and children.
Love me, and forever yours,
RICHARD WAGNER.

Then came the following : —

DEAREST: Come when you will!  Alas, everybody comes in the few weeks of the summer, and it is possible that you will find visitors already when you come.  In the quiet time not even a cock crows after you, but you will find your place prepared for you ; only, therefore, to our next meeting.

Yours,<br>
RICHARD WAGNER.

LUCERNE, TRIBSCHEN, 6th June, 1871.


In the summer I went to stay with Wagner.  How changed!  Fifty-eight years old, and yet but one year in the possession of what is called home.  His had been a roving life.  Not through choice, but necessity.  Energetic and persevering, never leaving a stone unturned or failing in an effort to preach his creed.  And so through the long years of early manhood and middle age had he struggled with adversity, never finding an abiding resting-place.  But the sunset of his life was setting in rich, warm colours.  A feeling of serenity, born of the conscious security from worldly anxieties, had taken possession of him.  His work had been acknowledged throughout Europe.  He was ambitious, and his soul was satisfied.  Now was he for the first time living in that warm-hearted, self-denying atmosphere of "home," where dwelt a remarkably cultured, intellectual wife and children.  *There* "bloomed for him a splendid son, strong and beautiful."  Yes ; he was happy.  His naturally buoyant temperament had not lessened with years.  I remember full well, one day when we were sitting together in the drawing-room at Tribschen, on a sort of ottoman, talking over the events of the years gone by, when he suddenly rose and stood on his head upon the ottoman. At the very moment he was in that inverted position the door opened and Madame Wagner entered. Her surprise and alarm were great, and she hastened forward, exclaiming, "Ah! lieber Richard! Richard!" Quickly recovering himself, he reassured her of his sanity, explaining that he was only showing Ferdinand he could stand on his head at sixty, which was more than the said Ferdinand could do. This was a ridiculous incident, but strikingly illustrative of the "Wagner as I knew him." I suppose there are few thinking people who will deny the seriousness and profundity of Wagner's mind, and that perhaps in earnestness of purpose and power of reflection, he may be said to have been the equal of Carlyle; yet who can picture the "sage of Chelsea" standing on his head at sixty, or indeed at any period of his life?

Wagner's tranquillity of mind was delightful to contemplate. He longed for "peace on earth and good will to all men." The desire of his heart, the dream of those early Dresden days, was about to be realized. A theatre constructed after his own theory was soon to be erected. The architect and engineer, Neumann and Brandt, came to Lucerne during my visit. I was privileged to be present at their discussions. It was another illustration of "to have a clear notion of what you want is half-way to get it." "The theatre must be so built that it can be emptied in the space of one or two minutes"; upon this Wagner insisted. Did the experts explain some detail to him it was marvellous to see how quickly he grasped the point and debated it with them. His heart was in his work, in this as in all he did, and there lay the secret of his success, for of this I am convinced,

that without his indomitable will, that untiring perseverance which would not be conquered, the genius of
Wagner would have availed him but little.

In writing of "Wagner as I knew him" I have touched
upon certain subjects and criticised him in a manner
which I am aware many of his worshippers might perhaps
shrink from.   But in this I have in no way offended
Wagner.   He wished to be known as he was.   Indeed,
he has written his own life, which, should it please the
Wagner heirs, may one day be given to the world to its
great gain.   I became aware of the existence of this
autobiography in the following manner.   Wagner and
his wife were going out, leaving me alone at Tribschen.
Before going, Wagner placed in my hands a volume for
my perusal during his absence.   "It is my autobiography,"
he said.   "Only Liszt has a copy; none other has seen
it, and it shall not be published until my Siegfried has
reached his majority."   I read it carefully, and I may
state, without touching upon any of the matter contained
therein, that in my treatment of Wagner I have not
uttered one word to which he himself would not have
subscribed.

To see Wagner surrounded by children was a pleasant sight.   He was as frolicsome as they.   He would
have the children sing the "Kaisermarsch" at the piano,
and reward them with coins.   As regards their discipline and training, he effaced himself completely before
Madame Wagner.   To his wife he showed the tenderest affection.   It might almost be said of him that he
was the most uxorious of husbands.

No matter the mood in which I found Wagner, it

was always the old Wagner. Did we set out for a stroll, he would take me into some wayside inn, there to eat sausages and drink beer. I must add that his drinking was of the most moderate description. It was during one of these rambles that we spoke of Liszt, and in the talking, he told me that Liszt had been more pained at his daughter Cosima's change of religion from Roman Catholic to Protestant, than at her divorce from von Bülow. Among other things, too, he said, speaking of Liszt as a composer, that "he [Liszt] had begun too late in life."

To me Wagner was all affection. He played to me, showed me everything received from the king (among the many presents were two handsome vases, the equivalent of which in money Wagner said he would have preferred), and did all that he could to make my stay agreeable. I did not stay the whole time I had purposed; I left somewhat unexpectedly. My departure brought the following letter from Wagner:—

Thou strangest of all men, why do you not give a sign of life? Is it right or just? After having lived among us, as one of us, to have left us so suddenly, and not without causing us some anxiety, too, on your behalf. How wrong if you were in a dissatisfied mood with us; but that cannot be; rather be convinced that we take the most hearty interest in you, and that this is the sole reason which induces me to make this inquiry.

Let me hear from you, and be heartily greeted.

From yours ever,<br>
RICHARD WAGNER.

From now to the day of his death I have but little to tell. He had arrived at a time when the world accepted him as one of its great men. His movements were chronicled in the press as though he were some minister of state. I saw him repeatedly since 1872, notably at the opening of the Bayreuth theatre in 1874, and at the succeeding representations there, and naturally on his coming to London for the Albert Hall Wagner Festival in 1877, when at the banquet given at the Cannon Street Hotel in his honour, he toasted me as the friend, "the first in this country to nobly support him," at a time when he was a stranger in the land and the target of hostile criticism. Later on, I saw him again at the "Parsifal" performances at Bayreuth, which proved to be for the last time.

My task is done.

Wagner's labours ceased at Venice on the 13th February, 1883. What he has accomplished is beyond the power of any man to destroy. Were Wagner himself to return to us, *he* could not undo what he has done. In future years, aye, in future centuries, men will come from all parts of the civilized globe to worship at Bayreuth ; that is the Mecca of musicians. There is the shrine of the founder of a new religion in art, pure and ennobling to all who have ears to hear and human hearts that can be touched. To use an old metaphor, but accurate and appropriate when applied to Wagner, his work is as the boundless ocean ; many will sail their craft upon it, from the majestic ship of tragedy to the winsome bark of comic opera, and then shall they not have navigated all the seas.

The key of Wagner's success is his truth. Look at his work from whichever side we may, that is it which ever finds its way into all hearts. While the musicians were, and some still are, engaged in the dissecting-room, with a bar here and bar there, with the people, the laymen, he is universally popular. And what is the cause? His truth, his earnestness. At bottom, it is this sincerity which has made him great. Speaking of the laymen, I am forcibly reminded of perhaps the most musically gifted and most devoted of all, one Julius Cyriax, a German merchant of the city of London, whose friendship Wagner contracted here in 1877, and with whom Wagner was in intimate correspondence down to the last.

And if this be the judgment passed upon his work, what shall be said of the character of the man? Without fear, I say earnestness of purpose guided him here too; that he was impatient of incompetence when it sought to pose as the true in art was, and is, natural in a great genius. Autocratic in bearing, and the intimate of a king, though democratic in music and a professed lover of the *demos* in his earlier career, this is but a seeming contradiction. Democratic describes his music; no domineering there of one voice; and democratic, too, in the last days, when he refused imperial distinctions, preferring to remain one of the people. An opponent in art, he was to be dreaded. Why? Because he fought for his cause with such a whole-heartedness that he drove, as Napoleon used to say, "fear into the enemy's camp." His memory, like that of all great men, was extremely retentive. He was a hard worker, as his eleven published volumes of literary matter and fourteen music-dramas abundantly testify. To accomplish such work was only possible to a man of method, and he *was* methodical and careful withal in what he did. Look at his handwriting and music notation, small but clear, neat and clean. He was not free from blemish or prejudice, — who is ? — but

Take him all in all,<br>
We ne'er shall look upon his like again.

Typography by J. S. Cushing & Co., Boston.

# THE STORY OF MUSIC.

## By W. J. HENDERSON.

### *12mo, Ornamental Cloth Cover, $1.25.*

"Mr. Henderson tells in a clear, comprehensive, and logical way the story of the growth of modern music. The work is prefixed by a newly-prepared chronological table, which will be found invaluable by musical students, and which contains many dates and notes of important events that are not further mentioned in the text. . . . Few contemporary writers on music have a more agreeable style, and few, even among the renowned and profound Germans, a firmer grasp of the subject. The book, moreover, will be valuable to the student for its references, which form a guide to the best literature of music in all languages. The story of the development of religious music, a subject that is too often made forbidding and uninteresting to the general reader, is here related so simply as to interest and instruct any reader, whether or not he has a thorough knowledge of harmonics and an intimate acquaintance with the estimable dominant and the deplorable consecutive fifths. The chapter on instruments and instrumental forms is valuable for exactly the same reasons."—NEW YORK TIMES.

"It is a pleasure to open a new book and discover on its first page that the clearness and simple beauty of its typography has a harmony in the clearness, directness, and restful finish of the writer's style. . . . Mr. Henderson has accomplished, with rare judgment and skill, the task of telling the story of the growth of the art of music without encumbering his pages with excess of biographical material. He has aimed at a connected recital, and, for its sake, has treated of creative epochs and epoch-making works, rather than groups of composers segregated by the accidents of time and space. . . . Admirable for its succinctness, clearness, and gracefulness of statement."—NEW YORK TRIBUNE.

"The work is both statistical and narrative, and its special design is to give a detailed and comprehensive history of the various steps in the development of music as an art. There is a very valuable chronological table, which presents important dates that could not otherwise be well introduced into the book. The choice style in which this book is written lends its added charms to a work most important on the literary as well as on the artistic side of music."
—BOSTON TRAVELLER.

## LONGMANS, GREEN, & CO.,
### 15 East 16th Street, New York.

# PRELUDES AND STUDIES.

### MUSICAL THEMES OF THE DAY.

### By W. J. HENDERSON,

Author of "The Story of Music."

_______

### *12mo, Cloth, Extra, Gilt Top, $1.25.*

"The questions which he handles are all living. Even the purely historical lectures which he has grouped together under the general head of "The Evolution of Piano Music," are informed with freshness and contemporaneous interest by the manner which he has chosen for their treatment. . . . The concluding chapter of the book is an essay designed to win appreciation for Schumann, . . . and is the gem of the book both in thought and expression."

—NEW YORK TRIBUNE.

"Leaving Wagner, of whom the book treats in a most interesting way, the evolution of piano music is taken up and treated in such a way as to convince one that the writer is a master of his subject. Mr. Henderson dwells on the performances of some living players, their methods, manner, etc., and closes his work with a number on Schumann and the programme symphony."

—DETROIT SUNDAY NEWS.

"The book is written by one who knows his subject thoroughly and is made interesting to the general public as well as to those who are learned in music."

—BOSTON POST.

"All lovers and students of music will find much to appreciate. . . . Mr. Henderson writes charmingly of his various subjects — sympathetically, critically, and keenly. He shows a sincere love for his themes, and study of them ; yet he is never pedantic, a virtue to be appreciated in a writer of essays upon any department of art."—BOSTON TIMES.

"Mr. Henderson's clear style is well known to readers of the musical criticism of the New York Times, and his catholicity of sentiment, and freedom from prejudice, . . . . . though this volume will be especially valuable to the student of music, it will be helpful to the amateur, and can be read with satisfaction by one ignorant of music, which, altogether, is surely high praise."

—PROVIDENCE SUNDAY JOURNAL.

"It is a volume of extremely suggestive musical studies. . . . They are all full of appreciative comment, and show considerable clear insight into the origin and nature of musical works. The author has a style which is adapted to exposition. The book is an attractive one for the lover of music."

—PUBLIC OPINION.

"Mr. Henderson studies carefully and intelligently the evolution of piano music and Schumann's relation to the development of the programme symphony. This is a suggestive, original, and well-equipped group of essays upon themes which interest musicians."—LITERARY WORLD.

_______

## LONGMANS, GREEN, & CO.,

### 15 East 16th Street, New York.

www.ingramcontent.com/pod-product-compliance
Lightning Source LLC
Chambersburg PA
CBHW051125120726
47905CB00005B/1432